The Reincarnation of
Winston Churchill

Dearest Scarlett,

Maybe our destinies are more connected than we will ever know...

Bill Rowe

xoxo Nevia & Craig.

Aug 2022.

BOULDER
BOOKS

Library and Archives Canada Cataloguing in Publication

Title: The reincarnation of Winston Churchill / Bill Rowe.
Names: Rowe, William N. (William Neil), 1942- author.
Identifiers: Canadiana 20220159459 | ISBN 9781989417584 (softcover)
Subjects: LCSH: Churchill, Winston, 1874-1965—Fiction. | LCGFT: Novels.
| LCGFT: Biographical fiction.
Classification: LCC PS8585.O8955 R45 2022 | DDC C813/.54—dc23

Published by Boulder Books
Portugal Cove-St. Philip's, Newfoundland and Labrador
www.boulderbooks.ca

Design and layout: Tanya Montini
Copy editor: Iona Bulgin

Printed in Canada

We acknowledge the financial support of the Government of Newfoundland and
Labrador through the Department of Tourism, Culture, Arts and Recreation.

Funded by the Government of Canada | Financé par le gouvernement du Canada | Canadä

To Shirley with thanks

❦

Sir Winston Churchill's grandson, Winston S. Churchill, said this about the family's Indigenous North American ancestry:

"Not only did Winston Churchill have Revolutionary blood in his veins but, possibly, native American as well … While it is unlikely that the question of the family's native American heritage can be firmly proved either way, I have little doubt as to the truth of the matter. For me physical features speak louder than any entry in a register of births …"

From "Churchill's American Heritage," 2008

＆

In 1937, Winston Churchill appeared before the British Royal Commission on Palestine during the Arab revolt there, and spoke in support of a Jewish homeland, while rejecting the Arab demand to stop Jewish migration to Palestine. Here are some of his words:

"I do not admit for instance that a great wrong has been done to the Red Indians of America or the black people of Australia. I do not admit that a wrong has been done to those people by the fact that a stronger race, a higher-grade race or at any rate a more worldly-wise race, to put it that way, has come in and taken their place. I do not admit it. I do not think the Red Indians had any right to say, 'The American continent belongs to us and we are not going to have any of these European settlers coming in here.' They had not the right, nor had they the power."

AUTHOR'S NOTE

All my life I've been gripped by two happenings, widely separated in time and place. The first was how and why, during the 1930s, Winston Churchill, nearly alone, became an unyielding foe of Hitler and the Nazis. The second, 100 years before and thousands of miles away, was the heartbreaking tragedy of the native Beothuk of Newfoundland.

After I learned of Churchill's North American Indigenous ancestry, I became driven more and more by an urge to connect the two. This is the result.

CHAPTER 1

In the heyday of my young manhood, mentors considered me one of the upcoming cohort of the clever and the knowing who were going to straighten out the mess their own generation was leaving behind. But, truly, what help could I hope to bring to humanity, if I would do this?

I was a student from the colonies reading law at Oxford University when Sir Winston Churchill, 90 years old and near death, had his man invite me, and me alone, to come and hear him unravel an unknown mystery at his core. Now he wasn't even acquainted with me, so the invitation was astonishing, until I realized it had nothing to do with me as a person; it was extended only because of my ambiguous heritage—from whom I was descended, and whence I hailed. Even so, it was highly flattering to be asked by the greatest man alive to go and listen to him, and my response did not denote sanity. I told the renowned war leader's go-between I couldn't do it.

During the brief time Churchill had available as he approached what he knew was his end, I'd already arranged with some other students, one of whom was comely and lovable, to go on a ski trip. And I was prepared to let that fortnight's jaunt to Austria, albeit in blithe company, trump my chance to record for posterity the secret essence of the man who'd saved humanity from Hitler. Mock-worthy as my reaction seems now at this remove of over half a century, I can only plead that, back then, to a lad of 22, my expectation of making merry under an Alpine eiderdown with my loving girl *was* the salvation of humanity.

In the weeks before Churchill's invitation came in November 1964, I was trying to fit in at Brasenose, my Oxford college. This splendid pile of stone and erudition was named after the 11th-century door-knocker in the shape of an animal's brazen snout affixed to the main portal. The place was not wrong-named: Brasenose College counted more than its due of famously brazen-nosed men among its alumni. A year before I arrived, one of them, the cabinet minister John Profumo, had to resign after lying to the House of Commons about sharing with a high soviet Russian official, the bed of 19-year-old Christine Keeler. And fast-forwarding five decades to when I was just starting to write this, the UK prime minister, Brasenose alumnus David Cameron, was forced out of office amid howls of execration over his brazen Brexit bungling.

Some unabashed arts also got their hothouse starts at Brasenose. The college yielded a magnificent alumnus in William Golding, who would win the Booker Prize and the Nobel Prize for literature. While he was a student at Brasenose, as his posthumous archives revealed, he attempted to rape a flirtatious 15-year-old girl. Winston Churchill greatly admired him.

Michael Palin was at Brasenose while I was there. A Newfoundland friend of mine at Oxford, Neil Murray, went with me to see Palin and his buddy Terry Jones of the college, Teddy Hall, in a hilarious Oxford comedy spectacle. But I confess that, in those days, whenever I exchanged passing hellos with Palin in our college quadrangles, it never occurred to me that in a few years he'd become world-famous in anything like Monty Python.

Two other students of the college, one delightfully brazen, the other revoltingly so, though decades apart, came together in forcing this book to be made. The first was a contemporary of mine and a splendid friend, the future bestselling novelist, and peer of the realm, and celebrated and denigrated, in equal measure, Jeffrey Archer. The other predated me by over three-quarters of a century, but his evil spirit was a constant, woeful presence to me there, the Butcher of the Somme, Field Marshal Douglas Earl Haig.

Walking to and from my lodgings in college every day, I suffered an uprush of bile at the sight of a metal plaque on the wall commemorating Douglas Earl Haig. The toxic sensation pushed me toward getting kicked out of college and sent down. The potential for that ignominy arose not long after I'd arrived and attended a welcoming sherry party for tutors and students hosted by the head of the college, Sir Noel Hall.

The reception room in Sir Noel's lodgings filled with students. I knew few of them in those early days, and I stood in the middle of the room rather self-consciously, emptying glasses of sherry far too quickly. I gravitated toward the young men standing around Sir Noel, listening to him talk from his chair in front of the fireplace. With them was the student who'd been pointed out to me at dinner in hall yesterday as the man who, in March past, had brought the Beatles to this same room in Brasenose to meet with Sir Noel and some dons and students. It was the extraordinary Jeffrey Archer.

Just after the Beatles' trip to the US had created Beatlemania there, Archer had somehow persuaded all four of them to come to Oxford in aid of an Oxfam fundraiser. Posted in the junior common room of Brasenose afterwards was a photograph that became famous around the world. It showed Paul McCartney, George Harrison, Ringo Starr, and John Lennon in this room talking to a tutor and to Sir Noel and to Archer himself. The text that accompanied the snapshot reported that none of the Beatles had ever been to a university before.

When I approached the group around Sir Noel, he glanced at me briefly as, I thought through my haze of sherry, he would have noticed a blue-arsed housefly that had flown into his range of vision. At the time I wasn't used to the effect of the 18 per cent alcohol content in fortified wines that went down so smoothly. I would grasp more clearly later in life that an excess of alcohol always tended to render me somewhat paranoid and too bold withal. And today my reaction to Sir Noel was perhaps a little extreme. Instead of standing diffidently by, a lowly first-year student just happy to be swelling the head man's audience, I found that his professorial mumblings around the pipe in his mouth, plus the plummy responses from the students, and the unwarranted volume of their laughter at his words, vexed me. Indeed, the scene before me gave rise to an impulse to emit some words myself.

I heard myself butting into the discourse. "Do you realize," I said too loudly, "how sickening it is for me to pass by that plaque to Haig every day?" In my own ears, compared to the intonations of the others, I sounded harsh and uncouth, in effect a colonial barbarian.

Sir Noel, in the middle of a hold-forth, stopped speaking, and sought out the source in wonder. The students turned toward my accent and assumed looks and grins of, "what fresh American gaucherie is this, then?" The principal said, "I beg your pardon, Mister ah ..."

I very much wanted to stop now and run away, but he'd forced me to push on. "There's a brass plaque to the memory of that psychopathic moron, Douglas Haig, incompetent in everything but planning the massacre of innocent boys, on the wall of our college chapel."

This caused Sir Noel to remove his pipe and display his chaotic teeth in a chortle of forbearance before speaking. "Please do me— do all of us—the honour of enlightening us as to who might be addressing us."

"William Cull, and I—"

"Ah yes, Mr. Cull, from overseas. Mr. Cull, it is sadly true that a certain school of historians has endeavoured to place Lord Haig's victory in the First World War in a less than heroic perspective. But this college is far too firmly established in time and place to sway, let alone bow, to every modern historical fad that might arise from time to time in the Americas. Now gentlemen, where were we?"

"You were saying, sir," said Jeffrey Archer, "that John Lennon told you of—"

"We were talking about Haig," I said. "Our college's illustrious military genius who slaughtered hundreds of my fellow Newfound-landers at Beaumont-Hamel; Haig, who sent them and tens of thousands like them out of their trenches along the Somme into a blanket of bullets from the thuggish Huns." I locked eyes with a gentle German scholar standing among the students; I'd had some enjoyable chats with him at dinner. I looked away and pressed on: "Haig, whose perverted personal relationship with his God told him to find out how very good the Germans were at slaughtering defenceless teenage boys for target practice with machine guns at close range."

"Quite," said Principal Hall. He had heaved himself to his feet now. "My good man, feeling as you do about Lord Haig, I hesitate to ask your sentiments concerning another of our great alumni, John Buchan, the celebrated writer, who was raised to the peerage as Lord Tweedsmuir before becoming Governor General of your own Canada, where he elevated the state of the arts there by founding your Governor General's Literary Awards. But let's disinter his remains, shall we, and hang him anyway, because he wrote speeches and communiques for Lord Haig." There were student chuckles all round. "Even Sir Winston Churchill early admired Haig's qualities as a commander. Sir Winston wrote that, if there are some who would question Haig's right to rank with Wellington in British military annals, there are none who will deny that his character and conduct as a soldier will long serve as an example to all. You'll find such a citation in the First World War literature if you'd bother to research it. But you're not reading history, are you? No, I should scarcely have thought so."

The sherry vapours warping my mind couldn't keep me from sensing that it would be easy to suffer a humbling defeat here. But the mushrooming crowd's chortles made me bawl back: "The words of one *narcissistic* elitist do not excuse the lethal idiocies of another." A student cackled, either in appreciation of my sentiment or because

I mightn't have gotten all the syllables of narcissistic in. I suspected the latter. "And we weren't talking about Churchill. We're talking about Haig. Field Marshal Douglas Earl Haig and his brass plaque out there make me want to throw up."

"Good heavens. Do spare us that, Mr. Cull, at least in the physical sense." The students laughed out generally now. The principal sat down again with his face turned away: "Now, yes, John Lennon ..." The students, in unison, showed me their backs.

I inched my way out of the principal's lodge without ceremony, and without notice, except for the occasional sidewise smirk. I walked to my room not feeling proud and sat back in my chair and closed my scalding eyes. After 15 disconsolate minutes, I lurched upright to a sense of doom caused by my own stupidity: I'd remembered suddenly that Churchill's words about Haig, just then quoted by Sir Noel, were not praise but sarcasm over Haig's incompetence. They were in a book I'd read on Churchill, and in it he'd also reviled Haig for managing to kill three British soldiers for every two Germans he killed. But I'd forgotten all that when it would have been useful in my response to Sir Noel, my brain having been reduced to porridge by the sensation that I was over my head and sinking.

I splashed some water on my burning face, and skulked over to the college buttery to put something solid in my stomach, empty save for the sloshing sherry. A dozen students were there, enjoying a pint and watching television. Two or three of them glanced at me and grinned at each other as I bought a sandwich. I was settling down alone at a table when the big man in college came in, flanked by two of his retinue, and followed by 10 or 15 other students from the sherry party. He had a quick look my way and came over, smiling good-naturedly. "Jeffrey Archer," he said, and stuck out a hand. "I say, Cull, thank you for providing my mates and me with your delightful cabaret earlier. You were not only persuasive but most entertaining as well."

I shook his hand. "I have my doubts that Sir Noel was as persuaded or amused as you claim to be."

"He should have been. But, no, he was not. He thought you an absolute boor, judging by his pithy remarks regarding shameless cheek afterwards. Be careful about sneaking birds into your room after hours from now on. You will want to avoid providing him with the slightest reason to have you sent down." Archer dropped smoothly into the empty space on the bench next to me and grinned. "No, it's not that bad. Sir Noel is a good and fair man. But my advice is that you ought really to apologize at an early opportunity. And don't blame the sherry when you do. That generation can't abide someone who's rendered injudicious by his inability to hold his booze." His grin widened charmingly. "If I were you, I think I should plead a case of overseas jitters in the face of Oxford grandeur."

He was certainly the kind of guy that you had to grin back at. "Well, that wouldn't be strictly true," I said. "Speaking of which, I only spoke the simple truth about Haig."

"Yes, but I've found that, in determining who the world's heroes and villains might be, the truth seems to have many facets. Your analysis of Lord Haig may have been less damaging in Sir Noel's eyes than your unpleasant remark about Sir Winston."

"Yeah, I didn't really mean to lump Churchill in with Haig. Sir

Noel's comment about Churchill admiring him took me by surprise. I only recalled afterwards that Churchill's words were meant to mock Haig, not praise him."

"Ah, yes, the devastating comeback thought of too late—that damned *esprit d'escalier*. One has to learn to be fast on one's feet in our pitiless world. Sir Noel takes enormous pride in having worked closely with the great man during the Second World War, and he will not hear an adverse word about him. Sir Winston may have been a bloody-minded loose cannon to his subordinates but he was our bloody-minded loose cannon. If you like, I can support you in getting back into Sir Noel's good graces. He and I have always been rather close since my school days, and after the success of the Beatles' visit, we've grown more so. Unless you object strenuously, I can help you make amends."

I leaned back the better to study Archer's open face. He gazed at me with unswerving eyes that looked constantly amused, but unsurprised, at the world's foibles. My wonderment at the man increased when I recalled reading in the student newspaper, the *Cherwell*, that he was a competitive sprinter at the national level. Why would a student prodigy like him go out of his way to rescue an inconsequential stranger from the effects of his own loutish gracelessness? Perhaps he was simply driven by innate goodness; after all, he was working for an international charity of renown. Or perhaps he liked to draw retainers to himself by extricating them from the consequences of their own idiocies and making them grateful. That seemed more plausible, and I was about to give his offer a "Thanks but no thanks" reply, even though it might leave me in bad books on high, when the miracle occurred.

Celebrated Canadian-American economist John Kenneth Galbraith appeared on the buttery television screen. He was narrating an episode in his must-watch series on money. I recognized him at first image, mostly from having met all 6 feet and 8 inches of him at the opening of the new campus of Memorial University of Newfoundland in St. John's three years before, where he'd been a special guest. The university's name commemorated the Newfoundlanders killed in the First World War. Now he was on TV, walking through Newfoundland's memorial park at Beaumont-Hamel in France and evaluating the Battle of the Somme. The students in the buttery were already riveted to the screen. I turned away from Archer to concentrate on it.

Galbraith was standing in front of our bronze, emblematic Royal Newfoundland Regiment caribou, exultant upon its rock, and he was describing the area and the horrendous events that had taken place there. The wholesale butchery of Newfoundland boys in this place, he was saying, was *the* most egregious event in a gruesome episode of a ghastly world war caused and maintained by callous military stupidity and uncaring capitalist greed and corrupt political inanity. He named Field Marshal Douglas Haig as a major culprit.

Every student in the buttery looked over at me. They must have all seen or heard about my half-drunken rant in the principal's lodge. One of them called out, "Well done."

Jeffrey Archer muttered, "Now there's a prodigious coincidence for us to contemplate." He looked at me. "Your good luck reminds me of myself. Are you always as jammy fortunate as that?"

"I hope not. Luck cuts both ways. The odds against winning a big lottery are about the same as crashing in an airplane. I'd like to avoid being a plaything of fortune, either way."

"Well, you're having a pretty good run the right way, so far. We both know we had to be blessed by incredibly good fortune, you and I, to land up here at Oxford among a mere fraction of a percentage point of the population. And now, in your case, Galbraith to the rescue, out of the blue ..."

"And I'm sitting here talking with Jeffrey Archer on top of all that. I'm afraid I may be pushing my luck."

"Not a bit of it. Your waggishness cannot disguise the reality. I think you and I need to drop in at Ladbrokes and test our hand at some serious wagering."

"If I were the devil, that's exactly how I'd suck in my next victim."

"Well, I've not yet achieved diabolical status, try as some might ... Oh you mean the temptation provided by your lucky coincidence to do something disastrous. Yes, an acute insight, that. One has to be careful about one's luck. It can lead to hubris. Coincidences alone are not enough, though. They have to be combined with audacity. Our Churchill said that the first quality needed for great endeavours is audacity. In the absence of your insolence to Sir Noel earlier, Galbraith's appearance on TV tonight would have been a merely interesting but meaningless coincidence of your happening to hear him talking about something pertaining to your own homeland. But instead, the lucky coincidence of Galbraith's appearing on the telly to condemn Haig, right on the heels of your seemingly gratuitous censure of the very same personage to Sir Noel, has become a breathtaking example of successful audacity, of effective *chutzpah*. And that sort of thing will become highly productive in moving you far forward in life. Just watch and see if I'm not right."

"And you reckon that this union of good luck and gall describes you, as well as me?"

"Bloody hell, William, yes. Just look at both of us sitting here at the top of the world. That didn't result from servile passivity on the part of either of us. We've seen what you achieved tonight. As for myself, think of the luck of my being in the principal's room with you earlier, and being with you here as well when Galbraith came on, plus my intuition in offering to help you when you were at a low ebb, before your sudden rise to eminence. All of that is remarkable, really. Almost as if it were fated to happen to us."

We watched the rest of the show, and parted with a promise to get together again soon. On top of my delight at the way the Haig fiasco had turned out, I was tickled at having begun to form a relationship with a student considered outstanding among notable students in this eminent university.

CHAPTER 2

After my tutorial next morning, I sauntered across the college quads, acknowledging with a casual wave of my hand the greetings of fellow students who suddenly knew me. The porter from the lodge puffed up behind me and called my name. The principal, he said, required Mr. Cull to wait on him.

I walked over to the site of last evening's infamy and knocked on the slightly ajar door to Sir Noel's office. I wasn't required to wait on him. He instantly pulled the door open and invited me in to sit down with him. Full of the generosity of vindication, now, I started to say that I regretted my impolite tone last evening, but he stopped me.

"Not at all, Mr. Cull, not at all," he said. "I do apprehend and fully appreciate the level of emotion aroused in you by my own indifference to your strongly held convictions. I saw part of the television program last evening, and a student who holds you in high esteem—Jeffrey Archer?—told me that students in the college were inordinately impressed by the juxtaposition of Ken Galbraith's position and yours. As it happens, I knew Ken well in America during the war, and greatly respected his views, even those with which I disagreed, especially the ones characterized to me by Joseph Kennedy—the martyred president's father?—as soppy Canadian socialist sentimentality. Ha ha. But our mutual respect for one another, Professor Galbraith and I, has obliged me to think your matter through carefully. Hence, I have decided to strike a committee of distinguished alumni to consider the best modern opinion on Haig's true military role and make a recommendation about the appropriateness or otherwise of his plaque remaining in place here."

I thanked Sir Noel for his broadminded thinking, and added, "But I do want to apologize, sir, for my gratuitous and erroneous outburst regarding your close friend and colleague, Sir Winston Churchill."

But he kept going about the Field Marshal. "The Haig matter is somewhat complicated, of course, by the fact that Haig was invited to Newfoundland by your government in 1924, as my research shows, to lay the cornerstone of your war memorial in the capital, St. John's, where he proclaimed that Newfoundlanders were the best of the best. The newspapers there declared at the time that Newfoundlanders would love him forever ... What?" Sir Noel sat upright in his chair. "What's that you say? My close friend? *Winston Churchill?* However on earth did you acquire that notion?"

"A student mentioned it to me."

"That sounds like our Archer again. Oh, he's a good lad—top-drawer money raiser, superb athlete—and he helped me put Brasenose solidly on the modern map by arranging for the Beatles to come up so soon after their epoch-making American tour, for which I'm grateful—did you see them on the Ed Sullivan show? Mind-boggling public reaction. And I do consider Jeffrey a protégé of mine from his school days, but he does have a tendency to romance a little. I am sometimes teased for being an incorrigible name-dropper, hence I trust I am convincing when I assert that, no, Churchill was not my friend at any level. I served in a senior position at the Ministry of Economic Warfare during the first part of the war and headed the War Trade department at the British embassy in Washington, and I came across the Right Honourable Mr. Churchill and his edicts from cloud-cuckoo-land more times than I care to remember. And most of my colleagues would agree: a more offensive and obnoxious man would be hard to imagine, or, indeed, a man more deficient and blundering in most of his strategies and tactics."

"It was fortunate for Churchill's reputation, then," I said with a poker face, "that he saved the world."

Sir Noel jerked his earnest face toward me, and then laughed. "Good. Good. That's very good. You have struck the nail on the head, Mr. Cull. You'll forgive me if I appropriate your words for conversational use in my club. Sir Isaiah Berlin—he's a great friend of mine; we were both knighted in the same year, 1957—after Sir Winston was no longer prime minister, you may notice—Isaiah might well have had Churchill in mind when he wrote his famous essay "The Hedgehog and the Fox." Isaiah divided thinkers into two categories: foxes who know many things, and hedgehogs who know one important thing, one single defining overriding idea. Churchill strove mightily to be a fox. He endeavoured to foster one cockamamie notion after the other, madcap ideas that were severely wanting in their conception and erratic in their execution. Hence, politically and militarily, he drove everyone to the very edge of insanity. But our

Sir Winston was a failed fox. He was, however, the very epitome of the hedgehog. He had one good big idea and he knew one good big thing: he had to defeat Hitler and save the British Empire and the civilized world. And he carried that through at the level of genius, with dogged determination—no, with veritable *godlike* resolve. Those of us who disliked him personally for his insufferable behaviour can pardon him for everything else because he possessed that one big implacable idea. I cannot fathom where it came from or how it arose in him, when so many of his social class, the strong and effective as well as the effete and feeble, thought otherwise. It was as if it had emerged wholly grown and fully armoured from the brow of Zeus. He was virtually alone in the British Isles in first conceiving of it— the whole idea of going to war with Germany again was anathema to the rest of the nation. And until Hitler showed his hand with blinding obviousness, Churchill was essentially alone in striving to carry through with his conception. It's easy to see his shrewd acumen clearly now, in retrospect, in the light of Hitler's actions and all the odious Nazi apparatus. But before that, hardly anyone but Churchill saw it, or wanted to see it. Was this a peculiarity of Churchill's mental makeup or had it been entrenched in his brain by some unknown persons or events?"

I would find out.

That evening I saw Jeffrey, about to have dinner in the dining hall. I walked over to him and he turned to welcome me. "Thank you," I said, "for talking to the man about Galbraith."

His face lit up. "Well, I wanted to make certain that our mutual friend had seen the program, and knew of the impact it had on people, or else everything—the coincidence, your audacity, the chutzpah, the astonishing good luck—would have all gone for naught. One must needs stay on top of events to make them bear fruit. Come, Will Cull, sit here"—he patted the narrow space beside him—"and tell me about your meeting. You're back in his good graces?"

His mate moved over to let me sit next to Archer. "Apparently so, thank you. Our meeting was enlightening. For instance, he says he admires what Churchill did, but he never wanted to be his friend."

"Well, as Oscar Levant said, he knew Doris Day *before* she was a virgin. And I knew Sir Noel *before* he never wanted to be Sir Winston's friend. I've teased him about that. Churchill out of office is now merely history without power."

"An aging political leader I'm familiar with back in Canada always resists retiring by saying, 'There's nothing deader than a retired politician.' Sir Winston should have conferred with him before resigning from the House of Commons."

"Your Premier Smallwood? They did confer some 10 years ago, but that was on his gargantuan hydroelectric proposal in Labrador."

I leaned back and looked at his face in surprise. "You're well briefed. Have you been studying up on my homeland?"

"I'm very interested in Canada, William. Always have been. Limitless opportunity. We must talk about all that soon." I'd remember his words years later, when financial disaster in Canada struck him. "But first things first: there's a party of some Christ Church blokes tonight. Should be amusing—lord this and the honourable that, and some likely birds. Care to join me?"

I did care to join him. Christ Church College was reputed to be a favourite academic haunt of the young aristocracy. And it had produced more prime ministers of Great Britain, over a dozen, than any other Oxford college. I wanted to see what a party there would be like. And perhaps it would lead to acquaintanceship with a promising young lady. But I had no idea.

CHAPTER 3

Archer didn't have rooms in Brasenose College. He lived in a flat on Banbury Road in a building I learned he owned. And unlike any other student I knew, he also owned a car, with which he picked me up at the college gate at the appointed time for the party. In the passenger seat sat a striking young woman. Jeffrey introduced her, meeting her lips with a peck, as our fellow student, Claire Perceval, and added, "Will's own life at Oxford is thus far uncomplicated by a trouble and strife."

"A wife?" I said, pleased to show I was with it in Cockney. "No, and not even a girlfriend here, yet."

"It's good that you comprehend his lingo," said Claire. "Sometimes Archer can't hold back his yearning for the east end haunts of his dear departed father."

"*Nostalgie de la boue*," said Jeffrey. He was longing to be back in the mud? What the hell were they were talking about? I only learned later about his notorious father.

"Perhaps William is just choosier than you are when it comes to lady friends," said Claire. This caused no reaction from Jeffrey. He kept his eyes on the street ahead. And I, since Claire was the prettiest woman I'd yet seen in Oxford, was rendered wordless. "Well, that fell flat," Claire said with a laugh. "Can't you two alleged scholars and gentlemen tell when a woman is fishing for a compliment?"

"You tackle this one, Will," said Jeffrey. "I long ago exhausted my lexicon of superlatives on my Claire." He reached over and squeezed her thigh.

Taken by surprise, I blurted out: "Well, if I was hoping for the most beautiful woman in Oxford as my girlfriend, I'd have to abandon that desire now, since, evidently, she's already spoken for." Great. Not only was that totally inane, but in trying to flatter Claire, I'd insinuated that I was lusting after Jeffrey's girl. No wonder he glanced at me quick in his rear-view mirror.

"Good one, Will," said Jeffrey. He was grinning, but his grin disappeared as he looked to the side at Claire.

She turned to him and said, "What? You think he meant me? Cor blimey, Archer, you have the nicest friends. This one confesses frankly that merely meeting me has driven him to romantic despair."

The party consisted of about 20 men and women and took place in the rooms of an Honourable Robert something. The guest of honour was Lord Jonathon someone, the fourth son of a duke. The women were students at Oxford and daughters of birth or wealth. One was a Lady Jane. Another was a daughter of the owner of a tabloid rag with circulation figures insanely high enough to make him a baron in the next honours list. Everyone but Jeffrey and me seemed to know everyone else, apparently from childhood. Even Claire knew most of them from somewhere, judging by the scintillating in-talk among them, although she didn't seem to be very familiar with their recounted memories of magnificent weekend balls at country estates, or with their laughing arguments over who'd been swiving and tupping whom at them from among their parents' generation.

Jeffrey chatted with me at the beginning, explaining Claire by her father's high position in the British bureaucracy. Then he was off and running, sometimes exchanging a word or two with Claire, but mainly holding forth to groups of two or three. Being an outsider posed no problem for him. On top of the Beatles thing, which everyone knew about, he was a natural in this company and weighed in with poise and aplomb. And Claire never had less than four men around her.

I had a couple of chats with guys that went nowhere. It seemed difficult in this company to come up with something interesting to them. Then, one chap, Lord Algernon, on learning my name, said he once had a tailor named Cull who took pride in claiming to be a descendant of Owen Rowe, the friend of Oliver Cromwell, and a member of the court that had tried King Charles the First, and signed his death warrant. Was I too related to that Rowe?

In the spirit of chitchat, I replied, "I can only hope so. I am related to Rowes back in Canada."

"My good fellow, you ought fervently to hope the precise contrary," said Lord Algernon. "Owen Rowe was a damnable regicide. He was explicitly excluded by name when my own collateral ancestor, Charles the Second, passed the *Act of Free and General Pardon, Indemnity, and Oblivion* in 1660. Your putative ancestor died in the Tower of London, regrettably, before he could be properly hanged, drawn, and quartered." Lord Algernon backed away from me smiling ominously, with fire in his eye. I could only wonder about the fate of his poor tailor. His facial expression was a bizarre combination of malevolence mixed up with fake politesse. Then he took no further notice of me, relieving me of any fear that I was consequential enough to die in a daft family revenge-feud from the 17th century.

Two girls approached me in turn, but after a few minutes, other men came by to chat them up, and in each case their ready banter, delivered in commanding baritone voices, eclipsed and sidelined me. Jeffrey would tell me later that they were taught an imperious tone of speaking, intimidating to the uninitiate, from their earliest years at elite schools.

I saw Jeffrey glancing over at me a few times as I stood by myself in the middle of the floor, to avoid looking like a wallflower. Then, Claire walked up to me, probably on a rescue mission. After I'd drawn from her that she lived in Beckenham, Kent, and was reading English Literature at Lady Margaret Hall, she said, "Archer tells me your home is on an island. That's rather romantic. I'd love to live on a little island and always be aware that I'm completely cut off from the madding Main."

"The island I inhabit is nearly as large as this United Kingdom isle we're presently standing on. Newfoundland ...?"

"What?" She laughed. "That bloody Archer! To hear him talk, your island was like Iona in size and remoteness. Okay, William, your turn: now you say something utterly mindless."

"Perhaps he thought you could be impressed by notions of ancient and adventurous locations. Newfoundland is England's oldest overseas colony."

"Yes, that's sufficiently inane. On two counts: Ireland is England's oldest overseas colony. At least it's across a sea. One of my early Irish ancestors received a Norman pike in the gut to prove it. And notions of adventurous locations? No. I didn't have to be lured over here by any enticement beyond the fetching colonial prodigy himself."

"Jeffrey has the nicest girlfriends."

"Girlfriends, you say?" Mock anxiety suffused her beautiful face. "How many do you reckon he has?"

I laughed. "No, I only meant—"

A Lord Marmaduke had sidled up, interrupting me by speaking directly to Claire and trying to muscle me out with his dulcet tones. She said hello to him, and turned back to me. He made one more attempt, also unsuccessful, and then inched away. She looked at me po-faced. "You were talking about all of Archer's many nice girlfriends."

"Purely a figure of speech, Claire, I assure you."

I felt a hand on my shoulder from the side. "This is the most animated conversation in the place," said Jeffrey. "What about my many girlfriends?"

"Will was struggling to convince me that his saying 'Jeffrey has nice girlfriends' was a trope, really meaning only one, me."

Jeffrey looked at me thoughtfully for a second. "Will, we must leave. The Brasenose gate will soon be closed and then you'll have to climb in over the barbed wire and jagged glass and spikes on top of the back wall, at great menace to your prospect of progeny."

"What a clever method the men's colleges have," said Claire, "to recruit castrati for their choirs."

"I climbed it once before and survived intact. I don't mind risking it all again so that Jeffrey can get you back to Lady Margaret Hall before the main door is locked."

They looked at each other and smiled. "No, I'll drop you off first, en route," said Archer. That could only mean she must have signed out and was spending the night in his flat. I couldn't believe my reaction: something akin to jealousy felt like a needle piercing my heart.

On the drive back, I said, "Thanks for the invitation to the party. It was interesting."

"I hope you weren't bored. You seemed a bit."

"Not at all, Jeffrey. But when you don't know anyone there, it's a little hard sometimes to fit in."

"That's never been Archer's problem," said Claire. "He'd fit in if it was the queen mother's boudoir."

"How'd you find out about me and the queen mother?" asked Jeffrey. "Is MI5 spying on me again?" Then he looked at me in the rear-view mirror. "But it was a very boring do, Will. Precious junior representatives—*cadet* members—of peerage and industry, merely. We went to indulge Claire's friend in the minor landed gentry who thought she could command us to attend."

"You can get back at her by commanding her to attend your soirée when you're elevated to the House of Lords." Claire turned to grin back at me.

Jeffrey swerved the car around the Radcliffe Camera and stopped rather abruptly at the Brasenose gate. He put his arm around Claire and kissed her on the lips. "One of these days, Sweetheart," he said in a not-bad Bogart, "you'll be looking down at me from the spectators' gallery of the Lords, saying, 'But I was only being sarcastic.'" He regarded me in the mirror again and continued his Bogart impression. "Okay, Willy, drop the gun. I'll see you tomorrow."

That night before bed, Claire's face, lovely and wryly amused, popped into my brain without my willing it there. But when I went to sleep, I didn't dream about her. I had disjointed images of my earlier promise of feisty chutzpah failing to emerge at an intimate party in Buckingham Palace. I could see that my failure to shine with the members of the royal family made Jeffrey disappointed in me. In the dream, my insipid performance was understood to be a huge disaster. When I awoke, I lay there astonished that those trifling imaginings, so ridiculous awake, could have evoked such profoundly important significance in my sleep.

At lunch in hall, I sat with some law students. When Jeffrey came in, he joined a group of his usual friends, without looking about. That was odd; normally his eyes made an unobtrusive but constant survey of his surroundings. As I left, I looked over at his table but he didn't glance my way. Was he deliberately not recognizing my existence? Perhaps I was tangled up with one of those passive-aggressive types— ebulliently companionable one day, moodily withdrawn the next.

I went out to the porter's lodge to check for mail. A square envelope, invitation-shaped and sized, addressed to me at the college, was waiting in my box. On its back was some sort of fancy insignia. I wasn't familiar with the symbol, but I knew immediately what it was. My father had alerted me to expect this correspondence. I slowly ran my thumb under the flap, careful not to damage the envelope. This was a valued keepsake to save in my archives.

From behind me I heard, "I didn't see you at lunch until you were going out the door." It was Archer, looking for mail as well. "I was sorry you didn't come over and say hello." Perhaps I was the passive-aggressive one. "I wanted to alert you to—Is that the de Rothschild's coat of arms?"

"Yes, I do believe it is." I nonchalantly pulled the card out of the envelope. "You have a good eye, Jeffrey, to spot that."

"Well, they are a very great house, pre-eminent as merchant bankers here and on the continent," he said. "That looks like an invitation."

"It is an invitation. It's from Edmund de Rothschild requesting the honour of my presence," I snorted as if at the ludicrousness of the formal language, "at lunch in the firm's premises in London." I passed the card to him.

He was frankly incredulous, eyeing the invitation from top to bottom, and turning it over to examine its blank back. "That is super, Will. Do you mind if I ask why you would receive an invitation from a partner in N. M. Rothschild and Sons to take luncheon in their private dining room?"

Why indeed? But it only *seemed* mysterious; it was not in fact so. In the early 1950s as mentioned by Jeffrey himself yesterday, the premier of Newfoundland, Joey Smallwood, had finagled a meeting with Sir Winston Churchill, who'd recently become prime minister again. Smallwood wanted to discuss the development of one of the last great hydroelectrical potentials left in the world, the Grand Falls on the Hamilton River in the wild heart of Labrador. Having heard Smallwood's pitch, Churchill pronounced it "a grand imperial concept—imperial, not imperialistic." My father, who was Minister of Resources in the Newfoundland government, had been there with Smallwood, and told me how everyone had laughed at Churchill's wit; he'd been under constant political attack in the Commons for his steadfast defence of imperialistic Britain—this sort of thing: "I have not become the king's First Minister in order to preside over the liquidation of the British Empire!"A Labour MP had called him the last of the Neanderthal imperialists.

Churchill had undertaken to put Smallwood in touch with his banker friends, the de Rothschilds, to see if they might be interested in assembling a consortium of adventurers to examine and perhaps develop the idea. The upshot was that Edmund de Rothschild formed a company for that purpose called the British Newfoundland Corporation, BRINCO for short, which had been striving ever since to get the thing up and running. But because of Quebec's resistance— that province always maintained that Labrador was part of Quebec not Newfoundland—and owing to the government of Canada's pusillanimity in not enforcing the federal right to let the project run a transmission line through Quebec's territory, BRINCO had so far been stymied. That was the state of affairs when Smallwood and my father notified Edmund de Rothschild of my arrival in England as a law student. They were hoping for a casual invitation to some function for me—a horizons-broadening thing.

"Oh, Eddie de Rothschild is a friend of my father's," I now said to Archer, embroidering the truth. They were in fact accidental and very occasional politico-business acquaintances.

"*Eddie* de Rothschild, you call him. What the hell does your father do?"

"He's only a minister in the government of a minor province of Canada, but his portfolio happens to include one of the largest remaining hydroelectric developments on the face of the earth. Hence the interest of the de Rothschilds, who are furthering the enterprise. You mentioned it yesterday."

"Yes, of course, the river in Labrador," said Jeffrey. "And I also mentioned that you and I would make a pretty good team regarding developments in Canada."

"You said you wanted to alert me to something?"

"I did. I've been advised to expect an agreeable little write-up in the *Cherwell* this week on your productive dialogues with Sir Noel concerning Haig and Galbraith. The whole thing was too good to let die without a broader audience."

CHAPTER 4

J effrey Archer began a habit of sitting down by me or waving me over to sit with him at every meal he took in the dining hall. Three times, he drove me to his flat for an evening hour of coffee and port and talk. When the *Cherwell* came out, he was pleased with the story, unbylined, on me and Lord Haig's plaque—William Cull's assertive but gracious approach to Sir Noel in the famous room Jeffrey Archer had brought the Beatles to last spring, Sir Noel's even-handed response to Cull, Galbraith's serendipitous intervention to condemn Haig, and Sir Noel's broadminded arrangement to follow through on having an independent committee look into the matter.

Claire was at the flat. "Crikey. That's somewhat more restrained than the story I heard." She looked at Archer. "Someone's a master of diplomacy."

"Perhaps there is some subtle diplomacy in the piece," said Jeffrey. "But no advantage in hurt feelings if we can still get the points across."

"I like the way it captures the all-important element—that everything started, as usual, in Archer's famous Beatles room." Claire grinned at me, and Jeffrey chuckled.

Each time I came to the flat when Claire was there, she overdid her delight at my presence, more than seemed strictly necessary for an infrequently seen friend of her beau. The third evening I was there, Jeffrey studied me silently for a few seconds and then her for longer, with a guarded look on his face. I was a little discomfited.

"Archer," Claire said. "Why are you giving me that 'My Last Duchess' look?"

Jeffrey laughed, and quoted sonorously from Browning's sinister poem on malignant jealousy: "I gave commands; / Then all smiles stopped together. There she stands / As if alive ..."

"Never forget, dear boy, that these days that knife can cut both ways," said Claire, showing no sign of stopping her smiles as she turned to me. "Is it true, as Archer has reported, that you've signed up to go on the same pre-Christmas skiing trip as me and my friends, the one to Zurs in Austria, sponsored by Oxford, Cambridge, and Trinity College, Dublin."

"He has reported accurately," I answered.

"A freakish aberration," said Jeffrey, "as Claire will agree."

"True, but this time a happy one," she said. "Will, my friends and I are organizing a small group to go on that trip together. Very companionable people, don't you think, Archer?"

"I do. Especially the two suitably unattached girls that might be of interest to Will and his mate."

"It'll be great fun. We'll all be in the same carriage on the train and in the same hotel in Zurs for après-ski delights. Come join us, you and your friend. Jeffrey met him in your rooms one time, I believe—a compatriot of yours ...?"

"Neil Murray at Oriel," said Jeffrey. The guy had instant recall of names he'd heard once. "Looked like a first-rate bloke. An English Lit sort like you, Claire. He can help you separate the dirty from the divine in Donne's poetry over a Glühwein."

"We may never see the ski lifts."

I broke in. "But Neil and I are already fully registered and paid up. The guidelines made it clear that the organizers assigned the berths on the train and the hotel rooms on a random basis, so ..." I didn't mention that my friend and I had been alerted about the trip by two charming students from St. Hilda's College we'd become chatty with in the close quarters of the Turf Tavern. I'd hit it off with one of them; we'd had a dinner date last week. No commitments, but we'd told each other that we looked forward to spending time together in Austria.

"Oh, you can leave all the coordination with the organizers' travel agent to me," said Claire. "A good friend of mine is head of the organizing committee. All I need is your names and receipt numbers on this authorization form to have your packets of tickets and reservations made up with ours."

"Sounds excellent," I said. "I'll get Neil's okay on it tonight and drop the information off at Lady Margaret Hall tomorrow morning."

"Or you could give it to me for her," said Jeffrey. "We're in for a couple of days of drizzle, and it's a bit of a trek from BNC. I'll be seeing her at LMH tomorrow lunchtime."

"It's not that far. And I need all the exercise I can get to top up my fitness for the skiing. I'll just drop it off at the porters' lodge in Claire's name."

Claire widened those lips over her teeth. "Done then," she said, with a first-rate my-last-duchess smile.

The next morning, with the registration particulars of Neil Murray and myself in pocket, I walked for 15 minutes along Parks Road and through Norham Gardens in a light but steady downpour. Even if I hadn't had an umbrella, I wouldn't have regretted turning down Archer's offer to deliver the documents I was toting. My hope was to encounter Claire in college, somehow. I had grown to like her company a lot, and vice versa, it seemed—as a friend, of course, as part of my power-couple pals, Jeffrey and Claire.

I was giving the envelope to the porter at the desk in Lady Margaret Hall when I heard from the corridor, "Good morning, Egon Zimmermann." It was Claire, calling me by the name of the man who'd won the Olympics downhill gold medal that year. I'd told her and Jeffrey last night that I'd hardly ever been on skis before.

I continued the silliness. "And good morning to you, Christl Haas." That was the female gold medalist. I turned as she came up to me and in my peripheral vision I could see her shorts and bare legs. I kept my eyes on hers. "We'll have to find a name for Jeffrey," I said, "unless he already *is* an Olympic-class skier."

"I'm glad I didn't miss you, Will. I was keeping an eye out for you before my morning run."

Now I used the excuse of her run to look down. She was in very short shorts and sandals. Her legs were lissom and strong and lovely. Without an unseemly rush, I brought my eyes up again. "It's very cool and rainy out for a run in that outfit."

"Oh." She glanced down at her limbs as if she'd just become aware of how she was dressed. "No, this is only my William Blake reading outfit. He makes me get overheated. Come up for a cuppa." She signed me in and led me down the corridor and up the stairs. Behind her, I noticed that her buttocks were strong and appealing, and, though perfectly proportioned to the rest of her body, they made her shorts seem a size too small. My heart reacted with an extra beat each time the toes of a foot raised her to the next step, causing the calf to go from lovely to beautiful perfection, and her bum to shift in a way that guaranteed the perpetuation of the human race.

In her room she left the door open 6 inches, showed me a chair, and put on her kettle. Then she kicked off her sandals and sat cross-legged in the other chair. As she moved, even slightly, there occurred under her overlarge T-shirt a free and gentle and substantial stirring. She showed no concern for the impact that her overall splendour, or the fineness of each body part, might have on someone. I ventured the opinion that she looked great in her Blake-reading ensemble. "But it would be impossible for you not to look great in a burlap sack."

She laughed, "Thank you, Will, but I can't take any credit, existentially, for my anatomy. It just happened." All the same, her disclaimer seemed not to inhibit her from following Dear Abby's advice to the modest sex: "If you've got it, flaunt it." Or, at least, don't be too scrupulously shy about it.

After 20 minutes of chit-chat and chuckles, she walked me down to the entrance where she said goodbye for now with a buddylike pat on my shoulder. I strolled back to Brasenose, echoing in my thoughts my first utterance to her: this gorgeous woman could never be mine.

But then solace seeped into my heart from that very impossibility; futility crushed all hope aborning and gave me relief.

At dinner in hall that night, Archer came in, looked around, spotted me, and walked over. He politely asked the student beside me if he'd mind shifting over so that he could sit next to me: he had some vital information to impart. The student obliged.

Archer sat down and murmured into my ear, "Good luck on your big day in London tomorrow." Then he asked in a louder voice if I could join him and Claire for a coffee after dinner. I said I'd be delighted. He squeezed my arm and then broke into his normal, charismatic group-conversation mode. I sat there relishing the thought that this leading student had sought me out in front of all the others to sit next to me for a tête-à-tête and an invitation to his digs.

Driving there, Jeffrey asked me if he could mention to Claire my lunch at the de Rothschild's tomorrow. Delighted that she'd learn of my big assignation without my having to mention it, I said, yes, of course.

Claire was already at the flat, and getting the coffee ready. She had a key, evidently. She'd jogged here from LMH, she said, touching her ratty sweat pants and jersey, confirming my conclusion that there was nothing the woman didn't look good in. Over coffee, Jeffrey described to her in detail how and why I'd been invited down to London, embellishing, as I'd done to him, first, the nature of my relationship with Winston Churchill: "Will's mentor, Prime Minister Smallwood, is an intimate of Sir Winston's"; then my "close" relationship with the de Rothschild firm—"Eddie de Rothschild is an exceedingly close friend of Will's family"; and finally my connection with the proposed Labrador hydro project—"and Will's father has complete governmental control over this last, vast power development on earth." Throughout, Claire looked from his face to mine, shaking her head occasionally in obvious awe.

At the end of his narrative, she said, "Jesus, you two yobs! You don't even have to look at a door, let alone knock on it, to have it open wide for you." She rose and went into the kitchen to get more coffee. Coming out, she added, "You know, if you two stick together, and work closely together, the whole world is your bloody oyster. I'm looking forward to writing the screenplay about it." She raised her hands in the air, the coffee pot still in one, and moved them slowly apart as if framing the title in the marquee of a theatre, intoning: "*The Great Gatsby Boys.*" As we laughed, I noticed a drip of scalding coffee coming dangerously close to landing on her head. Days later, I would recall that near accident, as my first inkling that this brilliant woman seemed sometimes careless, even oblivious, of the risk flowing from an impetuous action.

"There's something about that title that unsettles me," said Jeffrey now. "Why don't you try instead *Rosencrantz and Guildenstern: Their Many Successes*"?

We all laughed again, and Claire looked at the ceiling in thoughtful mode. "Seriously for a second, though, you two would really make a great team. And the pair of you acting together ... you'd be what some business writers are describing these days with the term *synergy*—two elements together being greater than the sum of their parts. I think that'd be you two."

Jeffrey was gazing at her … fondly, it seemed, and turned to me with his wry grin for my reaction. "Jeffrey, do you know how blessed you are with Claire? Not only is she beautiful and brilliant, but she spares no effort to further your cause at every turn."

"You'd think a man of his discernment would realize all that more fully, wouldn't you?" Claire said, with a laugh. "And by the by, just to show I have your best interests at heart also, Will, I'm going to suggest to Archer that he lay his hands on that E-type Jaguar he has access to, and drive you down to London in it tomorrow. Consider the impression you will make when he drops you off at the door. Doormen are the world's greatest gossips, so your arrival in such style would permeate the entire building within the hour."

"Good idea. I'd be happy to do that, Will, if you'd like."

My chary intuition reacted. "Thank you, Jeffrey. But there are some other things I need to attend to in London during the morning beforehand, so I'm going to take the early train."

He and Claire glanced at each other and they both regarded me closely for some seconds. Did I see in their gaze a flicker of awareness that I was not the self-starting, cunning, quick study I needed to be for real success in this life? It hit me, not for the first time, but firmer than before, that I was somewhat out of my comfort zone with Jeffrey as a friend. At least, at this stage of my life. That would no doubt change, I thought, as I became more experienced and self-confident, and we became even closer friends, and I did want that. I thoroughly liked being with him. He smiled warmly at me and said, "Whatever you think best, old boy. Have another port."

Claire had a grim smile on, almost tragic: "You have the royal jelly, Will. Don't neglect to use it to the maximum extent possible. It would be a sin to do otherwise."

"Well, any sins I commit have to be fun, at least."

"No argument from me on that one," said Claire.

"I'm going to take off," I said. "I've got an early rise in the morning." I turned down Jeffrey's offer of a drive to the college and walked back. For no reason I could put my finger on, I felt unsettled by Claire as I went.

CHAPTER 5

I reached London in the morning with a few hours to spare, intending to arrive at the de Rothschild establishment in good time. I killed over an hour in Foyles Bookstore and then hailed a cab. When I gave the driver the name and the address I'd memorized, he disputed its correctness. The de Rothschilds had occupied their premises at New Court, St. Swithin's Lane, for two centuries, he said. They were more time-honoured than the Bank of England. Over the years, he'd conveyed many a toff there. I gave way to him, the last time in my life that I would surrender to a claim of authoritative knowledge different from my own.

When we arrived at the cabby's choice of address, we found a building in the process of reconstruction. A sign said that the firm was rebuilding New Court and that the offices were lodged in temporary quarters at the address I'd given the driver.

"Oh Christ, I'm going to be late," I groaned.

The driver turned off his meter and broke speed limits to get there. All the way I interrupted his profuse apologies with a continuous chant of how my important meeting was going to be ruined, rendering the man, by the sound of him, semi-suicidal.

Dropping me off, he offered to waive the fare altogether, but didn't insist when I declined. I gave him the exact amount, and then added as a punishment for making me nearly five minutes late, a tip of three pence. I ran to the entrance, feeling a feathery hit to the back of my head and hearing something light drop to the ground. I looked back and saw that the cabbie had overcome his remorse enough to fire my three-penny bit at me, and glower.

Inside the door, at reception, a retainer escorted me toward the dining room. A shortish, bald-headed man turned a compassionate face to me at the door and introduced himself. Despite my embroidery of the relationship to Jeffrey, this was the first time I'd met Edmund de Rothschild. He noted my overheated state, and I blamed my delay on the cabbie, omitting mention of the projectile I'd furnished and its launch. "Poor chap. He has spent his life cramming his head full of the whereabouts of every street and established business in London, and thereupon we moved our headquarters temporarily from the site we've occupied for three or four lifetimes." He urged me to calm myself and enjoy lunch.

Inside, de Rothschild introduced me to the one other person present, a man of about 40, whose double-barrelled name was not then meaningful to me. It would soon be embedded in my brain forever. I was seated to the right of the host, as the guest of honour, and the other man sat to his left. When de Rothschild took his seat, I glanced at the door, surprised that there were only the three of us at the table. "A simple triumvirate," he said, "for a cozy tête-à-tête."

As Edmund and I chatted—what I was reading at Oxford, how

Premier Smallwood and my father were—the other man stayed quiet. But he never took his eyes off me. I felt as if he was an observer at my audition for a role; I had no idea for what. To impress them, I mentioned the book I'd found in Blackwell's bookstore in Oxford last week by Frederic Morton on the de Rothschild dynasty and had read for this occasion. "It was extremely thought-provoking," I said.

"That book," Edmund responded, "is full of inaccuracies. You'd be far better served if you spent your playful time attending theatre in the West End. Have you seen *A Severed Head* at the Criterion, yet?"

"The adaptation of the Iris Murdoch novel? No, not yet. But I will. I quite enjoyed the book; rather amusing in a farcical way: the growing sexual revolution hits the middle classes." I was really perking now, parroting a two-line review of the play I'd read a few weeks ago in *Time Out* magazine. "Did you enjoy it?"

"Tolerably. I went to see it because of the title. It struck me as an accurate prediction of the condition of my own head if we didn't get our Labrador hydro development up and running soon." De Rothschild smiled at me and turned to the other guest, who still seemed intent only on studying me. I figured I was going to have to disappoint him after the meal, if he was hoping that this might bloom into something more than a beautiful friendship. "Some nights, Anthony," de Rothschild said to him, "when I'm lying wide awake in bed during the small hours, staring disconsolately at the ceiling, and trying to muster some of Napoleon's 3 a.m. courage, I chastise Sir Winston for first involving me in that enterprise."

"I beg your pardon, sir!" said Anthony, grinning. "But it's a grand imperial concept."

I joined their chortles, and displayed my inside knowledge: "That's one of Premier Smallwood's favourite stories of Churchill. Second only, perhaps, to Sir Winston's remark during the First World War that Newfoundlanders were the best small-boat men in the world."

"Yes, he's always had a profound knowledge of Newfoundland and great affection for Newfoundlanders," said Anthony. "He considers that your rather challenging climate there gave rise to a vigorous race of settlers originally from the British Isles as well as a remarkable people in the form of the Aboriginal inhabitants. He told me that when he landed once at the airbase in Botwood during the war—it was the month of May—a raging snowstorm had just ended. He asked a stupefied airman from Washington state, 'How do you like the Newfoundland spring?' The poor American just shook his head and replied, 'But they told me we'd be on the same latitude here as Seattle.' To which Sir Winston replied, 'We are, my good man. And the climate is much the same—it's just that the *weather* is rather different.'"

We all chuckled at the hapless American, and fortunately, before I could display my gross ignorance by asking this Anthony how he knew Churchill so well, Edmund reverted to his project. "And it is a grand concept. But with the Canadian government impotent and the Quebec government intractable, it's somewhat slower showing its true worth, Mr. Cull, than our consortium originally believed."

"Indeed," I said.

There was now a lapse in the conversation, as we tucked into our veal. I felt tested to fill it with something diverting. "Speaking of novels," I said, "I see that a UK paperback edition of *Catch-22* is piled up in all the bookstores. I read it when it first came out a couple of years ago, but I must pick it up and look at it again." That was book number three in 10 minutes that I'd alleged I'd read. I could probably stop now, having convinced all present that my elementary school system had succeeded in teaching me my letters.

"Fairly amusing book," said Edmund. "Did you like it, Anthony?" The guest raised and lowered a noncommittal hand. Eddie turned to me. "Like the protagonist, Anthony was in the Air Force during the war."

"Eddie tells me you're attending Oxford on a highly coveted scholarship, Mr. Cull," said Anthony. "Congratulations."

"Thank you. But the congratulations would be more merited if the scholarship weren't restricted to men. I knew half a dozen girls at university who were more deserving than me. But their brainy big heads up top couldn't compete with my brain-free little head down below."

Dead silence. Sometimes my notion of a comical utterance didn't sound as amusing aloud as when I was formulating it in my big head. But then they both chuckled and Anthony said to Edmund, "I must pass that on to Sir Winston. He'll enjoy using it when he teases Lady Churchill about women taking over everywhere. Law, Eddie says, Mr. Cull? One would have thought, from your remarks here today, that you were reading English Literature."

"And I should be. It's my first love. I've always wanted to write. But my father convinced me that the *first* priority of anyone who imagines he's going to be writer of deathless prose is, quote, 'pay the goddamned rent.' Hence, law."

"And thank God for rational fathers," said Anthony. "I met your father, Walter Cull? with Sir Winston Churchill. He was in Premier Smallwood's entourage some years ago when they had a meeting with Sir Winston on the subject of the Labrador hydro power that Eddie was just fulminating about."

Who the hell was this guy? I must have telegraphed my surprise, because Edmund said, "Anthony is Sir Winston's private secretary, as you are doubtless aware."

I nodded my "of course," putting on a confident face.

"Sir Winston especially remembers him," said Anthony, "because your father said it was high time someone wrote a modern book, a myth-debunking book, about the Beothuk of Newfoundland, the original Red Indians. That was of exceedingly great interest to the prime minister."

"May I ask how the Beothuk of Newfoundland came up during a discussion about a power development on the Grand Falls of Labrador?"

"Oh, Sir Winston is fascinated by them and their ultimate plight—has been all his life, even before he was Undersecretary for the Colonies. They were so mysterious in their origins, language, customs, and senseless demise. His empathy with them made him raise the subject as soon as he heard your father's name, 'Cull,' which of course figured prominently in the person of your namesake, William Cull, in their last days. Are you named after him? Your father said he was an ancestor."

"Afraid so. He seems to have been a very ambiguous character, for better or for worse, historically speaking." This was all I needed now—a discussion on genocide, and my ancestor's uncertain role therein, in front of Jewish leader Edmund de Rothschild. "You mentioned Sir Winston's empathy with the Beothuk." I continued. "But didn't he say somewhere that no wrongs were done to North American Indians?"

"Yes, he did say something like that. He told the Royal Commission on Palestine in the late 1930s that he did not admit a great wrong had been done to the Red Indians of America because a higher race had come in and taken their place."

Edmund de Rothschild held up his hand. "But he didn't really believe that, then or now. Remember that he was always a great advocate of a Jewish homeland in Palestine and he was prepared to advance extreme views against adversaries and in support of his position."

"No doubt," smiled Anthony. "But we must concede that Sir Winston believes history has shown, by and large, that the upper classes of England were at the top of the Darwinian pyramid."

"Of which he happened to be a member, of course." I smirked. "I wonder what he would have thought if he'd been born with the same brain on an Indian reservation in the Arizona desert."

"Interesting you say that," said Anthony. "It's been asserted that Sir Winston has American Indian ancestry through his mother. He himself says he believes it is a fact. Which, of course, maddens beyond endurance some English-blood purists among his family and relatives, much to his delight. He has goaded them by asking what on earth they thought had made him rise so irresistibly, so *ineluctably,* from the seven generations of slumbering Marlborough mediocrity since the exploits of his one great ancestor, the first Duke of Marlborough. His most sincere belief is in the great man theory, the unstoppable man of destiny, of which, assuredly, he was one. And you, Mr. Cull? Are you as interested in the original Red Indians as your father is?"

"It seems to be in the genes—literally. My grandmother told me as a young boy of her own grandmother relating stories to her as a young girl of the Indians, the Beothuk, frightening the women half to death on Fogo Island in the early 1800s by clambering on the roofs of houses and breaking into storage sheds to steal things when the men were away trapping or fishing, and of the men then tracking them down to try to get their tools and goods back, usually with disastrous consequences for the Beothuk. My father claims we have ancestors on both sides of the tragic issue—the Europeans like Cull who allegedly pursued the Red Indians with murderous intent and the hunted Beothuk themselves who tried, with their own sporadic attacks on settlers, to avoid their extermination as thieving vermin in the eyes of the white man."

De Rothschild shook his head and I heard him mutter something unintelligible. I didn't ask him to repeat it. We'd already strayed too close to horror for a luncheon conversation hosted by him. But as Anthony stared at me without saying anything, I did have to ask quickly, "How did Sir Winston become so fascinated with the Beothuk, in particular, I wonder?"

Anthony sat back. "Mr. Cull, Eddie tells me you're at Brasenose." This was beginning to feel like a job interview, with its disjointed questions and comments to me. "Wonderful little college, right in the middle of things, Radcliffe Square with the delightful Radcliffe

Camera in front of it. A lot of good rowers, too—in my day, BNC was called the king of the river."

"Were you at Oxford?"

"I was at Magdalen. But I had to leave, reluctantly, to join the war effort. I spent some time in Canada and the US learning how to be a fighter pilot."

"Anthony was awarded the Distinguished Flying Cross for his acts of valour while flying in active operations, especially against the Japanese."

"A lot of DFCs were handed out, Eddie."

"And all deserved."

"After the war I went up to Magdalen again before joining the foreign service."

"Magdalen is a beautiful college," I said. "And clever too, apparently. A Swiss girl I met at a party, who had a boyfriend at Magdalen, told me they had more firsts in the examinations than any other college, whereas Brasenose is distinguished, she said, by our rowing-related charley horses—especially the ones between our ears." We chuckled.

"Like Field Marshal Douglas Lord Haig's," said Anthony. He met my surprised look with, "It was in the *Cherwell*. Sir Winston was intrigued by the article when I showed it to him, and the reference to a student of your name. He asked me to look into the episode, and I discovered that the actual exchange between you and Sir Noel was perhaps a little feistier than reported. Sir Winston was delighted with it. I was personally more interested, as a former diplomat, in how the story, as written, smoothed over possible animosities and hurt feelings of Sir Noel consequent on Galbraith's savage attack on the position he'd assumed and his support of yours. I take it you're familiar with Jeffrey Archer, Mr. Cull."

"I am. He's at Brasenose."

"I understand that he didn't actually write the piece but that he was a moderating influence."

"Jeffrey Archer?" de Rothschild inquired. "The name sounds familiar."

"Yes, he's the bloke who had the Beatles fundraiser at Oxford for Oxfam last spring. It was in the papers."

"Oh righto. My musical little daughter and her cousins wanted to go up to see them—the Fab Four, they called them."

"Interesting fellow, Archer," said Anthony. "Sir Winston still likes to keep tabs on politically ambitious young up-and-comers especially those with a Conservative Party bent, like Archer. He asked me to research him a little. But frankly it was the involvement of Sir Noel Hall with the Beatles thing that made Sir Winston most curious. He appreciated Sir Noel's contributions during the war and all that and didn't think he was the sort to want to be associated with a passing, popular-music fad."

"Well, as you said, it was an important fundraiser for Oxfam."

"Yes, and a highly successful one. But the more I looked into Archer, the more nasty rumourmongering turned up. In the first place, nobody in Oxford, or London, can seem to work out what he's up to. He's but a part-time employee of the charity, Oxfam, yet is said to own several cars and houses in Oxford. He's not in fact a member of your college but is doing some sort of Education certificate with the university and is associated with BNC through the machinations of the principal, Sir Noel Hall, who knew him from a previous situation—school, I believe. His qualifications for admission to his course of studies are alleged to be dubious, as his American university degree is said to have been granted by a body-building club. The certificate he's working toward is supposed to take one year to attain, and he has already started his second without finishing it."

"It sounds like you're reading from a tabloid scandal sheet."

"It does a bit, doesn't it? I was somewhat flabbergasted at the amount of it that came at me. A tutor at BNC who was at Sir Noel's reception for the Beatles told me that one of the band—the bloke with the name like the founder of the Russian Communist Party ...?"

"Lennon. John Lennon."

"That is the very gent. Sir Winston was amused by the similarity of names. It's exceedingly convenient, he said, to have one's abhorrence of communism and one's revulsion at the popular music of these 1960s summed up in the one name. My tutor friend told me that Mr. Lennon asked him who this Jeffrey Archer chap was, because, when he shook hands with him, Lennon said, he felt he should count his fingers afterwards to make certain he'd got all of them back."

Edmund laughed. "We could use Lennon's attitude on some of our boards ... if he'd just change his name to something less evocative of insurrection and revolution."

"There was comment from another member of the band, as well," said Anthony. "The curious-looking bloke—is he the drummer?"

"Ringo Starr."

"Right you are. A student at Merton, who attended Archer's fundraising event, has said that he found himself in the lavatory standing at a urinal next to your Ringo Starr. Mr. Starr asked him if he knew this Jeffrey Archer chap; he was a nice enough fella, Mr. Starr said, but he struck him as the kind of bloke who would bottle your piss and sell it back to you."

Edmund had to put down his coffee and laugh. "University politics is nasty indeed at the Other Place. Next time, we'll have edifying stories only from my Cambridge."

"Yes, I've noticed a fair amount of jealousy of Jeffrey there," I said evenly. "He's a superb athlete, too ... an athletics Blue, and heading for the presidency of the Oxford University Athletics Club. Have you heard any defamatory rumours about that?"

"Nothing actionable. Only that television film is said to exist of him making a false start in a 100-yard dash this year, but it was not immediately picked up at the time and he was not disqualified."

"I'm invited on a skiing holiday to Austria before Christmas that Jeffrey and his girlfriend have arranged. I'll let you know if he talks anyone there from Magdalen into buying an Alp."

Anthony laughed. "I didn't realize you were close to him like that. I hope I didn't injure your sensibilities. But I will say this: if he does sell someone an Alp, he will have bred true. His father, William Archer, was reputed to be a confidence man and a bigamist, who stole the identity of another William Archer, conveniently dead, and appropriated his war honours as his own. Later, he was charged with fraud as a London mortgage broker, and upon being granted bail, fled to the US under another assumed name."

"I understand the father has been dead for nearly 10 years. So we'll have to hang Jeffrey in his stead."

"The son shall not suffer for the iniquity of the father," said Eddie. "However tempting, sometimes."

"Quite right. Sir Winston would admire your loyalty to your friend, Mr. Cull. He's always been like that himself. Sometimes excessively so. For example, Anthony Eden was his friend and colleague—his second in command in the House for years, married to his niece, that sort of thing. Privately, Sir Winston thought he was a vain, blundering fool as prime minister, especially during the Suez Canal crisis in 1956. But publicly, to the despair of many of us around Sir Winston, he supported Eden's actions."

"That's a degree of hypocrisy that doesn't seem to accord with the great man's reputation for courageous integrity," I said. Anthony had got my dander up. "Or perhaps it was just a matter of British imperialism overriding all else in his mind."

"You don't appear to be one of Sir Winston's admirers."

"I do admire what's admirable in him, but I've also been amazed at his breathtaking, life-long arrogance. He's always done exactly what he felt like doing, personally and politically, come hell or high water, and regardless of the consequences to others." I hadn't fully realized how irritated I'd become by the rumourmongering about Jeffrey. I pushed ahead. "What old man would remain on and on as prime minister, sick, weak, and probably suffering dementia, unless driven by extreme arrogance, or absolute egotism to the point of clinical pathology? Perhaps Sir Winston's salvation of the world against Hitler was not the result of far-seeing insight and brave strength of character possessed by no one else, but simply elitist arrogance, ingrained self-importance, and egotism of psychotic proportions."

"I know you can't mean all that," said de Rothschild, smiling painfully. "And I shouldn't let your Premier Smallwood hear you say it, if I were you. He has told me many times that, in the phrase of Oliver Cromwell, he's a 'warts and all' admirer of Sir Winston, as am I. Mr. Smallwood even wishes to name our Labrador project, the great falls and its river, after Churchill when he dies: Churchill Falls. Sir Winston has been a most welcome luncheon guest here—he has sat where you're sitting—on countless occasions."

I couldn't resist. "But isn't he on the record as anti-Semitic?"

"He may have spoken and written the casual, general prejudice of his class and time against Jews, now and then, but he consistently supported the idea of a Jewish state in Palestine. And as far back as the early 1920s, he wrote that whether people are partial to Jews or not, there can be no doubt that they are the most remarkable race in the world."

"Well, what about his anti-Muslim stance? Didn't he write that Islamic fanaticism is just as dangerous in a man as rabies is in a dog?"

Anthony spoke. "He was talking specifically about the Mahdists of the Sudan in his book following the savage war he fought there personally in the late 1890s. Later in life, family tradition has it that he was so fascinated with Islam that they had to intervene to keep him from converting to it. I don't believe that—Winston has never been inclined to be a devotee of any religion. But it does indicate a certain bias in favour, not against. And during the Second World War, he had his cabinet grant £100,000 toward the building of a mosque in London in appreciation of Muslims who had fought to preserve the British Empire. Actions do speak louder than words."

"Oh yes, the preservation of the British Empire. Wasn't he also fanatical in his opposition to Mahatma Gandhi's fight for the autonomy of India? I read somewhere that he advised his cabinet colleagues not to release Gandhi from jail over his threat to begin another fast. Churchill said that they'd be rid of a very bad man and a big enemy of the British Empire if Gandhi starved to death. Giving India independence, apparently, was going to bring about the collapse of the Empire and the downfall of civilization in our time. One theory of why few people paid attention to Churchill's forewarnings about Hitler leading up to the German invasion of Poland was that, a few years before, he'd said precisely the same things about Gandhi."

"I don't believe Sir Winston would take great exception to some of those views," said Anthony. "But he might say about them, again with Oliver Cromwell, 'I beseech you, in the bowels of Christ, think it possible you may be mistaken.'"

"Yes, of course," I said, trying to grin insouciantly, grateful for the opportunity to back away from my rant. "I do think it possible I may be mistaken."

"I don't hear that round this table very often," said Eddie, rising abruptly to end the lunch.

At the door Anthony asked me for the dates of my planned absence from the UK before Christmas. I gave him the fortnight spread for the skiing trip. He frowned and said, "That's damned awkward."

"Why?"

"Premature to say." He gave me his card with his address and telephone number and asked me to let him know right away if my skiing holiday plans changed. Meanwhile, did I have a phone number where I could be reached in college? I gave him the number for the student phone in the lodge, and he said he'd very likely be in touch with me soon. "And by the by, Sir Winston was delighted by all that gossip I mentioned to you on Archer. 'There's a man who will go places,' he said. 'A man has to be exceptional to cause that kind of reaction.' He even asked Lady Churchill to consider inviting him to his upcoming 90th birthday celebration to enliven the place a little."

"Jeffrey'd like that for sure."

"But she won't invite him. She wants to restrict the list to family and old, longtime friends and colleagues, and the house will already be overstuffed with them alone."

I said goodbye and headed for the young woman downstairs holding a taxi at the front door. Edmund was apparently unaware that the acoustics on the staircase of this temporary place allowed for easy eavesdropping by departing visitors; as I descended, I heard Anthony ask him if his secretary could provide my mailing address in Oxford, and the reply, "Certainly, but do you really think Sir Winston would find him suitable, in fact?"

"Oh, I don't know. Probably. It's for a very specific purpose. He is, rather, a spirited young bugger. He might be just the ticket. And there's no requirement that they fall in love with each other."

CHAPTER 6

Jeffrey dropped in on me that night. He had a bottle of Sandeman port with him and while he filled two glasses, he asked, "How did it go with Mr. de Rothschild et al.?"

"Fine. It was pleasant enough. Nothing exceptional." I didn't feel like mentioning the slander—or bringing up the disappointing birthday possibility.

"Who else was there?"

"Sir Winston Churchill's private secretary."

"Anthony Montague Browne? Just the three of you? That was a highly exclusive lunch."

"I wouldn't call it the event of the year."

"Well, you were certainly occupying a rarefied atmosphere. Do you know why?" I shrugged and shook my head. "What did you talk about?"

"General chit-chat."

"Where do you go from here? What's next on the agenda?"

"Nothing, I'd say." I saw no need to mention Anthony's cryptic references regarding me.

"That's peculiar. A highly promising, auspicious, meeting that goes nowhere?"

"Well, I don't think I ingratiated myself with my host. He admires Winston Churchill immensely, and I kept bringing up the great man's Victorian era prejudices and his tendency to govern by whimsical impulse."

He grinned at me. "That's amusing, Will. You concentrated on alienating yourself from both Churchill's close factotum and his known friend and admirer by disparaging their great man right in front of them?"

"I'd say that's fairly accurate."

He gave a little chuckle. "And you didn't even have Galbraith standing by to rescue you?"

"Well, I generally have good reason for my follies, and I believe I did in this case."

"Wasn't it Sir Winston himself who said that the secret to success in politics is not merely to get elected but to get *re*-elected? I'd daresay that the same principle applies to success in life in general—not merely getting invited but getting reinvited."

I nodded wordlessly. Jeffrey studied me for a few seconds, and said, "Well, that looks like one avenue in Claire's plan for our brilliant success together, barred." Another mute nod from me. "Will, you're being strangely reticent, if not downright mysterious ..."

"Sorry. You're right. I wasn't going to get into this tonight. But, on second thought I should tell you. Your name came up."

"Really? In what context?"

"The article on Haig and me. Anthony Montague Browne zeroed

in on you as being somehow behind it."

"That was clever. So they did in point of fact actually know of me?"

"I wouldn't say Edmund de Rothschild was all that aware, but Anthony certainly was. He knew of the Beatles thing here, of course, and Sir Winston had heard of you as a young Conservative Party up-and-comer and asked him to have you checked out."

Archer stood up. "Sir Winston Churchill himself wanted me vetted! What was Montague Browne able to dig up?"

"Gossip and rumours, mostly. Nothing to place you on the pope's list of candidates for sainthood."

Archer laughed. "Bloody lucky you were on the spot, then, to debunk all the falsehoods."

"I did try. I debunked my little arse off." I gave him a summary of Anthony's account, and concluded with, "So, as you see, everything he kept bringing up about you was nearly entirely negative."

"Of course it was, Will. That is wholly unsurprising, but also wholly irrelevant. Thank you for trying to defend me—you're a good man—but it's impossible to come to the attention of the high and the mighty by meek and milquetoast conduct. The whole point here is that the great man saw the need to look at me and my prospects. That's all that matters, and I am exceedingly grateful to you for telling me that Churchill and his boots had been discussing me."

"There was also some good in it, along with bad. Apparently, Sir Winston thought you had to be exceptional to attract that kind gossip, and it showed you were going places. He suggested that you be invited to the celebration on his birthday to put some life in it."

"The 30th of the month. He'll be 90. That is good. What happened?"

"Lady Churchill said no. Old friends and close colleagues only."

Archer sat down again. "There might not be enough time for me to become an old friend, so I'll have to work on becoming a close colleague." He smiled. "Well, that's unfortunate. It would have been a phenomenal leg up. But thank you for telling me. It's good to know how the great ones are thinking. William, my friend, we won't always be just up-and-comers. Now I have a little bad news for you—the other reason I wanted to see you tonight—I can't go to Austria in December. I had hoped we'd be able to spend time there talking about our strategy for the future in England and Canada, but we'll have to do that after Christmas, now. Something personal came up I have to deal with."

His words "can't go to Austria" sent an electric shock through my body. Oh God. Claire would be there without him. Or—wait—would she be bowing out, too? I probed. "That's bloody awful for you—for both of you. Claire won't want to go if you're not there."

"Oh no, she'll be okay. I haven't told her yet, but I'd be very surprised if she'll miss that little jaunt. She'll have lots of friends there." He stood up. "Well, I'm off to tell her I have to depart tomorrow for Somerset for a few days with my mum." He gestured at his half full bottle of port. "I'll leave that for you to remember me by while I'm away."

"Take it for Claire."

"Normally I would, but I don't want her nipping into it tonight. We haven't been getting along recently and my news about the skiing trip may just be the last straw. See you when I get back."

"Thanks. Have a safe trip." I felt relieved at the thought of his absence for a while. I didn't want to feel guilty, every time I looked at him, over the thrill that went through me at the thought that he wouldn't be in Austria. I don't know why I experienced that excitement. What the hell was I expecting to happen between me and my friend Jeffrey's girl on this skiing trip, especially with their pals all around? I had to admit to myself yet again that the further I stayed away from Claire, the less I'd feel the pain of my futile desire. In Austria, I'd bail out of her orbit and stick with the easygoing Neil Murray and the girls we knew.

My reading of legal texts that night was interrupted by questions in my mind over how long I could stay friends with Archer, as much as I might want to. In his personal gifts and his street savvy shrewdness and his expectations for us two, he was out of my league. He was a couple of years older, and without doubt a product of a more know-how environment, a *savoir faire* milieu, which made me suspect that I mightn't be able to keep up with his own demands on himself. A touch of resentment started to arise in me over his signals, unstated but insinuated, I believed, that I wasn't measuring up as a bullshit artist.

The next afternoon, Sir Noel Hall sent a porter to fetch me to his lodgings for an important discussion. "Archer informs me," said Sir Noel, "that you had lunch yesterday with Edmund de Rothschild and Anthony Montague Browne. Had I but known, I would have given you a message of my personal good wishes for Sir Winston."

"I had no idea Montague Browne was going to be there."

"Oh? Well, you certainly seem with great frequency to happen by chance on some fascinating personages. Galbraith back in Canada, and then great friends almost immediately on your arrival here with someone as exceptionally promising as Archer, and now an intimate lunch with the head of the greatest merchant bank in the City and the long-time private secretary of Churchill himself—do you have anyone else of note up your sleeve?"

"I can assure you, Sir Noel, that, as you correctly suggested, it has all been pure happenstance." I explained to him the de Rothschild connection to my homeland. Jeffrey would have been dismayed at my naïve downplaying of the importance of my connections. But there was no persuading Sir Noel of my want of eminence.

"Be that as it may," he responded, "but you were in fact invited, which I am sure does not happen to every young man associated with all enterprises or governments doing business with that great financial house. Still less does it explain why Edmund de Rothschild would have invited Churchill's man to what seems to have been an intimate conversation with you alone."

"I'm as mystified as you are."

Sir Noel leaned forward. "Did you talk of anyone that might give us a clue? Did Edmund de Rothschild know you are here at Brasenose?"

"Yes, he sent the invitation to me here."

Sir Noel leaned back in satisfaction. He was zeroing in on his truth. "Did anyone's name happen to come up in relation to the college?"

"Yes, sir, Archer's did. Anthony identified him as responsible for the Beatles' visit here where you, Sir Winston's wartime associate, now happen to be the principal."

"*Happen* to ...? Didn't he know it was I who extended that invitation? Archer was merely the emissary on my behalf in the piece." He lurched forward in his chair. "Purely as a matter of curiosity, was my name used in any other context?"

"Apparently Sir Winston couldn't imagine the Sir Noel Hall he had known during the war being such a huge fan of a popular music fad, so he had Anthony check Jeffrey out as a young man of evident influence. Especially since he's emerging as a Conservative Party up-and-comer."

"Had him checked *out*! Good heavens, the residual delusions of grandeur." He paused. "Ah, did Montague Browne mention anything else that Sir Winston might have said about ... the college?"

I swallowed and embellished. "He did indicate that Churchill retained his exceedingly high opinion of you." I made a mental note to report my public-relations progress to Jeffrey.

"Well." Sir Noel settled back, smiling. "Evidently, our ancient exalted does maintain his grip on the essentials. What, by the by, did Montague Browne discover about our friend Archer? Nothing insalubrious, I trust."

"A few silly rumours he'd picked up."

"Please divulge, if you would. I consider Archer a protégé of mine who will indeed be percolating to the top, and I need to be prepared beforehand to strike down falsehoods, should they arise in my presence."

Stressing confidentiality, I gave the principal a full summary of Montague Browne's points about Jeffrey. I left him sitting back, gazing fixedly up at a corner in the ceiling where two walls joined.

That evening, someone knocked at my door. I opened it, expecting to see Neil Murray or one of my fellow law students. Claire Perceval smiled in at me. "I fancied une coupe de vin with my good mate,

William the Conqueror," she said, striding straight through the doorway. "Got any?"

"Some execrable Spanish 'burgundy,'" I said. "And some excellent port of Jeffrey's, hidden away from predatory law students."

"I don't want any of Archer's bloody port."

"Oh. Okay. Where is Jeffrey? I thought he said he was going somewhere to visit with his mum."

"He is. He's gone to see dear Lola and kin in faraway Somerset, which is why I'm here."

"What do you mean?" I laughed. "Taken the wrong way, that could sound scary."

She laughed. "Even taken the right way, you have every reason for disquiet. Are you still lacking a regular girlfriend here at Oxford?"

"I have no girl yet that I've sworn undying, everlasting devotion and fidelity to, but a couple of good friends who do happen to be girls. Would you like some of my plonk?"

"And would you like to make love to me?"

Despite the quake within, I managed to treat the conversation as if it were mere surface banter. "You answered my question with a question, Claire, and a non sequitur, to boot. Good God, dear lady, you're reading English Literature at Oxford."

"And this lad is in his first term of law at the same institution, and already he's a nitpicker. Well, would you, Will?" She came close and placed her hands on my shoulders.

"There's not a man in Oxford—correction, in the entire free world—who would not like to make love to you. But, if I don't have a girlfriend, you do have a boyfriend."

"Deliver us from obfuscating lawyers! Let me try again. Will you kindly oblige me, dear friend, by making love to me?"

"I would very much like to make love to you, Claire. But Jeffrey is my friend too, so, ergo, no, I will not make love to you."

"Well, this is a conundrum. Because I assure you, Archer is no friend of mine. Did you know he has bailed out of our skiing trip, left me completely in the lurch? Something important came up, he said. That incensed me exceedingly—something more important than me?"

"So you'd like to get back at him by bedding one of his mates?"

"No, this would not be a spite shag, Will. I would have liked to make love with you ever since I first met you, as, I have perceived, you would me. I should tell you that meeting you has been something of a *coup de foudre* for me." I emitted a snort of derision at her ridiculously inflated words. "No, wait. Earlier, out of loyalty to Jeffrey, I wouldn't have. Just as you claim you wouldn't have. Now though, after what he did, I have been released from my bond of loyalty. I told him we were finished. And now I may follow my desires, not out of spite or revenge, but because I am now free to do whatever, whenever, and with whomever, I bloody well like." She touched my cheek.

Without answering over my thumping heart, I dawdled by pouring two glasses of wine, spilling some with a shaking hand. She grabbed hers and drained it in one gulp, making a violent shudder and putting on a face of severe revulsion. She said, "Jesus Christ, Will, you need to cheer me up after that." We laughed and she said, "And please don't pretend that you've never wanted to lift a lawless leg upon me."

The woman was a formidable devil's advocate. I felt incompetent to refute her arguments, logically or even spuriously. Instead, I stepped to the door and locked it, and turned round to discover her lips heading for my mouth. Now we joined hands and advanced on my bed. I moved mindlessly, like a penile automaton on mechanical feet. But I found my reaction there human and discerned a mutual feeling of gladness and delight in both of us before, during, and after our lovemaking.

Within the hour, Claire and I were walking across the quadrangle outside my staircase, side by side, but separated by more than a yard. I felt, without being able to put my finger on it, that there'd been something doubtful about Claire's explanation in my room. I said hello to the two students we passed. They looked from me to Claire, and I told myself that, in the dull light, I couldn't have seen what I sensed—censorious looks on their faces: I was only suffering post-coital guilt or remorse, sensations which, in those days, were all the fad in earnest student discourse about sex.

At the gate, I phoned a taxi and we stood outside in Radcliffe Square, keeping a few feet away from each other to dampen any accurate speculation by passing students. Perhaps the double takes I got from some resulted from their recognition of Jeffrey's girl, or more likely from the surprise of seeing me with such a striking woman. Claire and I didn't talk; we seemed sunk in our own thoughts. But as she was climbing aboard the taxi, she whispered confirmation of our plan to meet tomorrow afternoon in her room at Lady Margaret Hall for tea. Then she gazed back and waved and, until the car disappeared behind the curved perimeter of the Radcliffe Camera, her face stayed turned to me.

Back in my room I sat at the desk and glanced at the essay which, before the interruption, I'd been preparing for tomorrow's tutorial. It dealt with some old-time legal actions, and the question was which of them might still contain a spark of life, and which of them were currently obsolete and dead. My eye lit upon the wrongful act of "alienation of affection." This tort involved the wilful or malicious interference with the relationship between a husband and wife by a third party, usually by adultery. Claire was not a wife, or even in a relationship now, according to her, and the cause of action itself was probably lifeless, but the descriptions of some of the perpetrators in the old cases, for some reason, seemed alive and well to me: blighter, bounder, blackguard, cad, knave, miscreant, rogue, rotter, villain. I had to resist a weird impulse to apply them to myself.

But if, at first, those words seemed to suit my dubious conscience, the usual biological miracle soon took over: the reloading below began to create clearer and clearer images of my visit to Claire's room tomorrow afternoon until they obliterated all other pangs but one.

Then my brain went into overdrive imagining Claire and me living for two weeks in the close quarters of an Austrian ski resort. The surge of joy in my whole body felt boundless. As soon as Archer got back from Somerset, she'd have to tell him we were in love and together as a couple. It was all very quick, for sure, and I hoped it wouldn't give rise to awkwardness in our friendship, but I could live with that, if need be, for the sake of our love …

Sometime during the night, I came to with my face resting on the desk. I stripped off my clothes yet again, turned off the lamp, and slipped between my musky sheets.

CHAPTER 7

A bang at the door woke me up in a sweat of foreboding. But it was only my scout who looked after my digs. I was wanted on the telephone, he said. I saw that I'd slept in; I'd barely have time to make it to my tutorial.

"Who is it? Did they say?" My voice surprised me with its ill-omened tone.

"They did not, sir."

"Male or female?"

"I'm told it's a woman." My scout's voice contained a chortle as he moved off. He'd already told me, earlier in the fall, that history precisely repeated the shenanigans with every new generation of students.

My heart stopped. Her. Oh God, she was calling to cancel. Then my heart jumped and beat with wild hope: no, she wanted me to come to her room right away this morning. I'd have to miss my tutorial, but that was okay because, even if I went to it, I'd have to excuse my uncompleted essay by saying I'd been sick, so I might as well use that lie to dodge the tutorial altogether. Love always finds a way.

I pulled on a pair of jeans and boots and threw a raincoat over my naked torso, buttoning it as I ran to the phone. There I emitted a loving, sing-song hello into the receiver. For my pains, I heard, not her melodious mezzo-soprano, but a flat goddamned baritone. He must have had a female assistant make the call. "Oh! ... Is that you, Mr. Cull? Yes? I won't beat about the bush. Anthony Montague Browne here. Are you still on for that skiing trip in the Alps?"

The searing disappointment now replacing the indecent image of Claire in my mind, made me snap, "Well yes! Of course I am. Most definitely. Absolutely."

"Did I reach you at a bad time, Mr. Cull?"

"I was on my way to an important tutorial."

"Let me call you back in one hour. Sir Winston asked me to speak with you. He wishes to see you without fail."

"Pardon? Sir Winston Churchill? Are you serious?"

"Exceedingly so."

"Whatever about?"

"Back in one hour."

I walked over to the Torts tutor, assumed a death-mask face, and excused my sick self from the tutorial. Then, rueing my missed breakfast and the consequent hunger pains, I fidgeted for an hour in my room.

I was waiting by the phone in the lodge when it rang. Anthony recognized my voice from my hello. Without preamble, he asked, "What are the precise dates of your trip, again?"

I gave him the dates from the end of the first week to the end of the third week of December, and said, "It would be a great honour to visit Sir Winston Churchill. But why in the world would he want to see me?"

"My question, precisely, when he first broached it. But I have come to understand his need. I shall tell you why after you have agreed that you can do it."

"Oh, I can do it, no question. I have plenty of free days before and after my trip. I could drop everything and come down almost any day before I go."

"It's more complicated than that. He has calculated that you and he would need to be together at least three or four hours a day for about five clear days to complete the project he has in mind for you. In his physical and mental condition, he wants the continuity, with no gaps. His 90th birthday is coming up on November 30th. That's a Monday. Your Michaelmas term won't be finished before then, and he will not interfere with your regular studies. Many family and friends and former colleagues will be visiting for his birthday and some close family will be hanging about the premises for a few days after that. Then you'll be departing a couple of days later for two weeks. The days just before, during, and after Christmas would be hopeless; the word is out that his doctor and family believe this will be his last Christmas, so we'd have to be prepared for troops of visitors all during that period. No. The work week from the 7th of December to the 12th would be the only suitable and dependable time, which is precisely when you plan to be gone."

"That is rather complicated. If you'd been in charge of logistics for Napoleon's army, the invasion of Russia would have been a cakewalk. Sorry. I didn't mean to be so flippant."

"Sir Winston has always demanded simplicity in proposals to him, but nothing is ever entirely simple with him, in execution. I don't suppose you could drop out of your skiing trip this year and do it next year instead?"

Was the man mad? "I'm all paid up, Mr. Montague Brown, and it wasn't cheap. If I dropped out now without a doctor's certificate saying I'm too ill to go, I'd lose it all."

"Please call me, Anthony. I'm sure Sir Winston would wish to save you harmless from that expense. That shouldn't deter—"

"Oh I couldn't do that, Anthony. I very much want to go, and, besides, I've made commitments to other people."

"Yes, you mentioned Jeffrey Archer and his girlfriend at lunch. Would that be the young woman by the name of Claire Perceval?"

"She has been his girlfriend, yes, but I fail to see how that's relevant. Suffice it say that I'm very much committed to going. She made all the arrangements, went out of her way, to include me in her group."

There was a longish pause at the other end. It only became meaningful to me when I looked back later on this conversation. "Sorry," said Anthony, "I should've mentioned that I saw the pair of them, Claire Perceval with Jeffrey Archer, listed together as a going concern in a gossip column about a Mayfair party in September past. They were described as being a new, thoroughly modern, power couple, socially and politically smart, and ambitious well beyond merely becoming famous for being famous. Her name jumped out at me because I knew her father well when I served in the Foreign Office."

For an instant I felt a sensation of tumbling down a precipice. "So, Anthony," I pushed on, "I've been looking forward to this trip with friends who are counting on me to go. Really, I can't bring myself to give it up just to suit, with the greatest respect, an unreasonable imposition out of the blue by someone else. I mean to say, why would the eminent Sir Winston Churchill want the presence of me, a young student and an utter stranger, over such a long continuous period of very specific time?"

"He's secretive about it. I believe he fears you would find the whole thing rather silly unless he has an opportunity to plunge right into it with you and him, face to face, and keep it going to its conclusion."

"Silly? My God, Sir Winston Churchill? I don't care how silly it is—I do want to accept his invitation. What about in the new year? Hilary term doesn't start until the middle of January. Wouldn't the period soon after New Year's Day be nice and quiet as far as visitors are concerned?"

"Reasonable point. But Sir Winston is not at all well. He hasn't really recovered since he broke his hip in that fall a few years ago in Monte Carlo. He came home from that to die in England. Moreover, just a year ago, last October, his beloved daughter, Diana, committed suicide right here in London, which nearly finished both him and Lady Churchill. And right now the aftermath of that anniversary is upon us with devastating effect on both him and her. And this past summer, the House of Commons gave him a vote of thanks on his retirement from parliament. An unprecedented honour. But for a man who had spent his entire adult life there and was now irretrievably out forever, it sounded to him like the final nail going in his coffin. His physician, Lord Moran, will not predict when the fatal stroke or heart attack is going to occur, of course, but he feels certain that, because of all I've described, it will be sooner rather than later. Moran has even asked him if he has all his affairs in order. Sir Winston joked with him that he has just three more mistresses to dismiss, which he wants to announce in *The Times* to confound his friends who have whispered for years that he was undersexed because he wouldn't join them in their debaucheries. You can see that he's still in reasonably good spirits. But he claims with some justification that the strain of these well-meaning 90th birthday and Christmas celebrations will be the self-fulfilling prophecy that kills him off. And on top of everything else is the certainty he has had in his head for years that he will die on the very same day of the year that his father, Lord Randolph, died, which is January 24th. He believes that it will be this January coming up that contains that fatal day, and he says he fears from his earlier strokes that he will be reduced to a turnip for some days, perhaps weeks, leading up to it. That's why he has a great sense of urgency to do this with you between his birthday and Christmas. For the grand old man's sake, Mr. Cull, I really do wish you'd do it. I believe that in a few years, as a mature man, you would be astonished and appalled at your dogged rejection."

As a mature man in a few years! Well, that was sufficiently galling. Looking back, in a few years, though, at the opportunity Anthony was presenting I did recognize in myself the built-in pig-headedness in youth to resist having fantasies of love and lust interfered with by the absurd whims of ancient codgers, however greatly venerated. This old guy, while idolized for his intellect and feats, was predicting, soothsaying no less, his own death on the exact day of the same month on which his father had died decades before. Honest to God, what next? I said over the phone to Anthony now, "Look, I'm absolutely obligated to going to Austria. But my offer to meet any time before I go, or after I get back, stands."

He sighed. "Well, so be it. We'll see what happens. Please let me know if events alter or if you change your mind."

"That's not likely to happen, Anthony."

That afternoon, I walked to Lady Margaret Hall, careful not to work up a sweat, keeping myself fresh from my bath for the close encounter to come. There I told the desk I wished to be announced to Claire Perceval. She came down immediately, fully covered in slacks and sweater, the better, no doubt, to disguise her rascally intentions. "Oh good, you're here—we can discuss our arrangements for the ski trip," she said for the benefit of staff. "Come up for tea."

She closed and locked her door. I don't recall tea. She seemed to be in a great hurry, practically ripping the clothes off her body and mine, which I took at the time for uncontrollable desire. When we finished our lovemaking, she abruptly jumped up from a blissful but too short pause, wiped her tummy with tissues, and put on her clothes in a rush. There was something important she had to do, she said, so she had no time for pillow talk. Did I mind getting dressed a bit faster? "Sorry to be so pressed for time, but I didn't want to miss our lovely little cuddle."

"What's so important?"

"I'll tell you later." She fidgeted impatiently while I dressed.

"Okay, I'm off," I said, "I'll call you tonight to make plans."

She kissed me on the cheek and said, "Thanks for being a trooper, Will. You were super."

As I walked back to Brasenose, my whole being still full of ardour and eagerness, I wondered about the peculiarity of our last few minutes, the oddness of her thank you, and the ambiguity of her compliment cast in the past tense. But I accepted it all as part of her jitters in transferring her affections to me. For the hundredth time since last night, the thought flashed through my brain of her and me together, home free, unconstrained, in Zurs.

When I arrived at the college, a telephone message from her was waiting. She took my return call right away. "Will, Archer phoned me. He's on his way back from Somerset."

My heart pounded against my ribs for no clear reason. "Two days early? Why is he doing that?"

"I made a big mistake. I did act out of spitefulness, or vindictiveness, or vengefulness or something equally stupid when I went to your room. I thought he was dumping me. But I misunderstood. I don't know if he's heard anything about us, but he sounded rather edgy. I thought I should alert you."

"What? Edgy? How would he've heard—? When is he getting back?"

"This evening. Soon, I'd say. It's usually a three- or four-hour drive, I think, but he sounded as if he wasn't going to waste much time either leaving or on the road. I'm expecting him any minute."

"That seems fast. When did he phone you?"

"Just after lunch."

"You mean before I got there and we ...? Why didn't you tell me then?"

"I didn't want to alarm you before we ..."

"Alarm me? What did he say, exactly?"

"Will, I have to go. I've got to prepare myself for this."

"Are you going to tell him tonight that you and he are finished?" I waited for the answer, but I was listening to a dead telephone receiver.

I had no idea what Jeffrey would be capable of if he suspected something. He was a superb athlete with a gritty family past. Instead of having dinner in hall, I skulked out through the college gate, eyes swivelling about me, and walked to the little coffee shop on the Turl. There I sat, chewing at a sandwich, facing the door. Leaving it half finished, I crept back, close to the walls, seeking the shadows, relieved to encounter no hostile faces en route to my room. There I locked my door and resolved to remain silent if anyone knocked. But no knock came that night.

CHAPTER 8

The next morning, after sleep, albeit fitful, I had grown within my gut a courage based on anger. What the hell was I feeling anxious about? That had arisen only because I'd felt guilty. But I had no reason to feel guilty. I didn't seek this. Her relationship with him had already been ruptured, she said, when she had come to me in the first place. She'd no doubt completed the breakup with him last night; that was why she had to prepare herself. I should've called her back last night to see how she was making out. Too early to call now; I'd do it right after breakfast.

In hall there was no sign of Jeffrey—not that he regularly took breakfast there—and he was not in evidence as I walked out to the telephone. I peeked around the main door at one of the spots where he usually parked. No car. I called Lady Margaret Hall and asked for Claire. Ten minutes of waiting yielded only a voice to say she was not available. Did I want to leave a message?

Yes, please ask her to call William.

I proceeded unmolested to my tutorial, and to lunch, and then to the Stallybrass Law Library in college. I began writing my essay in

Roman Law on the proper procedure for gaining your freedom from slavery. In walked Archer.

"Hi," I said, hiding my surprise and studying his face. It was as friendly as usual. I queried like a moron, "Aren't you back to Oxford early?"

"Didn't Claire tell you I was coming back last night?" He murmured, catching me in canard number one. "She said she did."

"Oh yeah, right." I only hoped my face didn't look as red as it felt.

He smiled. "I gathered from Sir Noel this morning that you regaled him with every evil rumour you've ever heard about me."

The unexpected switch of my thoughts, from fornication with his girlfriend to a chat with his mentor, was like a last-minute reprieve from hanging. The other three law students in the library were looking over, glad to be diverted from their legal tomes by something that sounded vaguely dramatic. "Let's go outside and talk," I said, rising and leaving abruptly.

We stood face to face in the quad. Archer had half an inch of height on me, but today it seemed more like a foot. "Sir Noel probed me about my lunch in London. Which, by the way, he mentioned *you* had regaled him with. What I told him was on a purely confidential basis, and only because he said he wanted to be prepared in order to counter any lies he might hear about you." I was so relieved that Jeffrey's beef was not about my trysts with Claire that now I'd become cross and cocky. "And by the way, I thought you said it's better to be talked about in negative terms than not to be talked about at all. Please make up your mind."

"Will, it's one thing to be talked about, even adversely, in the dining rooms and clubs of the high and mighty. That creates a mystique that can only be advantageous to one, as you saw from Churchill's remark. It's quite another matter to risk having one's reputation bandied about by a band of judgmental academics. That becomes merely distasteful and unproductive. Not that Sir Noel would do that, and you are absolutely right—please excuse my momentary pique—as you say, he did probe you. Which in turn raises the question of whom, precisely, you were probing in my brief absence."

Oh Christ. "I beg your pardon."

"You lifted your lawless leg upon her, Will." Claire's words to me earlier from Rabbie Burns.

"I did *what*?"

"Behind my back, you and she did the wink-wink, nudge-nudge, say no more."

"Jeffrey, what the hell are you talking about?"

"You said you saw Michael Palin and Terry Jones on stage last month. So you know exactly what I'm talking about."

"Are you saying that I …?"

"That is precisely what I'm saying."

"What is?"

"That you, Will, bonked my bird."

"You're saying that Claire and I …?"

"I didn't say anything about Claire, but thank you for the confession. That was too easy, Will. You need to work on that area."

"Jesus Christ, Jeffrey, I'm confessing nothing. I mean, I didn't confess anything. Where did you hear that horseshit, anyway?"

"The aforementioned Claire told me."

"Claire told—why would she tell you a lie like that? I don't believe it. You probably heard some bullshit rumour because she visited me here in college the other evening."

Jeffrey's grin widened. "William, William, do contain yourself. It's not a matter of great magnitude. Claire and I both agreed at the beginning of our relationship that we value love and friendship far above mundane sexual fidelity. That's not to say we would cheat on each other frivolously and Claire did not do that. She acted in error. My withdrawal from our trip to Austria was for legitimate reasons concerning my mother, but she thought I was using it to part ways with her. Thus, it was an honest mistake on Claire's part, and I'm not blaming her for acting on it by visiting your room the night before last. The problem that has arisen, though, stems from your visit to her room yesterday afternoon."

"There were a couple of loose ends I had to straighten out regarding the ski trip."

"That is at considerable variance with her more playful version. Which one am I to believe—yours, that you passed part of an afternoon behind her closed doors discussing train tickets and hotel reservations, or hers—that you spent the entire hour alternating between making the beast with two backs, and going at it like the two idyllic village goats I saw yesterday in the West Country? You see my dilemma. But, Will, I have chosen on a balance of probabilities to believe honest girlfriend's raucous tale over good friend's insipid account. So, although I can understand her sleeping once with my friend in error as a tit-for-tat, yet then she turned around, *after* I'd exposed her mistake to her, and slept with him again. What kind of a fucking tit-for-tat is that? I frankly confess that I didn't like it very much. In fact, I didn't like it at all. I fear I became incensed with rage."

"You didn't hurt her or anything, did you?" I asked for the sake of gentlemanly form, as if I gave a sweet shit if he'd even throttled the perpetrator of my discomfort.

"What? Who Claire? Good heavens no. I wasn't enraged at her. She explained everything to me. The first time with you she happened to be wrong, and that was understandable. And the second time she wanted to—well let her tell you next time you're speaking to her. Look here, are you interested in knowing whom I became enraged at, or not?"

"Ah, let me make a wild guess. Could it have been I?"

"Well, examine it from my point of view, Will. One betrayal by you in your own room that first night, I could easily live with. After all she can be exceedingly persuasive. Her very surname indicates she's probably descended from warriors who were capable of piercing the strongest armour. But then your second betrayal the next afternoon? Bloody hell, Will, that took planning and malice aforethought. You had to walk to LMH for that. You were not simply a willing dupe in that episode; you were one of the primary designers and executors. Hence, we're left with your two betrayals in a row the moment my back was turned as I attended to my dear mother. Now each of the two acts of disloyalty in itself might not have been conclusive. But two together, one after the other, bang-bang, within hours of my convenient absence? That bespeaks, not just a slip, or a rash mistake, but a universal tendency, an inbred proclivity, to betray your best friend and counsellor at every turn. As Claire herself said, 'It does look exceedingly fiendish, Archer—even Judas Iscariot was satisfied with betraying his lord and master just the once.'"

"I trust you were impressed at how well I'm coming along in the duplicity department."

"More at her off-beat sense of humour, to be honest. She did try to exculpate you, by the way. She claimed she took you by surprise that first night. She'd love, she said, to see how I would have reacted if I'd been in your identical situation. The woman has an unnerving talent for zeroing in on one's most fragile character traits. And then, your second time in her room? She was under the strong impression that she'd inadvertently caused you to fall in love with her, she said, and that you were suffering a similar delusion about her attitude toward you. So all of that did take the edge off my reaction, and it has allowed me to think, especially now that you and I have cleared the air here, that nothing has been lost between us." He stuck out his hand. "Our relationship was developing toward a friendship for the ages. We shouldn't throw that away, Will. Overcoming this slight derailment ought to make it even stronger. I'd like to try to preserve it and strengthen it."

I took his hand, and nodded, all the while thinking, Not likely old buddy; there's only catastrophe in store for me with you as a friend. After he'd squeezed my hand hard, looked me earnestly in the eye, and turned and walked away, I felt shame over what I'd done to him, and then nausea over what Claire had done to me. A sudden moment of new angst came over me: an intuition that I wasn't out of this pickle yet.

I rushed toward the phone to get Claire's version of what had passed between her and Jeffrey. But half way there I stopped and thought: you pathetic fool, you're hoping to keep a relationship going with a woman who made you her chump. Strolling back to the library, I wondered how we would manage, thrown together at close quarters in Austria. But surely, that didn't have to be awkward. I would just avoid her whenever possible, and carry on with distant courtesy when I couldn't, and concentrate on other female and male friends ... Unless, now, she became sincerely contrite and offered serious amends ...

That evening I was summoned to the telephone and my heart leapt. Yes, it was Claire. And, yes, as I'd surmised, she was already contrite. "I'm very sorry about everything, Will. I can only say I was irrational with frustration and possessiveness over what I thought Archer was doing, and I acted thoughtlessly. I'm afraid I may have hurt you both badly, and I'm so sorry."

"I think I'll survive, Claire, and Jeffrey seemed rather blasé about it this afternoon."

"Believe me, Will, I hurt him, especially after I told him you and I got together the second time in my room. He actually told me I had to choose between him and you."

"Oh did he? And how did you explain our second rendezvous?"

"I said it was to confirm how good I had it with him as my lover."

"Oh for God's sake! Well, the next time you feel the urge to contrast my bedtime abilities with all the other men in the world, you don't have to make an idiot like me work up a sweat. You only need to ask them. And what did you reply to Jeffrey's alleged ultimatum?"

"I said, 'Archer, don't be so bloody daft. There's no choice to be made there.' Will, I don't mean to be unkind ... I like you a great deal, you must know that, and Archer certainly knows it, probably too much from his viewpoint. He and I have been close for many months and I've only known you for a matter of weeks."

"Well, that all sounds cut-and-dried enough. I'm glad my delusion, as Jeffrey says you described it, only lasted a couple of days. But it was more like your deception than my delusion. Look Claire, I've got to go."

"Oh let's come down to earth, here, shall we, Will? As one of you American boys said to a friend of mine who was besotted with him after a night of intimacy, 'Honey, it was just a piece of ass. Don't let it throw you.'"

I couldn't even be bothered to protest, with the usual insignificance to the listener, that I was Canadian. "Righto, then, Claire. Thank you for calling and setting me straight on everything. I'll see you—"

"Wait, Will. This is the real reason I called. I'm worried about Austria. Our close quarters there may be discomfiting."

"Christ, I forgot all about that. But don't worry. I'll be doing my own thing."

"It'll be hard to avoid each other. After what happened between us, I don't want to raise any suspicions there in Jeffrey's absence."

"He and I are very copacetic, Claire. No concerns there."

"Yeah, you two will always be just ducky. I'm more worried about me there without him. It'd almost be better if I were stuck in the middle there between two bloated phallic egos in après-ski pants."

"Don't flatter yourself, Claire. Bye." As she drew a breath to continue, I hung up.

I congratulated myself on my hardnosed attitude. Nobody was going to mess with my heartstrings. Then I pondered our conversation with the impeccable logic of love. If she needed to divulge to me her worry over our being too close in Austria, our bond could not be as irrevocably cut as she was claiming. After all, her attraction to me over the past few days had been relentless. Now, my attitude softened toward understanding, and I had the sensation that our unquenchable passion was still in lockstep. In my benighted head, I knew confidently that I could expect a call or a note from Claire within 24 hours.

My instinct for these things was unerring. The next afternoon, I received an envelope in the mail, addressed to me in her handwriting and containing on the back her return address at LMH. My heart bounced and my hand quivered with eagerness as I thumbed it open.

Inside was a typewritten note from the travel agency that was managing the ski trip. Herewith, it stated, was a cheque payable to William Cull representing a full refund for all payments he'd made. All the usual penalties were being waived, and the cancellation was final and irrevocable.

I had to lean against the wall, flabbergasted. The porter behind the desk asked me if I was quite all right, and I nodded at him. After a few deep breaths, I telephoned Lady Margaret Hall. Miss Perceval was not available came the immediate reply. Did I have a message for her? I hung up and stood there dumbfounded, without strategy, until another gawp from the desk scurried me away to my room to look in my file.

Along with the brochure, there was a receipt from the travel agency for my payment, guaranteeing my placement. I ran back out and phoned the agency and inquired about my status. My name was not on their list, the woman replied. But I had a receipt, I protested. We'd have to check the actual file, she said … right, there it was: the organizer I'd authorized to act on my behalf had yesterday cancelled my participation for a full refund—a highly unorthodox privilege, incidentally, at this stage, since ordinarily I'd be charged a large penalty for cancellation, but an exception had been made because of her excellent relationship with the agency. I asked for the organizer's name. She gave me the name of Claire's friend who'd arranged the cozy togetherness for the half dozen of us on the trip. Oh no, sir, the agency woman snapped, there was no possibility of revoking my cancellation at this point; someone else had already been slotted in from the waiting queue. Moreover, I should have received the refund by now. It had been put in the post immediately, yesterday.

In a state of high anxiety I asked if my friend Neil Murray was still registered to go, and received a snarl: Sir! It was entirely against policy to give out information on whether another person was even a client of the firm.

Thinking I had very likely buggered up Neil's trip too—the man who had initiated it for the two of us in the first place—I bolted out the college door, across the High to Oriel College, and up to Neil's room. He wasn't there, and I left a note telling him to see me right away.

That evening at dinner in hall, I was so worried on Neil's account that I couldn't engage in conversation with anyone or even finish my favourite weekly dessert—those canned purple plums swimming on a plate of thin yellow custard, weirdly English and somehow delicious. But tonight the concoction looked as ugly as my day, and I had to get up and leave it untouched.

Neil was just arriving at my door. Inside, with trepidation, I asked him if he knew whether he was still registered for the trip. Yes, he said, he'd received notice from the travel agency in that afternoon's mail to pick up his envelope of tickets and reservations at their premises. I told him what Claire had done to me and apologized for leaving him in the lurch like this, but I assured him that I was entirely blameless.

Neil looked at me with dubious amusement at my "entirely blameless" protest; I'd told him of my trysts with Claire. Then he summed up the essence of my ridiculous quandary with a paraphrased line of verse: "La Belle Dame sans merci had thee in thrall."

"Don't waste good poetry on the woman," I said, "unless this qualifies: 'FUCK HER.'"

Right after I'd bellowed the two words, Neil's grin was cut short by a knock on the door. Whoever it was would have heard my obscene roar. I opened it, prepared to be embarrassed. But standing there by himself was Jeffrey Archer.

"I don't blame you, Will," he said, walking in past me. "May I talk to you? Oh, sorry. I didn't realize you had company. Hello Neil."

"Yeah, I often lock myself in my room by myself and shout misogynistic obscenities into the vacant air."

Jeffrey struggled to keep his face stolid, but Neil chuckled his appreciation of my words and said, "I was just leaving anyway." He raised his hand to bar any objections from me. "I'll see you tomorrow." I walked him down the staircase to the outside, where he stopped. "Do I need to lurk near your door for any reason?"

"No," I said, and squeezed the good man's arm.

"I'm counting on a full report from you tomorrow," Neil said. "There could be a mildly entertaining short story in this." We snorted our farewells.

Back in my room, Jeffrey said, "I came to say how sorry I am over what happened regarding your reservations for the ski trip. I personally disagreed vehemently with that result, but Claire told me she'd be devastated by the awkwardness that would ensue by having you so close to her in the train and the hotel."

"Oh golly, it's too bad she didn't prevent her 'devastation' by simply removing *herself* from the awkwardness altogether."

"I suggested that, but she said she was sure you possessed the broadness of empathy and fellow feeling to understand."

"And that teaches us how defective in judgment a clever brain can be."

"Will, I grasp how disappointed you are, but I wanted to say that my feeling of friendship toward you persists. So much is that the case that when Claire told me she'd had your reservations cancelled, I told her that in light of all she'd done with you and to you, we really had to ask ourselves how she and I could continue to go with each other. My God, if we want awkwardness! She agreed and we broke off with each other forthwith and irrevocably." I'd been slowly pacing the room, but his revelation stopped me dead in my tracks. Jeffrey went on: "I told her she should now have her friend get you back on the trip. But she said there was no way that could be done. I said, of course there was. And she said there was no way she, Claire, could do that. Don't ask me, Will—she wouldn't tell me why. I can't figure the woman out." Jeffrey took my hand for a firm shake. "We'll weather this." He headed for the door. "Our friendship is too valuable for us not to. I'd be sincerely saddened if we didn't."

I passed a dismal night. If I'd stuck to our original plan with Neil, instead of plunging out of my depth with Claire and Archer, I'd still be going on this delightful skiing holiday. Simply for a mission touted by Anthony Montague Browne to be of extraordinary historical significance with the greatest man alive, my 22-year-old body would never have passed up this Alpine adventure, especially the off-Alps part. Every time I woke up, I alternated between cursing Claire and damning myself as the overreaching author of my own calamity.

The next morning I dragged myself to the telephone and called Anthony. When I told him I'd withdrawn from my skiing holiday to accommodate him and Sir Winston, he replied tonelessly, "That is handsome of you." He didn't seem surprised, and he confirmed instantly the precise dates, five days toward the middle of December. "Just pencil them in your calendar for the nonce, lest something untoward should occur."

"Why? Is his health deteriorating?"

"One never knows at 90, does one? Find some lodging near a station on the Piccadilly Line for convenience of transportation to and from his house. And let me have the phone number. I'll be in touch. Perhaps we can have lunch somewhere before you see him."

"Anthony, you don't seem to be as enthusiastic about this meeting as you were before. Did something happen?"

"No, no, William, no, no. Sir Winston will be very pleased. He considers this to be the last important act in his life before he dies."

That sounded eager enough. Anthony's apparent lack of enthusiasm just then, I'd discover later, was not over the event itself, but only because the practiced diplomat had pulled this meeting off, just another routine bureaucratic accomplishment successfully behind him.

I didn't see Jeffrey much during the rest of November. He was preoccupied, he told me when we passed in college, with his various organizations and his race training, and I didn't seek him out. Once he came over to me at dinner in hall to tell me, without sitting down, that he'd received an invitation—telephoned because of lack of time—from Anthony Montague Browne to Sir Winston Churchill's 90th birthday party. "Anthony said it was your keen endorsement of me at the de Rothschild lunch that tipped the scales in favour of inviting me. Thank you, Will, you're a good mate."

CHAPTER 9

On December 7, 1964, a week after Churchill's birthday party, I met Anthony Montague Browne in London for lunch at The Sands, a trendy restaurant on New Bond Street.

When he asked where I was staying in London, I told him I was quartered in a bed and breakfast off Russell Square.

"You might find an ancient member of the Bloomsbury Group bumbling about."

"Well, if John Maynard Keynes wanders inadvertently into the place I'm staying in, he'll have enough material for a new economic theory of last-ditch destitution."

Anthony laughed. "What's the use of being a student if you're not forced to live in digs unfit for human habitation from time to time?" (The man was prescient: when I'd tried to stay there again for a day or two before travelling during next year's summer vacation, a municipal notice tacked to the door declared the premises closed as unfit for human habitation.) "But you may wish to go a little more upscale," he said. "You know that Sir Winston insists on covering your food and lodging and other expenses during this project."

"I would've stayed somewhere similar down here during vac, before and after the ski trip. This is fine." I waited for Anthony to renew the offer to cover the cost of my cancelled trip; I couldn't see how he'd have known I'd received a refund. But he didn't mention that.

He said, "The convenient thing for our purposes is that you have a direct Piccadilly Line from Russell Square to Gloucester Road Station, and then only a six- or eight-minute ramble to the house at Hyde Park Gate." We ordered lunch.

"How was Sir Winston's birthday party?"

"I'm a bad one to ask. When I was in Paris as a diplomat just after the war, doing political reporting—that is to say, spying for the British ambassador, trying to predict when the communist coup was finally going to take over France—I had to attend yet another dazzling diplomatic party every night of the bloody week. It put me off such carousing for the rest of my life."

"Jeffrey Archer told me you invited him, after."

"Yes, and a damned good thing, too. Sir Winston was more subdued than at his 80th, naturally, but his conversation with Mr. Archer perked him up for a while."

"Did Claire Perceval go?"

Anthony studied his knife for a moment. "I invited him to bring her with him, but he said they had parted ways. I told him to bring her as a friend. But she didn't come. Mr. Archer said at the party that she responded to his invitation by saying she had no good cause to be there on her own merits and she had no desire to be there as someone's appendage. Her father always said that in the main she did as she pleased but that, fortunately, she possessed the brain to carry it off. She missed little. Basically, family and close friends, and cheering crowds on the pavement right outside 28 Hyde Park Gate. The birthday boy appeared at his window in his siren suit from the war. The crowd went bonkers and kept singing Happy Birthday over and over. He had to go to the window again. Finally, Lady Churchill opened the window and asked them to be quieter, please—he had to save his strength for his party. Over 70,000 birthday greetings were received at last count."

"Amazing. I saw the picture of him in the newspaper at the window, standing there smiling out. I thought he looked great."

"When I told him the same thing, he said, 'Well, don't look under the bonnet, Anthony. I fear the motor is racked beyond repair.' But the fact is, since he learned that you could come see him, his faculties have revived a great deal. Before that, he had slowed down terribly, mentally and physically. But now he possesses good energy, and his memory from long ago is extraordinary, which, he says, is what's crucial for you and him. The other day he recited Lincoln's Gettysburg Address, and then Macaulay's 'Horatius at the Bridge,' both of which he'd learned by heart as a child. Lord Moran, his physician, supposes that this mental resurgence is the last one he'll have before he dies. Not an unusual occurrence in some who are approaching death, he said. Perhaps that's all it is. But I believe he's drawing upon his last prodigious reserves of energy and intellect to carry him through this project of yours and his."

"Which would be?"

Anthony stayed mute while the waiter brought our food. Then I focused on devouring avocado smothered in succulent shrimp and delicious house dressing, and wolfing down the Dover sole meuniere with our glasses of champagne. This was the bloody life.

"I think our timing is perfect," Anthony began again. "We should not be bothered by anyone for the rest of this week. Lady Churchill may come in to check on Sir Winston from time to time, and perhaps a daughter or grandchild may pop in to say hello, but none of that will be intrusive. Randolph the son can be a terrible nuisance but he won't be disturbing us. I once ate a full fortnight of dinners alone with Sir Winston without his turning up once, even though he wasn't far away. Moreover, earlier this year Randolph was rendered *hors de combat* by a brutal case of bronchial pneumonia, which nearly killed him. Then, on top of that, he had a tumour removed from his lung. It was benign, which nobody could comprehend in view of his three or four packets of cigarettes and his couple of bottles of Scotch a day for the past two decades. He puts to shame his father's own consumption of tobacco and liquor, which has been grossly exaggerated. Sir Winston confessed to some of us at the party that his own drinking is a bit like Dean Martin's reputation as a drinker—mythologized as a lovable drunk but whose intake was in fact exceedingly self-controlled. Your Archer then told Sir Winston that Dean Martin was able to knock the Beatles' record 'A Hard Day's Night' from the top of the US hit parade earlier this year with something called 'Everybody Loves Somebody.' He was over the moon. But back to Randolph ... for all his excesses, Randolph is a superb writer and Sir Winston has given him the go-ahead to proceed with his biography, except for your piece, of which he knows nothing."

"Which makes two of us."

"Yes. Sorry to be so cryptic about it, but it's on the Old Man's orders. First, we need to know you are agreeable to his conditions. I'm sure you will be. They're not onerous, but if you absolutely can't abide any of them, we'd better know before we get started. He doesn't want you to record on tape anything he says. He's always been exceedingly vain about the quality of his public pronouncements and has always practiced and polished up his speeches for delivery. During the war, in one or two speeches he made for radio when he was extremely fatigued, he came off sounding inebriated. He jested about it, saying that people were confused because they'd just heard what he sounded like when he *hadn't* consumed his usual quota of cognac; he'd be careful to remedy that in the future. But in fact he was mortified by some of the critical reaction to those presentations. So, he doesn't want any recordings around of his verbatim babblings as a feeble old man. You'll have to take notes as if you're at a lecture and edit them into publishable shape later. Are you content with that?"

"I'd be happier if you'd provide a tape recorder. I'd rather have backup tapes for accuracy, and for proof of what he might tell me, even if I agree to store them in a vault, never to be divulged unless ordered by a judge."

"No, he won't have that. He doesn't think the weak and feeble voice of a decrepit old man will do anything to enhance the fascination of his story or add to its mystique. He doesn't expect the story to be accepted as a certainty, but he's intrigued by the idea of it coming across as a credible possibility."

As I was mulling that notion over, Anthony rushed on: "You will keep your notes confidential and safe, and at some point in the future, you will assemble them, edit them, and have them published in coherent form. But he doesn't want you to do that for many years to come. He'll tell you how long you must wait, but I already know he doesn't want any of it made public until all the adult members of his family—wife, son, daughters, grandson Winston, and anyone who arranged for this to happen—Eddie de Rothschild, myself—are all dead and gone."

"Why on earth is that so important?"

"He's afraid family members and close associates would be embarrassed by it, that it will be considered the hare-brained last babblings of an antediluvian Colonel Blimp who's gone completely barmy. He wants us all out of the way."

"But it's just super for me to be the proud author and editor of what may be nonsensical babblings, with absolutely no evidence or proof to back up that he said it? Why can't you sit in on our meetings, look over my notes, and certify them as an accurate rendition of his narrative?"

"I raised those possibilities with him as his private secretary. He says I'll have a long public career ahead of me when he dies, and it would be too dangerous for me to append my name to notes not under my control. Of course, we do trust you, William, not to publish before the agreed time, but on the other hand one never knows, does one? He wants this matter executed entirely outside of his family and circle of friends and advisers."

I sat there with a forkful of sole halfway to my mouth, gazing out the window. Anthony laughed. "I don't blame you for being somewhat perplexed, William, but look at the whole grotesquerie in this way. First of all, you will undertake not to publish for decades to come, and even then it will be entirely in your own hands whether you ever publish it or not. At that stage, no one will be holding a gun to your head or even know about it."

"I suppose that's true. But it almost makes you wonder, what's the point of doing it at all?"

"Well, on the other hand, you will be obliged to promise him that you will in fact publish it. Then it will be up to you whether you break your solemn promise, after he's dead, to one of the most heroic men who ever lived. Pud?"

"What?" It took me a moment to gather that he was asking, not about my privates, but about dessert. "Oh. Yes, that crème brûlée looks good. What about if a fire destroys my notes? What sort of precautions am I supposed to take? What if I croak before the time is up?"

"Don't be anxious about that. As Sir Winston would say, 'If it be not now, yet it will come—the readiness is all ... blah blah blah ... Let be.'"

"Oh goodie, another dithering quote from Hamlet to guide us."

"If it's any consolation to you, he actually prefers Doris Day's 'Que sera, sera.'"

"I didn't realize Sir Winston has a soft spot for old-time popular singers."

"Well, yes and no. He's always loved Frank Sinatra's songs. Then, one time at the casino in Monte Carlo, Frank Sinatra walked up to him with his entourage, unannounced, very self-assured, and seized his hand and wrung it, and proclaimed that he'd been waiting a long time to do that, and then left. Sir Winston, even before Frank was out of earshot, growled, 'Who the hell was that yob?'"

"Sounds like a man I could warm to."

"We'll see. Look, William, place your notes in a file folder with your property deeds, your will, and your investment certificates, and keep them somewhere secure, and forget about the damn things till the time comes. Sir Winston believes that nothing catastrophic will happen to them or to you. Just as he knew all his life that he was an unstoppable man of destiny—good heavens, as a reckless youngster, and then as a wartime journalist, soldier, and politician he survived, relatively unscathed, several serious mishaps of his own making, and numerous attempts to kill him—he believes his secret narrative is destined to be told to the world at large. I'd suggest that's a pretty decent guarantee you'll be alive for a good long while yet. So. Let's go and view the great man himself."

CHAPTER 10

A uniformed policeman approached our taxi as Anthony and I got out at Hyde Park Gate. After a sign of recognition and friendly word between the two of them, he withdrew a short distance. "A precaution against belated birthday celebrants," said Anthony, "or worse." We walked toward the street number 28, high on black double doors in an attached, red brick house. "It doesn't look exceedingly imposing for the man who was offered the Dukedom of London by the queen, but it's in fact quite commodious: nearly 6,000 square feet, with a very spacious drawing room and a large dining room, and a smaller sitting room and family dining room, and I think, seven bedrooms. Lady Churchill uses one on the second floor as her sanctum sanctorum. He bought this after the electorate kicked him out of 10 Downing Street as prime minister in 1945. Number 27, right there, is for staff and storage. Lady Churchill threw a fit when he bought it. But he's always managed to muddle past insolvency, with the royalties from his prodigious writings, and loans, in quotes, from friends, and the occasional Nobel Prize. Quite an interesting street, this. Virginia Woolf lived down there and Lord Baden-Powell somewhere near here."

Because Anthony pronounced Powell to rhyme, un-North American, with Noel, I had to confirm. "The Boy Scouts guy?"

"The same. He and Sir Winston were soulmates till his death during the war, in spite of Baden-Powell's mantra, 'A Scout smiles and whistles under all circumstances.' Sir Winston has always held an intense dislike of people whistling. But their bond stemmed from their South Africa war experiences. Sir Winston wrote about him in his *Great Contemporaries*. Some people whispered that he was a secret homosexual, but Churchill wouldn't listen to a word of it. He'd roar, 'Alan Turing was a homosexual, and he shielded Great Britain at Bletchley Park from the Nazis, only to be hounded to death by some of the same goddamned English pygmies whose skins he saved.'"

Anthony used a key to enter the house. "He'll be in the smaller sitting room. Much cozier in these temperatures. But let's take a peek in the drawing room first. Fairly impressive." There was no sign of life as we walked down the chilly hall. Anthony opened a door and stood aside for me to peer in. The room looked huge with its very high ceiling, and at least one wall was shelved nearly all the way up with books. There was no fire in the fireplace. The air inside was even colder than the hall's.

Anthony shut that door and led me to another one, on which he tapped. An inarticulate rumble emanated from inside, which Anthony took as a signal to enter. I espied the crown of a pinkish head with sparse white hairs sunk down behind the back of an armchair facing the blazing fireplace. Anthony brought me over to the front of his chair, so that I was standing between the old man and the fireplace, and introduced me to Sir Winston Churchill. I heard a thunder-like growl up at me. "Come not between an antique relic and his fire!"

I looked at Anthony, uncertain, and he chuckled and moved me to the side. Sir Winston took reluctant eyes off the fire and turned his head as much as he could in an attempt to set them on me. Then, reaching for Anthony's hand, while pushing on the wooden armrest with his other hand, he gradually gained his feet. Anthony passed him his cane and, leaning on that, he held his hand out to me. "Hodge do, Will Cull," he said. I took a step toward him. My pace was too long. Now I was all but pressing belly to belly up against the living legend. He pulled his head away and I took a step back. Then I leaned in, stretching for the hand he was withdrawing, nearly toppling over on him in the effort. When we at last clasped hands in a brief shake, he chortled, "Colliding head-on with pre-eminence and renown does tend to unbalance people. But I quickly discovered that they get used to it in a day or two, as contempt begins to replace awe."

Anthony said, "I'll turn your chair around, Sir Winston."

"I expect you'll have to, for tolerable communication, although I frankly own I'd rather gaze at the fire than at two fine looking young men sent by the devil to mock, by their youthful presence, my own decrepitude." As the three of us sat down close together in the overwarm room, he went on, "I trust you will agree to wait until there's a future generation who never heard of me before readying for publication what I am about to tell you. Very much like Ulysses travelling with an oar so far inland until he met men who never heard of an oar."

"Anthony prepared me for a request of a long wait, but a generation that never heard of you?" I smiled wide. "Sir, that day will never come, so we might as well abandon the project."

"Sir Winston, you and I talked about that," said Anthony. "I understood you're satisfied with a delay of at least 50 years."

"I am. But I wanted to see how William would handle an old blighter's pathetic attempt to have his monstrous ego bolstered even more by flattery. And he passed with flying colours. But the 50-year wait, or greater, is not a request, William, it's a requirement. So you must swear to honour it. I want everybody close to me dead and buried before this sees the light of day. Anthony Montague Browne, here, I especially want him dead."

"Thank you," said Anthony. "I didn't realize you cared so deeply."

Churchill grinned. "You see the contumely I have to put up with these days, William, from what is euphemistically termed my help. I meant, Anthony, not that I absolutely want you dead now, at any rate not necessarily this minute, but that you must be dead when William makes this public, to spare you any embarrassment. Although I don't know why I concern myself with such thoughtful consideration, suspecting as I do the blot already staining your own copybook."

Anthony's eyes flicked my way for an instant. "Thank you, sir, I'm grateful for your thoughtfulness *and*, if I may insist, your discretion." Evidently, contrary to Anthony's boy-scout demeanour, he'd been up to mischief in the past. I wouldn't find out till later about the insinuation—scandalous and vociferously denied, yet true—that Churchill was making.

"That's why William must swear to maintain secrecy for half

a century about everything we say here. Swear, William. You're probably an atheist like everyone else in these times, so we shan't require a bible. The swearing is for dramatic purposes merely, to etch the occasion on your brain forever. *Swear.* Good God, I'm starting to sound like the ghost of King Hamlet. Well, after all, I *am* near that state. It's propitious that we arranged this rendezvous now, for it's not a moment too soon. Do you swear?"

"I do, sir."

"And that sometime after 50 years you'll write it up and make every effort to publish it."

"Yes, sir."

"And you, Anthony, will you stay in the room throughout my narrative, on the condition that you won't speak a word of it to another soul during your life, except William here?"

"Yes, Sir Winston, of course."

Churchill became all business. "Then we are ready to begin. This is an account of the most searing of my childhood memories. One early spring, roughly round the year 1780, a boy, eight or 10 years old, was asleep with his family in their shelter—they called it a mamateek— when white men came upriver before dawn with their guns. The Indians had pitched three mamateeks the previous afternoon on a bank of their big river, the Exploits River, not far from where it empties into the Bay of Exploits, in Notre Dame Bay. The Indians were about 20 in number and they were intending to set out toward the sea ice this morning to prosecute their ancient activity, the hunting of seals. They well knew of the hazard of white men in the Bay of Exploits, but they planned to evade them by using their concealed trails in the woods along the shore of the bay until they were close enough to the ice floes to take seals and then quickly retreat out of danger.

"Among the half-dozen or so white men approaching the mamateeks, William, on this fateful morning, was your own namesake, one William Cull. He was young, probably not yet 20 at the time, but he was already a successful trapper and highly experienced in the woods. He was what you North Americans would call a 'natural' in the wilds and, even at that early age, he was intrepid when it came to venturing by himself into Red Indian territory. Other furriers were more fearful of travelling there unaccompanied by well-armed mates. But Cull put his whole trust, he always said, in his Fogo Island long gun.

"It had been he who, snowshoeing alone upstream, near the mouth of the frozen, snow-covered river, approaching dusk the day before, had sensed quiet activity well off to the side under cover of trees and brush. Surveying methodically the crests of the trees and the spaces between them, his eyes gradually focused on the top 2 or 3 inches of a new mamateek in the distance. He abandoned his plan of erecting a tilt, the rough and ready shelter of the trapper, for the night, and retraced his steps back to Ship Cove—that's present-day Botwood. I visited the place and explored it on my stopovers at the seaplane base there during the Second World War.

"In Ship Cove, Cull reported his discovery to other furriers who were gathered in the settlement, preparing for a safety-in-numbers trapping expedition upriver. They could scarcely believe their good luck. Along with taking fur animals, they had also been intending to track down and recover tools and traps which, last autumn, the Red

Indians had stolen during raids on their premises in Notre Dame Bay. And now this opportunity had fallen into their laps.

"The night was bright with stars and part of a moon shining on the snow, and right away, within a half-hour of Cull's report to them now, and without sleep, the men left Ship Cove at double time, following Cull's lead. These men and their ilk were exceedingly sturdy and skilled frontiersmen, capable of improbable feats of endurance and hardship. Well practiced in travelling fast and soundlessly over long distances in the woods on snow, sometimes they were capable of taking a band of unsuspecting natives completely by surprise.

"Now, this morning before daylight, as they moved over the sound-muffling snow, they were able to get close to the Indian structures. Using silent gestures, they divided the mamateeks among them and, without troubling the occupants with a warning, they fired a salvo from their long guns directly into the walls of the shelters, aiming downward where they knew the Indians would be sleeping in their hollow niches in the ground. Your forebears, William, knew their stuff.

"The boy's 12-year-old sister, sleeping next to their mother, was killed outright. His aunt and uncle and some others escaped from the mamateeks while the whites were reloading. They struggled to run through the deep snow into the dense woods, but several, some already wounded, including his uncle, were cut down before they could make it. His mother, at the first burst of gunfire, had jumped up and then fallen. She crawled upon him and covered his body with hers, mortally wounded. Then the settlers came in and inspected their handiwork in the gloom. Two Red Indians, who, the whites concluded from their groans, were still alive, they shot.

"The boy lay silent and motionless and scarcely breathing under his mother's body as the whites finished, in the barely dawning light, inelegantly ransacking the mamateeks. They recovered what they could find of their stolen tools and traps and other gear, and gathered up some furs and dried caribou meat. The boy remained terrified; if he got up to try to escape, he'd be shot, but if he stayed quiet till they set fire to the mamateeks, as he knew they habitually did, he'd be burned to death."

As Sir Winston spoke, my ire kept rising. I knew that my ancestor, William Cull, was no saint, and had a dubious, at best ambivalent, reputation in modern minds regarding his dealings with the native people, but Churchill's details of appalling atrocities as fact without giving any source for his information were too much to bear. "Sir Winston, sir, sir, sorry, but, really, where did all this come from? I must ask where you got—what your source is for—this gruesome account of a massacre of, I assume, the Beothuk of Newfoundland."

"Your venting of spleen is readily understandable, young William Cull, but all will be made clear in good time. And your namesake may even appear in a better light. Might I continue with our task?"

"Yes, sir, but excuse me, this particular story, I do need to know—"

"Of course, of course." He raised his hand to silence me. I decided to wait and see where this led, especially since there appeared to be no stopping the gravelly voice. "After a time, the boy heard the white men leaving the campsite. He waited for many minutes in the horrifying, heartbreaking silence, and then tried to crawl out from under his mother's body. He couldn't do it at first. Her body in death had flattened closely over areas of contact with his. At last, he managed to push and squirm his way out. Then he forced himself to peep about in the sunrise, inside and out. Dead relatives lay everywhere. Though he wore the blood of others, he had no injury himself. The ghastly pain he felt was from his heart within his chest.

"He saw that the whites had left behind a number of their tools and some furs and skins. That was why they hadn't burned down the mamateeks. They'd be back later today or by tomorrow to do that, with sledges to drag off the items they couldn't take this morning.

"The boy knew that, depending on weather, he was eight to 10 days walk upriver by himself, over rough ice or deep snow, from his home camp on Red Indian Lake. He didn't know if he was the sole survivor of the massacre, or if others had managed to escape. Some or all of those whose bodies he couldn't see might be dead of their wounds in the woods. But he was hoping there were other survivors who would come back for him.

"In fact, three in his greater family, a man, a woman, and a 15-year-old lad, all wounded, had successfully dashed into the woods and lived to get home. But they thought, on good grounds, that everyone left behind, including the boy, was dead. Some days would pass before any Beothuk made it back in sufficient numbers to recover the remains for ceremonial burials.

"Meanwhile, the boy hid in the woods all that day and night, waiting for the return of the white devils. He'd been brought up in his people's dogma of wreaking mandatory revenge on murderers of members their tribe, no matter how long into the future it took. Only then would his slain family be at final peaceful rest among the good spirits. He knew he was too young and weak to act when they came back, but if he now made himself familiar with their features, he'd be able to recognize them as he grew older and stronger, and seize good opportunities to kill them all.

"Next dawn, he came awake to silent forms of white settlers taking shape before him like foul and loathsome ghosts. They had entered the campsite so stealthily he couldn't hear them from his hiding place. There were only four now, known from the historical record: William Cull the trapper guide, John Peyton Sr. the salmon fisherman and entrepreneur, and two of Peyton's servants, all carrying long guns. Without a word or other sound, Peyton and Cull peered into the woods surrounding the campsite, each slowly making a complete revolution of surveillance. Cull looked directly at the boy's blind in the bushes, causing heart palpitations, but his eyes didn't linger there. Peyton now sauntered about the clearing, stopping to look at bodies. Two of the smaller forms, he turned over with the toe of his boot. Something about that action, his two men found funny. They muttered a word to each other, following up with snorts of laughter. Peyton snarled at them in a furious whisper and shushed them quiet.

"Then the men entered each mamateek and recovered the rest of their purloined tools and traps. Next they set to examining furs, silently pointing out to each other where some were too badly tainted with human blood, and reluctantly threw them down. The frozen meat hanging from poles, out of the reach of animals, they lowered and inspected. Everything they wanted, they loaded aboard two sledges. Finally, they set fire to the mamateeks and watched as the structures burned quickly to the ground. The boy could smell burning flesh.

"With John Peyton leading the way, his servants began to pull the sledges back over the path on which they'd come. William Cull stood for a time near the glowing embers, glancing casually around into the trees, as if to enjoy a last gratifying sight for his memory's sake. Then he too vanished.

"The boy was glad he'd hidden himself so well behind his screen of bushes. Now, with a clear picture in his head of the four men for later vengeance, he could escape upriver and head for home camp—he felt hands hoisting him in the air from behind by his caribou skin garment and dumping him on his back in the snow. William Cull loomed over him, contempt and disgust on his face, and nudged his rifle into his ribs.

"The boy felt a mighty urge to scamper into the underbrush. But his instincts stopped him; he'd certainly be shot down like the others. Cull's face softened into a near smile. He pointed his finger at the boy and at the woods and shook his head vigorously, waving the gun barrel over him. From his pocket he pulled out a rag, crisp with snot, and reached for the boy's arm to yank him to his feet. He tied his wrists together behind his back with the rag and marched him out past the smouldering mamateeks and prone bodies, down to the three waiting white men.

"The words that now passed between John Peyton and William Cull rapidly turned into a strident argument. Anecdotes, told later about the event, had Peyton contending that, if the boy were allowed to come with them, he would rat on them about the massacre. This would cause no end of troublesome accusations from the magistrate when he visited Twillingate, and more from the governor in St.

John's, when word reached there, since there was already blooming in England and Newfoundland a vociferous 'spare the Red Indian' movement. Peyton raised his rifle and pointed it directly at the boy's chest, as he stood next to Cull. 'Move aside, boy,' barked Peyton, 'lest you be splattered with the Indian youngster's blood and guts.'

"But Cull pushed the rifle away. He was known in the Bay for being feisty and stubborn in talking to his elders, even at such a young age—not so much bloody-minded as exceedingly independent-minded. He asked Peyton now how many damned magistrates and governors he knew who could understand the boy's tongue. Peyton countered that he would learn English soon enough; look how fast that little girl who was captured a few years ago picked it up. He brought the long gun round again, to the boy's face.

"Cull pulled the boy behind him and told Peyton, the entrepreneur, that he might be rich enough to forgo the prospect of a large reward for the capture alive of a Red Indian, but he, Cull, the young and simple trapper was not. There'd been £50 on offer from the governor before for one of these prize captives, and it was no doubt still available now. They should place the boy with a clergyman in Twillingate and have the holy man write the governor and collect the reward for them. Moreover, the fact that they'd brought the Indian trophy in unharmed, having found him lost in the woods and rescued him, would dispel any slanderous rumours going round of a massacre of Red Indians. Peyton acknowledged that in his zeal to rid the land of another thieving river rat, he'd allowed the reward to slip his mind. He yielded the point and put his rifle up."

Churchill went silent and gazed sideways into the fire, lapsing into contemplation of something. I glanced at Anthony; he was studying the toes of his shoes. His face bore no expression. "Sir Winston," I ventured after a few seconds, "you mentioned a childhood memory ... did that vivid vision or nightmare, that horror, come from something you read or were told as a young boy?"

"It's a clear memory of actual experiences I had as a child round about, as I said, the late 1700s."

The old man had just made an autobiographical error of nearly a century. If we were to get anywhere in this project, whatever it was, we'd better correct that at the outset. "But, sir, just to be clear, you were born in the late *1800s*—1874, wasn't it? So your childhood memory would have been—"

"Yes, according to the records in Vital Statistics, that birth date is correct. But you're perplexed by my reference to the late *1700s*. William, do you believe in Pythagoreanism?"

"You mean, like, the square on the hypotenuse of a right-angled triangle is equal to—"

"What? No no no. Isn't that Euclid? Whatever it is, I never stayed very much interested in mathematics after Sandhurst and can't say my lack of it impeded my progress in life at all. No, I'm not banging on about mathematical truths, William. Heaven help us if we should need Bertrand Russell's presence here. He's only two years older than I, but twice as dogmatically opinionated. Which is frightening. What I have in mind is something somewhat dodgier than math. Metempsychosis? Pythagoras's belief in the transmigration of souls and their reincarnation after death. Do you believe in any of that?"

Christ. What could I say to the ancient geezer now? He

was on his last legs and rumoured to be severely depressed, and probably verging on dementia. As an admiring young person, I should mollycoddle him with comforting assurances regarding his memories—his hallucinations?—as he faced the final abyss. When I opened my mouth to lie, though, it felt like an act of contempt. "No sir, I do not believe in any of that."

"Nor do I. But that doesn't mean it doesn't exist, simply because you and I don't believe it. For all I know, my Clemmie, Lady Churchill, may believe in it, and there's no one more hard-nosed than her. She used to tell me in those good old days before women got the vote that she looked forward to being reincarnated as a man so that she could go into public life and straighten out the bloody mess we male prodigies had made, especially the worst of my own muddles. So, perhaps it's better to be agnostic about reincarnation and the like rather than a hard and fast non-believer."

"Good idea. I'll apply to the notions of transmigration and reincarnation and channeling, and such, the verdict of 'not proven,' as a Scottish judge might do."

"Excellent observation. I've always esteemed the canny Scots, and apart from my election loss in Dundee, they've often esteemed me. Or perhaps, on reincarnation, we might echo Osric's pronouncement on the hits during the sword play between Hamlet and Laertes: 'Nothing neither way.' Which, of course, was just before they killed each other. So, reincarnation and all that ilk ... we don't necessarily believe in it. Then what about ancestral memory, William, or perhaps one's memories of experiences one didn't have personally in this life but which were actual events from an earlier life, lived through by some related family member long dead before one was born? Do you believe that such phenomena might exist?"

"I suppose there's some kind of ancestral memory in a spider being able to spin an intricate web spontaneously, or a bird capable of building the same elaborate nests as its ancestors and relatives without ever having seen one built, something in the genes. But—"

"The genes? Oh dear. Having just escaped Bertrand Russell by the skin of our teeth, must we now send for Watson and Crick?"

"Ha ha. But if you mean our being able to somehow have an actual memory of an ancestor's or earlier relative's specific experience in life, then no, I don't believe it exists."

"Nor do I, at least not rationally. Although, as I proceed with my narrative, you may conclude that I do have good reason to so believe. For I have some difficulty in reconciling my rational beliefs with my actual memories from a previous time, a time before the date on my birth certificate."

Churchill stopped speaking, or growling, and turned his head to gaze steadily into the fireplace. I looked at Anthony. No doubt my eyes proclaimed a belief that we were sitting beside an antique madman, in the grip of some seriously wacky delusions. Anthony gave me a quick smile back, raised his eyebrows for a second, and stayed silent.

Churchill turned and leaned forward in his chair. "Anthony, if you please." He held his hand out toward his private secretary.

As Anthony moved toward him, I asked, "How old were you, Sir Winston, when you first started experiencing your visions or dreams from an earlier life?"

"They were clear memories, I say, not visions or dreams." His reply was rather testy. He held Anthony's hand and readied his cane for pushing with his other hand. "My very earliest memories of that former life began when I was perhaps four or five. And I've carried my memories of that life in my head since my earliest years of this current life. I used to tell my mother, Lady Randolph Churchill, about them; she'd listen and even talk about them with me—I recall asking her where she was, why she wasn't there, when such and such happened. She seemed highly interested, often amused, by our conversations. I attempted to tell my father as well one time, but he was neither interested nor amused. He attributed them to a feverish, overactive imagination, and he was frankly appalled by what he called my gruesome fantasies, like the one I just related to you. Hence, I quickly learned to keep them to myself rather than acquire a name for being a child with problems even greater than those I was already notorious for." He pushed and pulled himself to his feet and started for the door, jerking his hand free of his private secretary's. "Do sit, Anthony. I daresay I can still make my water without officious intermeddling."

They both cackled—it sounded affectionate—and Anthony came back to his chair. We sat for a few minutes in silence as I got my brain to register, at least for the record, what Sir Winston had just told us. Then I said, "Are we sure 50 years is long enough for me to wait before telling this to the world?"

Anthony controlled a laugh from his gut. "I don't believe he's insane or suffering from dementia. What he was talking about is no doubt connected in some way with the family legend that his great-grandmother on his mother's side was half, or at least partly,

North American Indian." We heard Sir Winston shuffling back. "I'm expecting him to tell you all about that."

"I shall indeed tell you all about that, and more," said Churchill, scuffing through the doorway. "You're doubtless unsettled by my memories of an earlier life. Well, disconcerting and distressing as it might be at this moment, I believe you will be convinced of the verisimilitude, the *authenticity*, of those memories, as we go on."

Anthony said, "You were actually able to hear me from that distance. Sir Winston, your hearing appears to have improved considerably."

"It has." Churchill settled back down in his chair. "Whatever has happened of late to my faculties, generally, it's the opposite of the calm before the storm, or the deepest darkness before the dawn. My brain, and its appurtenances, appear to be a *lively* storm now before the dead calm comes, a *bright* dawn before the smooth black velvet of death descends forever. I already know when that will come and it won't be long now. Yesterday, I heard my physician, Lord Moran, covertly intimating to Clemmie, to my wife, that this present-day lucid interval of mine is very likely my last. Yet, I am not dismayed by my looming extinction; I'm gratified to have lived for 20 additional years, after seeing that very bad man off, the monstrous Nazi führer. I can only hope that, wherever he's been suffering since, he has also been painfully aware of that. And were you aware, by the by, William, that Herr Hitler and I possessed a characteristic in common when we were darling little children?"

"Nothing springs to mind, sir,"

Churchill smiled at me. "Well, Hitler and I, both of us, as boys, loved to play at cowboys and Indians in the Wild American West. But there the similarity between us ended, for, even as youngsters, long before the brutal realities of our later life occurred, we had entirely different objectives and outcomes in our play-acting. In my own battles between the cowboys and Indians, I always contrived to have the Indians defeat the cowboys. My sympathies were forever with the Red Indians. Herr Hitler, on the other hand, in each and every battle, even as a young boy, delighted in causing his cowboys to massacre the Indians to the last man, woman, and child. Herr Hitler would have been elated at what happened, for example, to your Beothuk tribe, the Red Indians of Newfoundland."

"And he didn't have to lift a finger to accomplish it. We English, with our guns and diseases, managed to do it all by ourselves long before Hitler arrived on the world scene."

He gazed at me for a time. "But with more than a little self-help, as well."

"You mean by the Beothuk themselves, sir?" He nodded. That seemed a harshly unbalanced pronouncement to me, knowing of the ignoble role sometimes played by my own ancestors in their decline. I couldn't let his blame-the-victim comment go. "Are you familiar with the entire history of the Beothuk, sir? Your earlier story indicates you are acquainted—"

"Exceedingly familiar. After I became Undersecretary of State for the Colonies early in the 20th century, I researched extensively many of the Aboriginal peoples of the empire. My interest partly sprang from my own family's peculiar history. Did you know, William, that my American mother, Jennie Jerome, Lady Randolph Churchill, had

North American Indian blood in her, and that, therefore, so do I?"

"I've read about the speculation, sir, and I do love the idea of it. But I understood it'd been debunked and shown to have no credible basis."

"Never credibly debunked at all, though some would like it to be. My mother believed that her grandmother was half Red Indian and her mother believed it and I believe it. My grandson Winston believes the story, and so does my son, Randolph, although he has never been particularly fond of the fact. My mother told me as a child many times that her own mother informed her and her sister, as if she were revealing the secret of the Sphinx, that there was something they should know, which was not very fashionable but was rather curious: the family knowledge of Red Indian ancestry. My mother used to say to me that the photographs of herself clearly portrayed her as such, and I would make her laugh by replying, 'Yes, that is so, Mama; they show that you are a very beautiful Indian princess.'

"My niece, Anita Leslie wrote a book about 10 years ago entitled *The Fabulous Leonard Jerome* about my mother's American father. In it, his daughter Leonie, my mother's sister, is quoted as accounting for her famous energy by whispering, 'That's my Indian blood.' Jennie's and Leonie's mother, Leonard Jerome's wife, my grandmother Clara, is in a family portrait in my possession in which she very distinctly stands out—the oval face, the problematical dark features—as a person of a race different from, exceedingly distinct from, Anglo-Saxon descent. She, my grandmother, Clara Jerome, the daughter of our half Indian, was nicknamed Sitting Bull as a schoolgirl and a sister was called Hatchet Face. One need only look at the photographs of my mother, Jennie Jerome, and her sister, Leonie, and the portraits of their mother, Clara, and their grandmother, Clarissa Wilcox, to see their Red Indian traits. Such characteristic facial features do not lie. Indeed, the pictures of all the women in my family who are descendants of Clarissa Wilcox, the half-caste, have an uncanny resemblance to certain portraits of other Red Indians found in history. That is especially true of my mother. I have pictures that I will show you soon, in which you'll see that clearly. They will take your breath away."

"I look forward to seeing them, sir. When do you intend to show—"

"Bear in mind as well, as corroboration of its truth, that in the exalted social circles in which these ladies, my mother and her mother and the others, moved, it would have been nothing short of disgraceful at the time to have been considered a member of a Red Indian race, especially with the scandalous implications that my mother and grandmother had descended from a cryptic cross-breed of dubious legitimacy. They certainly would not have been stating that circumstance as a fact—Red Indian ancestry—unless it were unquestionably true."

"I had no idea that your entire family not only accepted the idea but rather relished it."

"Not entirely everyone in the family absolutely relished it. My father, Lord Randolph, once said to my mother when I brought home yet another bad report from my school, 'Is that your damned dim-witted Indian pedigree coming out in him?' He seemed unmindful of the fact that, as intelligent as he was, my mother had far more brain power and ability. But no mind—let the interpreters of history try to debunk or demean the idea of native American blood in me as they will—there is no doubt in my mind whatsoever about it. So much is this the case, that when President Roosevelt boasted to me during one of my wartime stopovers in Washington, 'You know, Winston, my Dutch ancestors were among the very first settlers in New York, in what was then called New Amsterdam,' I answered, 'But, my dear Franklin, it was my ancestors, the American Indians, who greeted them on arrival.'" Churchill chortled at the memory.

"Roosevelt must have been surprised."

"He was astonished. But when I told him that my American maternal forebears had lived in upstate New York, he assumed that my Indian ancestors must have been the noble Iroquois, that is to say, that I shared the bloodlines of one of the most warlike tribes of them all. Roosevelt joked that such a theory of my warrior ancestry went a long distance toward explaining my conduct in my wars." Anthony and I joined him in his chortles.

"Do you have any genealogical evidence, sir," I asked, "a reliable family tree, say, indicating that the story of your descent from the Iroquois is true?"

"None whatsoever. And, in fact, it is not true. One speculation was that Anna Baker, my great-great-grandmother, was raped by an Iroquois, which produced her daughter, Clarissa, as a half-Iroquois, in the late 18th century. But any allegation of rape is a defamation of the Iroquois. There's absolutely no evidence of any rape of Anna by anybody, or that it was the Iroquois that we are descended from. What we have is the clear family tradition that my mother's grandmother, Clarissa Wilcox, the daughter of Anna, was one-half North American

Indian. And we do have on paper that Clarissa's mother, Anna, was in fact born and grew up, not in New York state but in Nova Scotia, in what was to become Canada. She would marry one David Wilcox in New England, in 1791, and move to his farm in Palmyra, in upstate New York, and my mother's grandmother, Clarissa, our half-Indian, was the presumed, putative daughter of Anna and this David Wilcox. Clarissa was born there, to the south of Lake Ontario, in the homeland of the Iroquois confederacy of six nations. Hence the later supposition of Iroquois ancestry. I know many of my family have wished mightily that, if we absolutely must have the blood of natives in us at all, it be of the splendid Iroquois warrior. But it's not so. Our family tradition of Red Indian ancestry, based on practical evidence, is, to my mind, conclusive … it's just not Iroquois, but more likely it's derived from a handful of splendid, ancient people, vanishing in the backwoods of an ill-starred and pitiless land."

Churchill's backhanded reference to what I presumed to be my homeland irritated me a little. During his pause now, I jumped in somewhat peevishly. "Sir Winston, I'm wondering what your point might even be in stressing your North American Indian ancestry from such a place." He levelled his eyes at me. He certainly knew how to silently daunt someone. I rushed on. "Admittedly, in and of itself, it's an interesting—a *remarkable* facet of your personal family makeup and history, and your belief in it deserves to be better known. But beyond that, does it have greater significance to the world? Are you saying that it contributed in some essential way to the bigger picture, namely, your salvation of Britain, and perhaps your deliverance of the entire human race, from Nazi conquest?"

"I beg your pardon, suh!" he growled. "You say *perhaps* I contributed to the deliverance of the entire human race? I'm not sure I am gratified by your belittlement of my accomplishments, young Cull." Churchill rumbled out a laugh. "No, no, be not alarmed. I appreciate your moderation and self-control. And yes, it was an essential contribution to my wartime role, my guidance of this nation during the Second World War."

Having started the point, I pressed ahead. "Not to denigrate any aspect of your makeup or background that inspired or enabled your leadership during that war … but wouldn't it be more logical to attribute your wartime leadership to the courage and vision and resolve which you inherited through your father from the great first Duke of Marlborough, or even from your mother through the fabulous Leonard Jerome? I read a law case recently where a medical expert testified that when a physician hears hoofbeats on the racetrack, he should diagnose horses before zebras."

"Occam's razor," said Churchill. "The simplest of competing theories that fits the facts is to be preferred. An Englishman, of course, our Occam, and a great seeker after truth. We'll suppress the truth that his famous principle can be traced back to Aristotle. And we'll ignore the perverse chap who destroyed Occam's principle with, 'The simplest explanation for this murder is that the woman down the road is a well-known witch: ergo, she did it.'

"But let's consider, as you suggest, the Marlborough side of the matter. My father, Lord Randolph Churchill, was off to a brilliant, energetic career in politics and government. He might well have become prime minister if his career and his very life had not been cut tragically short by syphilis, by syphilitic paresis—locomotion ataxia, the child of syphilis. But, bear in mind that he was the first Churchill of the Marlborough line, since the first Duke of Marlborough's magnificent succession of triumphs over France in the early 18th century, to rouse himself to a semblance of brilliance, after a half-dozen generations of sleepy ducal mediocrity. My father was brilliant, yes, and I admired him immensely ... indeed I loved the man and do honour his memory this side of idolatry. What I got from him, both by inspiration and innate inheritance, perhaps lent me success in my early political career, but it also lent me failure as my career progressed. What kept me going and what made me prevail in the last war did not come from him. What I got from him, for the most part, was an impetuosity and rashness and disagreeableness that nearly finished my political career." Sir Winston stopped. After 30 seconds of silence, I leaned forward to cut into it with a comment, but Anthony touched my arm. Sir Winston muttered, "Great tragic man." Then he raised his head as if coming out of a trance.

"And Leonard Jerome, my American grandfather ... I certainly inherited some good traits from him, and some flawed ones, to boot. He had the vision and energy and flamboyant nature to be involved in everything of interest in his time and place. He was a highly successful speculator in corporate stock—the king of Wall Street, some called him—but he lost as many fortunes as he amassed. His house on Madison Avenue encompassed a theatre of 600 seats and fountains spewing champagne, but of course he didn't fail on occasion to declare bankruptcy, before picking himself up again and carrying on. He was a partner in railroads and a friend of the nouveau riche Cornelius Vanderbilt and other financial up-and-comers: he owned a large interest, for example, in the *New York Times*. Indeed, he helped hold off with a Gatling gun the working-class racists who were determined to ransack the *Times* building in the New York riots, as they resisted the draft by President Lincoln during the American civil war. I remember at an early age telling my Grandfather Jerome that the Gatling gun he used then was also employed in the Anglo-Zulu War in southern Africa five years after my birth, and that if only we'd had the Maxim gun at Khartoum, General Gordon would not have been wiped out by the Mahdi when I was ten.

"Grandfather Jerome was beguiled by my knowledge and interest. When he heard that my school reports portrayed me as a backward pupil, he told my mother and father, 'Let him alone. Boys get good at what they find they shine in.' A brilliant insight, but he died in Brighton of galloping consumption when I was just 17, and he therefore missed the fulfillment of his prophecy when I wrote about Kitchener's reconquest and revenge of Gordon that I personally participated in during my 20s in the River War. Grandfather Jerome was many things, good and perhaps not so good, and I inherited much of both from him, but the wherewithal of brain, heart, and soul to take on the Nazis nearly alone against insuperable, unspeakable, odds, was not one of them.

"Bear in mind that, from the record, the parents of Anna, the mother of our family's half-Indian, were living in Nova Scotia for years before Anna was born there in about 1771. And that's where Anna grew up. The family had many connections with New England which may explain why Anna married David Wilcox there in the 1790s and why their daughter, Clarissa, the half-Red Indian, was born in upper New York state. Meanwhile, however, Anna is known to have spent a great deal of her young womanhood in her beloved Nova Scotia, where there were no Iroquois. And it was in Nova Scotia that Anna became impregnated with a Red Indian baby, right before her marriage to Wilcox."

"Was it caused by sexual assault, Sir Winston?"

"No, the act was purely consensual."

I sat back in my chair and breathed in and out noisily. First of all, how the hell would he know that? And second, didn't he grasp that a tale of a pregnancy by a consensual affair with an Indian in Nova Scotia just before her New England marriage to a white man sounded more than a little strained? Churchill picked up on my doubt. "Yes I agree, the logistics required for that to take place are, from start to finish, hard to accept." He turned to his private secretary. "But then, it's not unknown, is it, Anthony, for a woman to become pregnant by a man other than her husband right before her marriage, with nobody suspecting a thing at the time? Would you happen to know something of the actions involved in accomplishing such a feat?"

Churchill was grinning. His questions sounded like a devious insinuation again. I looked at Anthony. His head had dropped. When he raised it again, his face displayed resigned irritation. He spoke acidly. "Judging by the billions of human specimens scrabbling about the face of this ravaged earth, I very much doubt that the feat of impregnation by any man requires a grand strategy, whether he be Red Indian interloper or royal paramour."

Churchill issued a guffaw, age-belying in volume, and spoke directly to me. "Anthony's sly regal reference is to the rumour that I am the product of a liaison between my mother and the then Prince of Wales, later His Majesty King Edward the seventh. Unfortunately unfounded. No, I fear my royal blood derives from one of the dusky races. But, Anthony, you neglected to mention among your examples of impregnation, its occurrence as a result of an illicit collaboration between two of a certain eminent man's trusted helpers."

Anthony almost rose from his chair: "Good heavens, Sir Winston! *If I may*! William must be wondering why we're talking in riddles like this. Sir Winston's mischievous reference is to the vile rumour, *fortunately* unfounded in my case, that I, a happily married man at the time, was responsible some years ago for impregnating one of his much-esteemed female secretaries, causing her to elope precipitously with her fiancé, without so much as a 'by your leave' to Sir Winston, and to his great vexation. I fear he has held her action against me over the years, in spite of my continued assurance that I am entirely blameless in the matter. Does that more or less sum up the dreary episode, sir?"

"It does, thank you, Anthony, except for your exaggeration that I have remained resentful in some way. I raised the matter only to buttress the credibility of my great-great-grandmother Anna marrying while pregnant by another man. In your case, I accepted all along that the allegation against you is without foundation." Churchill gazed sideways into the fire for a few seconds before turning back to conclude, "And that the uncanny resemblance of my secretary's child to you is purely coincidental and does not denote your active participation."

Anthony hove up a heartrending sigh of exasperation. I found Churchill's needling amusing, if a bit mean—the very idea that this straitlaced guy might have an offspring running about who, though born within the mother's wedlock to another, had been merry-begot by him outside, was beyond crediting. At least, that's what I thought then. "Please, Sir Winston, may we move on?" said Anthony now. "My only point was that paternity can be a mysterious thing. For instance, it's entirely possible that the Indian features of your ancestor, Clarissa, may have sprung from something hidden in the parental background of Wilcox, her father."

"And it was an excellent point, Anthony, were it not for the fact that I know for a certainty how Anna became pregnant by a Red Indian and whence came the Indian blood in me. And soon I'll enlighten you on how the dastardly or noble deed—take your choice—took place. There's not time to do justice to that tale at this hour. I must nap. Clemmie and our daughter Mary have some people coming for dinner as part of their campaign to make me keep one foot in the real world. They thought my birthday party rejuvenated me marvellously, especially the conversations with the one or two young political aspirants that was so enlivening. I believe you know Mr. Archer and his lady friend, Sir Gregory Perceval's—" His eyes slid toward Anthony and he abandoned the thought, but he continued to speak without pause. Why would he be about to mention Claire? She wasn't even at his party. "William, will you join us at 11 a.m. to learn the fate of the Indian boy and how the vigorous red blood of a North American Indian made its way into the effete blue blood of an English patrician?"

CHAPTER 11

In the morning, I was getting ready to leave my room for the Russell Square underground station, when my landlady called from the bottom of the stairs: I was wanted on the phone. It was Anthony. Sir Winston couldn't receive me this morning. Lady Churchill and Mary had ganged up on him last night at dinner to cajole him into feeding the deer in Richmond Park today, now that the rutting season was safely over.

I practically sputtered. "But what about our essential meeting today? Remember? Our indispensable sessions all this week?"

"I know. His family is rather overbearing and not to be diverted when they imagine they're doing the right thing for paterfamilias."

"Couldn't the great leader have said no to those ...?" I stopped myself before my sarcasm degenerated into misogyny.

There was a smile in Anthony's voice. "Well, it so happens that Sir Winston also dearly loves to feed the deer. Nothing to be done, I'm afraid. Come tomorrow, same schedule."

I left my squalid abode in a pique. I'd been so looking forward to hearing Churchill's yarns of the Beothuk boy and of his own Indian ancestry. Walking along, however, I told myself in consolation that it was all bullshit, anyway. Where could he possibly have gotten all those details of the boy's capture? And, obviously, the idea of his ancestor's pregnancy by another man just before she married her husband had come into his head as a result of his suspicions about Anthony.

I bought a newspaper containing an entertainment guide, put together a schedule, and took off. By evening I'd crammed in three films that had come out that year, *A Hard Day's Night,* and *Goldfinger,* and, for the second time, *Dr. Strangelove.* When I got back to my lodging, buoyant with humanity's artistic inventiveness, the landlady passed me a message from Anthony: Whatever the hour, call him immediately.

He answered on the first ring: Sir Winston had been looking for me this afternoon. He wanted me to come for tea, and get back to our session afterwards. He couldn't believe that I'd been incommunicado all day.

"And I couldn't believe he'd disrupt our absolutely vital sessions to feed the bloody deer. I could have been skiing in Austria."

Anthony didn't miss a beat. "One gets used to this, William, when one mingles with the mighty. So, tomorrow midmorning, then."

"If it has suddenly become so important again, I can materialize there in half an hour."

"Ah no. I'm not getting into those all-nighters again. I had too many years of that."

"Sounds like everybody's convenience is being catered to, except mine."

"Tomorrow morning, then, old boy."

I arrived before 11 and Anthony ushered me in without conversation, grinning just perceptibly, and we sat down silently in front of Sir Winston. He had on a sulky-baby face. His lower lip was actually protruding, and he glared at me. "I'm rather severely put out by you, young Cull," he growled. "What did you mean by disappearing off the face of the earth yesterday?"

My irritation had disappeared by dawn this morning. But now, the very idea of my being expected to gratify slavishly the whimsical fancies of the grand and illustrious brought it surging back. "And sir, what did you mean by cancelling our session on a whim? I gave up a delightful trip to the Alps with my friends to be here. The least—"

"Now that's not strictly accurate, William. I understood you were, as Kipling might say, 'turfed out' of your holiday group before agreeing to come here."

I stood up. "What? Who on earth could have told you that?"

The old codger had a good poker face. He looked off in the distance and mused, "No, upon reflection, I was mistaken. I was thinking of something else entirely."

I studied Anthony. He was leaning forward in his chair too eagerly, and made as if to take charge of a disorderly meeting. "May I suggest we revive our raison d'être?"

I sat down again. "Well, yes!" I snapped. "I, at least, put aside this entire week to get this job done."

Sir Winston eyed me critically. "I could have used your rather aggressive attitude, William, in June of 1942, when we suffered our worst month to date of shipping losses, almost a million tons of supplies sent beneath the waves, courtesy of the Hun, without adequate payback. But you were otherwise aggressively preoccupied at the time, I believe."

"Yes, I was fighting my way out into actual existence that same month and year, sir."

"Right. That was 68 years after I myself was born. Good heavens. That's a lot of water ..." He stopped, no doubt concluding from my contrite look that he had gotten his point across without actually having to call me a saucy, callow, young pup. "Are you still angry with me, William?"

"No, sir, I've been completely disarmed—nearly as fast as the Italian army."

Sir Winston laughed till he coughed. "This young man is clubbable, Anthony. It's too bad it's so late in the day for me. But I'm still a little vexed at you, William, and, of course, I have every right to be, as a *great man*." I'd read somewhere that he'd already used that line on his valet, but I chuckled along with him anyway. I wondered how tired Anthony was by this time of listening to the same old bons mots issuing from the legendary wit.

Now Churchill became all business. "I trust, gentlemen, we are ready to hear whence sprang my native American blood? This is what I've reliably pieced together from what seems to be lodged in my memory from an earlier life, and from what I may have learned from my mother and grandmother at a young age, all blended and coordinated with what I've read from every scrap of information available in the public domain. It was exceedingly fortunate for me, as you shall see, that our friends Cull and Peyton suffered the Indian boy to live.

"They took him to a clergyman in Twillingate, who named him after the holy day near which he'd been captured, Easter, plus Eli from the Old Testament for euphony. Eli Easter. The name, the minister hoped to his parishioners, would be a constant reminder to the young barbarian of his need to be Christianized and civilized into proper society. Years would pass before Eli heard anyone say his Beothuk name again.

"He lived under the care of the clergyman and his wife for a few weeks, with intermittent whippings for failing to follow the instructions they gave him in English. Then, the largest merchant there, Mr. Slade, was in contact with them. He had retail outlets and collected salt fish in communities in Notre Dame Bay and Bonavista Bay, and elsewhere, and enjoyed a reputation for, not meanness, precisely, but more for the hard-nosed fair play of a successful frontier trader. He asked for a private viewing of the Beothuk boy.

"Slade's request to see him had been made at the behest of his wife, a person of uncommon character for the times. The Slades had two beloved daughters to share secret joys and sorrows with their mother, but no son to comfort and follow his father. And she couldn't seem to have any more children. Mr. Slade had often told his wife, before she'd ceased breeding, how much he yearned to have a nice boy to accompany him everywhere and learn his skills. They even contemplated taking and bringing up some foundling child but no wholly suitable boy arose to fill the bill.

"Mrs. Slade had glimpsed the Red Indian boy being led out of the church by the clergyman's wife, where he'd been exhibited soon after his arrival in Twillingate. And she'd been straightaway struck by his beauty and gracefulness. She knew an Indian boy could never fill the need of her husband for a substitute son, but she wasn't bothered by that because, truly, after gazing upon him, she wanted this beautiful boy for her own.

"The clergyman's wife brought Mrs. Slade into the stable next to the manse and showed Eli to her. He had a long chain around his neck, fastened to a thick timber. 'He tried to run away twice,' said the reverend lady. 'But as you can see,' she raised a stick above her head, causing Eli, as trained, to turn his back and bend to receive the blows, 'I've pretty near got him civilized by now.'

"Mrs. Slade stepped between her and Eli to preclude further demonstration of the value of the biblical rod on the back of a child. She looked him straight in the eyes for a long time, feeling his arms and legs up and down. There was such a delicious expression on her face that he was afraid she was going to eat him. Eli knew tribal stories and songs about the whites eating each other. So, how much more would they want to eat a tender young Beothuk child? She'd tell him months later, when he could understand her words, that he did look good enough to eat that day and that she'd never seen in her life before a more fine-looking, well-formed boy.

"She prevailed upon Mr. Slade to go with her to meet with the clergyman and his wife and undertake responsibility for Eli's lodging and all his expenses, and the cost and time needed to travel with him to St. John's that summer, when the ice floes retreated, to discuss with the governor about establishing contact with the remnants of his tribe. Following a donation to the church for the expenses of his care to date, Eli was released into the hands of Mr. and Mrs. Slade.

"To the initial consternation of the household servants, Mrs. Slade rejected all advice to relegate him to the barn and chain him on for the night. Instead, she put a cot in the back porch for him to sleep on, and locked the outside door to keep him from escaping. To placate her maid—'Missus, you knows he'll be creeping about the house all night looking for white people to murder in their beds'— she also barred the inside door.

"In the mornings, Mrs. Slade found him on the floor, wrapped in a blanket from the cot, either sitting or curled up on his side, his knees drawn up to his chin. And that was the way, although she always started his night in the cot, he'd end up sleeping till dawn. All his people slept like that, he'd tell her later, in a ball within their shallow hollows on the floor of the mamateek.

"She started out the first morning ordering the servants to give him breakfast with them in the pantry, and then his other meals there as well. But when she discovered their tendency to treat him as a slave, owing to his status as a captured prize, she brought him into the kitchen for all his food, over the initial protests of her daughters. But soon, they and the help were treating him as occupying a station intermediate between family members and family pets.

"The outside workers on the Slade premises included some Mi'kmaq Indians. From the start, they considered Eli almost as if he were a little brother. This was a startling contrast with the horrors recounted in the tales and songs about Beothuk and Mi'kmaq he'd heard since birth. As soon as he could speak rudimentary English in a matter of weeks, he disclosed to them what his mother had told him in whispers, that he was part Mi'kmaq himself, an ancestor of hers having been a member of their nation. They found this information only mildly interesting; historically, they said, there'd always been recruitment of husbands and wives, back and forth, between them, especially before the Beothuk became more withdrawn and hostile. Even now, a lost or injured Beothuk child, discovered in the woods, would be without question adopted fully into a Mi'kmaq band. Yes, there had been battles between them in the old days over hunting territories, they said, but they needed to remember that the Mi'kmaq and the Beothuk were cousins.

"They asked Eli about current Beothuk customs. They were good-natured about it, but indicated that they found some of his people's habits ridiculous and unbelievable: Why did the Beothuk insist on forever staying hidden away in the woods, shunning everybody else in the world, Indian and white man alike, instead of trying to come to some kind of arrangement with other peoples? As an alternative to stealing tools and metal from the whites, why didn't they learn to trade furs with them for such items and materials? And didn't it occur to them that if they burned to ashes the white men's boats and vessels and everything in them, just to acquire the nails in the wood, the whites would go on murderous rampages against them? Why didn't the Beothuk learn from the Mi'kmaq that if they traded their furs to the settlers, such an arrangement would help keep the whites from invading Beothuk territory to trap their own? And did they really have a stupid rule that any Beothuk who spent time among the whites or the Mi'kmaq was automatically polluted and could never return to his tribe, except to be sacrificed?

"Every Mi'kmaq knew, they told him, that the Beothuk possessed great skills on land and water and admirable hunting abilities, so why didn't they steal some guns, just as they stole everything else, and learn to shoot them, as the Mi'kmaq had done, for hunting and even for protection, instead of trying to depend on those bows and arrows from the olden days? Was it because, as some whites claimed, the Beothuk were too backward and witless to learn how to shoot a gun? But they stopped asking that last question when its irony started to become too obvious.

"Eli, after a few bird hunting trips with Mr. Slade, became known, at 11 years or so, as one of the best shots with a rifle on Twillingate Islands. Sometimes, the Mi'kmaq would tease him about it in private, though: his deadly aim, they claimed, was just 'the Mi'kmaq coming out in him.' They also ribbed him by arguing with each other over who they thought was Mrs. Slade's favourite pet, Growler her water dog or Eli her Beothuk. Clearly, everyone, whites and Mi'kmaq alike, loved him.

"Eli never disclosed the Mi'kmaq in his background to white people. It wasn't just that he enjoyed, as a 'genuine' Beothuk, being an object of fascinated curiosity, with settlers actually going out of their way to come and look at him. What he really liked was how some of them openly expressed their spellbound distress over a powerful mystique he gave off by his appearance and bearing, their palpable fear of him and his kind.

"As he grew into his adolescence, the Mi'kmaq continued to treat Eli with affection and consideration, and protectiveness. Whereas they displayed arm's length politeness toward the white fishermen and trappers and their white fellow workers and their children, they always treated Eli with the familiarity and closeness of one they regarded as their own. Eli's feeling of security about this was only shattered on the occasions when a certain young Mi'kmaq from elsewhere, perhaps Bay St. George on the west coast of Newfoundland, or perhaps Nova Scotia, swaggered into settlements on Notre Dame Bay.

"His name was Noel Boss. Eli already knew of him for his abilities as a guide and trapper, and he could readily see the respect, perhaps apprehension, the other Mi'kmaq had for him. Leaders among fishermen and trappers, even Mr. Slade, welcomed him heartily, and vied to have him guide them upcountry. It was a toss-up whom they wanted with them more on their treks into the wild, Noel Boss or William Cull.

"Boss never appeared to take the least notice of Eli, save once. Eli was startled to see him, 30 or 40 yards away, in the middle of a group of trappers in Ship Cove, Bay of Exploits, staring at him intently for 10 seconds for no reason, before at last averting his eyes. After Boss left the area for Gander Bay, Eli asked some Mi'kmaq friends about him, and they told him that Noel Boss loathed and despised the Beothuk. Why? They didn't rightly know—some mortal family set-to maybe—but he already claimed to have killed a good few of Eli's kind, and would not rest, he vowed, until he etched the figure of 100 on his rifle stock. There was no need for Eli to be on guard, though—he couldn't be touched; he belonged to Mrs. Slade and enjoyed Mr. Slade's protection.

"Eli gradually became Mr. Slade's general factotum. He worked around the store and the house, and Slade brought him along whenever he went hunting sea birds and land animals, and he often sent him out in a fishing boat with a crew. The businessman told Eli he would soon be as good as the man June at fishing and working. June, or Tom June as some called him, was a Beothuk, named after the month in which he'd been taken. Some Irish hunters from Fogo had stumbled on a mamateek and fired into it, killing a woman and child, but allowing the boy, then nine years old, to survive. June was protected and trained by a family in Fogo, taken with them on a trip to England, returned with them to Fogo where he was used in the fishery, and developed a reputation for brilliant success in all aspects of the business. Slade told Eli he'd intended to bring him to Fogo to meet his fellow tribesman, but before he could do so, William Cull arrived in Twillingate with the bad news that, as June had entered the perilous gut leading to Fogo Harbour during a storm, he had capsized his skiff, trying to avoid the rocks and islands, and drowned.

"Mr. Slade started taking Eli with him to communities where he had retail stores and other operations. One evening at home Eli heard him, alone with his wife in the kitchen, murmur to her, 'He's great company and very dependable.'

"Mrs. Slade replied, 'I know, I love him. It's too bad he's an Indian or I'd adopt him as our own.'

"By 16, Eli was over 6 feet tall. And according to the remarks of older women who didn't hold back on their thoughts at the store in Twillingate, he was 'wonderful handsome.' One venerable matron from next door joked to a friend in the store, when Eli happened to be concealed by oilskins hanging nearby, that she knew the 10th commandment told you not to covet your neighbour's ass, but she hoped the bible didn't apply to a certain young native, because if so she was doomed to damnation. And the Slade daughters and their friends tittered and whispered whenever he was nearby and sometimes engaged him in bantering conversation almost as if he were a teenaged white boy.

"Spotting such tendencies among the girls, Mrs. Slade told her husband she was frightened for Eli's sake, and he'd best instruct the boy in the brutal realities of life. So, the next time Mr. Slade took Eli out in boat to shoot hagdowns together, he told him that he and his wife were very concerned for his well-being, his very survival, as a young Red Indian man in the white man's world. First, Eli had to make certain that he resisted all temptation placed in his way. Although it might be acceptable, or at least endurable, in people's eyes for a white lad to get a little too handy to an Indian maid, or even for a white man to live with an Indian woman—you saw the like of that stuff happening these days—the opposite situation was not acceptable at all. No Indian lad or man, Eli included, could even think about a white woman in that way on pain of dire injury, and most likely death.

"Eli assured Mr. Slade that there was no danger of that. But he didn't say why: for six years, whenever he was alone in the woods, or lying awake at night, he grieved, he ached, in his mind and body, for his murdered family. He whispered his mother tongue to himself— stories, songs, accounts of daily activities—to keep the sacred words alive within him, and he said his name: and he longed and hungered and burned in his heart to go up the river to the big lake and be with his own people, and have his own family. And so it was that, in the dark of one night in autumn, Eli forsook his home and security on Twillingate Islands and set out alone to become himself, the eagle called Gobodinwit, again, a true Beothuk once more ..."

I was sunk so deep in Sir Winston's tale that I felt physically jostled by the knock on the door. A tall, stately woman, even imposing, walked into the room. He introduced me to her, Lady Churchill, and the fleeting thought went through my head that she looked too good for him. She greeted me in cordial words but with a dull tone, and reminded him that they were to have lunch alone together today in the dining room, a tête-à-tête away from distractions. "I know he didn't neglect to inform you, Anthony," she said, "of so noteworthy an occasion." Anthony returned her smile, his ebullient, hers weak.

"Of course I didn't, Clemmie," said Sir Winston, taking her hand. "I've been very much looking forward to it all morning. These lads know they have to forage in the galley today."

After they'd left the room, Anthony said, "Confidentially, Lady Churchill is not well. She's been suffering spells of deep depression, even requiring hospitalization on occasion. Her children, apart from Mary Soames, have been a terrible burden for herself and Sir Winston to bear: Diana's suicide last year, Sarah, a long time alcoholic, now, after three disastrous marriages, becoming involved with a jazz singer, and Randolph of whom the less said the better. And she foresees the light of her life going out any day."

CHAPTER 12

Churchill came back from his lunch and his nap cheerful. "She still retains her curiosity," he murmured to Anthony. "She was wondering what in the name of God we three are doing down here with the door closed hour after hour." He settled in his chair and resumed precisely where he'd left off.

"Making his escape, Eli toted his rifle and a few provisions, borrowed small boats without difficulty, and paddled and walked his way to the main island of Newfoundland. There he relied on remnants of his childhood knowledge of secret paths, and what he'd learned from fishing, hunting, and travelling for Mr. Slade in the area, plus sheer instinct, to avoid all people, and trek carefully beyond the Bay of Exploits and the mouth of the great river.

"On the third day, travelling on a trail upriver, he caught sight, on the opposite bank, of a band of Mi'kmaq. They were about to cross the river in canoes. He'd run out of food and had been loathe to fire his rifle at game this close to the well-frequented mouth of the river. He was tempted now to hail the Mi'kmaq, proclaim his kinship and his friendship with their kind in Notre Dame Bay, and let them offer him a morsel of meat. But seeing these men and women here in the wild, now, so independent in poise and so in control of themselves and their surroundings, so authoritative, he became apprehensive and wary as all the lore of his people concerning their mortal enmity now rose in him and he dragged up from his memory their Beothuk name: Shonack, Bad Indians.

"Songs and tales of hatred and conflict between Beothuk and Mi'kmaq told of how, generations ago, the hostility had all begun with a chance meeting of bands in canoes on Grand Lake when both peoples were friends and considered themselves kin. That lake being Beothuk territory at the time, they invited the Mi'kmaq ashore and began preparing a feast of friendship. During their convivial palaver, a Beothuk child told his father that, under a pile of furs in a Mi'kmaq canoe, he'd spied the severed heads of two of their own missing tribesman. This confirmed in Beothuk minds the rumours beginning to spread among them that the French, then numerous in Newfoundland, had placed a bounty on Beothuk heads, and were encouraging their Mi'kmaq fur suppliers to kill as many as they could, the better to encroach on Beothuk terrain and extend the limits of their hunting and trapping without hindrance.

"The Beothuk spoke not a word of the discovered heads. Each man sat next to a Mi'kmaq to eat in a circle of companionship. At a given signal, every Beothuk without warning stabbed his Mi'kmaq neighbour to death. A few girls were spared and brought into the Beothuk band and adopted. Eli's own ancestor, his mother had told him, had been one of them. Only one Mi'kmaq, an adolescent boy, who'd happened to be in the woods on a private matter, escaped to relate the dire news of the massacre. And that was sufficient to cause the implacable blood feud between the two peoples forever after."

Churchill stopped in his narrative and looked at me. "You may believe, if you like, that hoary old story of mass murder at a fellowship feast. It looms large in the mythology of every people in every time and place in history. But whatever the root of the hostility between them, most likely territorial competition in origin like everywhere else in the world, pitched battles and guerilla warfare between Mi'kmaq and Beothuk thereafter ensued.

"At the beginning of the general conflict, as the tales from both sides confirm, the Beothuk, with their far superior knowledge of the land and waters, and their swiftness and cunning in their own forests, but mainly because of their nonpareil expertise with bows and arrows, won every confrontation hands down. But then, the Beothuk tales lamented, the Mi'kmaq acquired more and more of the evil firearms from the French white devils, and became just as devilishly adept in their use. And they grew more familiar with the Beothuk lands they'd invaded with their traplines, and soon every battle became a rout of the Beothuk and often a general massacre of all present. These events occasioned much bitter singing and storytelling in mamateeks on winter nights for years afterwards, and were laden with exhortations to retaliate, to hit back and avenge, avenge, avenge, always avenge.

"Eli, now years later, on the river, stayed hidden from these modern Mi'kmaq in their canoes. His memory, here in the wild, of the old stories and songs, sent shivers of hatred and dread up his spine. Even the accounts, repeated by his Mi'kmaq friends in Notre

Dame Bay, of how they had over the years adopted Beothuk into their bands, and sometimes intermarried with them were portrayed in the songs lingering in Eli's head as violent capture, kidnapping, and enslavement. And the sight of them now, so confidently familiar and at one with nature, so poised, so clearly knowing exactly what they had to do on the water and the land, overawed the boy. He waited till they had crossed the Exploits and disappeared overland into the birch and shivering aspen stands, portaging toward the abundant waters on the other side.

"Eli continued his trek upriver for two more days, once shooting an arctic hare for sustenance, feeling he could risk the noise in the downriver wind. Then, out of the mists, midmorning, he glimpsed a cluster of canoes in the distance, descending the river. Beothuk. From behind a thick copse of spruce saplings, motionless with thudding heart, he watched them approach and pass him, silently paddling, thrilling him from head to toe with their noble composure and dignity, and so mysterious looking with their ochre-covered faces and arms and garments.

"To his delight, they put in at a large glade just below him, on his side of the river. The children jumped out and raced each other into the woods. Eli recalled having to hold his water as a boy during similar travels by canoe. The adults followed sedately. A man posted himself on the downriver side of the dell as sentry. With nature's demands answered, the children frolicked about the meadow, and the adults carried containers of food from the canoes and started a fire.

"Eli recognized from six years ago some men and women from his own band. But others were unknown or only vaguely familiar and must have come from other bands. And the children were complete strangers, having been unborn or very young when he'd been captured. All of them, adults and children, their skin and garments, smouldered with a rich deep red in the sunlight. The sight brought back childhood nostalgia in Eli as he remembered how tenderly his mother and father had coated his entire body—his face, hair, and hands—and all his coverings and belongings with red ochre. The heartbreaking sense of sorrow, the excruciating pain in his core, which had receded somewhat in Twillingate, surged up in him.

"Abruptly, a man went down on one knee, loosened the caribou skin from his shoulder, drew his bow, and let fly two arrows, all so close together that the entire action was a blur of speed. A boy left the man's side and ran the wide distance to the edge of the glade. There, with a shout of triumph, he raised over his head two hares, each impaled by an arrow. The adults glanced at him casually, commented with a word or two, and went back to their tasks. Eli recalled that he himself as a boy had considered such fast and accurate archery a commonplace. But now, at this distance in time, he was astonished at the swift precision. The two small animals were as far away from the archer as Eli's one hare had been from him, and less open, when he'd shot it with his highly accurate long gun.

"He'd heard many times in Twillingate alarming tales among trappers and fishermen about how true the Beothuk were with their arrows at remarkable distances. And how devious. They'd fire arrows at a group of settlers so that they'd fall short—dumb arrows—thus luring the white men closer, but apparently still out of arrow range, to get a better shot with their rifles, only to have the next salvo of arrows reach them easily, doing dreadful damage to white bodies. And he recalled stories of Red Indians placing carved decoy ducks in the water as white men arrived on the scene, and if the whites failed to shoot at the ducks, it showed that they didn't have their rifles with them, and the Beothuk would emerge and loose their arrows at them with impunity.

"Eli knew that the failure of the Beothuk to master firearms was a great disadvantage to them, but he could feel in his blood why they were so loathe to abandon their bows in favour of guns. Indeed, his actually seeing the feat with the bow today brought back such pride and homesickness that he could not contain himself. He lay his rifle down, spread his arms wide, and showed himself, greeting them with Beothuk words he still retained, and saying his name aloud to others for the first time in six years. 'I am Gobodinwit.' Three men turned fully flexed bows on him. The sentry, on the far side of the clearing from him, shot an arrow up in the air that came down and punctured the turf with a startling, piercing thud, and stood almost vertical, just 18 inches in front of his toes. It was a shockingly precise and effective brake on his movement. None of the other men let fly their arrows.

"'You're speaking our language, but with strange sounds,' said a man, 'and you're dressed as a white devil. There have been stories from our spies ever since the River-mouth Massacre that a boy lived on Twillingate Island who, from the distance, looked like Gobodinwit. And sometimes he has been spotted from afar near the river. Are you that boy?'

"'Yes. The whites murdered my mother and sister and others in my family that day and I was left for dead before being captured.'

"A woman spoke up. 'His mother was my best friend. I remember him well.' Eli recognized the woman whom he used to call aunt. He nodded and smiled at her.

"While two men kept their bows trained on him, the other adults bent their head together. Then one of them said, 'Gobodinwit's body was never identified for sure because two dead children were burned beyond recognition. But we agree now that you are Gobodinwit. We won't harm you today if you don't come close but you must turn round and leave.'

"'I have never stopped yearning to rejoin my own people,' Eli said. 'I couldn't do it before now because I was too young to escape from the white settlement by myself.'

"'After living among the white devils, you cannot come back to live among us. We are giving you a chance to go away and not come back.'

"'There was a young man, I remember from when I was a child, who lived among the whites for years on Fogo Island but who would be allowed by our people to come back and visit his mother and father from time to time.'

"'Yes, but he had to meet them outside our campsite,' said the man. 'Even back then, he couldn't come in, and our law is much stricter now as more and more of our people sicken from the white devils' evil. You cannot return. If you were to enter our home camp, we would have to burn you to ashes to stop you from poisoning the rest of our people with the sickness you bring back with you from our enemies.'

"'But I'm not sick, and I can help you. I can teach you how to use firearms so that you can protect yourself properly, and hunt better. I know how skilful you are with your bows. I remember it and I just saw it. But bows cannot stand up to men with guns. If every Beothuk had a gun, there'd be no more sneak attacks on our camps and no more massacres. The white devils would respect us and would be much more afraid than they are now to come into woods and up our rivers.'

"'Did you bring a rifle with you now?'

"'Yes, I left it over there, where I was hidden.'

"'Show us." Eli's hopes rose as walked back and pointed at the rifle on the ground. Two men waved him away and strode to the weapon. A look of utter disgust and disdain came over their faces. One of them picked it up by the end of the barrel and hardly glancing at it, carried it to a nearby boulder, where he gripped the barrel with both hands and brought the stock down like a club on the granite, in two mighty blows. The gunstock split and some metal parts separated and bent.

"The other man picked up the remnants of the rifle and walked over to the edge of the small brooklet nearby and carefully placed the pieces in it, choosing his spots. Then he rubbed his hands vigorously, front and back, on his thighs. Most of the pieces of rifle poked above the water and remained clearly visible, which, Eli recalled, was the Beothuk technique for showing their contempt for all guns they seized and smashed. 'For bringing near us that weapon of white devils' murder,' said a man, 'and being so proud of it, we have to kill you right now.'

"Led by the men with their bows at the ready, the entire group moved toward Eli. But the woman who'd been his mother's friend thrust herself between him and them. 'We can't properly kill him out here like this,' she said. 'It will make the spirits furious. He's not truly our enemy, neither a white devil or a Mi'kmaq or an Esquimo, and he hasn't fully returned among our people as a Beothuk tainted with pollution.' The men with their bows trained on him did not look convinced. They stepped to her side for a clear shot around her. 'Besides,' she said, moving in tandem, 'it would be better to send him back to the white devils with a strong message: Stop coming near our lake or our river in our heartland or we will kill you without warning and without mercy.' She turned to Eli. 'And the same applies to you. Leave here right now, and remember that if we ever see you again within range of our arrows, we'll have to kill you, as a danger to our people, without question or warning.'

"Eli looked at the men. There was no indication that they agreed with her. Their bows were still up and ready. Slowly he turned and walked away, keeping his back straight and proud but already feeling a foreboding of the pain between his shoulder blades where he would take the first arrow. How could men as full of fear and loathing as they were, and as deadly with the bow, resist the temptation to execute their brilliant marksmanship right into the centre of his back. The woman ran after him carrying a skin sack and hurled it behind him. 'For you in memory of your mother,' she shouted. 'I loved her. We all did.' His heart was thumping out of his chest as he turned and fetched the sack with thanks, noting through the sweat half-blinding him that, despite the gift, the blurred figures of men were nonetheless holding their shoot-to-kill posture. He made it to the thick brush before breathing, and then speedily moved behind the trunks of some shimmering aspen trees. He opened the sack and found it full of a delight to his eyes: cured caribou meat.

"That day and that night in the woods, with a full stomach and a brain fuelled by the meat, he contemplated his fate. At daybreak he decided that there was nothing else to do but go back to Twillingate and take whatever punishment came. He made his way along the river, staying under cover till he reached the Bay of Exploits, where he knew it would be safe to present himself to people as merchant Slade's Red Indian.

"The first man he encountered told him that 'Mister' was frantically looking for him. His prize worker, Mr. Slade was saying, had disappeared into thin air. He was demanding everywhere if anyone had heard of an accident involving him. He was even offering a reward for news leading to Eli's return. He was carrying on, said the man, not as if he was a servant, but a family member. Eli had no trouble procuring a boat ride to Twillingate Harbour.

"Mr. and Mrs. Slade were overjoyed to see him. Mister clasped him to his chest in a first-ever strong embrace. The hug from Missus was even more ardent. Eli started to apologize, saying that he'd been overcome with an urge to visit his people upriver and, being afraid he wouldn't have been allowed to leave, he'd lost his head and departed without permission. But that yearning was gone now, he said, and he could not wait to get back to the kindness he was shown here. He was sorry for depriving them of his services. It wouldn't happen again.

"It wasn't Eli's services they lacked, said Mrs. Slade, but Eli himself. The whole family, and even the other workers, missed him. Mr. Slade had asked a Mi'kmaq guide to search for him, and he did travel upriver to the first falls, but he was understandably reluctant to penetrate too far into Beothuk country without a group of experienced armed men with him like John Peyton Sr. and William Cull. Mr. Slade had even sent a message to Cull on Fogo Island, asking his help in forming an expedition. Cull was finishing up some business and, to oblige his friend and patron, was due to arrive in Twillingate today.

"Eli wondered what would have happened if he'd still been in the woods with his rifle when Cull or Peyton came up. Six years after the slaughter, his heart burned yet for vengeance. It wouldn't have been a sure thing, of course; they were skilled and wily survivors. But he had no doubt that he would have tried to kill Peyton at least.

"Over the years, Eli had kept his own counsel and shown no emotion whenever he occasionally encountered John Peyton Sr. It wasn't much of a strain. There was no talk between them, and no relationship beyond the white man's flickering smirk of contempt. William Cull, on the other hand, stopped and chatted with Eli whenever they met. Sometimes he spoke of the white man's attitude regarding the Beothuk. He could understand, he said, if Eli hated him and the rest for their attack, but remember that, looked at another way, they had only been preserving law and order. The magistrate here, said Cull, had chastised men he called 'West Country buccaneers' last year— Harry Miller and John Peyton and Thomas Taylor—for reports that they'd travelled upriver heavily armed to recover some of the nets and traps the Indians had stolen. They told each other with a wink and a nod, his Honour lamented, that it would be only right and proper to impose just retribution for the thievery, and when they surprised a Beothuk campsite, they were constrained only by the number of their guns and time for reloading in butchering as many as they could. And ever since, they'd not been ashamed of their brutal treatment of the

Beothuk but, in fact, had been exulting over their highly useful and prosperous trip. Peyton reminded the magistrate that in England and her colonies, the law required execution by hanging for 200 crimes, including such robbery and thievery as the Beothuk were so good at, and even youngsters were not spared the rope. Thus, the punishment they inflicted on the Beothuk was only what English criminals would get in the homeland for identical crimes.

"Eli, who had absorbed much of the lore of the white man, replied, 'Yes, but only after a trial in court.' Cull's face lit up in delight. He found the Indian boy endearing."

Churchill stopped his narrative and looked into the fire for 30 seconds. "The pitiless Peyton was regrettably right. I was appointed Home Secretary at 35 years of age, early in 1910. It was one of the great offices of state, a cabinet position, and I was there for nearly two years. I was highly involved in law enforcement. As one of my American friends described it, I was England's 'top cop.' Among my other responsibilities was the appraisal of death sentences for the possibility of clemency. Now I've been an advocate of the death penalty all my life, partly on the grounds that anyone but a blockhead would prefer a death sentence to a lifetime in prison. Nevertheless, of the 43 cases of capital punishment submitted to me for consideration, I saved nearly 50 per cent from the noose, a substantially higher number than those reprieved by my predecessors during the previous decade. I spent a great deal of time and energy on those reviews, including a painstaking examination of death sentences in England throughout history.

"By 1800, there were about 220 crimes, including theft of goods over 12 pence, for which the penalty was hanging; and lawbreaking youngsters were not exempt. In the early 1800s, for instance, a 15-year-old girl was convicted of infanticide in the death of her child—she'd been seduced by a member of the gentry—and hanged.

"Late in the 18th century, a 15-year-old girl was convicted of setting fire to a barn and a haystack near Gloucester, and hanged. A local newspaper criticized her bad manners for refusing to shake hands with her wronged master just before her hanging.

"In Dorchester in the 1790s, a 15-year-old girl was convicted of murdering her grandfather. Therein lies a tale, I'm sure. She was hanged by the neck.

"Children continued to be sentenced to hang well into the 1800s, although public agitation against hanging children increased to the point where younger children's death sentences were commuted for less serious crimes. I believe the youngest person to be executed in the United States was 12 years old. She was hanged in 1786 in Connecticut for murder. Her hanging was eased in the public mind by virtue of her being an Indian.

"Back in this country, in 1800, a huge crowd watched a 16-year-old girl hang for infanticide in Hertfordshire. A few years later, a 17-year-old girl, who'd been made pregnant by a member of the local gentry and abandoned, was found guilty of murdering her illegitimate baby and hanged in Radnorshire. A year later, a 15-year-old boy was hanged at York Castle.

"In 1819, a 16-year-old girl was publicly hanged in Derby for allegedly poisoning someone. And that year, a 15-year-old boy was hanged at Newgate for highway robbery.

"In the 1820s, a 16-year-old boy was hanged in Somerset for

stealing from a dwelling house; a 16-year-old boy was executed in Surrey for alleged rape; a 15-year-old boy was hanged at Newgate for burglary; a boy was hanged at 17 in Newgate for housebreaking; a boy, aged 16, was hanged at Chelmsford in 1829 for arson; another 16-year-old boy was hanged in Westmoreland. A year or two later, a boy of 17 was hanged at Worcester for setting fire to a haystack.

"Fourteen-year-old John Any Bird Bell was hanged in Maidstone for murder in 1831. I remember his name because I believe he was the youngest person to be hanged in England in the 19th century. A boy of nine was in fact sentenced to death in Maidstone for housebreaking a couple of years later, but his hanging was stayed after some tender-hearted members of the public caused a fuss.

"Sixteen- and 17-year-old boys and girls were hanged well into the 1800s. One girl was 17 when she poisoned her husband to whom she'd been married for less than a month. Ten thousand people turned out in holiday mode in a meadow in Bury St. Edmunds on a beautiful spring day round about the middle of the century to see her hanged from the New Drop Gallows. She made a speech from the platform, and the crowd cheered her mightily when she beseeched other girls not to follow her example but to remain true to their marriage vows, before watching the teenager drop and strangle to death.

"A year or two later in Bristol, an 18-year-old girl showed less aplomb. With the noose around her neck, she became distraught—the reports described her as hysterical at the end—and even the veteran hangman of many years standing was markedly upset by the teenager's execution. That will suffice. I trust you catch my drift, William, somewhat laboriously made."

"I do, Sir Winston. I thank you for the reminder of how brutal the era was, whether we are talking about a civilized nation or the backwoods of Newfoundland. Your research must have affected you greatly, for you to retain all that in memory so well."

"Some things stay in one's memory forever without effort. Yes, I saw clearly that the law took a dreadfully long time, almost into our own era, for even this enlightened country to stop killing our own children for minor as well as major crimes. Hence, what hope of clemency did the poor Red Indian have? Our oft-cited barbarian William Cull said to Eli once that he was 'awful glad' he'd rescued him and saved his life that time; sometimes your ancestor was a man ahead of his time. But he wasn't alone. Many people in England and Newfoundland, high and low, decried the brutality, when elsewhere in North America the government policy was often to impose bloodbaths upon the Indian.

"Eli came almost to like Cull, as he approached manhood. Consequently, although killing Peyton or his men would have presented no moral problem whatsoever, if only Eli could contrive an accident, or an untraceable rifle shot from the woods, Cull might be another matter. Then came a perfect opportunity to test Eli's lingering attitude of vengeance toward William Cull."

CHAPTER 13

"Slade and Cull and Eli were due to go out birding near Change Islands, between New World Island and Fogo Island. But that morning Slade's wife woke up with a fever. He told Cull he needed to stay back and tend to her. He didn't want Cull to waste his trip in from Fogo Island, so he suggested that he and Eli go out by themselves. 'Now the wife just told me, though,' said Slade, 'to make sure you bring him back alive and well, or you and I won't need a case of her grippe to kill us.'

"Cull put a hand on Eli's shoulder and smiled, 'Tell the missus I brought him here alive and well the first time. And I'll do no less this time.'

"Out on the water, Cull's words to Slade ate into Eli's brain. The man was proud of saving Eli from the massacre in which he himself had taken full part! Eli was sorely tempted, and soon he got an excellent chance to shove Cull overboard.

"Like nearly all settlers, Cull couldn't swim, and he'd instantly sink in his heavy clothes and boots. An explanation of the drowning, Eli thought, would be child's play: Not often, but occasionally, a fisherman would be knocked overboard from his small boat by a rogue wave, what fishermen called 'a cowardly wave' for the way it sneaked up on the boat and broke without warning far higher and stronger than the other waves. Often, the overboard fisherman could be quickly hooked with a gaff by his mates and pulled back in, but in the strong tidal current where they were located, Eli could credibly report that he wasn't able to reach Cull with the boat before, tragically, he went under. Eli had no motive in the eyes of the whites to kill the man who'd rescued him years before, and now appeared to be his friend. Everything urged him on. There'd be no suspicion."

Sir Winston Churchill paused in his narrative. "Cogitating further on it, William, and passing up opportunities for the moment to shove him overboard, Eli started to doubt that Cull's people would hold him blameless in your ancestor's death. The man was a survivor on land and sea—he'd often been out in boat all alone without anything untoward happening, and, suddenly, when he's out in boat with Eli, he *accidentally* drowns? Believable? One thinks not. Eli visualized Mr. Slade's face, mistrustful as he turned his back on him. He doubted he'd survive future encounters with any of Cull's clan, or with John Peyton and his crew. Destiny is always a close-run thing, and if tipped, so easily, one way, it would have caused Eli's crucial role in my family and in my life to be lost.

"Eli came back to Twillingate with Cull, their boat full of seabirds. They met with acclaim and Cull never stopped commending Eli on his skill with the gun and the boat. He gave every appearance of feeling closely bonded to Eli in something like companionship as a result of this highly successful hunt together. Mr. Slade was impressed and told Eli he was ready for an important task. He said the magistrate had mentioned to him that the governor was inquiring when Eli, now that he was grown up, was going to be used to establish good relations with his tribe.

"Mr. Slade had already asked Eli, when he'd returned home after running away, if he'd met with any of his people upriver. Eli replied that he had, but only very briefly. Mister told him that any time he felt the homesick yearning to visit his people for a while, just let him know and he would be permitted, indeed helped, to do so. Slade had heard of other Red Indians who'd made such visits while living among white settlers. The one named Tom June was said to have travelled upriver occasionally to visit his family.

"Another Beothuk boy—it must have been round the time of Eli's birth—was being carried on his mother's back, said Slade, when some fishermen shot and killed her. This was in response to a reward posted by the governor for 'a live Indian.' They left the dead and brought the live child home with them and dubbed him John August. He was about four years old. Someone took charge of him and then brought him to England where, as the historic record reveals, he was 'exposed as a curiosity to the rabble at Poole for two pence apiece.' Back in Newfoundland, as a young man, he worked for a merchant in Trinity and become skipper of a boat out of Catalina. In the autumn, said reports, John August would canoe upriver for a fortnight to visit his family, and then come back to his employer. Eli should think about doing something like that. Slade offered to arrange a meeting between them, as long as Eli would disregard John August's oft-expressed desire to meet the murderers of his mother so that he could have his revenge. But Slade learned that August had died recently at 24 years old and been buried in Trinity.

"Eli now made a clean breast of the fact that he'd been met with hostility verging on the lethal by the members of his tribe he'd encountered, and Mrs. Slade became emphatic that she was not going to allow him to travel up the river again by himself. Mister suggested that Will Cull accompany him, as he seemed to have a charmed life in his ventures into Indian territory; he could protect Eli during his discussions with his people. To which Missus retorted, no, it was ruffians like Cull and Peyton and their ilk that had driven the Indians deep into the wilderness and turned them into what they were today. Eli was not going to be given over to any such so-called protection. Mister didn't force the issue. Instead, he offered Eli an advancement.

"Slade had come to recognize the skills of the Red Indians he'd heard of, he said, and certainly he'd observed first-hand Eli's abilities. He now understood that Beothuk were highly intelligent and industrious and quick to learn, and not ignorant, untamed, and stupid, as commonly thought. Therefore, Eli was to receive a big promotion: from now on he would be known as Mr. Slade's chief assistant.

"'Chief?' said Cull to Slade, on hearing of it during a visit, with his hand on Eli's shoulder, 'no pun intended, I'm sure.' The merchant had little sense of humour. While Cull and Eli chuckled, he said earnestly that the name only meant that Eli would be gradually put in charge of all elements of the business, bar none. And Mrs. Slade added that they wanted him to consider their home his home, permanently and everlastingly.

"Thenceforth, almost everywhere Mr. Slade went, Eli travelled with him. In his vessel, they sailed all over Notre Dame Bay, and to Trinity Bay, Bonavista Bay, and White Bay, and even down on the Labrador, where he met Nascopie and Montagnais Indians. He found it easy to make friends with them. Their way of life seemed similar to what he remembered of his own childhood, as they followed the caribou, seals, and salmon. It was as if they were family.

"Now, Slade had some cousins on Ile Saint-Jean, which the British would re-baptize, a few years later, Prince Edward Island. He had business arrangements with them trading salt cod for farming produce, and he visited them every two or three summers. The July that Eli was nearing 20, Mr. Slade asked him to come with him on the trip and made him responsible for provisioning the vessel for departure.

"They sailed across White Bay, up the eastern side of the Great Northern Peninsula, round Cape Bauld, past where the Vikings were reputed to have created a colony 800 years before, through the Strait of Belle Isle, and directly down to Ile Saint-Jean. After a short stop there, Slade's cousin persuaded him to cross to the colony of Nova Scotia and proceed to a place called Sackville, where excellent business opportunities were to be had with a respectable family he knew well, with roots in Nova Scotia and Massachusetts. The family, named Baker, operated a farm and a sawmill operation near Sackville and had fishing interests back in Boston; they were attracted to the idea of a reciprocal connection—farming, saw logging, and fishing— between Nova Scotia, Boston, and Newfoundland. In Sackville, with Eli tagging along, Mr. Slade met with Joseph Baker and his wife, called Experience, and family members and workers.

"During the time they stayed on the Baker farm, Mr. Slade and his cousin slept in the big house. Baker suggested that Eli sleep in the cabin with the handful of Mi'kmaq who worked on the farm, but when Mr. Slade looked he said that it would be too crowded in there, and insisted, for unspoken reasons of his own, that Eli have a place to himself at night. Eli himself suggested that he sleep on hay and blankets in the loft of the barn. Baker laughed that he couldn't guarantee it, but he thought that site would be mostly away from the rats.

"Eli helped out at everything, and received compliments from Mr. Baker and his family and workers for his diligence and strength. He was well over 6 feet tall now, towering above nearly everyone else, and he heard the usual remarks of the women and girls, who weren't aware of the sharpness of his hearing, about how beautiful he was. Too bad, they whispered, that he was only an Indian. It was a slur that rankled with Eli and brought out his proud Beothuk feeling of nobility and resentment. He was as good as any of them—indeed a fair sight better.

"Eli remained polite but reserved with everybody there. Hence, only Mr. Slade and, later, one member of the Baker family were fully conscious of his penetrating intelligence. And nobody on the farm but Slade knew of Eli's skill, taught by his wife, in reading and writing and cyphering. In his loft, he secretly made notes of his observations and calculations regarding the farm and neighbouring sawmill, which was why Mr. Slade had wanted him alone at night. The operations generally looked satisfactory, but Slade and Eli did see some wasteful procedures on the farm that bothered the merchant a little. And as Eli whispered to him, if that was happening even while Slade was here on the spot as a potential investor, what else might go on in his absence? But it was not important enough to be a barrier to agreement, and he told Eli of Baker's invitation to visit Boston and Worcester next year over a possible salt cod deal with him and his associates. He'd go, he said, provided Eli accompanied him. Then, a minor arrangement was struck between Slade and Baker that, improbably, would cause consequences far beyond the ken of that generation and even that continent.

"During the final days of their visit, Joseph Baker let Mr. Slade know that he was temporarily running short of help. The Mi'kmaq, who were some of his best workers, were leaving for a while to attend one of their important commemorative gatherings on Cape Breton Island. Could Baker keep Eli's services on the farm, and pay for them, for another four to six weeks? He'd see to it that he got back home safe and sound that fall.

"Mr. Slade could scarcely believe his good fortune in the timing. He told Eli it would be a godsend if he could stay on in Sackville for another month in his absence to size everything up secretly, and report on it, playing the role of an obliging servant with a weak mind and a strong back. He didn't have to stay if he didn't want to; Mrs. Slade would be infuriated if she learned he'd been forced to stay here by himself in a strange land, against his will. But Eli agreed with alacrity.

"Eli's motives were more than a little selfish. Two days after their arrival, while he'd been helping in the fields and looking after the animals, Anna, a daughter of the Bakers, had courteously approached him. She was about 18 and he'd learned that she'd grown up here in Nova Scotia with her family but had been living and learning in

New England with her mother and relatives for the past two or three years. Each of those summers she'd returned here, usually with her mother, to the home she loved, to visit her father for two months. Anna asked Eli if he could help her with some of her own odd jobs.

"Eli was surprised and, instead of answering, looked across the yard at her father. Anna smiled into his eyes at his uneasiness, and moved her hand toward his arm in reassurance, but stopped and withdrew it before touching him. 'He said it's all right,' she told him, and when Eli didn't speak, she called out, 'Papa, can Eli help me sometimes with my chores?'

"The white workers in the yard looked up, and Eli could see them glancing at each other. Her father walked over. 'If it's all right with Mr. Slade,' he said, 'he can help you with weeding your vegetable garden, and bringing water and firewood into the house, and with caring for your horse, and he can drive you and Matilda into town in the carriage to buy provisions.' He turned to walk back to his task before tossing over his shoulder as an afterthought, 'If Eli doesn't mind.'

"'I'm happy to help in any way I can,' said Eli. 'I have time in the evenings.' The whites grinned at each other, and he saw the lone Mi'kmaq worker nearby take a quick glance at him, his face stolid. Eli felt that he had sounded like a naïve child.

"Late that afternoon, Anna asked Eli if he could drive her and her maid Matilda to town in the wagon. They had a lot to buy and bring back to the house and would appreciate his help. During this first drive, Eli learned from Anna how to hold and control the reins. He took to it instantly, as he did with anything new. He also gleaned from the conversation between Anna and Matilda that her maid was her close confidante. They both had ardent suitors back in Boston, and freely asked for each other's advice about coping with them— mainly how to gain the whip hand over them, while still appearing to be the little woman.

"The next day, Eli viewed the inside of the big house for the first time. Anna had asked him to help her and Matilda to bring in firewood for the kitchen stove, and guided him minutely on where to stow it. Earnestly pointing out the right spots behind the stove and in the porch, she came close enough for him to smell the exquisite fragrance of her bath soap. He felt awkward and embarrassed with the thought that perhaps his own fragrance mightn't be so delicate. She asked him if he cared for a cup of tea, which he declined. But then, with Matilda present, she had him sit at the kitchen table and put his hands up, spread apart just so, and she placed a hank of yarn around them to unwind and roll into a ball of wool.

"That ended abruptly when her father came in, froze in his tracks at the sight, and snorted with laugher. He told her to stop that this minute. She should know that turning a big young strapping Indian into a lady's maid like that was a grave sin in the eyes of God. Let Matilda help her with her yarn. Anna replied that Matilda was busy cooking his dinner, and besides, Eli said he didn't mind. Her father countered that he himself wouldn't mind either sitting down and getting a good spell from sluicing out the barn, as Eli had undertaken. And as for dinner, he'd rather starve than ever have to witness a strong young buck doing the like of that again. On the way out of the house, Eli fabricated for Papa a look that said thank you, sir, for rescuing me from a fate worse than death.

"Soon after, though, as Anna and Eli started performing other small tasks together, their conversations, even with Matilda present, became full of detailed frankness. She was aware of many connections between Newfoundland and Massachusetts. The father of a friend of hers in Boston was the master of a vessel that plied a trade route between St. John's and the West Indies, bartering salt cod for Jamaican rum. She was full of intimate questions about existence in Newfoundland, fascinated by his living on a relatively small island in Notre Dame Bay—Twillingate, she loved the name—and even more so by his descriptions of his early life in his native tribe of Red Indians at the centre of the great island. She had found a map of Newfoundland among her father's charts, she said, and was surprised by the lack of detail on it inland, away from the coast. She half expected to see 'Here be dragons' written in the wide, empty spaces.

"When he told her of how his nation, the Beothuk, were being squeezed from their ancient lands, rivers, lakes, and seashores, and hounded, often to death, by the English trappers and settlers, she became sad and said that the same crimes, and worst, had been committed over here against the Mi'kmaq. A British general even gave the Indians smallpox-infested blankets. The Americans, she said, often called Nova Scotia the 14th colony, and many thought this colony should rebel against England too, and join the United States. But she doubted that the lot of the Indians would improve much even if they did become part of the US. He told her he thought that a great deal depended on the leadership of the Indians themselves, since many of the whites were too fixed in their arrogant, superior, and predatory ways to ever change. He hoped one day to go back to his own people and help lead them in a way that might save them, since the direction they were heading in now seemed likely to lead to their destruction.

"Sometimes, as they talked, she would sigh that she was expected to marry in New England and enter society there, and then be glued to her kitchen and nursery and bedroom forever after. That made her melancholy, she said. One time, when Matilda was out of hearing, she gushed out that, in bed last night, she yearned to be a Beothuk so that she could live their noble life in the beautiful wilderness and help them on the path to their salvation. Her fervour startled him so much he kept himself from reacting at all and, for five minutes, he couldn't look at her.

"Out of her presence, Eli thought of her constantly. He would have fallen in love with her if he hadn't known how hopelessly witless that notion was. As for her feelings for him, he was only conscious of realizing she must think of him as being the lesser part of their relationship, and that she played the dominant part, the lynchpin part, of an unbalanced friendship, a pleasing mistress-servant friendship, not unlike that between her and Matilda, but even less equal. Her sudden, blurted, Beothuk fantasy he took to be a reaction against her coming domestication; he'd gathered from vague talk between her and Matilda, and chit-chat among workers outside, that she was in fact already promised in marriage to, betrothed to, a man in New England.

"People noticed her easy ways with him, and a couple of white men made laughing comments among themselves, not troubling to keep their words from him, about her friendliness with him. One snorted to his mates that he never reckoned her to be an 'Indian lover,' or he would have made a few war whoops himself. Eli received the men's comments without resentment, in the spirit of absurd humour, just so much clowning to be added to all the perennial old jests about the farmer's daughter. It was absolutely irrational to everyone that there could be anything remotely intimate between Eli and Anna.

"He heard Matilda mutter to her once, as he was entering the house with a pail of water he'd offered to bring in for the houseplants, 'I know, Anna, but be careful. He's only a ...' He couldn't hear what she thought he was, but he knew it was a belittlement. It should have caused him pain, but it made his innards lurch with pleasure at the inkling of awareness, but awareness loved for its own sake alone, awareness without result, that could have no result.

"In late summer, the day before she was to leave for New England, she wondered if he could bring her small trunk from the shed into the house so that she could pack. As he came in the door, she called him from upstairs, asking him if he'd mind carrying the trunk up to her room. Matilda was in the kitchen, but now she immediately mounted the stairs behind him. Anna was in her bedroom, and she directed him to place the trunk on top of her cedar chest for packing. When he'd done that, and with Matilda's obvious presence in the hall, Anna put both arms around him, and hugged him wordlessly, her face pressed to his chest. 'Thank you for everything, Eli,' she said, stepping back. 'You made my visit this summer an absolute delight. If ever you come to upper New York state, where it looks like I'm going to end up, please visit us. And if I'm ever shipwrecked in Newfoundland, I'll expect you to rescue me.'

"Even Matilda laughed, albeit briefly, before saying, 'Anna, let's get cracking. Eli, your master just went in the barn. I think he's looking for a pair of strong arms.'

"The next morning Anna left in the carriage with her father and maid to join her vessel for Boston. Many waves and fond goodbyes went to and from the retainers assembled to see them off. Her smiles for all were equally warm, with nothing special for Eli. It was a clear signal they'd said farewell forever. He would very likely never see her again—at most, perhaps, a glimpse of her as a married woman if she happened to be there when he accompanied Mr. Slade to Boston.

"A week later, Eli departed by boat as planned for Cape Breton Island. There, he was put in contact with a vessel carrying some Mi'kmaq across the Cabot Strait before the fall storms, to engage in the Newfoundland hunting and trapping seasons. His trip home took days, touching in at Flat Bay in Bay St. George, and Bonne Bay, to let off some Mi'kmaq, then up the Great Northern Peninsula, and down the other side, following the same route by which he'd come, until he reached Twillingate, and Mrs. Slade's waiting embrace.

"He brought back to Mr. Slade a report showing some relationships by Baker with some buyers of the farm's produce that Eli thought might be too cozy. Mr. Slade couldn't praise him enough. Eli pushed out of his mind the touch of guilt he felt at reporting on Anna's father behind his back; there was nothing between him and her to unsettle his duty to Mister. Besides, although she might be buried deep in his heart, and probably always would be, he soon acquired a little help in easing the ache.

"That fall, on a trip to some settlements in Bonavista Bay with

Slade, he met a lovely, smart Mi'kmaq girl called Minnie Paul. She was 17 years old, and helped out running the boarding house in a place where they were stranded by stormy weather. She and Eli hit it off right away, to the point where Slade told him at the dinner table on their second night there that he could do a lot worse in a few years than to make Minnie his woman. Eli did not demur.

"When they got home again, the merchant conferred with Mrs. Slade and then sent a message to Minnie Paul's father proposing to bring her to Twillingate for the winter, during downtime for the boarding house, to train and work under watchful eyes in Slade's store. Minnie proved to be keen on the proposal, and charmed Eli 10 days later when she stepped off the vessel onto Slade's wharf and had fun directing him minutely on the careful conveyance of her rough-hewn luggage up to the house. He was exceedingly happy that she was there. But then, the bolt from the blue.

"Upon receiving the accounts from Sackville in the fall, Mr. Slade told Eli he was bothered by the saw-log side of the operation. It was turning a profit but was not performing up to his expectations. There might be something less than the best going on there. He was going to write Mr. Baker to say that he was close to deciding on a partnership, but that, first, he wanted Eli, who had learned so much about the farming operation there last summer, to spend six weeks from the beginning of July in Sackville next summer at Slade's own expense, making himself more familiar with the sawmill.

"Now Eli didn't know if Anna would be there during any of that period, but probably not, owing to her upcoming marriage. Still, from what he could gather from all the palaver this past summer, the wedding wasn't expected till next winter, so there was always a slight possibility she'd be visiting Nova Scotia beforehand. There was no way he could find out for sure, of course, but the barest hope that she might visit brought on a surge of excitement. He kept it concealed and looked over at Minnie Paul, carrying groceries from the store to the house. Mr. Slade caught his glance and winked at him. 'Your pretty little friend won't be delighted to see you depart, and I'd understand your own reluctance to leave her. And Mrs. Slade won't let you go if you don't want to. But you'd be doing a big important favour for me. What do you say?'

"'I'll be more than happy,' said Eli, 'to go back for you.'"

CHAPTER 14

"**D**uring the winter in Twillingate, Eli helped prepare equipment for the cod fishery and the salmon netting on the rivers, but he was most content out hunting and visiting traplines; he revelled in the wilderness and how it challenged his ability to survive every day. When home, he responded eagerly to Minnie's frequent calls to help her move something heavy from the warehouse to the store. Mr. Slade patted him on the shoulder and told him to give her requests priority: Eli needed to spend time with her before he left. Mrs. Slade, seeing Minnie's desire to be close to him all the time, and her difficulty in keeping her hands off him, warned Eli in a crabwise way not to do anything dishonourable until he obtained her father's formal consent to marry her, and a day was actually set.

"That spring and early summer, the ice floes from Labrador were the worst in living memory. The seal hunt from the land was excellent and Eli exulted in going out on the icefields nearly every day and bringing in fat carcasses, but still, even out there, his thoughts were always on the holdup in his departure for Nova Scotia.

"When the delay reached nearly a month, both Mrs. Slade and

Minnie Paul told him it was far too late for him to leave now. But Slade had sent a letter to Baker in the fall that Eli would be coming, and, to Mister's joy, Eli insisted on living up to the commitment he'd made to him. As soon as the wind blew the ice offshore, Mr. Slade put him aboard a vessel with a Mi'kmaq companion, and Eli set sail in front of two sad female faces. By the fourth week of July he arrived in Sackville, and Anna was not there.

"But her father was there and delighted to see him. He told Eli he was lucky this time: he wouldn't have to do double duty, tending to his regular work on top of seeing to Anna's demands; she was not planning to visit this summer. She and her mother had too much to attend to in Boston, getting ready for the winter wedding. At the thought of having to spend a month and a half doing nothing but bugger about in a bloody old sawmill, Eli concealed his disappointment. The Beothuk were good at putting on a poker face. Then, to his shock one evening a week later, up the lane in a strange wagon came Matilda the maid.

"Judging by Mr. Baker's reaction he wasn't expecting her, either. Eli waved to her in greeting from across the yard, but she ignored him with a stony face. Going into the house, she told Baker that there had been no time to send him a message of her arrival, but she did have a message from Anna. She closed the door behind her before Eli could hear Anna's message.

"He was sitting in the barn with his anxious thoughts, trying to make his surreptitious notes, when he heard Matilda calling his name from the front door of the house. He hid his writing implements and walked over. As he drew close, she asked him aloud if he could help bring in a few pails of water for her wash. Then she whispered to him, 'Don't bust your buckskins, Eli, but, yes, she's coming. Remember, now, she's an engaged woman. She's getting married over Christmas. So, do not—hear!—*do not* forget your place.'

"Matilda's vehement, demeaning warning irked him. He might have said he was too busy to tote water and walked away, standing on his pride as Mr. Slade's man. But, of course, a thrilling curiosity over Anna's visit had seized him. The thought went through his head that this near coincidence of timing in their arrival here had been ordained by fate, by destiny. If it hadn't been for the late Labrador ice, they might have missed each other entirely. He said to Matilda. 'I didn't even expect her to visit here this summer.'

"Matilda looked at him closely. 'She didn't either. At least she kept saying she wouldn't come. But then, all of a sudden, last week, she had to have one last visit before becoming a wife.' Unsmiling, as if in dismay for some wrongdoing of his, she slowly shook her head and moved back toward the door. 'Would you please fetch the water.' Then she stopped and whispered again, 'I shouldn't even be telling you this—she changed her mind after Mr. Baker mentioned in his regular letter to Mrs. Baker last Tuesday that you had come for a few weeks.'

"All now became clear to Eli: neither coincidence, nor fate, nor destiny had anything to do with Anna's visit. She had deliberately decided to come for him.

"The day after he saw Anna driving up the farm road in the carriage, they were back in their old groove. Her father said to her in his presence, 'Don't work him so hard this year, Anna. Save a piece of him for the sawmill.'

"With Anna beside him, and Matilda sitting on the bench behind with her back to them, he drove the wagon to town next evening for household dry goods. Anna told him she'd been intending to stay in New England this summer and make herself ready for her future life. Then she'd had an incontrollable urge, her last chance, to spend time in her childhood home before the responsibilities of married life piled on her, and she'd scrabbled and clambered to get here before he left. She was delighted to find on arrival that he still had over a month remaining in his visit. Eli stayed silent, embarrassed at Matilda hearing this. She breathed out noisily behind them.

"Then he felt Anna's fingers on his hand holding the reins. He glanced over his shoulder; Matilda was looking at the dust behind the wagon. He passed the leather straps to his other hand and held hers for minutes, low enough that, even if Matilda did turn round, she wouldn't have been able to see their clasp. Eli couldn't look at Anna but he heard her breathing deepen beside him. He wondered if Matilda heard it too above the clatter of the wheels.

"On Sunday morning, Anna's family and some workers got ready as usual to go to the Methodist church. The Mi'kmaq workers on the farm went on their own to the Catholic church. Having lived in the house of Methodists in Twillingate, Eli was considered to be of that persuasion. He always went, and sat in the back, often by himself, recalling throughout each service here, as he did in Twillingate, what he'd learned as a young boy about the gods of the sun and the moon and the good and bad spirits of the Beothuk.

"Eli was waiting to drive the Baker household to church this morning when Mr. Baker told him Anna was staying home with cramps in her abdomen. Matilda would remain with her in the house, but a trusted man was also needed to stay back on the virtually empty farm as a safeguard while everyone else was off the property. Anna, the headstrong girl, he said, had argued with him that she didn't need anyone else there besides Matilda. But he had insisted, and he now asked Eli to keep an eye out from the stable to ensure the safety of the two women. Meanwhile, he laughed, Eli could catch up on forgiveness for all his sins at the evening service.

"Yesterday, Anna had threatened, jokingly Eli thought, to shock him out of his boots one of these days by showing up unexpectedly in his barn. Now, this morning, as he stood in his door looking at the house he was guarding against misconduct, he saw her quietly come out, carrying a tray. He stepped toward her, awkwardly, to help, but not knowing quite what to do; she shook her head vigorously at him without a word, and continued to creep gingerly across the space. He was discomfited that she was dressed only in her nightdress, bathrobe, and sandals.

"When she came close, she said in a low voice that this was his special breakfast treat for all his help. Her tray contained fruit, cream, toasted bread and jam, and a cup of tea. He took the tray from her with thanks in front of the barn door and started to back in. Her hand covered his and she brushed past him, nearly upsetting the tray. She pulled him into the barn by the arm and whispered right into his ear, 'I can't stop thinking of you, Eli ... in ways I know I shouldn't. Matilda says they're shameful ways, but I don't believe they are, and I can't help it anyway.' She took the tray out of his hands and placed it on a bench.

"He hadn't touched a morsel on the tray before, there and

then, guided by Anna, they made urgent and clumsy love under her garments, standing up in the stall nearest the door. The whole procedure lasted less than a minute. Which was a good thing, because right after they finished, he heard the door opening and saw Matilda coming out of the house. By the time she'd stomped across to the barn, he was sitting on a bale of hay sipping his tea and Anna was standing on the other side of the stall, her bathrobe all arranged and orderly, but her face and neck were flushed.

"Matilda practically yelled, 'Anna, I thought you said you were going to get me to invite him to the kitchen when it was ready.'

"'You were busy upstairs stripping the beds, so I reckoned I might as well bring it over myself.'

"'What happened to your cramps?'

"'They come and go, Matilda. You know what they're like.'

"Matilda eyed Anna and then Eli, up and down, with great suspicion. Her gaze lingered on the front of his garments. He kept himself from squirming. He'd find out later that part of her anxiety came from her clear awareness that it was not actually the time of the month for Anna's cramps and her serious doubts that either he or Anna possessed the wit to do anything at all to preclude a biological disaster.

"'Hurry up and finish that, Eli,' Matilda ordered, 'so I can bring the tray back to the house. And, Anna, back to bed with you.' She sounded more like an exasperated older sister than a maid. 'We can't have your father finding out that you were traipsing about the farm in your unmentionables all morning visiting everything in two moccasins.'

"Anna laughed and said, 'Oh Matilda. What nonsense.'

"Anna and Eli liked what they'd done so much they tried to contrive to do it again. But, with family or workers about, and Matilda keeping a sharp eye on her as self-appointed chaperon, no further occasion arose on the farm. They hoped to arrange to drive to town alone together, perhaps if Matilda were to get sick and have to stay home. They intended to stop the wagon behind some trees for a few minutes, or pull off the main road onto a deserted path. Not only did Matilda stay sickeningly healthy, but they noticed on their last routine drive to town that there always seemed to be workers in the fields, or homesteaders on the verandas of houses, or wagon traffic going and coming. She longed, she whispered behind him, as he was toting some hardware into the house from town one evening, to run away with him.

"The weeks went by agonizingly fast toward Eli's date of departure, redeemed only by the tasks they did together chastely, out in the open or under Matilda's vigilant eye in the house. They plotted in murmurs two or three different, but similarly cockeyed, plans to escape to somewhere, somehow. A few days before he was due to leave for home, she told him, as they were brushing down her horse after supper, that she had missed her time of month by nearly a week. It had always been like clockwork before, she said. This was the very first time it had happened in her life. To his nonplussed face, she explained directly what the female phenomenon might mean: she thought she might be with child. Eli's child.

"Far from causing them the desperate concern that the consequences of their childlike love warranted, they eagerly used it to make concrete plans. They would secretly sneak their way through Nova Scotia, they imagined, and one way or another, driven by their love, make their way back to Newfoundland. To obtain her good advice, Anna told him she'd be confiding her plans to Matilda; her maid and confidante had never once let slip any of her secrets.

"That night, Eli, in the barn, spinning the future in his head, heard an unnerving commotion of male and female voices from the house, together with the sounds of the farm manager and the Mi'kmaq foreman, coming and going outside in the dark. Before dawn, he made out the crunch of wagon wheels leaving the farm, and saw the light from a lantern on the receding vehicle and silhouettes of human forms on it, but nothing else was visible in the moonless black. The house was dark. Until Matilda came over to the barn at daybreak, Eli remained ignorant.

"The maid looked at him with a disgusted face. She wouldn't even be over here, she spat out, talking to an uppity Indian, who was an idiot to boot, if Anna had not made her swear, in the name of *love*, for God's sake, to explain to Eli everything that had happened in the house last night.

"When Anna had told her she thought she was pregnant, and by whom, Matilda had gone deathly silent, nearly fainting from the shock. Then one thought alone echoed in her head: protect Anna, rescue Anna, *save* Anna. And the solution instantly came to her. Hadn't Anna implied to her that she'd been intimate with her fiancé before she'd left Boston for here? Yes, Anna said, a few nights before, he had seduced her, forced himself on her, actually, claiming it as his right since they were engaged and that it would serve as a little memento for them while they were apart. But she didn't want to talk about that awful stuff: she'd had her period right after that; if she was with child, it was not his.

"But he wouldn't know that, Matilda replied, and she urged Anna to tell her father it was her fiancé's and that they should hold her wedding a little earlier than planned. But Anna refused. It was Eli's, she said.

"'Don't say that,' Matilda screamed at her under her breath. 'Never ever say that. Never never never say that.' But Anna groaned that she was going to run away with Eli, and that was the end of the discussion, and she wanted Matilda's help as her friend.

"So the maid, to stop her beloved Anna from doing something that was sure to end in disaster in every way, told Anna's father about the intimate encounter with the fiancé and that his daughter thought she might be pregnant. Papa was unperturbed. It was too soon after the deed to be certain, he said, and he knew from experience that there were myriad false starts in that business. But, ever practical, he summoned Anna and told her they were going to write her fiancé and her mother in Boston of her suspicions to put them on guard, and if her time of month did not return to normal in a few days, they would leave for the States right away and arrange to get that wedding behind them quick. To Matilda's horror, Anna became frantic and screamed, no: the baby was not her fiancé's, it was Eli's, she loved Eli, and she was going to go away with him and marry him.

"Her outburst flabbergasted Papa into a bug-eyed, purple-faced, spine-chilling silence. After 10 or 15 seconds, he exploded and went off his head completely. Howling unintelligibly, he lunged forward and grabbed Anna by the upper arms; if Matilda hadn't forced herself between father and daughter as he raised his hand, she was sure that, for the very first time in Anna's life, he would have struck her, and not gently. Instead, now, alternating between swearing under his breath, and emitting falsetto screeches, he clomped about the kitchen, stopping only long enough to punch the wall and put a crack in a thick board. Finally, holding his right hand, dripping blood from the knuckles, in his left, he stood over Anna, as she wept on the couch, and spelled out his strategy in a low, controlled, terrifying voice: If she didn't leave for New England with him tomorrow morning without another word to her violator, and if she didn't claim to her fiancé there that he'd made her pregnant, and marry him immediately, he would arrange to have her rapist killed for assaulting her. It was her father's wild eyes and eerie calmness of voice that made Anna believe him without question, and between sobs she nodded her assent to everything he demanded in order to save Eli's life.

"Matilda told Eli that she herself was going to leave for Boston tomorrow, after she'd packed or stored Anna's remaining things today. But before she started that she had one last piece of information for him, not for his own stupid sake but for the sake of poor Anna and her misguided love for him. After her father had barred Anna in her room, crying, he sent Matilda with a lantern over to the Mi'kmaq lodging to ask the headman to come to the house.

"When Matilda arrived with the Mi'kmaq foreman, father sent Matilda to her room, but she still managed to overhear him confiding that Eli had attempted to rape his daughter. He'd been unsuccessful, but the capital offence was in the attempt—and, if left unpunished, would bring disrepute on the entire Mi'kmaq people here in Nova Scotia.

"The foreman replied that Eli was not a Mi'kmaq from Nova Scotia, but a Beothuk from Newfoundland.

"That subtle distinction would be lost on white people here in Nova Scotia where the attempt was made, said Mr. Baker. To them he was just another Indian. But it could be a useful motive for certain Newfoundland or Nova Scotia Mi'kmaq. Keep everything quiet and do nothing until after Anna was safely married in a few weeks. Then he would send the Mi'kmaq headman a one-word message from Boston: 'Now.' That would be the signal that the goodly sum of £50 would be paid to any enterprising Mi'kmaq who might find Eli the Beothuk here, or in Newfoundland, or anywhere else he decided to hide, tragically dead under unsuspicious circumstances ... a hunting accident, a drowning, a fall off a cliff. Anna's reputation had to be kept free from any possible blot, blemish, or besmirchment by ridding the world of her attempted rapist.

"Anna was already at the end of her tether, Matilda told Eli. She'd screeched at Matilda last night, and threatened to kill her and herself for informing Mr. Baker that she might be pregnant. If the poor girl were to hear later that Eli was dead—killed?—she'd fall apart completely, and God alone knew what she would actually do or say— maybe really try to harm her father or herself, and certainly she'd blurt everything out and ruin her own life and her child's. But her father was so stunned and unsettled by her and Eli's treachery that he wasn't thinking straight about any of that happening. Hence, Eli must hightail it out of here this very day, go into hiding somewhere, and try to save his skin, for Anna's sake, if not his own.

"Matilda started for the door out of the barn while Eli, dazed and heartbroken and unable to reason, mumbled, 'Anna wanted us to be together, to go away together.'

"Matilda turned on him with a fierce look: 'If you and she had run away together yesterday, you'd be dead today as an Indian kidnapper and rapist. And Anna ... My God, fornicating with a—! Her family would have disowned her and she'd probably be dead herself soon, or at best unmarried for the rest of her life. At least be a little happy now that she's still alive and on the right course. Get out of here by tonight, Eli. Vanish! You selfish benighted fool.'

"He kept to the barn all day, stewing in suicidal thoughts. There was no activity by workers in the yard. In the afternoon, up in his loft, he heard his name whispered below. It was the Mi'kmaq headman: 'Disappear from this place,' he muttered when Eli appeared above, 'and leave Nova Scotia. There are good Newfoundland Mi'kmaq in Cape Breton to help you.' That evening, at twilight, Eli walked across the yard to the open kitchen window and called Matilda. There he said, 'Please tell Anna I wish her happiness, and tell Mr. Baker I said I'm gone from Nova Scotia for good. I'm heading for the Montagnais in Quebec.'" Sir Winston stopped speaking and pushed at his armrests to get up. "And I'm heading for preprandial libation and nap," he muttered. "We'll resume in the morning."

Walking out of the house, I asked Anthony, "Does he do that on purpose? I mean breaking off at a point of maximum suspense and leaving us hanging like that?

"He has always loved to do that," said Anthony. "It has been very effective in his writing. But also generally in life: For example, the date and place of the D-day invasion were kept top secret, of course, as a necessary strategy, but Sir Winston's greatest joy was to make sure that Hitler knew it was coming, as it drove him crazy with the prolonged suspense of not knowing when or where."

CHAPTER 15

In the morning, Churchill met my good morning with a barely raised arm and said, "I don't know how much longer I'll have for this. We'd best move along without overdoing the civilities." After dark, Eli made his way, felt his way, off the farm, and began his trek, laboriously and clandestinely and grief-stricken, up toward Cape Breton Island. From time immemorial, Mi'kmaq had sailed in little boats from there to Newfoundland.

"When he arrived days later, half-starved, he managed to meet up with some local Mi'kmaq. They fed him and directed him to a few of their fellows from Newfoundland. They knew of him from talking with friends over the years from Notre Dame Bay, and latterly from Sackville, and welcomed him. But word was percolating through to them that he was a fugitive of some kind, that a private bounty was about to be placed on his head for an attempt to commit a violent, immoral act on a white woman.

"'The accusation is not true,' said Eli.

"'Then why are you running?' asked one.

"His friend turned on him. 'Where have you been all your life? If one of our kind is accused of that, he runs or he dies.'

"Another asked, 'Do you know Noel Boss? He's a young Mi'kmaq who travels between Newfoundland and Nova Scotia a lot.'

"'I've seen him in Newfoundland.'

"'They say he's going to take on the job.'

"'I'm not afraid of Noel Boss.'

"'I would be if I were you. You're going to help him carry out his boast that he'll kill 100 Beothuk vermin before he's done.'

"'One of my ancestors was Mi'kmaq. Does he kill Mi'kmaq too?'

"'You're Beothuk enough for Noel Boss.'

"'Am I Mi'kmaq enough to get a ride to Newfoundland?' Eli discussed with them a boat trip across the Cabot Strait. They said that this time of year there were lots of Mi'kmaq going home to Newfoundland. But they didn't think it was a good idea for him to trap himself there on the island that Noel Boss also knew so well.

"Eli prevailed upon them, nevertheless, to take him on board. He was at sea when he learned from them that Noel Boss had already offered half the coming reward to any Mi'kmaq who would report back to him that he'd witnessed Eli meeting with an accidental death. Eli asked the men if he was going to fall overboard accidently. One replied that if he slept with one eye open, he'd find out. They all laughed. Then the skipper said they were not about to profit from a white man's accusation against a fellow Indian. If they started doing that, they'd never stop killing each other.

"Eli's fear of being heaved overboard soon tapered off by comparison with the perils of the voyage. They were traversing this expanse of 60 miles and more of ferocious sea in a fragile 30-foot shallop. And only one haven of shelter existed, at tiny St. Paul's Island, 15 miles out from Cape North. From that to Cape Ray, Newfoundland, the skipper said, there were 50 miles of sudden gales, choppy waves from the contending wind and tide, blinding mist and fog, and huge swells that threatened to swamp the boat. 'We have to hope that our dead reckoning is not too far off for making safe landfall on the other side. A few of our Mi'kmaq can still make this ancient voyage by canoe. We only do it to keep you Beothuk from getting big-headed admiring your own skill and courage in travelling by canoe to the invisible Funk Islands, just 40 miles out in the North Atlantic Ocean. By the way, the seagoing canoes of the Mi'kmaq and the Beothuk are very similar, nearly identical. I don't know who copied who, but I think it shows we are all brothers.'

"After the shallop sighted Cape Ray and then moved up the coast to put in at Flat Bay in Bay St. George, Eli jumped into the shallow surf, and helped to pull the craft ashore. Then he shook hands all round, and joked and laughed, bursting with survivor's delight. An elder in the Mi'kmaq community greeted him on the beach, asked him his name, and invited him to his home.

"Eli sat with him over tea and thanked him for the big-heartedness of his people. The old man said he was welcome to stay here for a while and share stories and relationships with the several Beothuk or part Beothuk, men, women, and children, among them who had, by marriage or adoption, become highly esteemed members of their nation. They were safe there under Mi'kmaq protection, even from the likes of Noel Boss, but, in truth, Eli himself might not be secure in this place for long. Not because of any accusation against him, since most Mi'kmaq would just consider it more white man's slander, but because of the secret price reportedly on his head, and it would take only one impulsive young man to act on that.

"Eli replied that he intended to leave Flat Bay immediately to make his way back to Twillingate. He was sure that Mr. and Mrs. Slade would welcome him. He even had a Mi'kmaq girlfriend there they wanted him to marry.

"The elder smiled at him. Eli was a bright young man, he said, but very unworldly and had been kept extremely innocent all these years under the wing of the Slades. He needed to ask himself with brutal honesty what their reaction would be in the face of direct allegations from their partner in Nova Scotia of an evil attempt by their trusted Indian against the virtue of his daughter engaged to be married. How welcoming would the Slades be after serious accusations that Eli, their all-but-adopted son, had betrayed their trust and their honour in such a wicked, criminal way? Perhaps they'd take Eli's word over their white colleague's, but the elder's experience told him he shouldn't count on it. And add in the fact that, although most by far of the Mi'kmaq who frequented the bays of the northeast coast of Newfoundland were good sensible people, not all of them were. Numbered among the latter, he'd place the implacable Beothuk hunter, Noel Boss, and although he and his methods were not well liked by most Mi'kmaq, some of their young men here and in Notre Dame Bay considered him their idol, and white furriers appreciated his celebrated guiding skills, especially up the Exploits River where the Beothuk still survived as a remnant.

"If Eli went back to the islands of Notre Dame Bay, said the elder, it would be childishly simple for him to die by mishap. Even the father of his Mi'kmaq sweetheart waiting for him in Twillingate would more than likely bring her back home now to spare her from becoming a widow with young children.

"Eli might consider joining his own people at Red Indian Lake, the elder continued, but the Beothuk living here in Flat Bay said they could never do that and expect to survive. Hadn't Eli already tried that five years ago, according to the stories, only to find them to be a very stiff-necked people, and disinclined to embrace him as a long lost son? Perhaps his only hope, and that a bleak one, was to head up the Great Northern Peninsula, unobserved with luck, cross the Strait of Belle Isle to Labrador, and join a band of Naskapi or Montagnais there. They were good people, and would take him in among them as an endangered, forlorn Beothuk brother.

"Eli and the kindly elder talked all day and much of the night about travel inland. The old man described alternative trails, those that led up north to Bonne Bay and beyond, and those that tended east toward Grand Lake and on to Red Indian Lake, and those that veered south and allowed trekking along the coast all the way over to Bay D'Espoir. The elder described landmarks—tolts, mountains, large rocks, streams, ponds, bogs, lakes—and Eli visualized them on a map in his head and learned them by heart.

"The few Beothuk and part Beothuk in the community, and some Mi'kmaq, drifted in to see him. The Beothuk especially urged him to stay in this place. They were welcome and safe there and could help protect him, they insisted, even in spite of the odd thug like Noel Boss. The elder countered that no Indian was safe with a price on his head.

"The next morning, with provisions, and a rifle and ammunition supplied by the elder, he set out, declaring to all he intended to travel up the Great Northern Peninsula. But instead, he veered northeastward and kept trekking until he reached Grand Lake, the biggest body of fresh water in Newfoundland with its great island, an area containing old haunts of his Beothuk ancestors, now abandoned, but still celebrated, he remembered, in story and song, for victorious battles against the Mi'kmaq before they acquired their wicked rifles.

"He turned east along Little Grand Lake, following the waterways and paths until he hit the bottom of Star Lake and then Lloyd's River, as described by the elder without their white man's names, that ran into the southwest end of his Beothuk home lake, now called by the settlers Red Indian Lake. This end of the lake was opposite to the end most frequented and inhabited by his people these days, from which their great sacred river, called the Exploits by the whites, flowed out. He would have to trek the length of the lake, but he was nearly home, the home where, if he ever came back to it, he'd been warned by his kin as a 16-year-old on the riverbank, he'd be killed.

"In his heart, he didn't truly believe the threat. How could they destroy someone as valuable to their tribe as him? And, even if that notion had no hold on them, how could they deliberately, consciously, make away with someone, one of their own, whose history was so tragic and who so desperately needed their help? Besides, he flattered himself, when it came right down to it, he'd be able to escape the ordained fate through his persuasive talk. People liked to listen to him when he talked, whether Mi'kmaq in Newfoundland or Nova Scotia, or white people like Mr. and Mrs. Slade, or William Cull, or Mr. Baker, or Anna.

"Anna had told him she was first attracted to him because he was such a gorgeous creature to look at. But she'd actually fallen in love with him by listening to him talk, especially about his adventures and escapades—just as Desdemona had fallen in love with Othello, she said, by listening to his tales of his tribulations and dangers. She neglected to tell him how Desdemona's and Othello's story ended.

"He planned to surrender to the first Beothuk band he met and begin ingratiating himself as one of them. He convinced himself now as he trudged the trails that, in the end, his winning talk would save him with his own people. But the real strength of his plan, he acknowledged to himself under the boughs of his sheltering tilt each night, was that this operation was do or die. It rested on his absolute resignation: he no longer cared if they killed him or not. Yes, he would, out of habit, strive to survive, but in fact death was preferable in his mind to any of the other alternatives he'd discussed with the Mi'kmaq elder. If he couldn't be restored to his place as a Beothuk, he'd just as soon be dead. But, in fact, his faith was robust that they wouldn't kill him, and that he'd be able to use his knowledge of both worlds to lead them into practices that would stop the mutual murders and allow both sides to develop live-and-let-live relations, like the Mi'kmaq. As imperfect as such a relationship might be, it could at least lead to some kind of a future for his tribe.

"He made his way warily along the southeast side of Red Indian Lake, exhausting the last of his provisions, but supplementing his diet with berries. All along this trek he was surprised by the frequency of native Newfoundland pine trees. They were straight and tall, looming high above the spruce and fir. He was familiar with the tree from Notre Dame Bay and along the rivers but most of them were gone from there now, cut down and prized by the settlers for the excellent spars they made for their vessels.

"He saw animals—beaver, otter, hare—but he couldn't risk the sound of gunshot near Beothuk territory. Instead, he fashioned a long spear and, after a day and a half without eating anything, he stood hidden and motionless by the mouth of a brook for hours, until an otter he'd earlier glimpsed, came back in sight, followed by her two babies. The mother disappeared for a while, but the adorable pups stayed, squeaking, cavorting, and playing with each other, diverted from his presence by their joie de vivre. He was able to impale one on the end of his spear, and it squealed to break his heart. Anyone hearing it, though, would have thought it had fallen prey to a lynx or weasel. He created a small fire, virtually smokeless from the dry twigs he used, and roasted the poor, succulent, little thing.

"He was leery of encountering a large campsite on the lake. A sizable band of Beothuk might be too hard to manage. He did see several clusters of three or four mamateeks, but no sign of anyone in or around them. They'd been abandoned. There was also much evidence of campsites of white trappers with their tilts and lean-tos and huts. Some were old but many were recent. The extent of this deep encroachment up here right along the lake shocked him. He'd heard in Twillingate this past summer that the governor in St. John's had issued another edict that no settlers should venture away from the coast or their own traditional inland territory into the Red Indian homeland without official authorization. That new decree was obviously working as well as ever.

"He pushed on, and a short distance from where the Exploits River left the lake, he all but stumbled on an occupied mamateek. It was hidden behind trees just a few feet from the lake. He might have walked right into it if he hadn't sensed a presence ahead, and then a low murmur of voices. Creeping closer and hiding motionless in the brush, he saw three women and two children beside the structure, butchering a beaver. He watched and listened for a while, and was able to overhear parts of their conversation.

"He made out that their men had gone downriver in canoes, planning to reach the salt water, and to hunt birds out among the islands. The women discussed what detours over brooks and ponds at the lower end the men might use, to avoid sites occupied by the white devils. They wondered if the weather was going to be right, that is, if the fog or rain would be dense enough to hide the men and let them avoid being shot at by whites on the water. If so, the men intended to paddle out to sea, even attempting to reach the Funk Islands. They had to find out if the settlers had left any Great Auks still alive there.

"Hearing mention of the Great Auks, Eli recalled flashes of talk with Mr. Slade about how those flightless birds nested by their thousands and thousands on the Funks before the settlers exterminated nearly all of them for their fat and soft down or simply because they were right there in front of them on the rocks, helpless, awkward, unable to escape, and easy to kill.

"Eli listened now to the Beothuk women talking about the hazards of their men's expedition: the open ocean was dangerous enough in canoes on a clear day, let alone when you couldn't see a hand before your face. Eli was filled with wonder, as he always was, at the thought that his own people were capable of such a journey in birchbark canoes to those fabulous bird islands so far out. Even on a sunny day, you couldn't see the Funks from the mainland. How did his ancestors even discover them and then survive to report back that they existed with all their abundance? And then regularly prosecute the hunt for the Auks. The teasing comparisons by his Mi'kmaq companions, sailing over from Cape Breton to Newfoundland, couldn't diminish in his mind this almost unthinkable feat of his people.

"Crouching there, listening, Eli's yearning to talk to his own people about all that, rose in him again. He'd been captured too young to be fully versed in tribal knowledge and ways, and his aching need ever since to probe into that of which he was ignorant never left him. He felt that his having encountered this single, unthreatening mamateek was the good omen he needed. It made him stand up from his blind. He walked slowly toward the women and children, calling out gently in their language, with his gun held high over his head in, he hoped, an unthreatening manner.

"The women turned toward him and stood close together, shouting at the children to run into the woods. First, he thought the women were paralyzed with fear, until he saw that their bodies were situated precisely between him and the children scampering behind them into the trees. It was a practiced shielding manoeuvre, executed at the possible sacrifice of their own lives. His realization that brutal events had caused such a child-saving tactic, unknown a decade ago when he'd been a boy, to be conceived of and perfected since then, stabbed into his heart.

"He assured the women that he meant no harm; he came in friendship and kinship—he was one of them. He gave his Beothuk name, Gobodinwit, and stated that he wanted to re-join the tribe and live among them. They demanded that he throw his rifle behind him, away from them, which he did. They drew closer to him, each bearing the large knife with which they'd been making short work of the beaver, and peered at his fly-bitten face and neck and examined his hands. He remembered, as he looked at their bite-free faces and necks under the ochre, how every Beothuk would apply it, combined with animal grease, to their entire bodies for religious reasons, as required by the good spirits. As a result, members of the tribe would be mostly free of blackfly, mosquito, deer-fly, and stout bites all the time: religious faith arising from practicality.

"One woman murmured his mother's name and stopped studying his face. She turned to the others and said, 'Yes, it's him.' There was no joy in the recognition and no words of welcome back. But one of them offered him some dried caribou meat from a bag around her neck. It seemed to him to be the most delicious food he'd ever tasted. Another woman casually walked to his rifle and picked it up with disgust on her face as if she were gathering bear droppings. He called to her that the weapon was dangerous to handle, and she looked at him as if to say, tell her something she didn't already know.

"She walked to a nearby rock protruding from the ground, and prepared to raise the rifle over her head by the barrel. He thought of rushing to her to prevent her from striking it on the rock, which would very likely cause the loaded weapon to fire, with deadly results to her. But his action would be misunderstood and destroy his chances. Before he could act, anyway, she quickly brought the stock down on the rock with great force, over and over, like the Beothuk man on the river when he'd been 16. And again, the wood splintered and the metal bent, but without discharging. She dropped the battered rifle into the little brook that ran into the lake. It poked up from the water in plain sight, as usual, in keeping with the Beothuk custom of showing the whites and the Mi'kmaq their utter contempt and loathing for these evil devices.

"One of the children peeped around a young birch and called out to his mother. 'Can we come out of the woods yet?' She waved him forward, and he asked her why they didn't keep the gunmetal, as they did with nails and bear traps, to turn it into useful tools. She replied that every bit of the gun was too wicked, cursed, and sinful to keep among their people. Then she turned to Eli and said that whatever slim hope he might have now of not being instantly killed, he would have had none at all the moment any man saw him holding the rifle.

"Eli asked them if their main camp was still up the lake on the other side of the river. Yes, it was, they said, as his friend John Peyton well knew: He and a gang of devils came upriver last winter and they knew exactly where it was for their raid. Eli responded that he hadn't heard about that in Twillingate; they must have kept it secret. Most whites wanted nothing to do with hurting Beothuk and were in fact dead set against it. Were any Beothuk injured this time? No, the white devils had been spotted and everyone got away before they ransacked the mamateeks and took traps and tools. Unfortunately, none of the whites were killed or injured either; they fired their rifles into the woods a lot, which kept the archers too distant to get any good shots away with their arrows.

"Mostly to temporize, Eli asked the women whether the Beothuk had ever considered keeping some dogs around to warn them of the approach of intruders. They replied that one family had a dog once, and its yapping had attracted some white trappers to their mamateek, which would otherwise have stayed hidden in the woods, and a death and injuries had resulted. So, no: dogs were no longer a consideration. Silence was better, both in their camps and on their own raids.

"Eli hoped he might get a chance to talk to his people about the evils of that vicious circle of mutual retaliation—theft raids followed by recovery raids followed by revenge forays, leading to death on both sides, but overwhelmingly on the Beothuk side. He said nothing about that now. He asked the women if they would conduct him to the main camp, for a decision on his fate as a Beothuk. They replied that they'd be going back as soon as they packed up the butchered beaver to bring with them. He could tag along behind them if he wanted to and they'd announce him to the camp to try to prevent his getting shot full of arrows on sight.

"Despite the dire prophecy, Eli felt confident as he walked. He was a strong healthy man and an excellent hunter. No, he didn't have much expertise with a bow, beyond what he'd learned until he was nine or 10 years old, but he would work at it as he tried to introduce them to the benefits of obtaining rifles. The Beothuk would have to be insane not to let him re-enter the tribe, if for no other reason than simply to strengthen their numbers by adding his skills. He became less confident of his value when they reached the place where the Exploits River streamed out of the lake. There, they crossed the river by means of a clever pull-rope and rafting arrangement, and the women and children laughed uproariously at his ineptness in trying to help them operate the ropes in harmony.

"Approaching the camp, Eli was struck by the small number of mamateeks in contrast to his memory of even 10 years ago. Yes, said one of the women, this was nearly the entire tribe, except for a few who hadn't arrived yet from up north. There were just over 100 of them in all. The entire people were gathering here at this time, according to custom, to repair the miles of caribou fences that would direct the migrating animals to their slaughter later this fall.

"Upon the announcement of his entry, everyone in the village stopped to stare at him. One or two briefly waved and looked like they wanted to come over and welcome him, but none did. Most of the adults were employed at tasks, but some were sitting or walking slowly about, lethargic and apathetic, and obviously ill. A few were coughing incessantly.

"They all knew who he was. Since his encounter with the band on the Exploits five years earlier, he learned, his existence had been a frequent topic of conversation. He recognized a man and a woman from that time. Then a man appeared in the door of the largest mamateek holding the oar of authority. He rested the end of the oar on the ground and leaned on it as if he truly needed the support. A man next to him motioned Eli over, where he introduced the chief and himself as the chief's brother-in-law, and told Eli without pause that the chief would preside immediately over the customary talk-circle to decide his fate.

"The chief coughed into a square of soft skin, and he didn't try to hide the blood. Indeed, he held the skin up to display it to the people gathering round him. This was the reason, he told them, that the good spirits of murder victims commanded the Beothuk to kill any of our people who have lived among the enemy: they bring back sickness and death with them.

"Men and women formed a half-circle in front of Eli and the chief, and, one after another, they stated their opinions. All were poised and eloquent. Some of the men and more of the women said they should consider letting him live. He was healthy and strong, they argued, and appeared to have no sickness; he would be a good husband to a woman, and a good father to children—in short, a great help and support to the people. Some men described spying on him at his trapline and at the salmon nets and in his boat on the ocean fishing and hunting birds, and they saw that he was talented and skilled at all of it. One young woman, obviously held in esteem, said that it bespoke a fruitless, misguided, stupid ruthlessness, indeed a sickness in the head, to destroy one of their own kind at all, not to mention one so outstanding in qualities as he had.

"Others, led by the chief, contended that Eli had to die. Those much-vaunted skills of his were the skills of the white devils and the Shonack rather than those of the Beothuk. The fact that he was part Mi'kmaq was not a relevant argument against him, however. That had been overpowered by generations of Beothuk ancestors in him—his mother and grandmother and her mother, who carried the Mi'kmaq blood, were good people—and by his upbringing among the People as a child. The Mi'kmaq had been wrung out of him. No, the problem was that since his childhood he'd become far more of a white devil than a Beothuk.

"'Hunting skills?' shouted the chief's brother-in-law and spat in contempt upon the ground: his hunting was done with that instrument of the devil and guided by evil spirits. He wouldn't be able to hit that mamateek—it was about 10 feet away—with an arrow. His skill with the salmon? He'd merely helped the settlers, the white devils, to steal from Beothuk salmon rivers with their nets, leaving his own people to starve. And perhaps he could explain why, after he'd lived among them so long, those murderers of his people—Peyton and Cull and Noel Boss and the others—were still alive and thriving in direct contravention of the orders of the spirits to exact merciless vengeance on such vicious enemies.

"The chief commanded the intruder to speak now.

"Eli told of the tragedy of the massacre when he'd been too young to act defensively or with vengeance; of his yearning after to become a Beothuk again which had never left him; of his attempt at the first opportunity, five years ago, to rejoin his people; of the talents and experience he could bring them in attempting to rescue the tribe from extermination. That last point was a blunder. A murmur of displeasure arose; nobody wanted to hear that their noble people might ever go out of existence. He held his tongue about how he could teach the protective use of firearms or that there were good people among the whites and the Mi'kmaq who could help in saving the tribe, and he concluded with the love he felt for his people, and that there was nothing, in logic or in his own actions, to declare he deserved death at their hands. When he finished, he thought, judging by the respectful silence of the assembly, that he'd made headway in being accepted.

"But the chief closed the debate with brief but telling arguments: Nobody was saying that the Beothuk Gobodinwit, or even the white

Eli, deserved to die. No person ever got, for better or for worse, what he truly deserved. For the good of the people, they could not allow what Gobodinwit might or might not deserve to decide this crucial question. Appearances, or pity, or love, or guilt didn't enter into this question. The chief held high his bloodied piece of soft caribou skin: 'I am 30 years old, and I don't deserve to die, either. I am guilty of nothing. I have always appeared brave in front of our children. I am greatly loved by my wife and family. You all pity me in my illness. And yet I am going to die. Do you want your wives, your children, your husbands, your parents to end up like me? That's why Gobodinwit must die—to keep others from dying. It is not his fault, but he must die.'

"Even those who'd been against his death earlier stayed silent now, and the shaman-healer, an aunt of the chief, came forth and intoned that Gobodinwit should die when the moon and the sun were in their proper positions to appease the good spirits and frighten off contamination from the bad spirits. There was no objection from the group, and warriors bound his arms. Then she led the chief to the sweat hut for his daily cure. After that she peered into the sky for the rest of the day, while Gobodinwit stood there silent and motionless. With the descent of darkness and the lighting of the communal fire, she pronounced that his ceremonial burning must take place at sunset in either one day or two days, but no later than five days, depending on what the spirit of her grandfather, the great seer, revealed to her. Warriors now took him, trussed, to a mamateek on the edge of the campsite, where he was to remain until his day of doom."

CHAPTER 16

When I arrived at Churchill's door in the morning for the start of my next session, I held Anthony back and said to him, "Where in the name of God is he getting this stuff? A recalled memory from a previous life? Stories told to him as a young child? By whom? His mother? I mean, really? I can only conclude he's making it all up as he goes."

Anthony shrugged. "I'm no wiser than you, but I'm sure he'll elucidate in good time. He's waiting for you inside." Without further chat, he turned and led me down the hall.

In his room, before we'd even sat down, Sir Winston began again precisely where he'd left off yesterday: "Two women were assigned to take turns in bringing Eli his food. Both were chosen for their reliability. The older one was a cousin of the chief. The younger woman was soon to be married to the chief's brother-in-law, his wife's brother. They were commanded not to go close to Gobodinwit for fear of his pollution. But on the first morning, after his guards had tied his wrists in front so that he could eat, the young woman came in with his meal and sat right beside him. She was the one who'd spoken against killing him during the decision on his fate. She would talk with him as long as she safely could, she said, without bringing too much notice to herself.

"She was called Odusweet ... as quick as a hare, she said, and she brought him his midday meal as well. She told him she had volunteered to relieve the older woman by preparing and bringing him two of his three rations of food each day for as long as he survived. The other woman had a husband and two children to look after and was terrified of being contaminated. But what about the young woman's fiancé? Eli asked. Wouldn't he object to her greater contact with the captive? She replied that he was off in the woods hunting for two or three days.

"After he'd finished eating and talking, and Odusweet was picking up her beautifully carved wooden cup and bowl, he asked her if her fiancé's absence might mean he wouldn't be burned to death on this night. No, if anything, it meant the opposite, she said. Her fiancé had done his duty by arguing loudly for his death by fire, disagreeing with her in the process, and he wouldn't want, by watching him burn, to give the spirits the impression that he was taking any personal satisfaction from it. Hence his absence. As she left the mamateek, she threw over her shoulder that the other woman would bring his evening meal, so she was saying her goodbyes to him now; the next time she saw him, most likely, he'd be on top of a pile of smoking faggots and boughs.

"After his evening meal, served rather severely by the older woman, Eli waited for nightfall, feeling no small foreboding of his death. Twilight arrived and a warrior came in. He wanted to bring Eli to the latrine before dark. Then, after some hours of trepidation back in his shelter alone, when no one else came in to lead him to his funeral pyre, he was able to drop off into intermittent dozing.

"When Odusweet brought him his morning and afternoon meals on the second day, and sat with him for a while, Eli continued to describe to her his life with the Slades in Twillingate, and he detailed what had happened in Nova Scotia between him and Anna—their strong but thwarted love, the reason for her sudden, forced leave-taking, and the threat of death that her father had imposed on him. Odusweet's fascination with his tale, and his expectation of imminent death, encouraged him to hold nothing at all back.

"That night the singing and shouting and the crackling of the fire outside were louder than before, and he waited in resignation to be led out. But again nothing happened. As the outer limit of his life, day number five, loomed in his mind, he wondered if the delay was unintentional or whether his fellow tribesmen had become experts in torturing someone with the exquisite anticipation of horrible death.

"His friendship with the young Beothuk woman was a great solace in his desperation. And she was his ally, however impotent she might be. When he told her that Noel Boss the Shonack had been on his trail, her eyes widened in awareness. Our men had been wanting to contend with that murderer for a long time, she said, and if they had any sense, they'd spare Gobodinwit to join them in ambushing and killing him. He was as wily as a fox, though, and with his firearms, formidable. They'd need all the cunning and strength they could muster to conquer him.

"In the afternoon of the third day, Odusweet came into the mamateek with his food, and dropped a bombshell: she had decided she wanted to help him escape into the woods. He replied that he couldn't accept that; she'd probably be executed as a traitor. She countered that that would only show how stupid everything had become: execution of her as a traitor for saving the life of another Beothuk, and a good one, too! So the best plan would be that she escape with him.

"Eli was shocked: She was promised to the chief's brother-in-law! True, she said, but she never really wanted to become his wife. She had reluctantly consented because there were so few other available men. And, anyway, that was before all this craziness about killing Gobodinwit came about, which had poisoned her mind against the chief and his entire family.

"He asked her if there was a saying among the Beothuk like 'out of the frying pan into the fire.' They had a better one than that, she said, pointing at herself: 'The clever hare flees from the fox into the jaws of the waiting wolf.'

"Yes, that would appear to cover her suggestion, he said: if they escaped, they could never survive friendless and alone, beset on all sides—enemies to their own people, and probably being shot on sight by the whites, and even being hunted by a hired killer for the bounty.

"She was willing to risk it, she said. She could run faster than most of the men, and she could shoot a bow as accurately as the best of them, and she could prepare furs properly for clothing and meat for meals. Besides, whatever happened to them after they escaped, it could be no worse than his being killed here in the camp. She knew the chief well and there was no doubt he would see to it that Gobodinwit died, because of his brother-in-law and also because he was jealous of the welcome he had received on his first arrival.

"No, he replied, he could not drag her into such a dangerous undertaking—almost certain death for her.

"Well, he had to do something, she said. She thought her partner in bringing him food, the chief's aunt, was suspicious of their closeness and suspected that she wished to help him, and, by now, more than likely, had told the chief.

"Then, yes, it was time for him to act, he said, but without implicating her beyond necessity, and certainly not in escaping with him. Did she have a knife he could borrow?

"No, they had removed her knife and any other possible weapons from her person when she came in here, for her own protection.

"Did she think they'd be executing him this evening?

"No, his burning was due to take place the night after tomorrow. The end of day five. The witch had proclaimed that from the signs yesterday.

"What? Did Odusweet know that yesterday?

"Of course, everyone in the tribe knew.

"Except himself, obviously. Why didn't she tell him and at least temporarily relieve his anxious uncertainty?

"She stepped up to him and took his two hands in hers and spoke, smiling serenely into his face throughout: Did he believe she should let him off the hook, after what he'd inflicted on the woman in Nova Scotia and the woman in Twillingate? Perhaps he didn't deserve to be cooked alive over a fire for those sins, but he certainly deserved to be punished with worry.

"And she had certainly succeeded in that, he said. Meanwhile, could she bring him with his meal in the morning a knife that wouldn't be immediately missed? He meant to make his getaway tomorrow, when opportune, by cutting through the mamateek. He intended to take the rope and the knife with him as the only buffers between him and starvation. But would she be implicated, he asked, and punished for his escape? Because, if so, he wouldn't do it.

"Some suspicion might fall on her, she said, but she thought her fiancé wanted her too much to allow any harm to come to her. So, yes, she'd sneak in a knife.

"In the morning, he discovered he'd waited too long. Bringing in his food, Odusweet whispered to him that at daybreak the chief's wife had noticed that overnight she'd coughed up traces of blood. And the chief was saying to everyone that his wife's ominous signs showed clearly that the spirits were displeased at the delay in killing Gobodinwit. He'd conferred with the shaman, and she'd studied the signs again to make sure, and they agreed now that, in order to cleanse the camp and appease the spirits, Gobodinwit had to die by ritual burning that very night.

"The chief was already ordering his followers to gather branches and boughs right away and pile them high, and get their songs ready for their dancing and singing around the gigantic fire. Two warriors poked their heads in. They were to stand guard outside continuously until he was taken to the pile for the sacrifice, one in front of the door and the other in back of the mamateek, in case he tried to cut his way out with a hidden knife. It was obvious, Odusweet whispered to him, that the chief had surmised an escape attempt."

Churchill stopped speaking and struggled to stand up from his chair. As Anthony went over to extend his hand to help him up, I asked, "Sir Winston, that whole narrative about Eli, all that information about him—where did it all come from? Did someone report it to you ...?"

Churchill replied in a curt voice, "That is sufficient unto this morning. I must take a nap before lunch. We'll resume this afternoon." He sounded exhausted.

"You're on your own for lunch," said Anthony. "I need to do some paperwork with him." He walked me silently through the empty-feeling house to the door. There he said, "I was thinking about your question of the origin of his story. You know, he's famous for his non-fiction, but he has written some fiction, as well. At the turn of the century, when he was in his twenties, he wrote a novel called *Savrola*, which he didn't think was very good. He always said that he consistently urged his friends to abstain from reading it. But my point is that he is certainly capable of creating a sustained piece of fiction, good or bad. And some of his critics have alleged that a great deal of his historical writing is also fiction. I think he'll satisfy your curiosity in due course."

"I'm not hopeful," I said. "He didn't sound too good there at the end."

Anthony looked uncertain. "Well, one never knows at that age. But I think you'll agree he's been amazing so far. I trust he won't pile on too many unanswered mysteries as we proceed. We'll resume at 2."

When I arrived back from an idle stroll after my sandwich, I expected Anthony to cancel the rest of the day. I wouldn't have been surprised if the whole project were put on ice indefinitely. But right away he ushered me into the room where Sir Winston sat fidgeting, dangling his watch by the chain. "Lunch hour—*hour*, I say—would seem to be a euphemism these days," he rumbled.

I looked at Anthony who, rightly suspecting a reaction on my part, said, "He's here at our agreed time, sir."

"Well, perhaps so, Anthony, but the generations after mine, including yours, appear to possess a dwindling supply of energy and spirit compared ..." Without finishing his obvious thought, and with scarcely a pause, Sir Winston launched back into his story:

"Midafternoon, in his mamateek," the old man declaimed as if reciting, "with all possibility of escape thwarted by the two guards outside, Eli sat wrapped in the fur Odusweet had furnished, alone with his unearthly musings. His prospect of a gruesome death had grown more excruciating with the development of his bond of closeness with Odusweet.

"Now he heard outside a peak in the hubbub in the camp, which sounded well beyond even the spirited preparations for his demise. He called to the guards but got no answer. Odusweet pulled open the entrance flap wearing a grin on her face. She was bringing, she said, good news for him.

"The chief's wife had had a vision in the sweat lodge this afternoon: the spirits told her that if she wished to stop the progress of her sickness, her husband must show the blameless Gobodinwit mercy by not burning him alive. His heart leapt. Was he saved? he queried.

"No, Odusweet replied, the good spirits ordained that they must kill him with arrows first. Then he'd be burned, dead not alive, which was less painful. Eli stared at her happy face. If that was considered good news in these parts, then perhaps, through his long absence, he'd lost touch with the core nature of his people.

"She fiddled with the birch bark cup containing his water, moving it an inch or two this way and that, setting it before him just right. Then, as if in a postscript, she muttered, 'Oh. There's something else.' When the chief's wife had reported her vision to him, Odusweet said, he jumped up and ran out and started discussing with his cronies the cure for his beloved woman's sickness, which would be Gobodinwit's immediate execution by bow and arrow. But right in the middle of it, the chief suffered a coughing fit and spewed a stream of blood into the air. Thereupon he dropped mutely to the ground, bleeding profusely from the mouth, and swiftly died.

"This drama was causing great grief with everyone, she said, including herself. But based on it, she and her father had argued to the people that it was a sure sign that Gobodinwit should be spared and welcomed to live here among them. That they'd lost a good man like the chief was horrible and fearful enough; it would be utterly absurd for them deliberately to reduce their ranks by killing another good man. This was being taken by most as the truth. Even the chief's aunt, responsible for reading the previously lethal omens, stayed subdued and silent, and did not protest.

"Eli stared at Odusweet in great doubt. But was that now true? he demanded. Was he truly being spared? And she stared back at him with po-faced insolence. But she couldn't stop a big grin from spreading over her face like a spring sunrise. He asked why she'd nearly frightened him to death again with her delay in revealing his salvation. She laughed in delight. 'I already told you,' she said. 'I did it because what you told me you did in Nova Scotia and Twillingate really got on my nerves.'

"The two warriors now came back into the mamateek and untied him. They led him out the door and he walked warily between them through a throng that seemed large, crowded as it was into a small, cleared space between the mamateeks. This was an assembly, said one of the two beside him, of nearly the entire tribe. Instantly, what had just seemed large to Eli now appeared to shrink in size as he understood that it meant that his whole people now consisted of fewer than 100 men, women, and children.

"Everyone was quiet, except for the dead chief's widow and her brother, Odusweet's fiancé, and his family. They were groaning and intoning lugubrious songs as they stood around a bier upon which rested the chief's body. Eli received quick smiles from a few but their faces returned instantly to the downcast demeanour of the others. He spotted some hostile faces among them, and he was uncertain whether the two warriors beside him were still serving as his captors, or providing a guard of honour, or protecting him from any ill-disposed tribesmen.

"Two men jostled aggressively toward Eli. They had knives fixed to their waists, and he was weaponless. He looked to the guards at his sides for means of defence, but they stood rooted there and did nothing. The approaching men reached toward him and grabbed a hand each, but the guards still remained unresponsive. He was trying to free his hands to deliver some blows—at least he'd die fighting—when he caught sight of Odusweet. She was grinning at him, and shaking her head.

"And now the men holding his hands began to vie with one another in arguments, each appealing to him for his favour. He learned that they were the heads of two separate families and each wanted to adopt him as their son for mutual care and support. Thence, he would have a recognized place in the tribe and not be completely alone without siblings or parents of his own. In one family's favour was the fact that they were cousins of his dead mother. But the head of the other family urged the point that Odusweet, the young woman who had tended on him with such care and concern and had worked hard for Gobodinwit's liberty and salvation, was his daughter."

Churchill paused and I asked a question that had been bothering me and which the debate over Gobodinwit's adoption now brought back. "Sir Winston, what happened to Eli's father? He's never mentioned."

"For good reason. Gobodinwit never knew him. He was a baby when his father died—killed over a squabble about another woman, evidently, either by her husband or by the tribe in a cleansing action. Nobody ever spoke of him."

"It sounds as if Eli, if he had a roving eye, came by it honestly."

Churchill let out a small chuckle. "One might say that. And that he might have passed it on to some elements outside the tribe. Meanwhile back to more sombre concerns. The chief's widow now voiced her indignation over this disrespect for her dead husband's spirit. What should have been a period of solemn grief over him had been stolen by this unseemly competition of two families for the polluter's affections. Her brother, Odusweet's fiancé, roared that this was what came of going against their tried-and-true customs and beliefs—they never should have kept this enemy intruder, Gobodinwit, alive, even this long. There were a few mutterings of agreement.

"The commotion decidedly discomfited Eli: one family still

wanted him dead; and his choice between the two other families vying for him would leave one rankled, perhaps infuriated. Then he got a staggering surprise. Odusweet stepped out of the crowd to speak. The campsite went silent at her raised hands. This was the first time that Eli had enjoyed an unobstructed view of her whole person at a distance, head to toe. He marvelled to himself at the beauty and strength of her form and the poise of her lovely face and head on her graceful neck.

"She was going to put an end to this argument over the adoption of Gobodinwit, she said. She objected intensely to the very idea of her family adopting this man. Her fiancé's face beamed; he must have suffered moments of uncertainty about her earlier, but now he looked around in great satisfaction. Then she stated her reasons: she wanted no new brothers adopted into her family because that would diminish the number of her marriage possibilities. Her fiancé's head jerked toward her. She went on. Everything had changed for her with the chief's death, and she now considered herself free of her earlier commitment to him over his brother-in-law. That marriage obligation had been thrust upon her by the tribe under the chief's leadership, as a reasonable step to help advance her people's future generations. But circumstances had now been altered by the arrival of an additional man and had opened up an alternative possibility for unmarried girls in the tribe.

"Eli sneaked a glance at the man she'd been promised to. His pride kept him from protesting his rejection but he made no effort to hide resentment in the eyes he flashed at her and him. Eli was glad to spend that night in a mamateek among his mother's burly male cousins.

"The erstwhile fiancé had been one of the most vociferous in demanding Eli's sacrifice. And so, when he attempted the next day to replace his dead brother-in-law as chief, but was passed over by a consensus in favour of the head of Odusweet's family, Eli had to struggle to hide his delight. Odusweet whispered to him going by, 'Don't be too pleased. We'll need to keep a close watch on him.'

"Instead of being unsettled by her caution, Eli's spirits leaped. She'd said, "*We'll* need ..." She'd coupled him and her together again. He'd been enchanted with the young woman ever since she'd first begun to solace him in the death mamateek. Even as the hours had been then rushing by, pushing him toward his grisly fate, he'd felt joy whenever enough time had passed to bring her through his door again.

"For weeks after his liberation, nearly every day when he could spare a moment from his hunting or learning, working on canoes and mamateeks, or transforming white man's metal objects into useful tools, or practicing archery, he sought her out for a talk. She didn't disguise her eagerness to chat with him. Hence, one cold afternoon in late fall when he thought she'd especially welcome a warm and loving body next to hers these nights, he asked her with confidence to become his wife.

"No, she replied, she would not become his wife, and had no intention of ever doing so.

"Eli was flabbergasted. What? he blurted. Hadn't she broken off with her fiancé for him? What? she echoed him. No, she hadn't done that for him. Didn't he hear her say at the time she'd done it because of her changed situation after the chief died? He should stop being so full of himself.

"But hadn't she offered to set him free, and to run away with him? Yes, but that was to save him from a horrible death. Had he ever seen someone burned to death on a pile of boughs? She had seen it, she said—a woman guilty of faithlessness to her husband, and it was not an amusing sight. She couldn't bear the thought of it happening to anyone else. But that wasn't his situation now. She didn't need to save him from anything, now, except his lack of skill with a bow. She could certainly help him with that, if he wanted.

"But hadn't she protested against his adoption as her brother so as not to diminish her marriage possibilities? Yes, but she'd only done that to make it abundantly clear to her fiancé that they were finished. And while she did want to keep her stock of potential husbands as large as possible, the more she'd thought about it since, the more she realized that he should not be in her batch of eligible mates. There were just too many grave concerns about him that she didn't believe could ever be resolved. He was still only a youngster and already he'd had two disastrous loves in his life, the Mi'kmaq girl he'd left on Twillingate Island, probably still waiting for him with a broken heart, and the white girl across the water he'd made pregnant and then run away from, deserted, at the first test of his courage. Those two episodes, she said, not to mention what evil spirit he'd very likely got from his father, prevented her from taking even one step in his direction as a lover.

"Eli regretted now more than ever that he had become so excessively chatty with her during his expectation of death. He'd confessed everything about the two women to her as a sympathetic female, a friend at arm's length, about to be married herself. She'd been fascinated by how he'd ended up here among the Beothuk, and he'd held back no intimate detail. The story had astonished her and brought out tears at the tragic romance of it. Now, though, after he'd offered to marry her, her attitude had drastically changed. She had no desire, she scoffed, to be dragged in as another victim of his irresponsibility. But she didn't walk away in a fit of temper or even bad humour. She simply stayed and calmly blanketed him with sordid accusations. He had, she said, dishonoured the reputation of another man's betrothed and breached the trust of his own employer regarding his daughter, not to mention the incredible stupidity, as emphasized by Matilda the maid, of his getting himself tangled up with a white woman in the first place, to the utmost peril of them both. But, bad as that was, and it was absolutely terrible, there was something even more troubling to her right now: the existence of his Mi'kmaq girlfriend in nearby Twillingate. Eli had confessed to Obusweet earlier, in the face of death, that he'd given his heart to her and she'd given hers to him, and that, while she'd been waiting loyally for him to return to her from Nova Scotia as he'd promised, he'd betrayed her with another woman. Odusweet raised her head and spoke to the air, to the spirits surrounding them: Just what did all this reveal, she asked them, about this man Gobodinwit's character?

"Eli answered for the spirits: it revealed, he said, that he was capable of committing terrible sins and taking formidable risks for love. Yes, he'd fallen completely in love with the white woman, Anna, and if he could have stayed with her for life, long or short, he would have done so. But after he was forced to come to his senses about that, his intention had been to go back to his girlfriend in Twillingate, confess everything and beg her forgiveness, and renew his vows, if she'd still have him. But circumstances prevented that from happening.

"Would he go back to her now if he could? Odusweet asked. And he answered, no, after rejoining his Beothuk people and meeting Odusweet, he wouldn't go back to her now under any circumstances. He only wanted to stay here with his people, and marry Odusweet, and have a Beothuk family with her. She had replaced all other love in his heart.

"She jumped up and leaned into him and whispered fiercely at his face: What kind of a fool did he take her for? Could he really be as flighty and fickle and unreliable as that? Suddenly she'd replaced all the other careless love in his reckless heart? The only reason his tawdry affair with the white devil in Nova Scotia had ended was that he'd been chased away like a rat caught nibbling at a feast. And the only reason he wasn't now married to his Mi'kmaq maiden was that his out-of-control man-thing had made it impossible for him to go home to her from his Nova Scotia fiasco without being massacred.

"Then, as if to prove that the clichés of thwarted love were universal and that the banalities of romantic heartbreak had even reached deep into these impenetrable forests, she told him that despite everything, she still wanted to be his friend. They could talk about interesting events and ideas, if he'd like, but anything further than that between them was simply not feasible. Dismayed, he left her for a week to herself.

"One afternoon, miles from home, returning from a test of his abilities, a two-day hunt alone in the woods, he glimpsed on the trail ahead Odusweet's former fiancé. He was stepping into a copse of trees, and vanished. The sight was unnerving, and would have been more so, if he had not been diverted immediately by catching a view of Odusweet herself, unmistakeably, in the distance, high upon a tor. The wind was gusty and there was snow in the air, and he couldn't believe anyone had climbed up that steep craggy peak, let alone a young woman by herself, but he clearly recognized her stance and her characteristic gesture with one arm while she carried her bow with the other. It was definitely her. She waved at him before she slipped away. Then, later that afternoon, as he walked warily, watchfully, along, he saw her on the trail ahead of him. He shouted and ran to catch up to her, but she was gone.

"He spent the night sporadically dozing under his bivouac of boughs. In the morning, he rushed to get back to camp. There he found Odusweet sitting placidly in front of her mamateek with another girl, sewing a fox skin collar to a garment of caribou hide.

"She met his questions with surprised eyes. No, it couldn't have been her, she said. What on earth did he reckon she was doing up on a high rock outcropping all alone on a winter day in the middle of nowhere? And how could a mere girl outrun a stout-hearted warrior like him on a long trail? It must have been a vision by the good spirits to rescue him from nightmarish thoughts the bad spirits were conjuring up from his evil deeds. The girl beside her laughed quietly to herself.

"Yes, it must have been provided by the good spirits, he said, because it was a beautiful sight, and it taught him how much he had left to learn about swift running on their trails.

"'No argument from me on that,' she replied, causing a snort from the other girl.

"Next morning, at dawn, she sought him out, calling him away from his mamateek and the grins of his family. She'd had some thoughts overnight, she said: What had really bothered her from the start about his love for the white devil in Nova Scotia was the dead-end impossibility of it. It was so foolish, so irresponsible, so hopeless, that it showed clearly his overpowering desire for the woman. If she herself, Odusweet, married him, how could she ever live with her emotional conflict and jealousy over such an intense love? But last night she'd had some bad dreams about him that revealed to her the great depth of his feelings in general, not just for the white devil, but for everything he did; he was a man who always did what seemed right to him, fearlessly, regardless of the risks or even the apparent impossibility. That thought would have inclined her, she said, to let Gobodinwit into her own heart forever, were it not for her feeling that she wasn't sure she wanted that much pain in her life. She turned and walked away from him again.

"That afternoon, wanting to see her, he spotted her behind her mamateek, talking with her former fiancé. His heart lurched. She was leaning toward him and making forceful statements into his face that Eli couldn't hear. In the evening, at the tribal fire, she sat down silently beside Eli, surprising him, since she normally sat by her father during his songs and tales. He asked her what she'd been saying so strongly to her old beloved earlier. She looked at him and shook her head: 'You shouldn't be spying on the girl you're courting if you want to make any progress with her.' They stayed quiet for a minute while he tried to come up with a recovery statement. Then she said, 'I told him that if you, Gobodinwit, ever lost your life, whether by accident or design, then unless it was beyond a doubt not my former fiancé's doing, I would step out from behind a tree on a trail one day soon afterwards and shoot an arrow through his heart.'

"Eli couldn't speak for a moment. Then, 'Did you happen to see him a couple of days ago on the trail where I caught sight of you?'

"She ignored his question and murmured, 'Most of my misgivings and emotional doubts over you are caused by how you and your Anna gave up and left each other without a vast struggle, without showing the great strength and passion, without having the wherewithal within you both, to try, to fight, even if you ultimately failed tragically, to overcome the hopeless and the impossible.'

"He answered, 'Anna gave up and left to save my life. And I did too: I gave up and left to save my own life. I'm not proud of that. But I also gave up to save her from ruin. What else could I've done that was not utterly irrational and stupid?'

"'Yes, you'd both gone pretty far in that direction already. Very passionate and very foolish, but then you became very smart in your consideration for each other. I envy your Anna her baby. It will have strong characteristics from you and her for future greatness. My own fervent wish is that you and I, if we were to marry, and if we are not capable together of trying to overcome the hopeless and the impossible ourselves, will be fortunate enough to have a such blessed child who can do so.' She swept her hand in front of her to direct his eyes to the small vestiges of healthy people left.

"He said, 'A child blessed with the strength, the desperate passion, to try to overcome the hopeless and the impossible? Perhaps destined as a result to go through the very worse that the evil in life can put forward? Do you believe that would be a blessing?'

"'It's what we need to produce, if the People are going to have a chance of surviving.'

"Eli told her he prized those insights he heard from her as much as he loved her extraordinary grace and beauty. Here in the middle of the woods on a big remote island in the ocean, he said, among this shrunken remnant of her own people, she was the loveliest, most intelligent, and honest person he'd ever met. As her father walked up to the fire to begin the songs and stories, Eli told her, 'I love you, Odusweet, more than anyone I've ever loved in my life.'

"She studied his eyes and face hard in the flickering light from the flames. 'You said that well,' she said. 'But, then, of course, you've had lots of practice.' When Eli looked at her sadly, she put her hand on his arm and said, 'However, I believe you.' And then, after a moment, she muttered, 'I think.' It made them both laugh. 'There has to be a reason,' she whispered, 'that everything happened in your life as it did, and that then you ended up back here alive with me like this.'

"A week later, the entire tribe, save one man who said later he'd been detained by bad weather while hunting, celebrated their marriage. During the feasting, dancing, and singing around a gigantic bonfire, his bride bent toward him and whispered in his ear: 'We must tell our children how full of mysteries life is. They must hear how their father married their mother in ecstasy and joy in front of the big fire that their own people were going to burn him to death on.'"

CHAPTER 17

"Not overnight, but soon, Gobodinwit's fellow Beothuk stopped laughing at his ham-fisted awkwardness with the canoe, and bow and arrow, and raft, and at working hides and furs and birchbark, and helping to erect mamateeks and storage houses for meat and furs, and the long miles of deer fences. They began to admire him for excelling at all the skills. But he was also very annoying to some. That was because he would not leave off wheedling, even haranguing, them to stop their stealth raids on the whites. It would be better, he said, to try to enter into trade arrangements with them. When the Beothuk burned one of their boats and cargo just to obtain the nails for their arrowheads, or broke into sheds to steal animal traps and tools for the metal, they must imagine how exasperated and fearful the whites became.

"But Gobodinwit could discern no enthusiasm among the Beothuk to spare the delicate sensitivities of any white devils. They would rather recount the injuries and killings that had been visited on them by some settlers. Moreover, the theft of desirable tools and knives and rope and sails, or materials to fashion objects from, was so easy, and so enjoyable, compared to making them from stone or birchbark or rawhide or roots, there was no way he could persuade them to stop. But, if they must steal from the settlers, he urged, then let them steal some rifles and ammunition, so that he could teach them how to use them for hunting, and to ward off raids by the white devils.

"At first, he could not in the least overcome their aversion to the evil weapons. Only gradually, after many months, did he sense a certain curiosity developing as some of the boys and younger men asked questions about firearms. But the older men and women made it clear that they'd never allow anyone to progress to the point where they might be willing to use them, or even try one out.

"Not many babies were being born, so there was great jubilation when Eli's Odusweet gave birth to her first child, a daughter. They called her Demasduit. A year later, after hoping fervently for a son, they had another daughter, but there was still great elation. Females were necessary if children were to be born. They named her Obseewit, which meant something like little bird. This was the child who, as she grew up, became my eyes and ears and mouth, virtually my earlier self, Winston Churchill, in that life. Yes, you may cackle if you wish at the incongruity between our two lives: a female little bird among the Red Indians of Newfoundland and a male British bulldog among the leaders of the world. But mystifyingly, Eli, Gobodinwit, had created essentially the one soul, nearly the one identity, in two very different bodies at two exceedingly disparate times and places."

I looked at Anthony. What the hell was the great old man rattling on about? I was going to jump in with just such a question. But

Anthony made a discouraging face which kept me from interrupting, and I settled back to listen, at least for the moment.

"The Beothuk family thrived for a time. Neither mother Odusweet or father Gobodinwit nor Demasduit nor Obseewit had serious illnesses. But there was enough sickness around that an aura of doom pervaded the bands whenever they heard of another premature death. Every time a baby was born, male or female, the event created joy, beyond the birth itself to a buoyant feeling of hope. Among Obseewit's first memories were those alternating feelings of doom and hope transmitted from the band at an untimely death or a successful birth.

"Eli, Gobodinwit, continued his leading role in providing food for his band: in the autumn, funnelling migrating caribou through the deer fences into the river for slaughter with spears; in the spring, taking seals on the arctic ice with gaffs and arrows; all year, hunting other animals and birds; in the summer, slipping on the sly into the settlers' seining operations on rivers and streams to capture salmon. The white devils, led by John Peyton Sr., had taken over most of the traditional Beothuk salmon watercourses. They used fixed vertical nets, borne up by floats on top and weighed down with lead bobs to the riverbed on the bottom, thereby blocking nearly all salmon from swimming upriver.

"Rather than spending hours waiting upstream, beyond the nets, for a rare free-swimming salmon to spear, it was much simpler to take some salmon furtively from their nets. The settlers regarded that as theft, even though it was only the removal of Beothuk salmon from obstructions in their own traditional rivers. The white man's anger often led to the shooting on sight of any Beothuk encountered anywhere. Many families Gobodinwit had known in Twillingate and the Bay of Exploits deplored the violence. Others egged it on. He told his family that he'd heard one of John Peyton's men in the store arguing with Mr. Slade one morning, 'Well, do you want to eat or do you want to starve? If you want your family to eat, then we've got to shoot the thieving vermin to keep them away from our salmon operations.' Slade had looked over at Eli and ordered the man off his premises.

"Gobodinwit, among the Beothuk, refused to take part in the entering of settlers' homes or storehouses, or their vessels, to steal their belongings. He spoke against the burning of their boats, or the vengeful unmooring of craft just to let them float to destruction on the rocks. Those undertakings, he argued, served no purpose save to enrage the white devils into greater violence against Beothuk. The pilfering and destruction didn't scare them off at all, but rather fired them up to take shots at any Beothuk they spotted, and even spurred some of them to organize secret punitive raids.

"He had little success in stopping most of the other Beothuk from doing any of it. What was the difference, they'd ask, between our activities and Gobodinwit leading them down to take salmon from seines? He would reply that the salmon were theirs and they had a right to them, whereas the hardware of the whites was their own property, and to take any of those possessions without permission was outright stealing. But as Obseewit grew older, this opinion of her father's became more of a distinction without a difference. She argued with her sister, Demasduit, even as a young girl, that all their activities against the white devils were in reaction to the encroachments, the invasion of Beothuk land, rivers, islands, and seashores, weren't they? Truly, what was the difference?

"Gobodinwit became adept in canoe expeditions under cover of mist and rain out to the islands of Notre Dame Bay to hunt for birds and eggs. A number of times he even canoed out on the ocean as far as the Funk Islands. There, he would tell the family on winter nights, countless thousands of seabirds nested and flew overhead and rained a constant torrent of shit from the sky so thick that he and his companions had to wear special cloaks and hoods. When he came back, they had to soak these garments in the brooks for days afterwards to make them free of stink again. The stench on the Funks was so bad, he said, that some warriors on a calm day or night, with no wind to blow the reek away, bent over and vomited on landing. The number of birds that could be easily taken boggled the mind. Restraint had to be exercised on the hunt in order to keep from wiping them all out. But no restraint was shown by white settlers or passing vessels in their desire for the meat, oil, and downy feathers of the Great Auk.

"Every settler's household that Eli had visited in Twillingate and Fogo and elsewhere in Notre Dame Bay, he said, had numerous pillows and cushions stuffed full of down from the Great Auk. Mr. Slade always claimed that the families of these lowly fishermen in remote coves had the softest pillows in the world, pillows softer than those which the sultans of Araby, for all their wealth, could acquire. With the ongoing slaughter, however, Slade cautioned, it wouldn't be long now before there were no more Great Auks left at all. Each member of Mr. Slade's own family, Eli noticed, owned half a dozen down-filled pillows and bolsters, hardly taking notice of them as anything exceptional.

"Gobodinwit told his wife and daughters that settlers would laugh in recounting how they'd walk up to a nesting auk—its small wings rendering it flightless and awkward and unable to escape—and simply capture it by hand, and rip off handfuls of down from the live bird and put the fine plumage in a sack to bring home. Then, they'd set the auk loose and watch it scramble comically toward the sea to escape, the bird not realizing that, now lacking its robust insulation, it would soon perish from exposure to the frigid ocean water.

"One fisherman recounted that he'd nearly died laughing at a down-stripped auk reacting to the unexpected shock of the freezing salt water by flipping itself out into the air, over and over, continuously, until the silly bird finally succumbed to fatigue and cold, and drowned.

"Sometimes, instead of bothering to hunt around for wood for a fire to boil the kettle, the men would simply catch an auk and set it on fire, its down and feathers acting as kindling, and then, soon, its exceedingly oily body making a beautiful flame, all by itself.

"Demasduit was a sensitive girl, with a personality everyone liked. One morning, after an evening of hearing such tales of the Great Auk, she told her father and mother and sister of the nightmare she'd had the previous night: she'd dreamed that both the Great Auk and the Beothuk had vanished from the world at the same time. She saw two white devils in their boat, she said, looking at the very last auk sunning itself on a pan of ice. They took turns shooting at it, and pridefully watched its dead body float away on the tide. Then the very last Beothuk in her canoe nearby attracted their notice and they excitedly hastened to shoot at her, as well, and they watched her body floating out to sea in satisfaction.

"'But what about you?' her sister, my Beothuk soulmate, asked in her smart, often envious way. 'You said you were there seeing the last Beothuk getting killed, but you're a Beothuk.'

"Demasduit didn't answer. Her face took on a look of horror as if she'd seen or foreseen something too terrible to utter. Her father put his arm around her: 'That's not going to happen to the Beothuk,' he said. 'It may be too late to save the Great Auk, but I'm going to see to it that contacts between the whites and the Beothuk improve to the point where we can survive, if not in love and harmony, at least in a live-and-let-live way. Our cousins the Mi'kmaq have done it here and in Nova Scotia after years of great pain and suffering and treachery by the whites, and so can we. I'm going to devote the rest of my life to it.' And so he did, for the time that he had left. But as events fell out, Demasduit was a better diviner of the future than her father.

"Gobodinwit watched for opportunities to advance his cause. He hoped to spot William Cull by himself on the river, so that he could approach the furrier secretly and open talks with him. He did spy him once but the white man had other settlers with him. Then, on another trip downriver to gather eggs and seabirds, Gobodinwit saw his chance in an unexpected way. Nearing the Bay of Exploits, he and his two Beothuk companions heard some men on the bank of the river. They put their canoe ashore and crept near the men through the woods. Two Mi'kmaq were bent over, repairing a rent in their canoe. Gobodinwit recognized them from Twillingate where they'd been fellow workers. He saw that their packs and rifles were resting on the ground at some distance from them.

"He told his mates to keep themselves hidden because it could be dangerous, but by no means to use their bows and arrows unless he clearly asked them to. Then he called out to the Mi'kmaq by their names in English. They turned toward the sound, not in the least startled, thinking it was a friend hailing them from the trail. Only when he showed himself in his Beothuk dress and ochre, did they stand bolt upright and exchange looks of confusion and concern. It was not unknown for Mi'kmaq as well as whites to be ambushed sometimes and injured or killed by arrows. These two started to sidle toward their rifles.

"Gobodinwit shouted that he was Eli Easter, and he came in friendship. He walked to them with his hands in the air. They stared at him, clearly amazed. They hadn't recognized him, they laughed, in his Red Indian disguise. Joyful greetings and handshakes followed.

"They told him that people first reckoned he'd joined the Labrador Indians, but, since there was no talk or sight of him up there over the years, everyone concluded Eli must be dead. It had never occurred to anyone, because of the rule against rejoining the tribe, that he was living with the Beothuk. And no one had ever reported seeing him among any of the Beothuk occasionally sighted on the trails or in canoes on the river or out among the islands. But, of course, it would have been hard to identify him, they laughed, under all that red ochre, long hair and feathers, and the Beothuk duds.

"Eli asked them about Mr. and Mrs. Slade. They were fairly well now, the Mi'kmaq replied. But 10 years ago, when they'd learned from our Mi'kmaq people that their Eli had come back to

Newfoundland from Nova Scotia and, according to reliable reports from Flat Bay, would not be returning to Twillingate, they went into a state of distress and grief. They wouldn't believe the letter from Mr. Slade's partner in Sackville that Eli had attempted to assault his daughter, and they sent out word that they wanted Eli to come home to Twillingate. But Eli was lucky he hadn't. The next summer, when Mr. Slade met with his partner in person in Nova Scotia, and heard a fuller story of broken trust from his own mouth, Slade did seem to become more doubtful about Eli's activities in Sackville. But nobody was completely clear on what he had actually done, and there was a fair amount of rumor mongering about it.

"According to what Mr. Slade told his wife in the kitchen on his return, as overheard by a Mi'kmaq maid, if Eli were ever to venture back to Twillingate, Slade might have to disown him as a fugitive and outlaw, with a supposedly secret but in fact well-known bounty on his head. That could have been disastrous for Eli, especially since John Peyton Sr. and his cronies were still unyielding in their loathing of thieving Beothuk generally, and with Noel Boss showing up now and then, sniffing around for a chance at another notch on his long gun to go with the handsome reward.

"So, Eli asked, if he were to try for a peaceful understanding between Beothuk and whites, it would be hopeless to approach Mr. Slade for the purpose?

"No, not necessarily hopeless these days, the Mi'kmaq men said. Mr. and Mrs. Slade never stopped quietly talking about Eli like a lost son, and, with the passage of time, they seemed ready to forgive Eli's sin in Nova Scotia, whatever it might have been. The only obstacle to Eli's standing with Mr. Slade was the continued active partnership between him and Baker in Sackville. But despite that, the two Mi'kmaq agreed, if they were to tell the Slades that Eli was alive up here, they'd probably hire Will Cull—certainly Missus would insist on it—to go on an expedition upriver to look for him and bring him home.

"Eli asked about his former girlfriend, Minnie Paul.

"As soon as she heard, they said, that Eli mightn't be coming back to Twillingate, she couldn't take off for home fast enough. She and Mrs. Slade didn't get along, especially after Minnie overheard her say to Mister one time that she didn't think Minnie was good enough for her Eli. When Minnie was leaving, she said someone should tell Eli, if anyone ever laid eyes on him again, that, if he wanted her, he had to come for her within the month. Otherwise, she intended to carry on with her own life. A year later, she married a settler from the Straight Shore, a good, hard-working trapper, and they now had two or three children. 'Eli,' one of the Mi'kmaq men said. 'I don't care what Mrs. Slade thought, you missed the boat with Minnie—you had an excellent woman there.'

"'I know, but circumstances conspired against us.'

"'What circumstances, Eli? What did you do in Nova Scotia, exactly, that got all the whites up in arms against you?'

"'I was falsely accused of assault, of attempted assault, of a white woman.'

"'Well, the stories from our own people in Nova Scotia said nothing about assault, attempted or otherwise. They talked about the daughter of Mr. Slade's partner forever buzzing around Eli the Beothuk like a shit-fly the whole time you were there. That must have led to something interesting, they said, because that next thing they knew she and her daddy took off in the dead of night for Boston like scalded cats to arrange a hasty wedding ceremony. And then seven or eight months later they talked about her giving birth in New York State to a little daughter with beautiful light brown skin. Her husband, they said, revealed that his family had ancestors with noble Iroquois blood in them from the old days, which had now come out again after several generations. One of your former Mi'kmaq friends in Nova Scotia said that recently the little girl and her mother visited Sackville with her family, and, if the child looked just like Eli, that was not surprising because, as everyone knows, all redskins look alike.' The Mi'kmaq men burst into laughter.

"'That is all pure nonsense,' said Eli. 'Tell Mr. Slade, I'll try to meet him quietly within a few weeks.'

"'That should be interesting. We heard that Mr. Slade met his partner's daughter and granddaughter in Sackville or Boston.'

"On his return to Red Indian Lake, Gobodinwit told Odusweet of his encounter with the two Mi'kmaq. Having agreed to have absolutely no secrets from each other, he frankly described how Demasduit and Obseewit, in the wide lands across the narrow waters, probably had a half-sister.

"His wife thanked him for this additional information regarding his caper in Nova Scotia and said that in due course she'd be telling their daughters all about it, like everything else he'd told her. What was not so exciting, though, but was in fact extremely alarming, was the thought that settlers and Mi'kmaq downriver in the bay now knew he was alive up here.

"Yes, there was risk attached to the disclosure, he said, but he had to run that risk in order to help Beothuk and whites come to terms with each other. The very existence of the Beothuk depended on it.

"One afternoon that winter Gobodinwit and Odusweet and three other men and their wives took their five children a short distance down the big river from Red Indian Lake to snare hares. Demasduit and Obseewit and their young relation Shanawdithit were among them. When darkness overtook them in their fun, the children prevailed upon their parents to camp for the night in two old abandoned mamateeks surrounded by trees near the riverbank.

"Just before dawn the next morning, Obseewit woke up needing to answer the call of nature. She didn't relish the thought of going out into the night woods by herself, she said, with bears, lynx, wolves, and evil ghouls roaming about everywhere, so she woke her mother to go with her. By now Demasduit and the other girl in the mamateek, Shanawdithit, were awake, and they said they were coming too. They left Gobodinwit and the other father and his pregnant wife, who'd gone out earlier, and their son behind.

"Gobodinwit had always stressed to his wife and daughters that they should never underestimate the stamina and stealth of the white trappers and pelt-mongers. As a young man, he'd been with some of them on trapping expeditions when they would trek up rivers and streams, and traverse trails on snow and ice and in blizzards with astonishing speed, silence, and doggedness. And everyone knew, of course, that, as a boy, he and his band had been taken by surprise in the dark of early morning when white devils had stolen unheard and unseen upon their mamateek like soulless wraiths, an encounter he'd survived by freakish chance, or determined fate.

"His wife was certain that, this time, Gobodinwit would have sensed the white men and their Mi'kmaq guide drawing near, even as quiet and unexpected as they were, if she had not indulged the three children in puncturing the night's stillness among the nearby trees with their loud shouts and clapping to frighten away imagined wild animals. Thus it was that the raiders were able to take unawares the members of the families still inside the mamateeks, while Gobodinwit's wife and the girls, as you North Americans might say, by pure dumb luck, were off in the woods.

"The four females were on their way back to their mamateek in the bright moonlight, hand in hand and chattering happily, when Odusweet, the mother, came to a brusque halt and hissed, 'Quiet.' There was dead silence for a minute. Then white men's low, muttering voices drifted toward them. The girls stood paralyzed, waiting to hear her tell them what to do. But instead, they heard Gobodinwit's screeching bellow: 'Run, Odusweet, run girls, run back to the Lake. The white devils are—' His roar ended abruptly, cut off in the middle. Yet no sound of gunshot was heard."

Sir Winston interrupted his narrative to tell Anthony and me that he was able to reconstruct events at the mamateeks that morning from the images in his own head, augmented by hearsay records of the raiders' braggadocio when they returned downriver. The white furriers had been guided upriver by Noel Boss and John Peyton Sr.; William Cull was not with them. The expedition had been thrown together by Peyton and Boss, after word got around that Mr. Slade was about to act on reports that Eli Easter, the prize catch with a handsome bounty probably still on his head from a dozen years ago, was living up the Exploits River, among the Red Indians.

"Noel Boss was familiar," Churchill continued, "with the location of abandoned mamateeks on the upper part of the Exploits and knew they were sometimes occupied spur-of-the-moment, overnight. Thus, on the way up, he gingerly closed in on each location but found the structures empty. Then he came near Eli's and heard the chiming of childish voices from the woods. The sound was disquieting in the still dawn, and one or two of the trappers raised their rifles and started toward it. Boss silently stopped them. He motioned the men to the two mamateeks, which had to be secured first to prevent ambush.

"The men entered both mamateeks with great caution, their rifles cocked. They waved and prodded the occupants out—men, women, of whom one was obviously pregnant, and young boys. At gunpoint, Peyton motioned them to sit down in the snow. None of trappers could speak Beothuk; Noel Boss simply kept repeating to them, 'Eli Easter, Eli Easter.'

"The Beothuk were well aware from Gobodinwit's stories that this had been his name among the whites, but no one, including the children, looked at him now sitting there among them or otherwise identified him to the menacing gang. Clouds had now drifted over the moon and the light became dim. That and the red ochre covering the men's faces, and their low posture with their heads down, prevented Peyton and Boss from immediately recognizing Eli. Besides, as Peyton would whinge later, 'Who in hell's name would have expected to stumble on the very fella we wanted, in the very first shelter with Indians in it that we bumped into?'

"Some of the white men were clumsily poking about in the gloom of the mamateeks for stolen items, without much luck. But John Peyton emerged from one mumbling in a rage, carrying an old iron bear trap he'd found inside. He held it out, muttering that he recognized it as his, and made threatening gestures at the Beothuk men with his rifle. Noel Boss said something to him, and pointed to the spot from which he'd heard the children's voices wafting. Some surmised in Twillingate later, when rumours of this latest adventure of Peyton's leaked out, that Boss had said they couldn't have any witnesses escaping to the Lake and alerting Eli Easter. Directing the men to follow him, Boss started to move toward the trees behind which Odusweet and the girls were taking cover.

"It was at this moment that, suddenly, Gobodinwit broke the quiet with his roar of warning to his wife and the girls to run. This loud, unexpected shout behind Peyton, in the unknown barbarous tongue, so startled and terrified him that he lurched round swinging the metal bear trap at arm's length, and brought it with great force against the side of Gobodinwit's head. The blow tipped him over onto his side in the snow where, for a time, he jerked and shuddered.

"Gobodinwit's shocking yell and Peyton's terrific blow made the other white men turn toward them, and they focused for a few seconds on Gobodinwit's spasmodic movements. That distraction allowed the Beothuk, adults and children, practiced as they were in taking advantage of diversions, to scatter into the nearby woods. The raiders fired at their vanishing forms. The heavily pregnant woman lagged behind the others a little, and she received shots in her back. She died on her belly, face down in the snow.

"Because of a familiar look in the still visible part of the face of the brained Beothuk, one of the trappers was drawn to him. In the brightening morning light, the trapper confirmed his hunch. He knew the man well, he said, had hunted with him and Mr. Slade many times, had fished with him in the two-man crew of one of Slade's skiffs. The murdered man was Eli Easter.

"The identification brought bitter recriminations from Boss and Peyton. Why hadn't Boss recognized his prize from the beginning? Why had Peyton acted so rashly in braining their trophy? But they cut the swapping of accusations short, for sudden fear that deadly Beothuk arrows from the woods might soon rain down on them.

"The raiders destroyed any bows and arrows in the mamateeks and took off downriver at great speed. They strove to keep archers on hidden trails at bay by firing their rifles blindly and repeatedly into the trees. They might have saved their ammunition. The Beothuk were weaponless, and preoccupied with staying hidden until they were sure the trappers had left the site and were heading downriver. Then they crept toward the mamateeks, stunned and heartbroken over the two bodies lying on the snow."

Churchill stared into the fire with watery eyes. After some minutes, he waved his arm at his listeners. "Till next time," he murmured.

CHAPTER 18

"I shall not dwell," said Sir Winston Churchill when next we convened, "on the appalling grief felt over those deaths of a father and husband and a wife and young mother-to-be. Suffice it to say that the suffering of the Beothuk was identical to that felt by English persons over the violent, needless death of family members, and I am well acquainted with that terrible heartache in this life and from my knowledge of that life. But it was compounded and intensified in the case of the Beothuk by their stark knowledge that they were so few in number and diminishing still."

He stared into his fire again until Anthony asked if he could fetch him anything. Churchill said no, and returned to his narrative. "Taking only a fraction of the time they'd spent coming up, Peyton, Boss, and their team reached the safety of the Bay of Exploits. Before parting for their lodging throughout Notre Dame Bay, they swore each other to secrecy, at least for now, about their adventure. Boss and Peyton were resigned to probably never filing their claim to the bounty, owing to the obvious homicidal circumstances of Eli's end. Mr. Baker, Anna's father, could never be seen as paying out money for a known murder. Moreover, their identification of the man whose death they stood to benefit from financially might be deemed unreliable. Hence, they held their tongues for a time, especially in the vicinity of the magistrate and clergymen and other notorious champions of the Beothuk.

"But little by little, through loose talk over grog with friends in Sandy Cove, New World Island, Exploits Island, and Twillingate and Fogo during the long tedious spring, the details of how their expedition had turned into such a fiasco, leaked out. Noel Boss, in a squabble with one of the other men on the botched mission over who was the better shot, pointed to the latest notch on his gunstock to claim credit for bringing down that very winter a fleeing Indian at a great distance, with just one shot. The other man parried with the riposte that Boss's feat was like hitting a shithouse at 10 feet, since the fleeing Indian was a squaw, so big with child she could scarcely waddle away. After the general laughter, John Peyton couldn't resist boasting about his dexterity with a stolen bear trap in knocking the brains out of an enormous Beothuk thief with one blow. He didn't name the gigantic thief, but soon, William Cull got wind of his identity, and told merchant Slade why he might as well call off the expedition up to the Lake he'd been asking Cull to lead. Mrs. Slade, her hopes of reuniting with her beautiful boy, so close and now so horribly dashed, was beside herself with grief for days."

Sir Winston Churchill, over 150 years later, in December 1964, and over 2,500 miles away, in London, turned from Anthony and myself toward his fire, and quietly wept. After a few minutes, he said. "You'll have to forgive me, but about certain things—I often don't know what beforehand and sometimes it's trivial—I have a tendency to blubber like a baby. In this case, however, over the events of that dreadful day, I have good reason. It was the death of my great-great-grandfather, as well as his wife's best friend, that has affected me so greatly. When the survivors returned to the site of the slaughter, they found the pregnant woman and Eli lying in the snow as the raiders had left them. From the serene look on her face, when they turned her over, she might have been asleep. That's what struck me so hard. She was so peacefully dead for no reason. What remained of Eli's face was contorted into a hideous snarl, and blood and grey matter lay on the snow beside his head. His loss was unbearable to his widow and their two daughters, of course, but what has touched me even more profoundly, reflecting on it in this later life, was a sense of anger and outrage at what was done to them, what others dared so casually to do to them.

"As Winston, I had to come to grips with the fact that Eli, my spirited great-great-grandfather, a splendid example of humanity—with the strengths and the weaknesses thereof—had his brains beaten out in the backwoods of his own land by a low-life thug with the cunning of a rat, an intruder, an invader, from my own English homeland, and that it was a senseless and inglorious and utterly meaningless end for the man who was my direct ancestor. But that often appears to be the way of the universe for those who fulfill their destiny. Once Eli had contributed through Anna to the line that was to culminate in me and my deeds in the 1930s and 1940s, and once he had created his daughter Obseewit, who, together with her friend Shanawdithit, could contribute to mankind's knowledge of their last days, both facets of the man's fate were done. Thereafter, the sword of Damocles was hanging daily over Eli's life and, there being no reason for destiny to keep him alive any longer now, his life could end at any moment. A meteorite could hit him, a piece of pemmican could stick in his throat and suffocate him, or an odious ruffian from Devon could unintentionally brain him with a rusty bear trap.

"A similar termination could have been visited on me after the war ended in 1945, because fate or destiny or kismet appeared to have no further reason then to keep me alive any longer. Death couldn't have been visited on me before that time, of course, as a man of destiny. Although God alone knows how I tried. In New York in December 1931, for instance, a motor car struck me as I was carelessly crossing Fifth Avenue. Pure imbecility on my part. Anyone who saw the accident, and the doctors who dragged me back from my demise, could not comprehend how I wasn't killed. And numerous other instances during my whole life before the war and during it when death from my foolhardiness, my childhood mishaps, battles—I was shot at point-blank during the Boer War—my suicidal urges around cliffs, high windows, underground trains—the blitz, or assassins, or a heart attack or stroke, should have done me in. I never once in my life avoided a risk. But somehow the toxic fangs of fatality could not get a grip on my jugular before our victory over the foul malevolence in Europe. But after that victory, death should have taken me at any time, as my destiny had apparently been fulfilled.

"But extraordinarily, after 1945, a compulsion, an unquenchable need, arose in me to tell my true story, like the Ancient Mariner, of how it was that I, Winston Churchill, became, and knew early in life

I had become, a man indispensable to the salvation of Great Britain and the Empire and perhaps even beyond. Which need, painfully enough, fated me to stay alive until I had done so. Here's an example of that. When I fell and broke my femur in Monte Carlo a few years ago, and lay there like a dying stag, it was the common knowledge of all—myself, my family, and physicians alike, that I was going to die from it. Anthony thought I was going to die, didn't you Anthony?"

"I did, sir. It looked very grave, indeed."

"I had the very best surgeons in a marvellous hospital in Monte Carlo, but I told Anthony I wanted to die in England, and he had the RAF scramble a jet aircraft to fly me home. However, I didn't die, as may not be entirely evident to an observer—neither from that nor any other accidental nor medical catastrophe I have suffered since the war. I couldn't die until this, what we are doing here now, was over and done with. And it was thus that, after the Second World War, I squeezed out another 20 years of life, of mostly misery—fretfulness and angst and melancholia and family grief and an ever-deepening canyon of worthlessness. But once I've finished this with you, it won't be long then before the all-enveloping stygian velvet covers me, soft, black, and everlasting."

Sir Winston lapsed into silence and, as was his wont, turned his eyes to contemplate the inscrutable mysteries of the fire in the grate. After a minute, I asked, "Will I be interrupting your thoughts if I pose a question, sir?"

"Too late for permission now, since that was a question. But thank you for supposing I have any thoughts these days, Mr. Cull. High praise indeed from a young man of your mental and physical vigour. I recall when I was like that, at your age, only very much more so." I caught Anthony's quick grin at the back-handed compliment.

The old bastard. Piqued by the roundabout slight, I was sorely tempted to shoot back: "And I recall reading how you were also disliked intensely at my age for your snobbery, for always pestering Mamma to pull strings to advance your career, for your low sarcasm, and for your gratuitously cutting remarks. Some traits haven't changed." Instead, I forced a smile and said, "No quarrel with your comparison, Sir Winston, but may I proceed with my second question?"

He glowered at me. "I could see you wanted to say something else a little more combative. No quarrel, you say ... Never give in, Cull. I was down and out many times when I was not much older than you, and clawed and plowed my way back. Yes, proceed with your question, your *third* question, by now."

The exasperating old fart. "Sweet Jesus!" I whispered under my breath, causing two grins. "Was what happened to Eli, your putative Beothuk ancestor, his murder that day, as perceived by you—was that the experience evoked from the earlier life that made you the man you became in 1939?"

"That day was monstrous and shattering to my ancestral family and people and to me, but, no, it was but a waystation en route to the crucial incident, the central event, which I shall uncover for you."

"Well, what bothers me about all this, sir, this narrative of yours, is how you have brought everything together, the incidents and your *memories* of them, as you say you consider them, from that former life, and the historical material you've read in this life about the Beothuk of the same period ... how did you connect it all more or less coherently in your mind? How did you even come to the conclusion that those memories you claim you've had from those earlier lives were from Beothuks alive in the early 1800s? Wouldn't it be more reasonable to conclude that, having read about the Beothuk in your adult life, you somehow projected the tales back onto your childhood fantasies and came to believe that they were actual memories from an earlier time and place?"

I waited in trepidation for Sir Winston's answer to my fundamental undermining of his story, but when he continued to merely look sideways into the fire, I went on. "I don't wish to be crude, sir, but I must be honest, and regrettably the one word that keeps springing to my mind about the undocumented stories from that earlier life, as fascinating as they may be, is that they are contrived. I fear they are bullshit."

I felt Anthony stirring beside me, but Sir Winston seemed unfazed. "And that's as good a term as any to apply to most so-called historical accounts on any subject or era. As to whether it applies here, I'll leave to your judgment when all of this is completed. I should say that when I was the young boy Winston, and was experiencing those images, those recollections for want of a better term, of that earlier Indian life, I had no idea what or who they were actually about, or where, precisely, or when, they were taking place. I merely accepted them as children do. I knew nothing of the position of Red Indians in a larger world. I knew only what I saw and heard in my own mind.

"As I grew older, as a boy in England, I did, naturally, become somewhat perplexed about those memories from an earlier life, and on occasion I felt or suspected that I was insane. After all, those earlier memories were entirely disconnected from what was going on in my actual current life then—there was no continuum between those memories and my experiences as an English boy, but I knew without doubt they were real memories of what had in fact taken place, and that they were absolutely genuine. I didn't know anything about Beothuk or Mi'kmaq or Nova Scotia or Newfoundland, save vague snatches I picked up in my eclectic, free-ranging reading.

"I only began to divine a clear connection between those memories and my reading about the historic Beothuk when I was over 30, after I became Undersecretary of State for the Colonies in 1905. I occupied that office for about three years and during that time I ransacked the archives for reports and literature on all our colonies. Officially, on the job, I was preoccupied with the day-to-day challenges of that period in Africa. But also, without fully realizing why, I found myself particularly drawn in my research to Newfoundland.

"I believe my first fascination with Newfoundland began as a very young schoolboy when one of our roguish senior boys introduced us wee ones to an erotic poem of John Donne's, written around 1600, entitled, 'To His Mistress Going to Bed.' The boy called it Donne's dirty poem, and if you read it in full, you may see how easily the other boys were persuaded that it was exceedingly sexually lascivious, at least to their racy juvenile imaginations. In the poem, Donne incites his lover to take off for him, piece by piece, all her clothes. One analyst called it the ultimate verbal striptease in English poetry. Another says it is the most intensely erotic love poem or lust poem in our far-flung and profoundly expressive tongue. Some boys liked to masturbate while reading it. But not in my case. In the first place, I was a little young.

But also, one particular passage, which some other boys treasured for its lewdness, affected me differently.

Licence my roving hands, and let them go,

Before, behind, between, above, below.

O my America! my new-found-land,

My kingdom, safeliest when with one man mann'd,

My Mine of precious stones, My Empirie,

How blest am I in this discovering thee!

"Anthony, give William my copy of Donne from the other room on his way out so that he can read the full poem tonight. I cherished the reference to America, of course, because of my heritage from my mother, and the one to 'my empirie' because I was a young imperialist, but especially, for reasons then unknown to me, I prized the mention of 'my new-found-land.' I knew, naturally, as a child prodigy in English history that John Cabot had discovered the island in England's name very early, in 1497, and that Sir Humphry Gilbert had claimed her as our first transatlantic colony in 1583. But more than any of that, I was especially attracted to Newfoundland because of the Vikings. I became utterly fascinated with the encounters between the Vikings and the Aboriginal peoples in the North American settlement the Vikings called Vineland around the year 1000. Among the several theories at the time, about the Vikings' landings in North America, was the assertion that the place called Vineland, mentioned in their great epics, was located in present-day Newfoundland. I believed that. It made sense. You need only glance at a map of the northern Atlantic Ocean—of Iceland, Greenland, Labrador, and Newfoundland—to see that it is the only theory of the navigation to Vineland in their sagas that can realistically be true.

"The Vikings tried to settle in Vineland after settling successfully in Iceland and Greenland, but after a few years of striving to establish themselves there, they had to leave Vineland. But why did they have to leave? Because they were forced out. The ferocious Vikings, that marauding nation of looting, butchering, conquering barbarians, who prevailed and triumphed just about everywhere else they ventured, whether Britain, France, Russia, or the Mediterranean, were driven out of Vineland; they were expelled from Newfoundland. The great Vikings had to turn tail and run from Vineland. They were ejected by the natives there whom they called the Skraelings. I could not believe it. A resident group of mere uncivilized natives drove out the world-conquering Vikings! Who could these magnificent native people be?

"Before the advent of firearms, the Vikings and the Skraelings of Vineland were, perhaps, on a more equal footing regarding weaponry, each side with their bows, spears, slings. But the Vikings did possess metal-edged swords and battle-axes, and metal points, in contrast to the Skraelings' wood and stone weapons. Yet the Skraelings sent the indomitable Vikings packing. Little wonder I became enthralled, utterly charmed, by those splendid Skraelings. And I believed then and still do, in common sense and folk memory and historical grounds that they were the ancestors of the Beothuks of Newfoundland who afterwards encountered Europeans again 500 years later, at the beginning of the 16th century.

"As Undersecretary of State for the Colonies, I ordered up everything, historical and modern, that my ministry could provide on the Beothuks and, in retrospect, I was unconsciously, little by little, without fully realizing it, drawing a connection between my earlier-life recollections and the events and characters I was reading about.

"But then, in 1908, I left the office of Undersecretary of State, when the prime minister advised the king to appoint me to a full cabinet position, where I was soon up to my neck in one government crisis after another, each more ominous and menacing than the last. That left little time for reflection on any memories of an earlier life, as I and the rest of the ministry endeavoured to survive our then current life, the greatest trial of which became, within a few years, the onset of the First World War.

"With the advent of war, I stood in the thick of it as First Lord of the Admiralty. Then there occurred one of those events, unbearably painful in the experiencing, but perhaps fortunate in the outcome. The Gallipoli campaign in 1915, and its cockup, caused my disgrace, *temporary*, as it turned out, although it felt very permanent at the time. As a result, I was demoted to the preposterous position of Chancellor of the Duchy of Lancaster.

"There my energies and intellect were not overtaxed. It was an absolute sinecure, and time hung heavily on my hands. To curb my dark thoughts for a few months before I resigned to wage war personally in the trenches on the Western Front, I read everything I could lay these hands on. I became aware of the publication by Cambridge that same year of the remarkable book by James Patrick Howley, *The Beothucks, or Red Indians, the Aboriginal Inhabitants, of Newfoundland.*

"If I'd still been First Lord of the Admiralty at the time, immersed in all the pressures and hurly-burly of a war that we might well lose, I never would have found occasion to read it. As Chancellor of the Duchy, however, I had the time to devour it, and its nearly 500 pages of treasures provided a veritable epiphany for me, my moment of eureka. My earlier reading from the archives jelled with what I was reading in Howley, and everything became clear and distinct and defined. My personal ancestral memories connected and corresponded to an astonishing degree with all that I was reading, in compendious but full form, from his book.

"In his preface—I have it by heart—Howley says that at this distance of time, with such meagre material as we possess, it would be utterly out of the question to attempt to write an accurate history of the Aborigines of the island of Newfoundland. All that he could aim at was to gather up the disjointed and disconnected references to people that have appeared in print and to relate the traditions and anecdotes he had gathered from generations of fishermen. He says that despite his best endeavours to preserve from oblivion the principal facts relating to this interesting but unfortunate section of the human family, there are very likely numerous other traditions which have not come under his notice. He delayed publishing, he asserts, in the hope that at any time additional important facts might reach him, and he interviewed or wrote to everyone alleged to have any information whatever on the subject. When I saw those declarations of Howley, I felt torn between keeping my own memories secret and in fact meeting with him to disclose what I knew. But when I read next his admission, that a great deal of what he had acquired was of a very dubious character, I realized that his reaction to my memories of Beothuk experiences would be highly skeptical and that he would regard them as useless or unreliable. He would have been constrained to conclude that I was, in fact, the madman I'd already been branded as by many, while I was desperately attempting to regain my reputation after the Dardanelles. Hence, I held my tongue.

"One of the greatest revelations in this tale came to me when Howley referred to a book on Newfoundland, called *Wandering Thoughts*, published in London in 1846 by the Reverend Phillip Tocque. I tracked the book down and one particular picture in it was a prodigious eye-opener for me and a shocking thrill to my entire system. The picture was a copy of the painting of the Beothuk woman Demasduit, whom the whites called Mary March after they captured her in 1819. She was Obseewit's sister, and Shanawdithit's relation, and one of the last of the Beothuks. The portrait was painted by Lady Hamilton, the wife of the governor of Newfoundland, in St. John's soon after Demasduit was captured. Everyone who saw both Demasduit herself in actual life and Lady Hamilton's painting of her proclaimed the picture to be an authentic representation of Demasduit, a remarkable likeness of the woman.

"You may imagine my feelings when, as a man in England, nearly 100 years after the picture of Demasduit was painted, I first glimpsed it, and was struck, absolutely astonished, by the resemblance between her and pictures of my own mother, Lady Randolph Churchill, particularly the upper face, especially the large, widely spaced eyes. I'll fetch the photographs of both women from my file for you to compare." He moved to stand up.

"May I retrieve them for you, sir?" asked Anthony.

"No, I'll get them. They're in a private file in a locked cabinet. I have the key."

Before Anthony could help him up, the door abruptly opened and in barged a scowling man. Sir Winston glowered at him and growled, "Where's your mother? I told her and the staff I wasn't to be disturbed by anyone."

"How the hell should I know where she is? She doesn't appear to be speaking to me these days."

"What could you have said to have angered her? She visited you practically every day when you were in hospital for your surgery. Go up to her study and say hello to her."

"What's this grand conclave here all about then? I heard there was a stranger in the house for hours on end for no ostensible reason. Anthony, who is this fellow and who brought him here and what is the object of his presence?" He was speaking in croaks and whispers.

We were standing now, and Anthony introduced us, me as a student at Oxford from Canada, and Randolph as Winston's son.

"And?" Randolph croaked, without shaking hands, but coming closer, and bending toward me in an unpleasant way.

Sir Winston said, "Randolph, I want you to leave the room. I'm talking over a few things about Newfoundland with this young gentleman. In private."

Randolph looked at the notepad in my hand: "What's he writing down there? You told me that I and I alone am writing your official biography. I'm supposed to be the sole author with exclusive rights. And now here you are spiriting into the house some little interloping bugger from the colonies to trespass on my domain. Newfoundland! I hope you're not talking to him about wartime Argentia and Gander and Botwood in Newfoundland. I'm having all that researched and

I'm writing about all that. Bloody goddamn hell, Papa, you know I had pneumonia this year and I just had a tumour removed from my lung, and here you are now making me raise my voice at considerable risk to my health."

"Well, stop your damned shouting then. In fact, stop talking altogether and be off with you. I'm discussing with this young man one tiny aspect of Newfoundland history for his own benefit. It has absolutely nothing to do with your biography of me."

"Are you banging on about those fucking Red Indians, again? I don't know why you're so spellbound by them. Aren't they long dead and gone? I hope you're not giving him anything about the Iroquois in the US. I have yet to decide if I'll write about the family pedigree tainted by your alleged Indian ancestry."

"I'll bang on about anything I bloody well wish. And right at this moment what I wish is that you remove yourself from my presence. And do not come back without my express invitation."

"I trust it will be acceptable to you if I do come, without your special invitation, to your forthcoming funeral? Oh please, do not deny me that final pleasure. Hargh, hargh, hargh." Randolph turned to me. "A little touch of the legendary Churchillian wit, there, old boy." He walked out of the room with the arrogance, as one of his sisters was to say of his comings and goings, of Louis XIV.

Sir Winston sat there silently. I noticed moisture in his eyes, but whether of age, hurt, or rage, I couldn't say. Anthony asked, "Can I get you something, sir?"

"Most obnoxious man in England," muttered Randolph's father. "I am required to love him as my son, but if he were not my son, I'd have nothing whatsoever to do with him. When his tumour was taken out and discovered to be benign, even his friend, the novelist Evelyn Waugh, said that modern medicine had just removed the one part of Randolph which was *not* malignant." Sir Winston snorted in appreciation, then scowled, and next rumbled, "I wish to talk to Clemmie."

Anthony held out his hand. But Sir Winston yanked himself up by the armrests and shuffled briskly across the room and out the door that Randolph had left wide open. Churchill's normal energy during the war had been legendary. When fuelled as well by anger, of which this was an eleventh-hour sample, it must have been a terror to behold.

"Don't feel embarrassed by that father-son contretemps," said Anthony. We flopped back down in our chairs. "It's a rather commonplace event both in private and in company." Rumbling male voices from the hall and a loud, high female voice from the second floor came through the doorway, causing Anthony to roll his eyes before continuing. "Last year I was on board Aristotle Onassis's yacht in the Mediterranean with Sir Winston and Randolph and some others, mixed company, when Randolph took it into his head to bark and yelp invective and insults and general abuse at his father. A young lady guest among us tried to intervene, and Randolph turned on her, calling her, in some of his gentler epithets, a disgusting, gabby little doll. No one could stop his flow of vitriol, not even Onassis himself. He simply went on, erupting like Vesuvius. Sir Winston throughout was impotent and looked as if he was suffering another stroke, and afterwards he requested that Ari have Randolph removed from the yacht. But how do you put ashore, without a scandalous scene of physical force, a drunken, raving lunatic with a sense of entitlement? Onassis solved it by arranging immediately for Randolph Churchill, the journalist, to have an interview with the monarch of Greece, King Paul himself. The next morning Randolph left the yacht for the palace in Athens, weeping copiously, declaring his great love for his dear father. And poor King Paul of the Hellenes? This past spring, less than a year after Randolph's visit, he was dead of cancer."

Winston Churchill shuffled back into the room. "There wasn't necessarily any cause-and-effect connection," he said.

"I beg your pardon, sir?" said Anthony.

"There might not have been a connection, *necessarily*, between Randolph's noxious visit to the king and the king's malignant death soon after. But I'm not denying it either. Now where were we?"

"You were about to show William some pictures of your mother and an Indian maiden."

"Oh be damned ... I forgot to get them in the wake of those Third World War unpleasantries. She was no more a maiden than my mother was, since she possessed, for a piteously short while, a superb husband and a beautiful nursing baby. Yes, I do know now where we were. We're at the time for my tea and a good nap. William, may I depend on seeing you here at the same time tomorrow?"

Anthony said, "You asked me to remind you to invite him to sit down at table for an actual luncheon tomorrow, instead of our usual quick, catch-as-catch-can sandwich from the kitchen."

"I did, to be sure. If you're available, William ...? Tomorrow morning, then. You will be astonished, indeed staggered, by my pictures."

CHAPTER 19

The moment I arrived next morning, Sir Winston started right in without preliminary chit-chat. It was as if he had loaded himself up with memories overnight and was now bursting to discharge all of them at once. He had in his hand two pictures which he passed to me in turn. "This one is the likeness of my cousin from an earlier life, the Beothuk captive, Demasduit or Mary March, painted by Lady Henrietta Hamilton, the wife of the Newfoundland governor, in 1819. Remark how beautiful and intelligent she is.

"During the short time she was among the whites, despite the unspeakable tragedies of her life, and the fact that at the beginning she could speak no English, she soon became renowned in the capital, St. John's, for her magnificent personality. She seemed to have a quality which was often ascribed to me before and during the war—by other people I hasten to say—which the German writer Max Weber called 'charismatic.' He described it as a certain quality of an individual personality, which, by exceptional powers or traits, sets the person apart from the ordinary. It's interesting that my mother was endowed with exactly the same quality of personality."

"Wasn't your father considered charismatic as well?"

Sir Winston looked at me. "You're implying that, if I inherited any quality of charisma, it was more likely to have been from my father than my mother. Yes, he was charismatic, but not in the same way. He was a hard man to love. His charisma was not enchanting and endearing, in truth lovable, as my mother's was, and as Demasduit's was. I don't know many who loved my father unto death, who would have died for him." He passed me the other picture. "And here's a photograph of my mother, Lady Randolph Churchill. See how she is beautiful and intelligent in the same way that Demasduit is. And look at the hair and forehead and eyes and nose and ears of both women, and even their colouring. If you make allowance for the differences between an old painting of a native woman around about the time of Napoleon and a modern photograph of an upper-class British lady of recent years, the two women are close to identical. That even shows through the earthy simplicity of Demasduit compared to Lady Churchill's immaculate coiffure and makeup. When Clemmie viewed these pictures, she said that even their lips tend to be the same, and would in fact be the same in both pictures if Lady Hamilton had been better at painting lips. Demasduit is about 23 in that portrait and my mother is a bit older, and more mature looking. Eli, or Gobodinwit, was Demasduit's father, and he was also my mother's great-grandfather by way of Anna Baker, and his physical traits, his much-remarked-upon beauty, came through, bred true, in both women. What I find most extraordinary in the pictures is how both women, beneath their beauty and their poise, possess the same wistful look, the same longing and melancholy, bordering on tragic grief."

Sir Winston sighed and fell silent. "A remarkable people the Beothuk," he began again. "Their—our origins were a mystery. There was no clear picture of where we came from. You'll forgive me if I say we to include myself among them as I look at this portrait of Demasduit, my aunt. Our language seemed unrelated to other tribes in North America, even the nearby ones, the Micmac and the Labrador Montagnais and Nascopie and the like, but the amateurish method in which the vocabulary was recorded, and essences of the language ignored, makes that unprovable."

I interjected a question which I'd hesitated to ask, as his answer might tend to destroy his entire proposition. "Can you speak Beothuk, sir?"

"One would think I'd be able to speak it, from my recollections of that earlier life, but regrettably, in that respect they are like a dream in which one can speak and understand an alien language perfectly, but when one awakens one cannot. Although one does recall the content, the substance, of what was said in the dream, once awake one cannot employ the actual words in which it was then spoken. I find that the same phenomenon prevails regarding the Beothuk language and me in this life."

"Does not your inability, as Winston Churchill, to speak or understand Beothuk today undermine the reality of your actual memory of events? In other words, as your dream analogy suggests, your remembrances may be dreams or imaginings, all based on your readings, a throwback in your mind from what you later read."

"I can readily see how someone hearing my story might come to that conclusion, but I can only conscientiously reiterate that I am certain my recollections are of real events experienced by real persons." He paused to scrutinize my face. "William, is your skepticism regarding that claim of mine too great for me to go on, or are you content for me to proceed on that basis?"

"Yes, sir, I do want you to proceed."

"One creation story was that the first Beothuk had sprung from an arrow piercing the ground. That was why arrows were so sacred to us and why we would not relinquish our attachment to them in favour of guns, and why our creation contributed to our downfall. Also we had our stories and songs of arriving in Newfoundland an eternity ago from the eastern sea, the Atlantic, by trekking across the sea ice with boats we hauled over the pans and paddled in the water at the edge of the ice. That was a reason given in song why our leaders carried an oar as a sign of respect of ancestors. The explanation of our arrival in Newfoundland I'd favour was that we'd simply come across the Strait of Belle Isle from Labrador. Or we crossed over at an early date from Cape Breton in Nova Scotia. Either the Labrador Indians or the Mi'kmaq were our ancestors."

"If that were the case," I asked, "wouldn't the Beothuk language have been similar to one of their languages?"

"We don't really know that. Perhaps modern linguists, if they could compare the languages in actual life, would see similarities. If not, I can only suppose that the migrations were long enough ago that the languages became mutually unintelligible. How long does that take with preliterate languages? Or we are thrown back upon the arrival from Europe across the eastern sea, the Atlantic, especially since there were Beothuk stories and songs of devils and spirits of unimaginable evil emerging from the same eastern sea in pursuit of us. That might have been the Norse, of course, around 1000 A.D., with their form of diplomacy known as massacre, and 500 years later the Cabots, John and Sebastian, and the Corte Reals and the Jacques Cartiers, and the rest of the great explorers with their grand strategy of shooting the Indians and kidnapping a few of the rest to bring them back to England, Spain, or France as slaves or specimens to be exhibited in cages in the cities, or as pets for the monarchs till they died of European diseases.

"You had to admire the dauntless spirit of the English, too. One Richard Hore, a merchant of London in the 1500s, took several vessels full of gentlemen on a sightseeing tour of the New Founde Lande in the hope of adventure and of encountering some Red Indians. They did see some, who were observing them in amazement from the woods, after the Englishmen had run out of food and had resorted to killing and eating one another. The survivors admitted to that years later, after escaping back in England in a pirated French vessel. There were songs and tales among the Beothuk of the white devils being cannibals who ate their own. That must have been a reference to Hore way back then. It certainly made an impression on my Beothuk and helped to poison our attitude toward the Europeans barbarians. Hore, the man-eater? He must have been an ancestor of Hoare, the appeaser, the Conservative politician Samuel Hoare who helped Neville Chamberlain develop and defend the Munich Pact with Hitler, and caused me no end of grief and woe. But the earlier Hore. the cannibal ... as a student, didn't he attend your Brasenose College?"

"I'm not sure, but he sounds as if he would have fitted right in, along with Haig, and Profumo, and Golding, and the rest."

"Yes, Anthony told me of the fuss you caused up there over Lord Haig. Bully for you. It kindled my thought that you might be the right young man for this job. And Profumo? It was I who gave Baron Profumo his real start in life—in front bench politics, I mean, not in the sharing of young ladies with Russian spies for purposes of fornication.

"But my favourite was your magnificent fellow Brasenoseian William Golding. I met him at the end of the Second World War and was struck by reports of his courage and his candour, and we spent some considerable time talking. He was in the Royal Navy on a destroyer that helped pursue and sink the *Bismarck*, and he took part in the D-Day invasion of Normandy, in command of a landing ship under bombardment, and he saw action off the Netherlands where all but one of his assault craft—23 out of 24, I believe—were put out of commission. I never met a braver man, nor a more honest one. He'd been a schoolmaster, and we swapped stories on the true diabolical nature of schoolboys. He told me that he'd cruelly goaded his pupils to the limit—setting them against each other, bullying them sarcastically—simply to see how they would act in ghastly situations. He could scarcely credit the horror of what he saw, and much of it found its way, 10 years ago, into *Lord of the Flies*, a book he despised and was exceedingly sorry he'd written. I wasn't one of his pupils, of course, but I think I spotted myself as one of his characters in the book.

"When I complimented Golding on his courage in battle, he told me he'd truly recognized in battle the monstrous side of his own character. If he'd been a German during the war, he said, he would have been one of the worst Nazis in the country. He also told me that when he'd been home on the long summer vacation after his first year at Oxford, he tried to rape a 15-year-old girl who'd been naïve enough to lead him on. She succeeded ultimately in escaping his clutches by destroying his lustful mood. She shouted at him, 'You're not sticking that thing up into my guts.' I told him that if he wanted to be awarded medals, or prizes for his literary efforts, he should, like me regarding my Nobel Prize writings, leave some things unsaid."

"Which character," I asked, "were you supposed to be in *Lord of the Flies?*"

"I'll leave that to you to decide the next time you read it. I've belaboured Golding and his own character, and those he invented, only to stress how mixed up in us all are the good and the bad, the virtuous and the evil, the courageous and the cowardly, the brilliant and the wrong-headed. And that was true regarding the relations between the English and the Red Indians of Newfoundland. Some on both sides endeavoured to start well, but soon got off on the wrong foot. The remarkable John Guy of my beloved Bristol did try to do things right. He established a colony at Cupids, in Conception Bay, in Newfoundland in 1610. That was a full 10 years, as I told President Roosevelt, before the Pilgrim Fathers landed in the *Mayflower* at Plymouth Rock. Being a good patriot, he wouldn't believe it, of course, and had to have someone look it up before he'd accept it. John Guy and his men began friendly relations with the Beothuk they met near Dildo Pond and Dildo Islands, in Trinity Bay. By the by, William, Anthony here was wondering when he was studying your

Newfoundland map with me, if it was pure coincidence that the place called Dildo is not far from Spread Eagle and Backside Pond."

I kept a poker face on, with a hint of grin to show I was in on the low joke, a recurring one in Newfoundland. "I'm not sure I catch your drift, sir. Dildos are the thole pins, the pegs, in the gunwale of a rowboat used as a fulcrum for an oar."

Sir Winston said, "I'm sure rowing a boat is what Shakespeare had in mind when he used the word dildo—the first time in print—in his *Winter's Tale*, as he talked of the prettiest love songs for maids with delicate refrains of dildos and fadings, and jump her and thump her …"

"I suppose it is conceivable that a thole pin or dildo may have suggested other practices as a result of its convenient shape in resembling a man's cock." A big grin appeared on Sir Winston's face. Then I finished him off with, "I'm of a mind that the mapmaker who so often put Dildo on the map of Newfoundland—Dildo Tickle, Dildo Run, South Dildo, Dildo Pond—must have also been responsible for situating the place names Tongue and Wick on the map of northern Scotland close to the place called Twatt."

Men in small groups, even eminent men, are easy to amuse with a little dirt. These two burst out laughing, until Sir Winston's laughter turned into a phlegmy cough. After a minute, he said, "You're a diverting fellow, William, which I very much like. But before all this music hall comedy kills me, let us resume our discussion of the subject at hand. John Guy and his men in the early 1600s exchanged useful and pretty items with the Red Indians, and they all agreed in signs and gestures to meet in the same place for further trade on the same day in the next year. Lamentably, Guy was called back to Bristol, and about the same time next year some fishermen, different Englishmen, in another vessel, happened to arrive at the same spot and, seeing the Red Indians congregated on the beach, grew alarmed and fired their guns at them. In the songs and tales heard in mamateeks on long winter nights nearly 200 years later, that episode, and many others like it, were examples of how untrustworthy and treacherous and murderous the white devils were. Thus ended any hope of a trading relationship or a rapport of any kind, the heart-breaking story goes, between the seafaring buccaneers and the ochre-hued Red Indians. But I'm certain we don't need a tragic misunderstanding as fatuous as the plot of *Romeo and Juliet* to account for the atrocities committed by the white man against the Red Indian in Newfoundland, like everywhere else in the Americas.

"Red Indian. It was because the Beothuk covered their faces, bodies, clothing, weapons, canoes, and everything they owned, with that red ochre that the Europeans first called them Red Indians. As they were the first natives seen by the first explorers in the northern parts of the Americas, Englishmen extended the name Red Indian to all the tribes of Canada and America thereafter encountered. It was only a short logical leap from that name to the derogatory term 'redskin' for every Aboriginal.

"Before the incursions of the white man, my people the Beothuk lived in a rough and rugged paradise on earth, of forest, barrens, lakes, rivers, and ocean. The most challenging thing was the weather in the winter and spring, especially during the years and years of the little ice age that caused the Norse colonies in Greenland to wither and vanish, and caused the Thames to freeze over so that fairs were held on the ice-covered river in Shakespeare's day. But there are worse things than weather:

Blow, blow, thou winter wind,

Thou art not so unkind

As man's ingratitude ...

Heigh-ho! sing, heigh-ho! unto the green holly:

Most friendship is feigning, most loving mere folly:

Then, heigh-ho, the holly!

This life is most jolly ...

"The Beothuk survived that frigid era, although there were songs and stories about the heroic struggles against prolonged freezing and starvation, right up to the 19th century. The year 1816 was an extreme example of many. It was called the year without a summer throughout the Northern Hemisphere, when thousands perished from crop failures. In Newfoundland, the deer died in droves and didn't migrate, the salmon were frozen in the rivers, the seals were too far offshore on the frozen ocean. Our Beothuk traditions told of how only the strong and the vigorous and stalwart survived those years. My theory is that those Darwinian forces helped to create a people who were noted in the writings of white commentators as extraordinarily strong, erect, swift, handsome, and intelligent as adults, and whose children were the most beautiful they'd ever seen.

"They were always few in number, though—had to be to survive in a harsh terrain and unpredictable climate entirely on seasonal hunting and gathering. Perhaps never more than 1,000 souls—though far, far less than that in my recollections of gathering as a tribe to build and repair the miles and miles of caribou fences. For hundreds of years, small bands of 30 or 40 men, women, and children had travelled everywhere throughout the island. Camps and burial sites were widespread and numerous.

"Caribou migrated in their thousands through the great island from north to south every autumn. Many bands would come together from all round the island before that season to build and repair the astonishingly long and effective deer fences of felled trees, 30, 40 miles long, to conduct the caribou to places on rivers and lakes where it was easy to slaughter them. An overall chief was put in place by consent of the bands for the great annual caribou hunt. Meat was frozen over the winter, and dried and smoked at other times, to preserve it for the entire year. Large storehouses were built for that purpose from which bands could take provisions in accordance with their needs. There was an easygoing concept of ownership; borrowing from others in time of need was understood.

"Some apologists for Beothuk belaboured that point when there was stealing from the settlers. But Beothuk knew that what they were doing was considered wicked by the whites and very likely punishable by death. When boats were set on fire and destroyed, and other pilfering and destruction and occasional murder took place, the Beothuk knew exactly what they were up to. The white devils were the enemy and their theft from Beothuk of rivers and bays and hunting grounds and lives could not be countenanced. The Beothuk's error was that they went about opposing it in the wrong way, by seeking only revenge against them. And that sense of revenge, their compulsive need for it, was far too highly developed. It allowed for no harmonious contact between native and enemy at all, unless temporarily forced to it, and then Beothuk affability was entirely counterfeit.

"I learned from that how counterproductive implacable revenge could be. Hence in this life, after the First World War, I argued against applying such a policy of hardnosed revenge against Germany. But to no avail against a veritable wall of opposition, as evidenced in the Treaty of Versailles by the war-guilt clause imposed on Germany, their territorial concessions, their back-breaking reparations, and ultimately by the advent of the Second World War. But I digress.

"What surprised me in my research on Newfoundland, though, was how early the English governors in St. John's and some writers and observers in the colony urged benevolent treatment of the Aboriginals. This was happening there while policies of genocide, official or covert, were mostly applied against the Indian throughout North America. Mind you, the kindly course of action advocated at high levels in Newfoundland was usually on the grounds that they were miserable, wretched, benighted heathen, in dire need of being Christianized.

"Of course, the pilfering of white property by the Beothuk and the killing of savages by some settlers, and vice versa, didn't stop, and after more atrocities on both sides, the governor of the day, John Duckworth, and a few well-meaning English settlers, organized another attempt—there having been futile ones earlier—to try to establish permanent relations with the Beothuk and to bring them into contact with civilization.

"Governor Duckworth proclaimed an official cessation of mistreatment of the Beothuk. In the summer of 1810, he ordered a respected man, Lieutenant David Buchan, to sail a vessel to Notre Dame Bay and try to establish contact with the Red Indians during their summer migration. Buchan cruised the harbours and coves there for weeks without spotting one Indian. But the governor was dogged and full of hope, and charged Buchan with gathering a gang of men that winter to seek and find Beothuk up the Exploits River. This was the expedition that became marked by well-intentioned and heart-breaking folly ..." Sir Winston stopped.

The door had opened and a self-assured man strode right in. Anthony introduced us. It was Sir Winston's physician, Lord Moran. Nearly every day, apparently, he dropped in at all hours to check on Churchill's vitals. Without protest from anyone, I moseyed out to the hall, leaving Anthony inside with him.

A woman came downstairs, smiled, introduced herself as Lady Churchill's secretary, and shivered. "Can't have an honoured guest left wandering about in this chilly old hall all by himself. Come in the kitchen for a cuppa." In there, she tried, crabwise, to draw out of me what I was doing in the house to begin with. And why, she wondered, for such long hours?

CHAPTER 20

When Moran left after my agreeable 20 minutes at the kitchen table, I went back into the room with Sir Winston and Anthony. Neither of them mentioned his visit, but they both looked rather gravely thoughtful. Before I could hope that the doctor had found everything well, Sir Winston hoped I hadn't been too bored out there. No, I replied, I had a pleasant chat with a kindly secretary.

"I trust," said Sir Winston, "she wasn't able to torture a confession out of you. They're rather good at that, she and Clemmie."

"She did seem rather curious, but I succeeded in making her eyes roll up in her head. I said we were discussing Canadian history."

"Excellent. Clemmie knows that, as usual, I'm fostering some bizarre notion down here, again, but she doesn't know exactly what. If she knew, of course, she'd think I was being as silly as a box of bollocks."

"Interesting turn of phrase, that, sir," said Anthony. "Is it one of Randolph's?"

"No, I've found women much better at mocking men's parts, so these days I get my more colourful obscenities from Mary. She's the delight of my life. But let's get on with that white man's ramble upriver.

"Lieutenant Buchan's preparations for the winter's trek on the frozen Exploits were prodigious. In January, at Ship Cove, later Botwood, he and his men loaded up a dozen sledges with nearly 4,000 pounds of supplies, guns, and gifts. Then he set some 30 men to the backbreaking toil of dragging the sledges across the harbour ice and up the river ice toward Red Indian Lake, some 70 miles away. It was a hard-forced march for 10 gruesome days over mounds and peaks of heaved up ice in ghastly winter weather. The nights were so cold that the men could only get through them with copious drafts of rum. And there was scant sleep, as they waited in utmost agitation, restlessness, and dread, in the freezing dark, for murderous raids by the Red Indians.

"Meanwhile, some Beothuk hunters reported back to the tribe at winter quarters near the big lake that they had sighted the procession a short distance up from the mouth of the river. They described a large band of plodding men hauling ponderous sledges, looking altogether like a hideous, slow-moving, giant insect in a fearsome nightmare. The Beothuk had a healthy regard for the prowess, strength, endurance, and swiftness of the white devils. Some even said they were aided by evil spirits. But after watching this sluggish, eerie, and mostly silent procession from the trees for hours, Beothuk hunters began to think the sight more and more preposterous. Then, seeing them often stalled, and growling and shouting at each other quarrelsomely during the next days of freezing rain and gales of wind, the spies concluded that there was no way that these white devils, even with evil supernatural help, could make it up to the lake, dragging such a load, in these terrible conditions.

"Our hunters overcame the urge to kill a few of the whites with arrows. There were so many of them that the situation would become perilous if the survivors gave chase with their guns. Instead, the Beothuk stopped watching in order to hurry up to the home site and report. Demasduit and Obseewit and Shanawdithit were there playing games together when they came back and, although everyone was perplexed by the described spectacle, they ended by cackling in scornful contempt, adults and children alike, at the white devils' folly.

"However, the historical records of the English show that Buchan and his men did make it up the river, against all the expectations of Beothuk, to within 5 miles or so from Red Indian Lake. He halted the procession there and, leaving the sledges and half the team behind, led the rest quietly toward the lake. Early the next morning, with Indian attentiveness relaxed in the frigid winter darkness, the whites surprised their encampment at a place the English named Bloody Point. The trained guns of 15 men kept the adults from running into the woods. But the children scampered away in panic from the devils, parents expecting them to be shot in the back as they ran. They all made it to the trees without a gun having been fired, and, from under branches, the young ones looked out on the scene.

"Buchan and his men lowered their rifles and, according to accounts, he tried to get across signs of their friendship, hampered somewhat by not being able to speak a word of the native tongue. If Gobodinwit had been there, this would have presented him, as Eli, with an ideal opportunity to establish communications. But his fellow tribesmen were not thinking along those lines. His daughter

Obeeswit in particular was glaring out from under the branches at these men who belonged to the enemy that had murdered her father.

"Buchan handed out to the adults the few presents they had with them, but he had neglected to bring from the sledges nearly all the presents and provisions that he had intended for the Beothuk, and which had been the whole reason in the first place for this arduous trek. The terrible weather and the physical strain must have depleted their brain power.

"He did get it across that they had to go back for the presents they wanted to give the Indians. Meanwhile, Beothuk men and women were putting on an elaborate show to the whites of friendship and goodwill—shaking hands, backslapping, uproarious merriment—but it was all fake. Obseewit and her friends were laughing in delight over how well their parents were able to fool these hard-hearted killers.

"At length, after hours of gesticulating, signing, and pointing, two of Lieutenant Buchan's crew volunteered to remain unarmed with the native people in Bloody Point as a show of good faith, and four Beothuks, including Demasduit's lover, Nonobawsut, agreed to go back with Buchan and his companions to help bring up the presents and provisions.

"When they left, the arguments raged among those remaining, disguised under displays of continued friendship, as to whether or not Buchan's two crewmembers should be killed. An uncle suggested that these two be done away with right now while the chance existed, before their friends came back in greater numbers with their dreadful weapons. But opinions were divided. Others argued that the promised gifts from downriver were at least worth the wait to see them. All this was stated with smiles and pats on the back to the two marines, which they reciprocated with handshakes and friendly animation.

"Relieving them of all alarm had been the intention from the start of this encounter with the settlers, but although the Beothuk were all pretending to be friendly, and giggling and gesticulating playfully, in fact, every member of the people, child and adult alike, reviled and detested them. The girls were watching their uncle pretending to be in a *friendly* dispute with the pair of white devils. The uncle wanted for his own the handsome wool jacket that one of the devils was wearing, and he pulled at the sleeves and lapels while the devil resisted with voice and hands. The uncle and the white devil were laughing in enjoyment of their little game. The tone of voice and bodily movements of both white devils showed that they naively felt no fear of the dozen or more men and women and children, who surrounded them.

"Some Beothuk said that if they killed this pair, the white devils would kill the men who had gone downriver with the others. And in any event, the murder of these good-faith detainees would certainly bring greater revenge raids from the white devils later. The uncle countered, in the middle of his laughing game-playing with the marine over his jacket, that the band should not be so foolish: the attacks on Beothuk would continue regardless of the fate visited on these two. His supporters added that, anyhow, the Beothuk were lagging far behind the white devils in vengeance killings. But the standoff went on and no violence was committed at the time.

"What the girls noticed most was the remarkable contrast between the full, white, even teeth of their own people and the jagged, yellow-brown teeth, with great gaps, of the devils. Their loathsome, scraggly-bearded faces, and every sound and action from them, recalled, even to young minds, the absolute disdain and contempt of the whites, and their murderous occupation of Beothuk lands and waters.

"Suddenly, out of the woods, two of the four Beothuck emissaries came creeping into the site. On their way down over the river ice with the white devils, they said, the four warriors had become more and more nervous and suspicious of what they were up to. These two had slipped away to come back. The other two had decided to keep going. But soon they came running back as well. They spoke in excited, worried language. Their mistrust had peaked when they approached the camp and the sledges downriver and saw, off to the side, lurking among the trees, another large group of white devils—a veritable army capable of wiping out everyone here with their weapons. The two recognized among them some men who had been involved in massacres of Beothuk men, women, and children in the past. One of them, they would tell his widow and fatherless daughters, was the very man who had beaten Eli's brains out with a bear trap. In justice, and for security, the two white hostages needed to be put to death.

"Obeeswit, orphaned of father by his gratuitous slaughter at the hands of the whites, was among those who now stepped up her arguments for their immediate execution. But Demasduit and her mother, also orphaned and widowed, stayed silent. Some in the band still remained opposed to killing the two harmless, unarmed marines, whom no one had ever seen hurting their people in any way, and who were here with them in trusting helplessness. If this truce arrangement was not safe, everyone should just bolt into the woods and vanish. Obeeswit knew, even as she heard herself piping up in her young girlish voice and shouting for their death, that her own murdered father would have argued the opposite against her.

"The restless disquiet of the people and their increasingly agitated language, changed the faces and tone of the two devils from a kind of parental humouring of children to, now, uncomprehending trepidation. With the return of the second pair of Beothuk, and their vehement speeches to the assembled tribesmen, the atmosphere of hostility around the two white men had started to become unmistakable to them. Voices were raised and the uncle's playfulness with the marine over his coat ended as he pushed the marine back and walked away from him in disgust.

"Alarm and then terror spread across the marines' faces and they backed away. They had no weapons, having been relieved of them as part of the truce, and they started to gibber at each other in panic. The uncle roared, 'Kill the white devils,' and grabbed his bow from his son. The white devils might not have understood his words, but they clearly grasped his meaning: they turned and ran, heading across the frozen river. No one shot until grandfather did. But when his arrow found the centre of one devil's back, instantly afterwards the backs of both men bristled with arrows. The marines fell down, shrieking, then groaning, then dying, and lay in two crumpled heaps in the snow."

Churchill paused in his narrative and gazed into space. Then he murmured that he could never fathom the idiocy of a group of white settlers, his fellow Englishmen, on a mission of reconciliation and friendship with Red Indians, who would bring with them men who'd be recognized by those Indians as their assassins from the recent past.

Churchill looked at me. He had committed to memory from the literature, he said, the names of these two marines from Buchan's crew who had selflessly volunteered with noble intentions for their dangerous task: James Butler and Thomas Bouthland. The names of these two men, otherwise unknown and anonymous outside of this tragic episode, he said, deserved to be commemorated for their courage, and for what they were trying to accomplish, and should be repeated on every possible occasion. He held my eye with his. "William Cull, please make certain that their names appear at least twice in your write-up of this, my chronicle: James Butler and Thomas Bouthland."

I nodded and Sir Winston wiped away moisture from his eyes to take up the thread of his story again: "Their riddled bodies were stripped of any article deemed good—boots, caps, items of clothing—and the uncle acquired the jacket he'd coveted. He provoked broad laughter when he poked his fingers through the arrow holes in it and wriggled them. Before now, the girls said, they had never understood why these men and their kind were called 'white' devils. Their faces and hands and necks always appeared to be the same tan colour as the Beothuk. But today they saw that any area of their naked skin ordinarily covered by clothing and protected from the sun, but now exposed, was repulsively pallid … not unlike the glistening white belly of a slimy fish, or in some places like the off-white, yellowish maggots squirming in their refuse heaps. For one moment the girls' feelings bounced from the stark loathing for them they'd learned from life to a natural pity for their wretched end. But their pity didn't last longer than an instant, because their grandmother now went to work.

"With enormous knife in hand, she stepped forward and squatted down beside the two corpses. She called Demasduit, Obseewit, and Shanawdithit over to watch closely as she commenced to cut and slice and saw at the neck of one of the white devils. She described to them exactly what she was doing. She was instructing them in her shaman's art, and she told them how lucky they were these days to have a beautiful metal knife like this, justly purloined from the white devils themselves, to work with, compared to her own grandmother who'd had to make do with a stone tool. The image of her shining knife, though slick with gouts of bright red blood, embedded itself as a souvenir in my brain forever. Perhaps it's why to this day, that I myself love a well-crafted knife, including, contrary to grandmother, the stone chert ones she referred to, which were in fact sharper and more beautiful than the metal ones, but not as shiny, and much harder to possess, in that they had to be made—formed and hafted—rather than simply stolen.

"When she had removed the head entirely from the body, she held it by the hair, level with the girls' eyes, for a close view of the gaunt and bloody face. Then, she rose to her feet and started to sing the revenge song they loved, while hoisting the disembodied head high in the air, and turning round and round, as she displayed it to the other men, women, and children encircling her and now beginning to sing and dance in joy as well.

"Soon, grandfather held up his leader's staff, an oar-shaped length of wood he always carried, and stopped our singing and dancing.

The tribe would continue the revenge celebration, he said, at the home site, tonight, farther up their lake. But, now, before the dead devils' friends came back, they had to leave this place of vengeance for now; they'd return later to worship, and celebrate these deeds here at this forevermore-sacred spot. He nodded to grandmother, who quickly, and without ceremony this time, severed the other head and stuffed them both into caribou-hide carrying bags for the men to lug. Then they set out on their snowshoe racquets upriver over the ice and snow, and slipped into the forest, out of the sight of any enemies, on trails hidden by trees, with their secret, concealed entrances and exits that, even at a young age, the girls were learning to know intimately. On the way, grandfather watched the young girls closely and asked if they wanted to sit in the sealskin slide and be pulled along by the men. They spurned the offer and never once fell behind in the deeper snow.

"That night, in their winter home by the big lake, men hoisted the pale-faced heads on poles by the blazing fire and everyone danced round them again, singing about other deeds of vengeance by their people in the past, and of future deeds yet to come, for all the cruel acts by the untold merciless enemies who surrounded them.

"Lieutenant Buchan and his men, when they approached the lake cheerfully with an abundance of presents for their new Red Indian friends, could not grasp the meaning of the empty silence or of the distant dark stain ahead on the glistening white. Then gradually, as they got nearer, it dawned on them that they were looking at an icefield of blood, and in the middle of it they now made out the two naked and headless bodies of James Butler and Thomas Bouthland.

"Inside a circle of guns pointing out, Buchan's crew wailed their distress and grief, and loaded the freezing corpses aboard the sledges. Then, heartsick with shock and sorrow, they lit out downriver for the Bay of Exploits. With no little dread of the murky woods beside the river, they stopped neither for meals nor sleep, and, while it had taken them 11 days to come up, they now reached the river mouth in not much more than two days. They need not have been so afraid. Those they feared were miles away, busily celebrating their pre-emptive strike, their great victory, against these white devils who loved nothing better than to murder their defensless women and children."

Sir Winston lifted his head to look directly at me. "Your ancestor and namesake, William Cull, as you would know from the reports at the time, was chief guide on that disastrous expedition. From the start of his career, and all through his nearly 40 years of involvement with the Red Indian, your Cull had a very unclear and ambiguous relationship with them. Back in his early days, his more murderous days, as Eli Easter could have testified, he told an official by the name of Pulling, who was doing a report on the native inhabitants in the 1790s, that, when he was inland trapping, he was molested by Indians. Yet he wasn't killed or even wounded. And white settlers marvelled that, although he would live alone in lean-to tilts upriver during the trapping season, nothing untoward happened to him, even though the Beothuk could easily have killed him if they chose to.

"For example, during roughly the same period in which Eli Easter was captured after his family was massacred by whites, including Cull, the Beothuk ambushed a settler by the name of Rowsell. He had the reputation of being the greatest of the Indian killers. He was shot full of arrows and his head removed from his body for festive purposes.

"The Beothuk had gained a reputation as fierce killers of whites over the centuries. Sir David Kirke, an early colonizer and governor of Newfoundland, wrote in the first decades of the 1600s that Indians surprised and murdered nearly 40 French fishermen up north over two days of massacre and then returned home in great triumph with their severed heads to celebrate. It was unlikely to have been Beothuk who did that, of course. Such a mass killing wasn't their style of murder at all, and Eli, and later Shanawdithit, knew of absolutely no tradition in their songs and stories of any such magnificent victory over the white devils. Perhaps it was the Eskimo—they congregated in numbers sufficient to commit such a massacre—but the difficulty with that theory is that Eskimo did not sever heads, while the Beothuk, and some other Indian tribes, did. Very probably there was confusion or embellishment in the telling, and the mystery remains. But the Beothuk got the credit or blame and developed an undeserved reputation for absolute savagery.

"Mind you, my Beothuk ancesters didn't shrink from the occasional revenge killing. As late as 1809, some Beothuk attacked men and women planting crops on Fogo Island, the home island of our William Cull, causing a death, and also shot a boy on Twillingate Island. Those and other acts of ambush, while terrifying, were far less than were warranted, even as simple revenge killings, by the actions of some of the whites.

"Your great Newfoundland historian, Daniel Prowse, usually even-handed and meticulous in his magnificent history of the Island, which he published near the turn of the 20th century, decades after their disappearance, wrote that the Beothuk possessed an 'insatiable hatred of pale faces.' Yet who could blame them? Take the incident in Trinity Bay in 1775. Beothuk stole some goods from fishermen's families in Old Perlican. Such pilfering, it could be argued, was only a courageous act of retaliation in the first place. Next day a party of whites set out after the Beothuk. They spotted an Indian encampment by the rising smoke and surprised them in their sleep. It was amazing how many mamateeks the whites were able to sneak up on and take the occupant Beothuk in them unawares. The Beothuk kept no dogs, which might have barked and warned of approaching settlers. Why not? The theory was that barking dogs were more likely to allow white devils to discover mamateeks hidden in the woods. Whatever the rights or wrongs of that argument, in this case the Old Perlican fishermen were able to creep up and shoot seven Beothuk inside, including the usual colossal giant alleged to be present and whose fearsomeness always seemed, in such circumstances, to spur on and justify the whites' defensive massacre.

"The no-guns rule, the no-dogs rule, the no-truck-or-traffic with the whites rule, the breach of which precluded a Beothuk from admittance to the happy island after death and from any burial items for the journey, all went far in leading to extinction. One can easily perceive the reasoning behind it all. All the way back to 1501, Gaspar Corte Real, the famous explorer, under commission from the king of Portugal, reached Newfoundland and thereupon captured 57 natives, who had welcomed his vessels, leaving an unknown number dead behind him. He sent them back as a gift to the king, as slaves. Yet some historians have had the temerity to wonder why the Beothuk, from the earliest years, increasingly employed a general strategy of withdrawal from the Europeans peopling the Newfoundland shores."

I jumped in. "Sir Winston, there's a plan afoot to erect a huge statue of Gaspar Corte Real next year in front of the government building in St. John's commemorating his magnificent deeds."

"Thank God I'll be dead." He sounded so comical in applauding the prospect of his own death that neither Anthony nor I could help laughing. To which Churchill growled, "I'm gratified that the thought of my imminent demise is still able to raise spirits."

Waving away our attempt to say sorry for our reaction, Sir Winston continued. "Newfoundland governments, fairly early in the 1800s, during the same periods that authorities in much of the rest of the Americas were waging wars of subjugation and annihilation of natives, issued edicts against the inhuman treatment of the Beothuk, backed up with severe penalties, which were, regrettably, unenforced. There were also misguided offers of rewards of £50, and later £100, for the capture of Beothuks to establish amicable relations between Indians and whites. For example, Governor Palliser proffered a financial incentive to settlers for the capture of a Beothuk to be used for establishing contact with them. That encouragement resulted in the 1760s in the killing of a woman by trappers, who then carried off her small boy for the money prize. They called him John August and little or nothing came of it.

"During the decades that concluded with the end of Shanawdithit's residency in St. John's in 1829, some eight or 10 Beothuk lived for a time with settlers. At least four of them were children, John August,

Oubee, Tom June, and Eli Easter. A group of English fishermen in the Bay of Exploits toward the end of the 18th century were tracking down Red Indians who'd pilfered salmon nets and traps when they came across a mamateek. Two women disappeared into the woods, but the fishermen managed to kill a Beothuk man and wound a boy, who escaped, and to capture a little girl called Oubee, whom they took as a 'fair prize.' She was given to a family in Trinity, who treated her with humanity, it was said, though she tried to escape. My Beothuk ancestor, the aforesaid Eli, didn't know her—she was born after he had been taken from the tribe—but he heard of her and wanted to talk to her. Mr. Slade brought him to Trinity to meet her. But her family had already taken her to England, where she died a year later, leaving a few words of Beothuk vocabulary behind.

"In the 1790s, an official report on the treatment of the Beothuk, known as the Pulling report, detailed the violence against them, and asserted that there was no hesitation on the part of some settlers to kill Indians. By 1800, Beothuk control over their former domains had shrunk woefully, as Europeans extended their reach well up the coast and into the bays. The whites were permanently settled in Bonavista Bay and Notre Dame Bay, including Fogo Island and Twillingate Island, and continued their encroaching on the last coastal dominions of the Red Indians. The settlers proved themselves to be as at home in the wild and harsh Newfoundland settings and circumstances as the Beothuk were, with the additional advantage of deadly firearms.

"In 1813, the governor of the day reissued the offer of a reward to any settler who established amicable intercourse with the Beothuk;

this time it was £100. Mere lip service, of course. How effective it was can be seen from the fact that, just four years later, in 1817, at least nine Beothuk were murdered. Your William Cull was a mysterious character in all this: Not only did he survive often alone in Beothuk country, but sometimes vulnerable Beothuk women appeared to give themselves up to him in a way that indicated, perhaps, a desperate trust. Yet those events he was involved in were not always free of ambiguities.

"Take this case in point: early in the 1800s, shortly after the turn of the century, a Beothuk woman somehow came into Cull's custody. He told officials that she was about 50 years old and that she'd been paddling alone in a canoe in Notre Dame Bay, gathering birds' eggs from the islands. Of course, that explanation seems fanciful, even preposterous. She would not have been out there in a canoe by herself on the salt water like that. So one can only ponder what might have happened to any companions."

"Were there no tales among the Beothuk," I asked Sir Winston, "about women or men who had gone missing at that particular time and place?"

"Yes, there was always a plethora of tales about our people over the years who had left and never come back. I was too young to remember at the time specific details of different persons who might have gone missing from various family and bands.

"Cull brought this woman to St. John's and visited the governor, who arranged for trinkets and other presents to be given to her to be brought to her tribe, and ordered him to carry her back upriver to her people. But she lived on with Cull for a year on Fogo Island because, he said, he couldn't find enough men to join him in bringing her back. People on Fogo, he informed the governor, 'do not hold with civilizing the Red Indians.' Finally, a year after her capture, he reported that he conveyed her partway up the Exploits River and left her on the riverbank with the gifts for her tribesmen to find. Ten days later, he went upriver to the place again, and reported back that she and the presents were gone.

"A naval surgeon, who spent several summer months in Newfoundland round that time, wrote that he believed Cull had murdered the woman for the gifts and disposed of her body. And a rumour to that effect went around Notre Dame Bay and St. John's. Cull professed outrage and vehemently denied the allegation, and made a dramatic point publicly of seeking advice on suing his naval accuser for defamation of his character. Regrettably, the credibility of his denial was somewhat undermined by his earlier boast that he had shot more Red Indians than he could recollect."

"Did you ever learn the truth," I asked, "of what Cull in fact did with the woman?"

"Taken at its best, whether he murdered the woman or not, the truth is that, only an unthinking brute, or a moron utterly indifferent to her harm, would deposit a woman alone on the banks of a river in the wilderness of Newfoundland and leave to her own devices, abandon her to her fate. Your ancestor and namesake, William Cull, was not always a good man. The most that can be said of him was that sometimes, as time went on, he became the best of a bad lot.

"Yet, a few years later, a year before the disastrous Buchan expedition that left two marines beheaded on the ice, the governor commissioned Cull to lead an excursion up the Exploits to contact the Beothuk. It was fruitless, but Cull reported back that he and the others, including two Mi'kmaq, saw in a storehouse near Red Indian Lake the tin kettles that he'd left with the woman when he'd abandoned her on the riverbank."

"So, it sounds like she did make it back home."

"Well, that may be wishful thinking on your part, William, in aid of the reputation of your ancestor and namesake. Some of the trinkets apparently did make it upriver, but as for her, I don't know. Shanawdithit never mentioned her—I don't think the girls knew of her. The first I heard of her was when I read, in this life, about Cull's exploits."

"That seems ominous ... as if she'd become a non-person."

"Rather, yes. But my Beothuk relatives were preoccupied during all their childhood and adolescence with retaliatory raids, revenge attacks on the settlers' property, that succeeded, not in regaining territory or access to trails and waterways but in stirring up the murderous wrath of the white devils' worst elements. Their murders never stopped, as long as there were Beothuk alive and manifest. Leading up to the time that Shanawdithit and two other women would avail themselves of the mercy of William Cull in 1823, her cousin and her cousin's father were shot, gratuitously, by two trappers.

"But the most tragic event to strike the tiny remnants of the Beothuk race was caused by an act of goodwill. And my soulmate, Obseewit, the Little Bird, was responsible for it, for the bad and the good, both in its heartbreak at the time and in its salvation of civilized humanity over a century later. It started eight or nine years after the peace mission of Lieutenant Buchan upriver that had ended in the decapitation of his two marines. The chain of fateful consequences began in 1818 when Obseewit was now a young woman. She convinced Shanawdithit that the time was ripe for payback on the white devils for recent murders, and in turn, they persuaded the current chief, Nonobawsut, the husband of her sister, Demasduit, to go with them to the Bay of Exploits and appraise the raiding possibilities.

"Two other men accompanied them down and, unseen, they reconnoitred properties there that looked promising. They settled on the premises of John Peyton Jr., where a vessel was tied up at his wharf and being loaded to the gunwales with valuable goods and wares. This John Jr. was the son of the brutal Indian killer John Peyton Sr., but was himself reputed to be tolerant and peaceable in his attitude toward the Beothuk. Still, Obseewit planned and conducted with the others their raid on his fully laden vessel. Some writers have characterized that last notorious foray as merely another act of pilfering, a continuation of the filching and thievery, that the Beothuk were ill-famed for. But as you will see, it was in itself a daring and skilful and measured act of retaliation against the murderous whites, and if it happened to be misdirected and produced tragic effects for the Beothuk within a year, we shall see how, after more than a century, in my life as Winston Churchill, those tragic effects would in turn create momentous consequences for good throughout the earth—"

A brisk knock at the door of our room stopped Churchill's flow and startled me out of the Beothuk world. The door opened instantly, and a young man a few years older than me looked in, causing the old man to burst into a smile and sit up eagerly at the entry of this exasperating intruder.

"**G**ood morning, Paterfamilias," said the young man, "please excuse me. I'm here for lunch as commanded. I won't disturb you now. I just popped in to let you know. Hello, Anthony."

"Come in, come in, Winston," said Sir Winston. "Have you said hello to your grandmama?"

"I have done, already. I know the strict order of precedence in this house."

"Sit down. Sit down. This is William Cull from Canada. He's reading law at Oxford. William, this is my namesake grandchild. He recently came down from Christ Church himself."

"That was some time ago, now, Grandfather. Long enough ago that I've flown an aircraft around much of the world, written a book about it, and got married. How do you do, William? I'm pleased to meet you."

"How do—?" My greeting was cut off by the enthusiastic grandfather.

"Yes, this year has truly been an *annus mirabilis* for my grandson," said Sir Winston. "I was accused as a young man of being a wunderkind myself, but Winston here has beaten me hands down. He learned how to fly four or five years ago, William, as I had done later in life, and then, after just one year of experience, flew off with a mate to cover Asian and African territory familiar to both my father and me during our checkered careers."

"Twenty thousand miles at the controls of a single-engine Piper Comanche," said young Winston, "in the Middle East and over deserts, jungles, and mountains round the entire African continent. You have no idea how much larger Africa is in reality, in contrast to its disproportionately reduced size on the Europe-centric Mercator maps. I thought of that when we were about to crash-land in the middle of 12 million square miles of jungle, desert, and veldt, and I could see the utter hopelessness of ever making our way out."

"But by skill and good luck," said the proud Sir Winston, "you managed to spot on the ground at the last minute your miniscule landing strip and put the craft down."

"More by the Churchillian good luck you resurrected," said Winston, "than superior skill, I can assure you."

"Sounds like a great read," I said. "What's the title of your book?"

"It's—didn't Grandfather or Anthony see fit to mention my book to you? It's called *First Journey*."

"I intended to bring it up at lunch," said Anthony. "It's doing marvellously well in the bookstores."

"As usual our American cousins have invented an appropriate term for it," said Sir Winston. "They're calling it a *bestseller*. Winston is an adventurer and author, and a husband, all before the age of 25. He's trounced me in the husband category. As I'd hoped he would do in the MP category by running in the October election in my old seat, but that he couldn't manage."

"I have to leave a little of your legacy intact, Grandfather," laughed young Winston. "I can't supersede too much of it."

His grandson apparently did supersede much in Sir Winston's mind, though. Thirty minutes remained before the appointed hour for lunch, time in which to resume his narrative of the Beothuk tragedy and its international impact, which I dearly wanted, but he kept Winston in the room talking instead. Then, over lunch, we discussed British politics and young Winston's future in it. His path ahead was so bright and he was so easily and so early taking advantage of the pluses he was born with that I had to will away a twinge of envy. I was helped when it occurred to me that his privileged advantages might make him burn out too soon, as his great-grandfather, Lord Randolph, had done, and even like his grandfather, Sir Winston, before the Second World War dropped into his lap.

As things would fall out, I'd see young Winston again just three or four years later in Labrador. By then I'd already be in local Newfoundland politics myself, and he'd be a special guest at Premier Smallwood's sod-turning for the gargantuan hydroelectric project on Churchill Falls, renamed for his grandfather. Winston the younger was then either in, or headed for, a fairly long, fairly respectable, series of terms in the House of Commons in London. But granddaddy's legacy would never be in danger of being superseded by the grandchild.

At lunch, now, young Churchill asked about my presence there. Sir Winston replied that Anthony had met me at a de Rothschild luncheon where I'd been invited because of the Labrador hydroelectrical project.

"Oh yes, William Cull," said young Winston. "I remember the name coming up a few weeks ago here when you asked Eddie to invite Anthony to that lunch, because of William's Red Indian connection through his ancestors."

"Well, I can say that Anthony's report on William piqued my interest sufficiently for me to invite him here to chat."

"A good chat, too, by the sound of things from dear Papa. And Grandmother says he's been here for several days. No offence, William, but I fear you may be a victim of Grandfather's fascination, and mine, with our relatives, the native American Indians."

"And it's been fascinating for me as well," I said.

"We've especially been able to help each other with some insights into the demise of the original Red Indians," said Sir Winston. "But enough of that for now. Let's talk about what you've been doing in recent days."

"Well, if you don't mind, Grandfather, I'd like to take absolutely selfish advantage of your guest's company to talk about your involvement with Newfoundland. You'll recall that you asked me to represent you at the sod-turning for the Labrador project whenever that might get under way."

That was all the encouragement Sir Winston needed. He was notorious for taking over the table talk at the least opportunity. "Here's something few are aware of. Now, I don't wish to make too much of the inspiration I derived from the Beothuk regarding the First World War; however, we can take as an instructive example the development of the armoured vehicle, the tank, in that conflict."

Young Winston shifted in his chair and shot a glance at Anthony.

Beothuks again? And what! they inspired the development of the modern military tank?

"We didn't call it a tank back then," continued Sir Winston. "We called it a caterpillar. And by no means did I solely invent that fighting machine as some have averred, but I did foster and encourage and promote its progress by getting the Landships Committee going, and the development of the tank probably ended the war in our favour. You see, I knew how disastrous the failure to keep up with advances in weaponry can be. It was the failure of the Beothuk to progress in the use of advanced weaponry, like firearms, which helped doom them to extinction and made me so adamant in this life about seizing and encouraging such opportunities against the enemy." Sir Winston stopped and worked on standing up. "Will you excuse me for a moment? I'll be back with more vignettes."

Young Winston helped him to his feet, and he shuffled out fast, impatient about missing any time with his grandson.

"Is he all right?" Winston asked Anthony. "He seems rather fixated on the Beothuk."

"Yes, that's what he's been talking to William about, based on his extensive research in the Colonial Office. I'll go out to the WC and hint gently to him that broader allusions to his Newfoundland experiences might be a little more useful for your needs."

When they came back in again, Sir Winston started talking before sitting down: "Yes, Newfoundland was never far from my mind. During the Second World War, before the Americans even entered the conflict, I raised the prospect of our granting the United States long leases of land in Newfoundland for military bases, in exchange for the gift of some old American destroyers to Britain. As a result, the Americans installed bases in St. John's and Argentia, and at Stephenville on the west coast of Newfoundland, not far, William, from Flat Bay where a young Beothuk came ashore with his Mi'kmaq saviours after escaping from Nova Scotia." The grandson slid his eyes my way and grinned.

"Then," continued the grandfather, "when President Roosevelt and I decided to meet for the first time as leaders in 1941, it was I who suggested that we meet secretly by ship near the American naval base in Argentia in Placentia Bay, Newfoundland. That was in August, four months before Pearl Harbor. I steamed across the Atlantic on HMS *Prince of Wales*, and Roosevelt arrived from Washington on USS *Augusta*. There, off unremarkable little Ship Harbour, Placentia Bay, we agreed on the terms of the Atlantic Charter, which all our Allies would later confirm and which became the foundation for the United Nations and many other international agreements, including, at Roosevelt's insistence and to my chagrin, the postwar self-rule of our colonies.

"Between my meetings with Roosevelt on board ship in Placentia Bay, I went ashore near Ship Harbour to explore the area. Mild protests arose from my retinue—the heavens threatened a serious downpour of rain. But I insisted. When we landed on the shore by launch, and I saw and felt beneath my feet the grey, rocky, pebbly beach, I underwent an intense sensation of déjà vu, as if I'd come home. I all but dropped to my hands and knees and kissed the ground. The others thought I was going slightly barmy when I climbed embankments and rolled rocks down over the slopes, as if

I were a child at play, which I was. And they thought I'd lost my mind altogether when I wandered far and wide over a rough meadow gathering pink wildflowers into a bunch in my fist like a child, and when I insisted on bringing the small bedraggled bouquet back to the ship. But happily, to allow my advisers the satisfaction of muttering that they'd told me so, we got caught in a torrential downpour which drenched us all to the skin.

"I dearly craved to go up to the bottom of Placentia Bay to Come by Chance, which I knew was a sacred area where the narrow neck of land on the Isthmus of Avalon, only a mile or so wide, from Come by Chance to Bull Arm, separated the two great bays, Placentia Bay and Trinity Bay, and where the salmon had been so magically prolific on the rivers in ancient times. I wanted to walk that entire enchanted place, from the mist and fog of Placentia Bay to the glorious rays of Sunnyside in Trinity Bay. But we couldn't go. There was simply no room in our schedule for such an outing.

"Also in Newfoundland, as part of our war effort, I encouraged the airbase operation of the Royal Canadian Air Force at Botwood, in the Bay of Exploits, which was part of the old ancestral land and sea of the Beothuk. The early white settlers called the place Ship Cove—*Cove* this time—no wonder the Germans never knew where I was, there were so many places with 'Ship' in their name. It was an important place for wartime vessels and aircraft. After we declared war on the Nazis in September 1939, the first act of war in the New World happened right there in Botwood, Newfoundland. A German freighter was in the harbour loading ore from the Buchans mine, or perhaps it was a German pulpwood carrier. Whatever it was, I ordered the vessel seized one morning by local police and residents, and its crewmembers were sent to a prisoner of war camp, the first enemy German ship captured in the New World.

"During the war I travelled to Botwood myself. I flew in on one of the famous seaplanes associated with the war operations there. It was a stopping-off point for overseas flights, and there may well have been good military reason for my going there, also, but of course I was greatly motivated to drop in for old time's sake, to see what I remembered … reading about.

"In my mind's eye, there, I saw Demasduit, Mary March, being offloaded from the vessel in Ship Cove, Botwood, where she'd died of consumption, and her corpse carried upriver, as the abortive, macabre completion of an insane goodwill mission to the Beothuk territory." Sir Winston turned to his grandson. "You remember the reproduction of the painting of Demasduit I showed you, Winston, that so strikingly displayed racial features similar to the photographs of your great-grandmother, Jennie Churchill?"

"I do indeed, Grandfather, and I readily perceived your mother's beautiful American Indian features, although I frankly confess I've never really seen the striking resemblance to Mary March that you see. But that must have been my defective eye in these matters, as you are the artist." He grinned and stood. "Regrettably, I must take my leave to keep an engagement."

"Well, I trust I've given you some good leads about my New-foundland experiences."

"You have indeed, Grandfather." He made an indulgent smile. "I hope to have the opportunity to resume this conversation over

Christmas. Meanwhile, do you mind if I have a short word with William here at the front door about that hydroelectric sod-turning. I won't bore you two with it."

I followed young Winston out of the room. Walking down the hall, he said, "Could you give me an address through which I can track you down in Canada in the months or years ahead? I was hoping to get a few substantial items here today for my ceremonial role in Labrador, but as you can see Grandfather's mind wanders a little and he seems more interested, somewhat obsessed in fact, with random bits and pieces about the Red Indians."

When I went back to our sitting room, Sir Winston said, "I trust I didn't let slip too much tantalizing detail about the Beothuk. Did he refer to it at all?"

"No, sir. He wanted to know how to reach me before his possible trip to Labrador."

"Good, good." And Churchill resumed where he had been interrupted by his grandson's departure. "During one of my visits to Botwood as myself, as prime minister, during the war, I spent time wandering along the shoreline and into the still familiar woods, against the advice of my security people scampering after me. They wondered why I'd want to hike up to a particular hummock and place my hands on a large boulder all but teetering there, with a depression, a kind of cave, under it. I couldn't tell them it was a sacred burial place positioned there by the good spirits. Instead, we talked about the amazing locations of huge rocks dropped by the retreating glaciers 10,000 years ago.

"While I was in Botwood, I ordered a small aircraft, a single-engine aeroplane, to fly me up the Exploits River, over the falls embedded in my head—settlers and explorers had named them Bishop's Falls and Grand Falls—and over the logging village of Badger and its two major tributaries of the Exploits I knew intimately in my mind, Badger River and Red Indian River—Eli and his family camped on them many times long before they had acquired white settlers' names—and on up the Exploits to the big lake, Red Indian Lake. Its contours differed somewhat now from the map of the body of water Shanawdithit drew from memory: the great newspaper proprietors, my good friends, the Harmsworths—although Harold, Viscount Rothermere, was a Nazi appeaser during the 1930s—had dammed the outflow of the Exploits River from the Lake in order to benefit their paper-making operation downstream in Grand Falls, thus raising the water level of the lake. Many of the shoreline areas I could envision, where my native family was born and lived, or where some of the atrocities on both sides took place, were covered over. The mining town of Buchans was now a major operation on the north side. I couldn't put down near the spot where Demasduit's heartbreak would be perpetrated because we were in a seaplane and the lake was still mostly frozen over. But just to see from the air the expanse of water, 40 miles long and the half-dozen islands and the inflowing brooks and rivers, and the outflowing brooks and the great river, were matters of extreme nostalgia for me, and a sense of a great tragedy from that life, and the deliverance it created for me in this life. But I must ready myself for all that. Tomorrow then?"

CHAPTER 22

When Anthony met me at Churchill's door the next morning, I said, "I don't recall reading any reference to his small aircraft flight up the Exploits River from Botwood. Do you?"

"I don't. Perhaps you should ask him."

Inside I did. And Sir Winston replied that the flight had taken place in the middle of the war, after all, and he supposed that it might have been classified, merely to keep the enemy from focusing in on the full range of his rash, mad, and reckless escapades. He hadn't written about it himself because it was related solely to our secret subject. "Speaking of which, let us now relive that crucial raid on John Peyton Jr.'s vessel.

"Obseewit was about 20 at this time, in 1818. Her older sister, Demasduit, had been married for a few years to Nonobawsut, the most eligible Beothuk in the land. With such a small population remaining, that was not necessarily saying a great deal, but, in fact, he was a superb specimen of manhood, tall, muscular, fast, intelligent. He would have been a credit to a population of any size.

His qualities made him chief of the Beothuk by general consensus. Shanawdithit also had a man she loved dearly, a member of one of the northern bands and known to be a great hunter and probably the fastest runner in the entire tribe. He had just begun to court her and was always finding reasons to visit her band. One day, crossing a swollen brook too swiftly, attempting to escape some white devils who were firing at him, he slipped on an icy rock and struck his head. He managed to drag himself into the underbrush, but being soaking wet, and the weather being frigid, he froze to death."

Sir Winston looked at Anthony and me in turn. I expected a watery-eyed reaction to his relating of the death of Shanawdithit's lover. But he was on another subject entirely now. "Obseewit was the closest, of all my ancestors, direct and collateral, to being absolutely my kindred spirit," he said. "It was she whose mind and heart I entered, channelled, now and later in her life. Unlike her sister, she had no romantic attachment and wasn't interested in forming one. During a day, after her friends had teased her about being too fussy and particular, she saw her mother, Odusweet, contemplating her closely. Then her mother said to her in private, 'You and Demasduit look so much alike, you could be twins, but in fact you couldn't be more different in character. She is designed to be a wife and mother and very womanly doing womanly things. You are not designed for that. You are a warrior. Your father had an aunt like you. One day she looked out from behind some trees on the bank of the river and saw a group of white devils on the other side. One of them she recognized from the year before; he had fired his gun at her and wounded her in the leg. Now she stepped out from behind the trees and shot an arrow toward him over the water, high into the afternoon sun. He looked across the river at that moment and saw her and her bow, just in time to receive her arrow in the centre of his chest. Falling, his eyes met hers, and he was dead soon after his comrades saw him hit the ground. When the rest of the band praised her magnificent marksmanship, she credited the destiny spirit for leading the arrow so accurately to its mark. It had to be the spirit, she said. What other power could have made him lock his eyes on hers at the precise moment he realized that her vengeance was accomplished?' Obseewit's mother told her to keep following her own path, like that aunt: 'Your father would have been proud of your courage and your intelligence.'

"But one of the paths Obseewit followed, that her father would not have been proud of, was the organizing of raids on the settlers, for revenge and for booty. She and her mates especially prized the plunder of metal objects that they could then refashion into their own tools and weapons. Their raids entailed the robbing and often the destruction of vessels and storage premises.

"Obseewit was called upon from teenage years to help band members arrange and execute those raids. They believed she exercised creativity in organization and overcoming obstacles, and was able to explain clearly the strategies and roles she envisioned. The trophy she set her sights on now was that vessel belonging to John Peyton Jr., a successful furrier and salmon fisherman near the mouth of the Exploits River. His father, John Peyton the elder, was well known among the whites, admired by some, deplored by others, as an unrelenting Red Indian harrier and killer. John Peyton the son, on the other hand, was known for his broadminded views on the Beothuk, advocating leniency and understanding and communication toward them in their existential plight. But even if she and the other Beothuk had known of Peyton Jr.'s sympathy with them, they were not of a mind to seek out degrees of compassion and kindheartedness among the white devils. To a man, the devils were taking over their lands, rivers, and coves, and blocking access to their salmon, seals, and birds, and bringing starvation upon them. In the Beothuk mind, the whole modus operandi of the whites as a people was governed by one protocol, which was, in reality, practiced by only a few: shoot the redskins on sight; or, as some American frontiersmen would say, the only good Indian is a dead Indian.

"This latest raid was an incursion of opportunity. In the fall of 1818, Demasduit stayed back at Red Indian Lake, happily pregnant after four or five years of trying, with her first baby. Obseewit left home-quarters with Demasduit's husband, Nonobawsut, and her niece, Shanawdithit, and a few other men, to head downriver. At the Bay of Exploits, they sneaked out on a little peninsula at Lower Sandy Point to spy on the operations of the settlers and concoct a plan of despoliation. They were in desperate straits. The climate at the time has been described as the Little Ice Age, which lasted until the middle of the 1800s. But, added to that, just two years before this raid, there was no summer at all. In fact, that's what it was called in eastern North America and western Europe—the year without a summer, caused by a massive volcanic eruption in the Dutch East Indies. As a result, the Beothuk were suffering dreadfully from an acute shortage of food; indeed, they were starving.

"In their surveillance, they spotted John Peyton Jr.'s vessel tied up at his wharf as it was being loaded with his goods and products. For many hours they surveyed the activity undetected, sometimes from high trees behind his house. Finally, the vessel was full and looked ready to depart. Obseewit worried that they only had that night for the raid, as the men were acting as if she would very likely leave the next morning. They had stopped working but they and Peyton stayed and kept watch on the wharf during the first part of the night. Peyton reported afterwards that he was fearful of just such a raid as the Beothuk were planning. But after hours of quiet, he told his men to go to bed and get some sleep in readiness for the departure; he'd stand guard himself till dawn.

"The night remained black and still. No unfamiliar sound was heard and there'd been no sign of Red Indians in the area, so Peyton felt safe in leaving the wharf for a few minutes and going into his house nearby for a cup of tea. While he was away from the vessel, Obseewit was chosen to lead the start of the operation; she was noted for her vision at night and her excellent timing in evading notice. She led the band out of the woods and crept to their canoe on the shore. They paddled silently to the wharf in the dark, and hid under it. When Peyton came back and stood on the wharf again, Shanawdithit, Nonobawsut, and Obseewit were so close to him that they could have reached out and touched him. But he suspected nothing.

"As soon as Peyton strolled off the wharf again for a short spell, Nonobawsut cut the mooring lines and set the vessel adrift. The entrepreneur, so savvy and alert to guard his property against this very eventuality, came back after a few minutes, to discover that, right under his nose, his vessel and cargo had utterly vanished into the dark fathomless night.

"It was the next day before he discovered his vessel. She had drifted some 12 or 15 miles from Lower Sandy Point past Phillips Head and Point of Bay, between Indian Cove and Thwart Island, and past Sunday Island to nearby Charles Brook, where she ended her meandering upon the rocks. Having followed the vessel in their canoe by her sounds in the dark, the Beothuk saw where she rested in the dawning light, and they pillaged and plundered and ransacked, and left the craft destroyed. Contrary to their custom, this time they didn't burn the boat for its nails, for fear of attracting notice. But they carried off what they could, hiding their canoe as they went, and ran upcountry along their once-secret trails in a state of jubilation over their success. They stopped long enough to break against rocks the rifles they'd purloined, and threw the pieces into brooks where they'd be seen by pursuing or roving whites. Thus did they advertise yet again to the white devils their own lack of firearms and their vulnerability to their mortal enemies.

"Many neighbours bombarded John Peyton the younger was with one question: Did he not now see at last what came of treating the redskins too well? They all urged him, spurred on by his father, to take a gang of well-armed men upriver and recover some of his heavy losses of treasured personal property and valuable salmon. And no one could expect them to be too particular in the circumstances about the cost to life and limb of the thieving Indians. But, to the bewilderment and disgust of Peyton the elder, his otherwise clever and resourceful son simply would not do it. 'Those Indians,' he said, 'wherever they were hiding—under the wharf, in canoe, behind my house—could easily have killed me any time they wanted, and they didn't.' He was right: they had debated murdering him, and if he'd been his father, they would have killed him. But no one among them had any stories of brutality involving Peyton Jr. requiring revenge.

"Instead of direct action, which family and friends pressed on him against the heathen marauders, John Peyton Jr. sailed to the capital, St. John's, and sought out the governor of the Colony of Newfoundland, Vice-Admiral Charles Hamilton. His Excellency, having been briefed on young Peyton's nonviolent stance toward the Red Indian, consented to meet with him at once. In the governor's office, Peyton emphasized his constant attitude of tolerance toward the Beothuk. He itemized his losses from their raids and sneak thievery over the years, which till now he had been prepared to stomach as part of the cost of running a business out on the frontier. But this latest incident of Red Indian rampage had been too damaging altogether, and he asked for executive permission to journey upriver into their territory and recover, harmoniously and without violence, some of his purloined possessions.

"Governor Hamilton was greatly impressed by John Peyton Jr.'s moderation, and he gave him his authorization to retrieve by peaceful means the stolen goods. Meanwhile, the fortuitous visit brought into the light of day another notion, stemming from a long-standing policy of the colonial office, which was gestating in what His Excellency was pleased to call his mind: this younger Peyton, having been brought over from England by his father just a few years before, was much better educated and cultured than the generality of ruffians the governor was accustomed to receive as petitioners in his office or to meet on his cruises to settlements along the coast, and he appeared to be the very man for this proper Christian task.

"The governor thereupon suggested that while John Peyton Jr. was in Red Indian territory, he ought to avail himself of the opportunity to establish good relations with the Beothuk by capturing one or more of them to bring back to civilization with him. Once here, such Red Indian guest or guests would be Christianized and fittingly impressed by English culture as manifested by the better classes of St. John's society. Then each such captured Beothuk, now enlightened, would be loaded down with gifts and sent back to the tribe as a goodwill emissary. There they would assure their heathen fellow-tribesmen of the kindly and benevolent intent of the upper reaches of humanity, the Anglo-Saxon Christian. In that way would lines of communications be initiated between the white man's greatest empire in history and the poor, benighted inhabitants who cowered and whimpered in the wilderness. By assuming this task, Mr. Peyton would be doing an immeasurable service in the eyes of the finest elements of the human race.

"Peyton was dubious about the governor's proposal. The Beothuk were not known, he said, to take kindly to any personal contact with settlers, let alone capture by them. One needed only recall the reaction of the Indians to the gift-giving expedition of Lieutenant Buchan, just a few years back, which had ended in the murder and beheading of two of his crew. The governor acknowledged all that and the difficulty and danger Peyton would face, which is why, His Excellency stated, he wished to offer him much more on top of simple permission to recover some of his stolen items. As a reward for his exertions and altruism, Peyton's friendly capture of just one Red Indian, male or female, to be brought back to St. John's, would forthwith earn him from the treasury the more than goodly sum of £100.

"That sum of money, back in the early 1800s, possessed the purchasing power of many thousands of pounds in today's currency, and the enlightened but entrepreneurial Peyton the younger was straightaway persuaded. He undertook the mission and sailed home to the Bay of Exploits to recruit some experienced men to accompany him upriver. Thus was the stage set for incalculable consequences, narrow and broad, evil and good, for that century and the next."

"Does it surprise you, Sir Winston," I asked, "that no one, not the governor, nor his advisers, nor politicians, local or imperial, seemed to realize how stupid that notion was: The white devils were to capture a Beothuk, take a Beothuk by force, to establish good relations with the Beothuk?"

"No one who has excavated and ransacked the archives of the colonial office, as I have done," said Sir Winston, "would be surprised in the least by any fresh instances of official idiocy or lunacy. At home or abroad."

"Or out-and-out greed and avarice," I said. "Even the doubts of the better Peyton were easily overcome by the reward dangled before his eyes. And, on top of that, it's as if we, the English, considered all the inhabitants of the lands we subjugated, not to be human beings with lives of worth like our own, but brute creatures to be killed, enslaved, exploited, or in the most benevolent cases, tamed with bribes of trinkets and baubles and scripture as we improved their way of life by destroying their culture and—"

"Quite." Churchill interrupted my lecture with a truculent bark, just when I was about to conclude with a clever remark. "I don't believe you are breaking new philosophical ground there, my good man. Yet I freely confess that I, in common with many of the best sort here on this sceptred isle, have always had a strong bent toward, with some individual exceptions, the general superiority of the white races. And when one considers the brilliance of what we have accomplished, admittedly for good and for bad, in war and in peace, on these British Isles, and in America, Australia, and your Canada, and in the better parts of Europe, it's difficult to throw off the judgment that we Caucasians have won history's Darwinian sweepstakes. But that nowise implies that those perceived to belong to lesser races, as the Nazis falsely and erroneously considered the Jews, ought to be persecuted or exterminated. For, with our own good fortune, of course, comes Rudyard Kipling's white man's burden, the noble wish, and splendid acts, to uplift people of colour. I inaugurated Kipling's memorial two or three years before the war. Best speech, some said, I ever made."

"Yes, well," I said, "we'll simply have to agree to disagree on your point about white superiority." That caused Churchill to smile indulgently, allowing me to emit the line I wanted to earlier. "But on the governor's idea for the capture of a Beothuk, it reminds me of the journalist who recently wrote that an American military adviser in Vietnam justified an attack on a village there with the statement, 'We had to destroy that village, to save it.'"

Both Sir Winston and Anthony winced and chuckled scornfully. "I grasp your point like a nettle," said Churchill, "and it's as well to remember that while some journalists are tempted to paint glib and facile critical parodies of military action from their safe rooms—God only knows I've been on both sides of that situation—it is somewhat more difficult to take sane and rational decisions while under direct deadly fire from the enemy, which both Anthony and I have been subjected to. But I do think we can agree on the senseless folly of Peyton's goodwill mission to capture a Beothuk, even if it was the remote fallout from that mission that made me the man ... we'll come to that.

"Here's how I conceive of his expedition from the various reports and the memories of events in my own mind. Early in March 1819, John Peyton Jr. left Sandy Cove at the mouth of the Exploits to travel upriver, full of good intentions and the milk of human kindness, to meet with the Red Indians. He was accompanied by nine other trappers and furriers of varying experience, including his father, John Peyton Sr., the famous Indian killer. I don't recall that William Cull was among them; he'd told Peyton the younger and anyone else who would listen that he was fed up with expeditions to the Indians. In his experience, they led only to vexation and trouble, if not outright disaster. Everyone knew he was thinking about the dreadful Buchans expedition he'd guided, and the two headless sailors on the ice.

"To his friends Mr. and Mrs. Slade of Twillingate, he said that, if he thought Eli was still alive he'd agree to travel up in a trice, but he'd heard the rumours of Eli's death and believed them. And there'd been no sign of Eli on his earlier ill-fated trek up. Much later, Mr. Slade would tell Cull that if he'd been in charge of the Peyton expedition, he could have prevented the tragedy that occurred. But Cull replied that nothing could have prevented that tragedy: the whole idea was preposterous from start to finish and was bound to end in ghastly misadventure.

"Peyton's squad did include a member of the merchant Slade family. He was a nephew of Eli Easter's old mentor, and an acquaintance of Eli's when he'd lived in Twillingate. His aunt, Mrs. Slade, had encouraged him to go and keep an eye out for Eli up there just in case. It was out of deference for the feelings of Mrs. Slade, and pure curiosity, that young Slade agreed to join the tour.

"On departure, Peyton Jr informed his gang that the purpose of their trip upriver was to earn a share each of the prize of £100 from the governor by catching a Beothuk or two. The idea of that was to use the captives to make friends between the whites and the tribe. They would also aim, of course, with the approval obtained from the governor himself, to recover items the Indians had stolen from Peyton's vessel. But, Peyton decreed, in neither of these objectives, was there to be any violence involved. Then he outfitted each member of his team of pacifists with a musket, a hatchet, and a bayonet. As young Slade would write later, some also carried pistols; Peyton Jr. himself, the man of moderation, sported two pistols, plus a double-barrelled rifle and an enormous dagger.

"As they trudged far upriver, they came across some abandoned mamateeks on the banks, and recently used firepits and storehouses. In the structures, they found a variety of traps and a jib sail from Peyton's wrecked vessel. These discoveries gratified the men, and caused old Peyton to amuse the others by muttering over each and every item, 'See this? What'd I tell ye?' as if everyone else had been arguing all along that the Red Indians had *not* stolen them.

"Fired up now, the Peytons, father and son, turned off from the Exploits River and led their men with alacrity through woods, bogs, and brooks, cutting straight across to the north side of Red Indian Lake. Their clear sense of direction made their crew marvel at how familiar they were with this very heartland of Beothuk country. The entire trip up from the ocean, on the rough and irregular river ice and over the rugged terrain, to the great lake of the Beothuk, 70 or 80 miles of hard grinding slog, toting and hauling provisions, took the men only five days.

"And there wasn't a single straggler. They were remarkable men of strength and stamina, these Englishmen. They were of the same period, and from the same mould of manhood as the army of Wellington that defeated Napoleon—an immensely sturdy, bloodthirsty, and determined race in the face of incredible hardships. The Duke of Wellington himself described them in awe: 'Our army is composed of the scum of the earth—the mere scum of the earth.' And the day before the Battle of Waterloo, he inspected his troops and declared, 'I don't know what effect these men will have upon the enemy, but by God, they frighten me.' So manned, there's little wonder that England was able to occupy much of the primitive world, beginning with the New Founde Lande, and establishing, against cruel competition, the greatest empire known to mankind.

"Leading them cross-country in Newfoundland that March day in 1819, young Peyton would report later, he again stressed to his men that they were going to commence amicable dealings and exchanges with the Indians, and he ordered his team once more not to resort to violence. Only if the Beothuk themselves chose to persist stubbornly and uncooperatively in opposing his friendly invitation to some of them to come back with him, would he then be forced actually to resort to capture.

"Having sighted the big frozen lake, the Englishmen were sneaking and creeping toward the northeastern arm in order to surprise an Indian campsite of three mamateeks standing there, when a caribou dashed by. The witless ones in Peyton's team, which evidently comprised a goodly number of the nine, instantly upped rifles and shot at the animal, filling the still air with loud retorts and echoes. Young Slade wrote in an article afterwards that straight away the lake ice swarmed with Beothuk. There were, he said, at least several hundred of them. But I can avow that the number of men, women, and children present did not reach two dozen. One of our last Beothuk, Shanawdithit, would tell her questioner, William Eppes Cormack, a few years later, that, at the time of this raid of Peyton's, the entire Beothuk population throughout Newfoundland consisted of 31 people.

"Upon hearing the approach of the white men, the band ran away through the snow. They all would have readily escaped into the forest, but Demasduit had recently become a mother and was weak and ill, and she was carrying her nursing baby. She passed the baby to her husband, Nonobawsut, and tried to flee like everyone else, but she could only make slow, laborious progress in the deep snow. John Peyton Jr. chased her relentlessly for 200 or 300 yards, like the cunning wolf whose rapt attention is focused on the weakest quarry, and he caught up with her. She dropped exhausted to her knees and begged for mercy. That availed her nothing and Peyton seized her by the arm. She opened her caribou fur garment to show him the breasts of a nursing mother. Peyton responded by pulling out his handkerchief and binding her wrists. Yanking her to her feet, he started to drag her back to his pack of men.

"When Peyton Jr. told his story of this episode to a grand jury later, he did mention that Demasduit had exposed her breasts to him, but he failed to mention, or he glossed over, that she was a nursing mother and had been carrying a baby in her arms. One of the other white men on this expedition of reconciliation, a John Day, would report that the Indian woman, Demasduit, had looked very ill as she tried to escape with a baby in her arms from the doggedly pursuing Peyton Jr. But Peyton himself did not relate to the grand jury that the woman was visibly ill. No doubt, he wished to avoid being characterized as a jackal or hyena who had unerringly zeroed in on the most vulnerable and helpless of his prospective prey. This heroic capture, he was doubtless thinking, would bring in an easy hundred quid.

"None of the Beothuk knew what to do in these circumstances—a white devil holding a nursing mother captive, forcibly keeping her from her nearby baby. Who among humanity, good or evil, would do such a thing? Nonobawsut had the baby in his arms, and he held him high in the air now so that the whites could see him clearly. He waved the child back and forth and shouted that it needed its nursing mother. Demasduit was crying and struggling to release herself and straining to reach her baby, but Peyton Jr. paid no attention to that. He kept moving toward his men, pulling her along with him. As unbelievable as it seemed, it was becoming clear to the Beothuk that they were actually taking Demasduit with them without her baby. The white men walked as a gang toward the mamateeks, dragging her along. That enraged Nonobawsut. He and his tribesmen all knew the stories of atrocious abuse of captured women and girls by vile men like Thomas Taylor, Henry Miller, and others. One of them, William Richmond, had the temerity to report to a chronicler, Pulling, concerning an attack in 1790, 'The woman I catched was a young good-looking woman ... We came back to the wigwams and brought two women with us ... We stayed all night in one of the wigwams ...' Nonobawsut was having nightmarish visions now of the mistreatment of his beloved woman, Demasduit, by these brutal men.

"The Beothuk had archers who were skilful enough, despite Peyton's attempt to shield his own body behind the woman's, to shoot him dead with arrows. Obseewit and some men wanted to free Demasduit in that way and fitted arrows to their bows, but Nonobawsut forbade, with shouts, their use. That would only bring a fusillade of gunfire, he said, and many, if not all of the band, would be shot and killed. Demasduit herself would be gunned down when she tried to run away. Beothuk were all familiar with the white devils' proficiency in shooting women and children in the back as they ran.

"Nonobawsut passed the baby to Obseewit, and lay his own bow down in the snow. Then he picked up a small spruce branch protruding from a shallow drift. He would go in peace to the white men, he said, and reason with them. He would make them see clearly with signs and gestures that they were taking away his wife, the mother of their infant child, who would surely die without his mother's milk. No human beings, no matter how wicked and devil-like, were capable of doing that. He walked toward Peyton, one hand open and empty at shoulder height, the other bearing the spruce branch of peace and friendship before him. Two other Beothuk men, one of them Nonobawsut's brother, also lay down their bows and walked close behind him till he reached unarmed the pack of nine strapping white men, all brandishing rifles, pistols, and daggers.

"Peyton Jr. would claim later that, as he held the woman, some eight threatening Beothuk men came toward him. But according to young Slade's later article, in fact only the three unarmed Beothuk men advanced toward them. And one of them, Nonobawsut, the husband of the captured woman, Demasduit, made no menacing gestures but, while holding his spruce branch, made a long speech to Peyton. At length, when his words availed him nothing, he became agitated, 'his eyes shooting fire.' But he calmed himself and went round and shook hands with all the white men, and tried to release Demasduit from Peyton Jr.'s grip.

"Peyton described him as a powerful giant of a man. Doubtless, this was the ever-present, ubiquitous Beothuk goliath who was reported to make his appearance at every encounter between white trappers and Red Indians, triggering by his aggressive presence the ensuing massacre of Indian men, women, and children. This current Beothuk behemoth, Peyton Jr. said, had a shiny new hatchet concealed under his clothes, which he ferociously menaced the young Peyton with, and would have killed him, had not Peyton's crew reached him just in the nick of time, and disarmed him.

"When the Beothuk giant, Nonobawsut, then tried to grab hold of Peyton Jr., the young Peyton said he shook him off, which was quite a feat considering that the Beothuk was a colossal, enraged husband,

and Peyton was encumbered by a frantic woman battling to escape his clutches. Then the Beothuk man tried to seize a gun from some of the white men, said Peyton Jr., including from Peyton's father—a rather mysterious action, since the Beothuk abhorred firearms, had absolutely no use for them, and had no idea how to operate them.

"Thwarted at that, the Beothuk man reached out his hand for Demasduit's arm. She struggled against young Peyton's hold on her wrists, but he would not let her go. Peyton's men crowded around, forcing Nonobawsut away from him, and one or two helped Peyton restrain her. Nonobawsut stood as close as the men would let him directly in front of Peyton and curbed any violent action by his much-agitated brother and the friend who were with him. Again he spoke at length, initially in gentle but firm tones, insisting that the white man free his wife to him. Peyton spoke back, insisting equally firmly that he would not let Demasduit go. Neither man understood the words of the other, but it was clear from their gestures what they meant. Peyton indicated that he was going to take her downriver, and he made signs that her husband should come, too: 'Be a reasonable fellow, my good man, and join us.' Throughout, Demasduit never stopped struggling to escape, and kept screeching that she wanted to go back to her baby, she needed to get her baby. He would starve without his mother's milk."

"Some other Beothuk men started to approach to help Nonobawsut, which caused the white men to raise their rifles. The chief told his tribesmen to stop: the white devils would only kill them with their guns. But Nonobawsut's orations having accomplished nothing, as he spoke to Peyton, now, he himself was becoming angry and desperate.

He raised his voice until he was shouting and he made threatening motions with his hands. Over Obseewit's distance of 15 or 20 yards from him, his eyes were beginning again clearly to flash furious wrath. She saw him become more and more brusque in his dealings with Peyton and some of the other men. He grabbed a white man in front of Peyton and threw him bodily several feet away, forcing his comrades to scramble aside with anxious faces at Nonobawsut's great strength. He seized one or two others and became involved in wrestling tussles with them. He punched one man in the chest, causing him to aim his rifle at him, but the man backed away without firing.

"A couple of young Peyton's more experienced men suggested, according to reports, that he free the woman, since it appeared that her big man's escalating stubbornness might lead to the bloodshed strictly prohibited by the governor. But nothing could prevail upon Peyton Jr., supported by his father, to let Demasduit go. There was no way he was going to waste all the time and effort and expense they'd spent on this project and terminate it without obtaining the huge financial reward offered by the governor for a captured Red Indian.

"And nothing could prevail upon Nonobawsut to leave without Demasduit. As his shouted threats and scuffles with the whites continued, they raised their rifles and aimed at him. Beothuk men and women called out that he should retreat. Otherwise, the white devils would end by killing him. Nonobawsut shouted back that there was nothing else for him to do but free his wife. He was not going to abandon her to them at any cost, even if he faced death. He would free Demasduit or he would die in the attempt—there was no action for him to take between those two positions.

"The altercations between him and the white men continued to build in intensity, and after the hatchet under his garments had been discovered and seized, the white raiders became more and more distressed and panicky, shouting and waving their guns about. Nonobawsut was now working his way toward John Peyton Sr., who, all knew, was the biggest Beothuk hater and murderer among the entire population of white devils in Newfoundland. The inclusion of such a peculiar person in an expedition to establish reconciliation and understanding between Indian and settlers might give you an idea once again of how dim-witted the English settlers were regarding these excursions upriver, or how hypocritical or hidden their agenda.

"When Obseewit saw Nonobawsut grabbing John Peyton Sr. by the neck, this man who had brained her father with a bear trap, her heart leapt into her throat through mingled fear and hope of revenge. He shouted into old Peyton's face that he was a murderer of pregnant Beothuk women and small children. Accounts reported that the elder Peyton bawled out, 'Will no one save me from this scurvy savage?' The sanitized rendition of the John Day chap was that he shouted, 'Are you going to stand by and let the Indian kill me?' A young white lout, characterized by Peyton Jr. later as one of the stupidest and least experienced of his team, raised his bayonet and stepped valiantly forward ...'"

Sir Winston stopped speaking. I looked up from my notes and saw that he was weeping. Anthony didn't move and met my glance impassively, but I couldn't help stirring. "Pay no attention to me," murmured the old man. "I am prone to blubber like a baby during moments of emotion. Always have done. We shall discontinue for today. And tomorrow will be our last day. All of what I've told you thus far is prologue to the crux of my narrative, the essence and soul of my story, the reason I asked you here. It's not long, but I need to recover overnight to prepare myself."

The next morning, before I could leave my B and B for Churchill's house, Anthony telephoned. "Sir Winston is knackered and drained this morning," he said. "I think it's the emotional effect of reliving, if that's the right word, this narrative of his. Anyhow, he cannot continue with it today. Amuse yourself for a few hours, William, and we'll continue tomorrow morning." I felt disappointed. But the thought that we'd finish tomorrow did allow me a pleasant day of wandering about London.

In the morning Anthony called again. "Lord Moran says he's not at all well. He should not be agitated for fear of a heart attack or a stroke. He needs a few days of solid rest, no visitors. Then he should be well enough for you to see him again. But this is just as we feared from the start. In that few days, we'll be into the Christmas and New Year's mayhem with family and close friends. This project of yours and his will be shut out. My advice is for you to take sabbatical leave from it till early in January. In the meantime, we'll stay in touch."

I was flabbergasted—after coming so far with it! "What if he dies?" I blurted. "This will all be for naught. His entire object and purpose will be lost."

"He tells me he's not going to die before this is finished and that we have until January 24, the day his father died. That should give us time. Tell William it'll be done, he said, it's a matter of our destiny, his and mine."

"I don't put much stock in the destiny thing. It's an intellectually dishonest attitude for a couple of agnostics to hold, equally for him the doer of prodigious deeds, as for me the mere teller of his story."

"Well, I doubt that his brain's logic can overcome the destiny he feels in his gut, any more than your brain could defeat your heart's desire when I was struggling rationally to persuade you to forgo your Alpine rendezvous. I'll be in touch."

CHAPTER 23

I'd never felt as anxious and full of tension over anything in my life before as I did now over our interrupted project. I believed that, most likely, I would never hear its finish. But there was no remedy except to wait, and I idly knocked about for a few days in a London crowded and ebullient with Christmas shoppers, before travelling up alone to a mostly deserted Oxford. I had to prepare for spending Christmas week at a friend's home in Manchester. He'd invited me earlier, to correspond with my intended return from Austria. There was a note in my mailbox saying how much he and his family were looking forward to my visit. Still, if there'd been any hope at all of my seeing Sir Winston during that time, I would have cancelled. That bare hope forced me to telephone Anthony. There was no improvement in Sir Winston's condition, he said. It was still not good, but his prognosis gave every hope of our getting together again in January. He'd call me. Anthony's tone lacked conviction. I boarded a train north, despondent among the Christmas home-goers.

When I got back after New Year's Day, I checked into the Mitre Hotel for a night and went to my box at Brasenose. No phone messages awaited, but there was a note from Neil Murray. He was staying at the flat of a friend until the colleges reopened for Hilary term. I was to come over for a coffee. I went with alacrity to hear about the Austrian nights.

Off the slopes, Neil told me, he'd spent most of his hours at the hotel of one of the girls whom he and I'd met earlier. Her friend, he said, the one who'd originally enticed me into the ski trip—Emma—was very disappointed, not to say vexed, that I'd dropped out. But she did seem determined to assuage her woe at après-ski partying. He could confirm my earlier expectation that I would've enjoyed a delightfully good time in Emma's company. How'd my visit to Sir Winston go?

"Probably entirely futile. I'll let you know when I hear back from them. Did you get a chance to talk to Claire?"

"Once. Whenever I saw her on the train or spotted her at the hotel in Zurs, she was with her female friends, drinking wine. I saw her on the slopes a lot, but she didn't seem to spend any time carousing or frequenting the sites of merriment. The one time I did have a short chat with her at the breakfast buffet, she told me she hoped I didn't miss Will on this trip as much as she did."

"Yeah? What she really missed," I said, "was having both Archer and me there so that she could play us off against each other."

"Well, judging by her forlorn tone," said Neil, "it was just as well that you didn't come: I fear you'd have been torn to pieces by the two competing maenads, the raving ones, ecstatic devotees of Dionysus, Claire and the other beauty, Emma, in an erotic frenzy over you."

"Jesus. Sounds pretty good to me, especially compared to my momentous abortive mission to London."

"Speaking of which, when I said, yes, I did miss you and I wish she hadn't inexplicably yanked you off the trip, she turned and walked away, but stopped and muttered back at me: 'Neil, the saviour of the bloody world made me do it.'" He dug into his pocket. "I got tickets for us yesterday to Bach's St. Matthew Passion."

A day later, I ran into one of Archer's friends picking up mail at Brasenose. He said, "Well, our mate's rise in the political world is well under way. Good lord, Sir Winston Churchill himself!"

"You mean the 90th birthday celebration?"

"Apparently Churchill laid the hands on him in front of the Tory grandees and predicted a magnificent political future for our Mr. Archer."

"Yes, I understand Sir Winston was very impressed by Jeffrey."

"No surprise there."

For the second time in two days, I felt bereft and left behind: earlier by Neil's account of the trip I'd been deceitfully deprived of, and most likely for no purpose, now, and just then by the friend's awestruck report of Archer's advancement.

I went to the porter's lodge to see if Anthony had called—I had a few words ready for him—but he hadn't. There was a message from Jeffrey: "If possible, drop in on me today before 8 p.m."

He opened the door to his flat with delight. "Super ... you got it," he said. His suitcase was near the door. "I didn't know where to reach you. You're as elusive as the Scarlet Pimpernel." He looked at his watch. "Yes, there's time. Have a cognac. I'm leaving Oxford in a few minutes on business for a full fortnight. Where are you staying before term starts?"

"A nondescript bed and breakfast."

"Can you stay here at my flat while I'm gone, until you move back into your college digs?"

"I can. That's very kind of you." We sat down with our drinks. "I've heard some great reports on your attendance at Sir Winston's 90th."

"That's good news, because among other things, I'm meeting with some party organizers during the next few days. They want to feel me out on constituency possibilities." I felt strange because Claire wasn't there. Every other time, she'd been present. Jeffrey got up and went to his desk. "You won't be disturbed. No one else has a key." He passed me a fob with key attached. "This was Claire's."

"Aren't you two getting back together?"

"No. We're finished for good. And she agreed with me that we couldn't go on. She seemed to think I was being ungrateful over some big favour she did for me with Churchill. I told her you were responsible for that. Her parting shot was that she wished she'd known I thought more of you than I did of her." Jeffrey grinned and stood up. "I didn't argue the point." He put out a hand to shake and grabbed my shoulder with the other. "I'll see you when I get back. I want to hear all about your visit to the great man. And I have some promising ideas about opportunities in Canada."

Next term, during his irregular visits to hall for dinner, Jeffrey usually sat next to me, and a few times he dropped in at my digs or invited me over for coffee in his flat. Our chats still brought out some entertaining and insightful views but they were growing less enchanting. I could see that he was as dissatisfied with my reactions to most of his entrepreneurial ideas as I was tepid to the ideas themselves. Once I stated outright that I thought I was too risk-averse for him. He put up no strenuous argument. Gradually we spent less and less time together. I'd see him around, inside and outside of the college, and we'd wave or exchange a word of greeting, but both of us always seemed to be urgently required for something somewhere else.

By springtime, I sometimes saw him with another lovely woman. I met them together in the audience at a debate at the Oxford Union, and Jeffrey introduced her to me: Mary Weeden, a science student at St. Anne's College. He described me as his close friend. That made me realize that for a short while last fall, he was my good friend and, despite the scuttlebutt perpetually swirling around him, I always considered him a good man. But, really, I told myself, we were like chalk and cheese. And I wasn't fond of the twinge of guilt that sometimes rose up when I saw him.

Shortly after I finished at Oxford and went back to Canada, I received an invitation to the wedding of Jeffrey Archer and Mary Weeden. I was too far away and too involved in starting a law practice at home to go.

We stayed in sporadic touch by short letters for a while and I would keep track for decades of Jeffrey's convoluted personal and career trajectory. It was hard to miss. He popped into the United Kingdom news, and, latterly, even the international news, a lot.

Not long after he went down from Oxford, still in his 20s, he'd be nominated to run for Parliament as a Tory. But the Conservative leader, Ted Heath, had misgivings over his fitness as a candidate because of allegations by the chairman of the organization he'd been fundraising for that there had been discrepancies in his expenses. Jeffrey sued the chairman for defamation. The action was settled out of court, and he got himself elected to the House of Commons.

A few years later, he wrote to tell me he was coming to Canada on an investment opportunity. He wasn't advising me to become involved, he said, as it entailed a fair amount of risk, but a lot of money might be made, and if I wished to look at it closer, I could meet him in Toronto. I would have flown up, if only to see him, but I'd already made family vacation plans. That was lucky because God only knew what I'd have been willingly caught up in once we started talking. Jeffrey became a victim of a fraudulent investment scheme by a Canadian company called Aquablast. He tried to reach me by phone at some point during that painful episode, but only once. We missed each other and he left a message that he'd called just to say hello while in Canada. There was no return telephone number.

His financial fiasco put him half a million pounds in debt; he had to step down as MP to try to stave off bankruptcy. For some reason, as part of his personal salvage operation, he decided to write a book. Against all odds, he found his niche. Incredibly, a novel of his jumped to number one on *The New York Times* bestsellers list. Then, book after book became bestsellers, and several were adapted for television. He would sell several hundred million copies of his books and become a multi-millionaire.

Next, Prime Minister Margaret Thatcher appointed him high in the structure of the Conservative Party, overriding the opposition of some party bigwigs. Within a year, an article in a London tabloid alleged that, through a middleman, he'd given a prostitute a considerable sum of money at a railway station. The newspaper claimed he'd furnished her with £2,000 to encourage her, for undisclosed reasons, to leave the country. The allegation forced Archer to ease out of his lofty Tory Party position.

Then a rival rag, not to be outdone, ran a piece stating that Archer had actually paid for sex with that *fille de joie*. He sued the journal and in court he claimed that his payment to the whore was an act of charity rather than that of a man bent on sin. In the witness box, his wife, undeterred by the smirks from some observers, backed his story, and the judge clearly fell in love with her. He extolled her many virtues to the jury and then asked them, incredulously, if the husband of such a woman was really in need of cold, unloving, rubber-insulated sex with a prostitute in a seedy hotel at 12:45 on a Tuesday morning after an evening with refined friends at a high-end, gourmet restaurant. The jury scrambled, as fast as they could, with scant regard to judicial dignity, to find in favour of Archer, and awarded him hundreds of thousands of pounds in damages.

Archer now kicked off a big charity-concert fundraiser on behalf of an oppressed middle-east minority, and brought on stage Paul Simon, Gloria Estefan, Rod Stewart, and Sting. Shortly thereafter, his friend, new prime minister John Major, had him elevated to the House of Lords. As he'd prophesied to Claire and me at Oxford, Claire's own sarcastic forecast of his rise to the peerage had actually come to pass.

Soon he was considering top-level municipal politics. Allegations came against him of profit-making of nearly £100,000 from insider trading. His lawyers brushed it off as the mere inadvertence of a busy life doing good. Thereupon, he sought the Tory nomination for mayor of London. Two former prime ministers and eight former cabinet ministers backed his candidacy. But an erstwhile friend now declared that Archer had asked him to provide a false alibi for the night he was with that exiled prostitute. Moreover, his personal assistant, also erstwhile, displayed her diary, showing that Archer had in fact dreamed up a false alibi for his successful libel suit against the newspaper.

During his resulting trial for perjury and perverting the course of justice, a former mistress of his entered the courtroom to testify that he and she had been engaged in an affair throughout the time of the libel trial. This was taken as undermining somewhat the earlier evidence of Archer and his wife, as highlighted by the libel case judge, that they'd been "exceedingly happily married" all during that period. A newspaper quoted his wife as stating that she did not consider sexual fidelity to be an important factor in a successful marriage, and that friendship and loyalty were more important qualities.

With an alacrity equal to the earlier jury's award of fabulous damages, this jury found Archer guilty as charged. And this judge sentenced him to four years in prison, while obliging him to pay back his £500,000 in damages from the newspaper, on top of all legal costs and hundreds of thousands of pounds in interest. In jail, Archer salved his financial wounds by writing bestselling memoirs on life in the clink.

After early release, he was able to assume his seat in the House of Lord, that august body possessing no procedure for kicking out a delinquent peer. But he had to fight off insinuations that millions were missing from his charitable fundraising accounts and deny allegations by an obscure African country that, in cahoots with the son of a former prime minister of Britain, he'd financed an attempted *coup d'état* against the government there.

One gossip columnist wrote that Archer's wife, who'd recovered from a bout with cancer, drew sympathetic chuckles at dinner parties whenever she murmured indulgently, "Jeffrey has a superb talent for the imprecise summation of facts" and "for inaccurate précis." To which one of Archer's many reported friends, replied to congenial laughter, "So *that's* what has sold his 300 million volumes of fiction." I was happy to read that Jeffrey had recovered from his own turn with cancer.

When I'd stayed at Jeffrey's flat before college reopened in January 1965, I often fantasized for a few seconds that Claire might come round to get something she'd left there. But, of course, that didn't happen; she was home in Beckenham, Kent, for the duration of the vac.

Soon after the new term started, though, I glimpsed her from afar in Oxford. She was coming out of Blackwell's Bookshop where I was also heading. I was weighed down with emotion during that fraught Churchillian January following my final visit to his house, and had no desire to add more, so I slowed my pace. But she spotted me and waved. I had to wave back and she started to walk fast toward me. I swivelled 90 degrees, and marched at double time away for five minutes. When I turned and walked back to the bookstore, there was no trace of her.

I found a note slipped under my door at Brasenose: "Greetings Will o' the Wisp, fancy going for a drink? I can explain everything." I don't know what would have happened if I'd been in my room when she came. Nothing, I trust, because by then I was seeing a charming student from Somerville College, who became my girlfriend. But I wouldn't have guaranteed it. However, I was bloody-minded enough at that moment to write a nasty response on her note under her offer to explain, and mail it back to her at LMH: "Here's a good title for your memoirs, gentle Claire: *It All Looks Really Shitty, I Know, But I Can Explain Everything.*"

I never heard from her again until Neil Murray told me he'd run into her going into a lecture on Samuel Taylor Coleridge. They had a little chat, and she asked if Jeffrey and I were still mates. When Neil said, not really, not like before, she murmured, "I certainly bollocksed everything up."

Neil misunderstood. "Yes, I've seen Archer gadding about with his new missus."

"No, no," she said, "I don't mean him. Our split was mutual. I mean with your friend, Will." She and Neil sat next to each other in the amphitheatre and at the end of the lecture, she folded and passed him a sheet she'd filled on both sides with her handwriting. Would he give it to me? "And please tell Will," she said, "that what the professor just quoted from Coleridge applies equally to him and me: 'Silence does not always mark wisdom.'"

My name written in her hand on the folded paper made my

heart leap with anticipation of amorous potential and then made my stomach lurch with experience-based revulsion. In two seconds, my vitals had traced the entire history of our affair. With all my organs back to neutral apathy, I opened the sheet and read.

Anthony Montague Brown had telephoned her out of the blue at LMH last November, a few hours before our last rendezvous in her room. He had located her through her father. Their conversation was longish, but the substance was this: Sir Winston Churchill was absolutely adamant that he meet with William Cull of Newfoundland for several specific days that happened to coincide with our skiing trip, on a narrative of great importance to international history. Otherwise, the information would die with Churchill, which event appeared likely to happen rather sooner than later. She'd asked Anthony why it had to be specifically then and why specifically me. He replied that Sir Winston had his good reasons and was resolutely insistent on both counts—it was that time or never and Cull or nobody; surely they all could, and must, indulge the greatest man of this century in his last days regarding this relatively minor inconvenience to William.

Anthony said he believed that William was determined to go on the trip only because of his "closeness and affection" regarding her and Archer, and that, as a consequence, he was about to make a serious mistake, indeed a misjudgment of great enormity. Will Cull had mentioned to Anthony her involvement in the trip arrangements, and it was imperative that she prevent me from going in order to make sure that the vital liaison with Sir Winston take place. She had to keep her actions absolutely confidential from everyone, including

Archer, and especially Cull: "Otherwise, our rather headstrong Mr. Cull would be sure to make a big fuss, and spoil everything, not fully realizing where his greater duty and interest lay."

So she did it. "After all, for heaven's sake, we were talking about you and Churchill making immortal history here, and this was his chief assistant making a special request of me. I really did feel that I was in the way of your best interests and his and, for all I knew, the world's. I sincerely hope that whatever the big, earth-shattering meeting between you and Churchill turned out to be about, it was bloody well worth it, because I've agonized every day over this ever since. I lost your friendship and respect, and I know my actions must have caused you and Archer to become alienated.

"In case you were wondering," she concluded, "about Archer's attendance at Churchill's 90th birthday party," Anthony had told her that, "entirely unrelated" to his request to her about me, and whether she helped him in that or not, he would endeavour to have her and Jeffrey invited. But she could not tell William any of this before I met with Churchill, he said, because it would be so prone to misunderstanding. "You must think that it stinks of bribery," Claire wrote in her note to me, "but I didn't take it as such, and it never motivated in the least my actions toward you. In fact, I didn't even go to the damned birthday party. But you can take solace from having done Archer a lot of good: he told me that he made contacts and budding friendships at the bash that were invaluable and would greatly further his advancement in politics. I do trust that there may have been some benefit to you as well in what I did. But, as for the hurt I may have caused you, please forgive me. And despite what

I may hope, I am not expecting you to respond to this in any way. Farewell my sweet William, with my love, Claire. PS. I'll be looking for your epoch-making narrative about Churchill, when it comes out."

I said to Neil with bravado, "Well, that was interesting, to exaggerate wildly." I extended the sheets to him. "Like to read it?"

"No thanks, she gave me the executive summary, and I have already divined, just talking to her, what she appears to want. My distinct impression is that her main regret in all this, in retrospect, was the breach in her relationship with you. I gathered that she would like to resume where you and she left off."

"Yeah? Hm. What would you do?"

"If I were you, I'd go back with her, because she's so beautiful and so smart. But if you're asking for my objective advice as a friend regarding your future best interests and peace of mind, I'd apply your earlier two-word line of basic English poetry: 'F her.' And for the very same reason: she's so beautiful and so smart."

For the rest of that day and night, I suffered something like Archer's *nostalgie de la boue* over a lunatic notion of what might have been. She hadn't mentioned in her note why she had welcomed me into her bed that afternoon, after she had already put her plan with Anthony in motion. But obviously, recalling her quote from the American boy, it was just a roll in the hay. At the time, I was part of the pathetic prevailing notion that a man couldn't be exploited purely for sex by a woman, could he? Only a woman could be deceitfully used by a man for lust, while any red-blooded man would take sex whenever and however it was on offer whatever the circumstances, and be damned grateful. I laughed to myself later that I'd been in on the dawning of the days of burgeoning sexual equality.

By the next day, I knew only that I was well out of it. But I felt impelled to write her a note to assuage the poor woman's guilt: "Claire, you did the right thing. Thank you and all the best for the future, William." But I didn't mail it to her. I couldn't make myself let her off the hook. It would stay in my correspondence file till the day I cleared stuff out to leave for home. Then I ripped it up and threw it in the wastebasket. She never got a reply from me to her note of explanation.

Claire would graduate, I'd hear from Neil, with a First in English Literature and a Blue in Lawn Tennis. This woman I thought I knew and whom I'd have sworn I'd been in love with—I wasn't even aware she played high-level competitive tennis.

Back in Canada, with hardly a thought to Claire, I would tranquilly practice law, get married, dabble in local politics, and write. I never inquired about her and I never heard of her for years. I would have only one spate of painful nostalgia early on when the presence of Edmund de Rothschild reminded me of those brief days of romantic turbulence in Oxford. My father, upon learning that de Rothschild was going to be in St. John's at the time of my wedding, had insisted on inviting him. A closer relationship had developed between them during the snail-like pace of the planning for the Churchill Falls hydro project. But, more important, my father said, Edmund never failed to ask about me whenever they met. Still, I was extremely surprised when he came to the reception, and I told him so.

There was no need to be, he said. He had already flown the Atlantic several hundred times (he'd make over 400 transatlantic flights before his death) in connection with de Rothschild-Canadian interests, including the British Newfoundland Development Corporation. Gander International Airport was his second home, he laughed, and he was highly pleased that I had arranged for my wedding to coincide with one of his refuelling stops there.

He gave me a pictorial book called *The Churchill Years, 1874–1965* and said that Anthony Montague Browne often mentioned how enthralled Sir Winston had been before his final stroke that he and I had managed to complete our sneaky little hush-hush project. Anthony had asked Edmund to give me his regards and to tell me that there was one event on the day of Sir Winston's funeral that, as agonizing as it had been to Anthony, the great man and I would have enjoyed immensely: Anthony had returned home from St. Paul's Cathedral to discover that his house had been burglarized. Everything of value had been stolen. But a prized painting by Churchill had been left unmolested and in place, as obviously worthless. Anthony said he could hear Sir Winston from his coffin on the train to Woodstock, laughing.

About Anthony Montague Browne I would read scattered references after our last meeting and Churchill's death in January 1965, including the publication of his memoirs in the mid-1990s, and his knighthood around the turn of the century. But there was one other later event, a discovery that Churchill would have enjoyed as well. The great man had hinted broadly at our meetings in December 1964, that Anthony had had a fling with one of Sir Winston's personal secretaries, Jane Portal, before her precipitous marriage to Gavin Welby and that their son Justin Welby, born eight months later, was in fact Anthony's progeny. Fifty years later, in 2016, after Anthony had died and I started writing this book, DNA tests would prove that Anthony was indeed the biological father of Justin Welby. Sir Winston would have roared with laughter at the scientific confirmation of his own earlier suspicion, and especially at the fact that the merry-begot boy had become by then the Archbishop of Canterbury.

In this new century, a man I knew a little from Oxford, but who'd been a good student pal of Neil Murray's there, tracked me down at my law firm and emailed me a publicity blurb about a book he'd written. He would have contacted Neil, he said, but, like everyone else who knew him, he'd been terribly shocked by Neil's death in his 40s from a catastrophic asthma attack. He'd approached me now because Claire Perceval, whom he saw at literary symposiums now and then, had reminded him of my existence in Canada, and she thought I might be someone to help gain attention for his book there. He added that she sent me her fond regards.

I emailed him back to ask what and how Claire was doing these days. He replied that she'd been married for decades to the boyfriend she'd had before Archer came on the scene, a brilliant graduate in Honours Classics—"Greats," the course was called—and they'd both gone on to receive their PhDs from Harvard. Claire had written several well-received books of literary criticism. They'd been offered positions at Oxford and Cambridge and numerous other universities in the UK and in the US, but she'd decided on the red brick University of Bristol, and she'd refused for years to stir from it. "Mind you," wrote the friend, "it's a highly ranked, rather elitist, university. Winston Churchill was chancellor there."

After I asked him to send my best wishes to Claire, she emailed me herself to say, "Hello to my sweet William, from a guardian of the legacy of your old mate, Sir Winston. He was chancellor at my university for 36 years, from 1929, when as a has-been politician, he was unexpectedly installed, until his death early in 1965, mere weeks after I singlehandedly arranged for you to visit him and make history. You're welcome, by the way!! I was happy to be a mere tool of his destiny and yours. But where's your book, William? I've googled you a few times and noticed that you have published some novels and political tomes, but nary a one on him. Hurry up. I want to see if my martyrdom was worth the candle. Anyhow, add to Churchill's presence here the facts that John Cabot set sail from Bristol in 1497 to discover Newfoundland, and that John Guy, a merchant of Bristol, started the first English settlement in Canada at Cupids, Newfoundland, in 1610, and I trust you will have your answer to the question, why does she love Bristol so? As, I am sure, I would have loved Newfoundland.

"Yours, with some exquisite memories among the ruins,

Claire.

"PS. What are we going to do with Archer? I've followed sporadically the ups and downs of his roller-coaster career over the decades, and I can only conclude that we narrowly escaped, you and I, as you were wont to say, by pure dumb luck. Still, I can't decide if you should curse me or thank me for sundering the friendship between you and him. On the one hand, as I told you both in his flat, you and he would have had one hell of an adventurous ride together. On the other hand, it may be more pleasant for you, if more boring, to be outside the walls of prison. But like you I'm sure, I love him dearly still. Sitting here writing this, I'm putting Homer's Andromache to shame when it comes to smiling through my tears." And Claire certainly made me smile through my tears.

CHAPTER 24

Sir Winston Churchill died on January 24, 1965, 70 years to the very day after his father's death in 1895. It's a historical fact that Sir Winston had many times previously foretold his own death on that precise day of the month. He couldn't have willed or caused his own death on that particular day, because he'd had a massive stroke on January 15, and had been in a profound, vegetative, coma from then till his natural death nine days later. I am not a mystic or in any way superstitious; hence, if asked, I would have to say that the identical day of the month of his own and his father's death, just as he predicted, was purely coincidental. And the odds against it were not really that huge: One chance in 365. Still, in light of everything else Sir Winston had told me of a mystic or psychic nature, it was rather remarkable.

On Monday morning, January 11, 1965, Anthony telephoned Brasenose and left a message for me to call back. It was afternoon before I got the message. When I reached him that evening, I put on the surliest voice I could muster and said, "William Cull here, you telephoned?" I was exceedingly irritated at his tricks with Claire; if anything, the days going by were exacerbating my anger.

He said, "You haven't called to inquire since before Christmas, and you sound rather put out this evening. May I surmise that you've had a jaw-jaw with Miss Perceval?"

"Is there something I can help you with, Anthony?"

"No, not I. It's Sir Winston. He wishes to see you tomorrow morning without fail."

"And if I have other plans ... yet again? Did he put you up to that treachery last time?"

"Treachery. Good heavens." He didn't sound too perturbed. "William, he wanted something done that he thought important. I have been a public servant, a diplomat, all my life. I simply, as usual, found a way to do it. Nobody was hurt, except perhaps someone's overactive libido, and he believes much good was done for him and for you. Eleven tomorrow morning, then." When I remained silent, he did now become perturbed. "William, don't be bloody silly about this. The man is not well. This is in all likelihood the only opportunity you'll have. There will be no one else about the house here tomorrow, at last, and you will have several hours to yourselves to finish the damned task, if indeed he's still alive and conscious."

"Please tell Sir Winston I'll be there."

On Tuesday morning, three days before Churchill suffered the stroke that would kill him, I came down from Oxford and walked up to his door. Anthony opened it before I knocked, grinned too briefly, and started without pleasantries down the silent unlit hall.

Put off by the abruptness, I stayed where I was. "Anthony, if you don't mind, before we ... How is he?"

He stopped. "Fairly strong and talkative. But I do believe we need to get on with it."

"Yes, well, coming down on the train, I was wondering in all seriousness, absolutely puzzled, over whether all this has been, and is, an exercise in pointless delusion. So-called memories, or something, from an earlier life determining crucial actions in this life? Really?"

"You might as well hear his story out at this point." Anthony turned and led me to the small room where Winston, through Gobodinwit and Obseewit and other Beothuk, had been relating their story. When we stood before the 90-year-old leader, he looked from my face to Anthony's and back. He didn't know who I was.

"You remember William Cull from Canada, sir."

"Not Canada. You mean William Cull from Newfoundland, the eminent guide and furrier. Newfoundland didn't join Canada until 1949. Cull was a friend of Gobodinwit's, of Eli's, my great-grandfather several times removed." Then Churchill lurched, suddenly realizing what world he was in. "No, no, sorry, you were indicating the *modern* William Cull, the student, my Boswell extraordinaire. Apologies, gentlemen, my memory is nearly wholly in the distant past these days, and I mean the deeply distant past, the past before I, Winston Churchill, was born. Those remembrances have crowded out most others in my antique brain, I fear, and I seldom recall the morning's events unless prompted by ... by ..." He stared at his assistant.

"Anthony, sir."

"Yes, I knew that. I was trying to remember whether it was Anthony with a *th* sound or Antony as in Mark Antony."

"They are both pronounced with the t sound, Sir Winston. You need not be bothered by that distinction without a difference ever again."

"Except in America where the th is pronounced. You can see from this, gentlemen, how war is constantly waging within my breast between my English heritage and my American." He chortled and Anthony and I joined in. "Now add to that," he said, "the battle for ascendency by my Red Indian heritage and you may appreciate why we must finish my narrative before the residues of my sanity desert me entirely. So, young Cull ... where were we?"

I was about to respond to Churchill first with a question about his sources when Anthony stopped me with a raised hand. "Sir Winston, you asked me to remind you to deal with the remarks you made before the Royal Commission on Palestine back in 1937, that you do not admit a great wrong has been done to the Red Indians of America. Your remarks appear to be contrary to the evidence of wrongs against North American Indians you have recounted here in your narrative to William."

"Yes, I know that has bothered you, William," said Churchill, "and given you divided feelings, particularly the family guilt stemming from your own ancestor and his standing accused of perpetrating great wrongs against the Indians."

I stood up close to him, causing Churchill to crane his neck uncomfortably to look at me. Anthony stirred in his chair. "Sir Winston, I feel no guilt whatsoever from anything anyone else has done, family or otherwise, unless I somehow contributed to the wrongdoing. However, I would feel guilt if I had stated publicly, particularly from a position of influence, that no wrong has been done to Aboriginal and Indigenous peoples."

"And especially if you knew you weren't telling the truth—do sit down, William, before you have to bear the guilt for causing my neck surgery—especially if you knew at the time or realized later that you were not stating your honestly held opinion when you said it. That's the position I'm in. And I'm truly sorry for it. You will appreciate my full contrition here when you realize that I've never apologized easily or swiftly for anything I've done in my life."

"I understand how eager you were at the time to see a Jewish homeland well established there, and that your remarks were all part of your advocacy for that. But ..."

"Yes, I thought I was snared in one of my lesser-of-two-evils situations. I've been there many times before and since, especially during the Second World War. But I don't believe my appearance before that Royal Commission was genuinely one of them. In my zeal, and in my powerlessness at the time, I supposed I was. But I wasn't. They were two separate issues. I was simply wrong to say that."

"Was there any reason you didn't retract it later as erroneous or apologize for it?"

"Well, as I said, that doesn't come easily to me and, furthermore, you may recall from history that I got caught up in a number of other preoccupations soon after 1937. Besides, I'm counting on you to explain all that when you publish this. So, let's continue our story."

"Sir, since this is our last day, I must first satisfy myself on a point I asked you about before. Do you believe that your stories and images and characters from the long-ago Beothuk life are actual memories from that time, or do you think that they may be imaginings by you as Winston the child, buttressed and reinforced in your mind by your extensive reading later as a man?"

"It's a reasonable query. Yes, as a child I believed they were real memories that I had lived through, and for most of my life afterwards, I believed they were actual memories from my earlier life among the Beothuk. But ever since you and I began talking, and I've been dredging deep in my brain for these recollections, I seem to recall being in fact told these stories as a small child. And I seem to recall being told that Anna, the mother of Eli's daughter, came to Newfoundland—I believe with her father on business with Mr. Slade—years after Eli's Nova Scotia adventure. Anna had learned that Shanawdithit was living among the whites, either with John Peyton Jr. in the Bay of Exploits or, more likely, with Cormac in St. John's. And I recall vaguely an anecdote that Anna sat down with Shanawdithit and talked for hours and hours on end. I think— I'm fairly certain—I was told all this by my grandmother Clarissa Hall Jerome, my mother's mother. She would tell me an abundance of tales when I was a small boy. She was born in 1825, close to the same era in which everything I've told you happened—in fact Shanawdithit herself didn't die till 1829, four years later, so it's not really stretching one's credulity to accept that Anna had gone searching later in life for intelligence on her Eli, and if so, she would pass on everything she garnered to her daughter and granddaughter. Yes, it's all second- or third-hand hearsay, and no court of law would accept the least vestige of it as true, and there's no way to confirm any of it now—Grandmother Jerome died in 1895, but, William, let me say this about all that.

"Whether the stories I'm telling you are my true memories, or they were planted in my head by my grandmother, or even if they are purely a product of my fertile childhood imagination enhanced by deep study later, or a combination of all of it, I in fact acted on them in the 1930s and 1940s, with the same global result that changed the world; hence what earthly difference does it all make?"

I looked at Anthony. He raised his eyebrows at me as if to say, "Hard to refute that."

"Now William," growled Sir Winston, "that damned reconciliation expedition of John Peyton Jr.'s up the Exploits River—would you kindly remind me where we left off."

I opened my familiar last notes. "You said, sir, that some chap on the Peyton Jr. mission to save the Beothuk, by the name of John Day, reported that when Demasduit's husband, Nonobawsut, grappled with Peyton Sr. and tried to throttle him, old man Peyton shouted out, 'Are you going to stand by and let the Indian kill me?' That provoked a white youngster, later characterized by Peyton Jr. as the stupidest and least experienced of his team, to raise his rifle, with bayonet fixed, and step valiantly forward."

"Yes," said Sir Winston, closing his eyes the better to see the sight, "that's all true. And the young hooligan stabbed Nonobawsut viciously in the back with his bayonet. According to another member of the reconciliation team, the man Slade, who wrote about the episode later, the boy who spiked Nonobawsut with his bayonet was later fiercely reproved by the other team members. They said that the Beothuk warrior was only acting as a man in coming to rescue his wife from the hands of her captors. The wonder is that, although the whites all seemed to recognize the impossible predicament they had placed Nonobawsut in, thus implicitly condemning themselves as utter villains, their actual censure was reserved for a benighted young lout who had but carried the whole heinous enormity the one step further. Young Peyton and the other men all justified their own actions to each other throughout with self-serving rationalizations.

"Obseewit was standing there with Shanawdithit looking on with her sister's wailing baby in her arms, when the bayonet was thrust into Nonobawsut's back. He gave out a great bellow of surprise and pain, and knocked the young man down. He continued to struggle with Peyton Sr., as he fended off with heavy blows the men who were now clubbing him with the butts of their rifles and striving to seize hold of him. Old Peyton, the famous Indian killer, according to later tradition down in their bay, now screeched out to his son, 'What're you waiting for, man? Shoot this fucking savage.'

"In front of Demasduit's eyes, John Peyton Jr. shot her husband. He fell to the snow and ice with a mighty roar that reverberated into the trees and across the lake, and froze everyone's blood, Beothuk and white devil alike. Obseewit and Shanawdithit saw the expression of hopeless, futile anguish on Nonobawsut's face. He coughed and gasped as a torrent of red flowed from his mouth and nose.

"Lying in his own blood, and having known from the start that he was bound to perish in this endeavour, and hearing his young, beloved wife crying and sobbing and screaming in heartbreaking grief, and his tiny only child screeching out his fear and distress, her magnificent husband died. According to the eyewitness, Day, the Beothuk chief was so strong that he would have defeated, hand-to-hand, all the white men there. They had no choice but to stab, club, and shoot him down, and, as Slade would later write so preciously, he nobly lost his life in his attempt to save his wife.

"Dead on the snow there, Nonobawsut was measured, and his height was found greater than 6 feet. It is admirable to note that the white furriers' devotion to scientific anthropology was so compelling that they took the time in all that turmoil, while ringed by hostile and enraged natives with lethal bows and arrows, to measure the length of the Indian they'd just murdered. The whites reported that now the other Beothuk took off again and scattered far and wide, while Peyton Jr. and his men went into some of the mamateeks and discovered a great number of stolen items—kettles, knives, axes, fish hooks, fishing lines, and nets. As the white men gathered up and loaded aboard sledges this hoard of wholesale pilfering, they told each other that this treasure trove alone justified their arduous excursion. And they congratulated Peyton Jr. for providing the frosting on the cake by staying firm in his decision to take Demasduit downriver to employ her in developing warm and friendly relations between the whites and her people. And to secure for them their share of the handsome reward.

"Newfoundland Governor Hamilton sent an official report on the episode to London, containing his interpretation of events surrounding the taking of Demasduit. He wrote that at the commencement of John Peyton Jr.'s encounter with the band of Beothuk, the latter all sprinted off except for a woman, identified later as Demasduit, who exchanged welcoming and hospitable signals with the white men. The other Indians, however, did not display the same peaceful sentiments as she did. Instead, he reported, they came at the white men in great numbers, and engaged in hand-to-hand struggles with them. When Peyton Sr.'s life was threatened with grave danger, a Beothuk man fell to a musket ball. The Beothuk then scattered and the white men travelled back home, in company with the Beothuk woman. Peyton Jr. confirmed to him, Governor Hamilton wrote, that if he could have intimidated or persuaded the downed Beothuk man, Nonobawsut, to go away instead, 'we should have been most happy to have spared using violence.'

"That same spring, the governor submitted the death of the Beothuk man to a grand jury in St. John's. The jury decided that it was not Peyton's design to possess a Beothuk by bloodshed and violence. They decreed that 'the deceased came to his death in consequence of an attack upon the party and his subsequent obstinacy in not desisting when repeatedly menaced by some of the party.' Nonobawsut's pigheadedness in insisting that his wife not be kidnapped warranted their acting on the defensive. The grand jury concluded, Governor Hamilton reported to Lord Bathurst in the English government, that Peyton's party were 'fully justified under all the circumstances in acting as they did.' The grand jury found that there was 'no malice on the part of Peyton's party to get possession of any of the Indians by such violence as would occasion bloodshed.' Hence John Peyton Jr. was absolved of the killing of Demasduit's husband.

"Apparently, none of the white men reported to the governor that a second man had been killed, and Demasduit's baby was not raised as an important issue to the governor or to the government in London. But Shanawdithit was there at the encounter, and she reported later that she saw Nonobawsut's brother being gunned down with a shot to his back as he retreated, and she saw and heard Demasduit utter her piteous cries to be given back her baby. Every white man there had seen the baby in its mother's arms, and then in Nonobawsut's arms. And nobody had missed Demasduit's exposed, nursing breasts. Obseewit had been handed her baby during the uproar and she wanted to bring her baby to her, but the rest of their people there wouldn't let her. After the murder of their two men, everyone thought it would be certain death as well for anyone else who approached the white devils.

"The party left the men's bodies lying on the ice and snow, and dragged Demasduit away, down to the Bay of Exploits, without her baby. John Peyton Jr., famous in history for his reasonable, even compassionate, approach to the Red Indian problem, simply would not let concern for the baby, or concern for a mother torn from her child, or concern for a distraught husband trying to rescue his wife, or concern for a shocked and grief-stricken wife witnessing the killing of her husband, or any other humane concern, interfere with his reward from the governor for capturing a Beothuk to establish good relations with the tribe. Demasduit, her wrists tied together, tried desperately to escape many times, but failed. They would not let her go. The white men checked the calendar to confirm the month of the capture, and fondly dubbed their beautiful prize, Mary March.

"Peyton Jr. brought Demasduit from his home in Lower Sandy Point to Twillingate, where she lived for a while with the family of the Englishman, Leigh, a Church of England missionary. There Mr. Slade's wife repeated to people how much Mary March looked like her lovely boy, Eli Easter. Later that same spring, Demasduit was transported to the city of St. John's to abide under the care of the governor, Sir Charles Hamilton. His wife, Lady Henrietta Hamilton, painted her portrait, which you have seen, William. Everyone commended the picture as a striking likeness of the woman herself, Mary March, Demasduit. She was described in the records as about 23 years old, pretty and tall with delicate arms and beautifully formed hands and feet, and skin of a light copper colour. And she was discovered to be ill with consumption.

"Hence, the operation to put her back in contact with her people and establish those much-vaunted good relations was speeded up. Many inhabitants of St John's and Notre Dame Bay raised funds to cover costs. She was taught, and quickly learned, the rudiments of English so that she could hear about, as well as see, the grandeur of white civilization, and thus overawe her people with her descriptions. That summer she was put aboard a vessel, the *Sir Francis Drake*, which cruised up and down the coast of Notre Dame Bay while she was directed to keep a close lookout for members of her tribe. The whole time she protested that she didn't want to go back with her own people; she was afraid that, having lived among the white devils for months, she could not return to live with her tribe. She reiterated constantly that she wanted only to recover her baby. She claimed to have sighted none of her fellow Red Indians on shore.

"When the vessel suddenly came upon a canoe 200 yards or so away, containing some Beothuk, the captain ordered his crew to give chase. But as they didn't gain on the canoe, the captain ordered guns to be fired in the air to throw the Indians into confusion, he said, and make them stop and surrender themselves. That brilliant stratagem didn't work. For some reason, the Beothuk fled even faster. It is truly difficult to fathom the profound stupidity of even the well-intentioned English in charge of creating good relations with the Indians.

"Late the same summer, the dedicated Captain David Buchan was despatched to the mouth of the Exploits River, to take over the project of safely returning Demasduit to her encampment at Red Indian Lake. But she repeated to the end that her only wish was to get her baby back. Early in January, on board Buchan's vessel in Ship Cove, Botwood, some nine months after her capture, while her hosts were preparing to bring her back upriver to her tribe with abundant gifts and stories of her abductors' goodwill, the heartbroken wife and mother, shattered by tragedy, died. She was 24.

"Poor Captain Buchan, so often disappointed in his staunch devotion, some said obsession, to saving the Beothuk, had her body, and the ornaments she'd grown attached to, placed in a coffin, and he undertook once more the arduous winter trek up the frozen Exploits to Red Indian Lake. He trudged along, in company with John Peyton Jr. and some 50 mariners and trappers hauling sledges over the ice and snow. Behind cover, unseen by the white men, the few Beothuk, including Demasduit's sister, Obseewit, and her niece, Shanawdithit, watched in alarm and horror as the murderer of her husband and the army of white devils arrived days later at the winter quarters. Not surprisingly, they found the encampment empty.

"There they carefully and solemnly laid out her body in its coffin, and surrounded it with gifts, in the largest of the mamateeks. Shanawdithit, one of the last of her people, would later explain to William Eppes Cormack, as the historic record shows, how the Beothuk positioned the body of Demasduwit next to Nonobawsut in a hallowed resting place. When Cormack came up in 1828, on a desperate last search for Beothuk, he saw her lying next to her murdered husband in their funeral chamber. All about him, the winter home was utterly bereft of people, and the country and the shores of the Beothuk's Lake were deathly still.

"But Obseewit was among four of her people who were yet alive. They watched Cormac from the forest, unseen. She had no intention of surrendering herself to the white devils, to William Cull, as Shanawdithit and her two starving and sick family members had done during that terrible sunless year of famine. She knew that although Shanawdithit had lived for several years after her capture, the other two had soon died of the white devils' sickness.

"Obseewit would travel downriver to the Bay of Exploits and talk secretly to Shanawdithit. She was living with John Peyton Jr. and his wife and servant in Sandy Cove. Obseewit would send her a signal from the woods and she'd tell the Peytons that she needed to commune with the spirits of her dead family, and away she'd go and meet her sister/aunt among the trees. She told her proudly how she'd often trace her own steps near the house from the time they'd so brilliantly cut loose and ransacked Peyton's vessel. Neither woman, of course, had any idea that it was that particular action that had led to tragedy.

"Shanawdithit would urge Obseewit to give themselves up, all four of them, to William Cull or the young Peyton, and they would see to it that they were fed and sheltered properly. Those two could be trusted, she said. But Obseewit said no, she'd never give herself up to the white devils. She would die alone in the wilderness of sickness or starvation, first. And the other three were near death from the sickness now and were going to die on their own land.

"Obseewit asked Shanawdithit to promise never to tell any white devil of her existence out here. She wanted nothing to do with them, and no encouragement to any of them, good or bad, to come looking for her, to 'rescue' her. Shanawdithit promised, and, as open and honest as she would be in describing events later to Comack, the record showed that she never betrayed her promise to Obseewit. Unless you count whatever she told Anna privately when she visited Newfoundland. But telling the questing mother of Eli's daughter, Demasduit's and Obseewit's half-sister, what had happened to their father and themselves would hardly have been a betrayal.

"No day went by on the banks of the Exploits River or the big Lake that Obseewit did not dwell on the murder of her father and of her sister's husband and his brother, and the seizure of her sister and the separation of mother and baby. Demasduit's baby, which Nonobawsut had passed to Obseewit so that he could go and rescue his captured wife, she wanted to bring to his mother. But the others, who'd just witnessed two bloody deaths, prevented her. And so the last words she heard from her sister were her piteous cries to bring her baby to her. Obseewit and Shanawdithit told each other that Demasduit's cries would ring in their ears till the day of their own death. What kind of humans could do such a thing to a mother? But worse than all the rest of the evil was their memory of Demasduit's baby crying and whimpering as they brought him home, knowing as they did that there was no hope for him. They could not feed him. His sole sustenance had been his mother's milk and that was gone. There was no other nursing mother in their winter quarters.

"The nearest that anyone knew of was many miles away over rugged terrain in White Bay. Obseewit and Shanawdithit undertook to try to reach that mother, carrying the baby with them. Odusweet, the baby's grandmother, wanted to come too, but she was very sick from the lung disease, and a storm was already brewing. She'd only delay the other two, and even they, strong as they were, after a few miles, had to turn back. They attempted to feed the baby water mixed with some mashed up food but it was no use. For two days they listened without hope to the baby's crying, and aunt and grandmother and all the other people tried to comfort him. Though the long night he whimpered more and more weakly in their arms, against their empty, useless chests, and, at daybreak, while his own overflowing mother cried downriver to be united with him, her beloved little son died."

Churchill paused and turned surprisingly dry eyes on me. Anthony and I were silently weeping. He murmured, "I would feel such pain of bereavement again in this life. In August of 1921, Clemmie and I suffered the entirely unexpected death of our daughter, Marigold— we called her Duckadilly—before she was three years old. The grief of that has never left me during my entire life, and intensified, if such a thing were possible, my heartache at the death of Demasduit's son. Those experiences of grief brought terrible bouts of despondency and dejection to my life, my Black Dog of melancholia."

After minutes of gazing into the fire, Churchill went on: "They placed Demasduit's little boy next to his father in the hallowed resting place, and when, some months later, Demasduit's body was brought upriver in a coffin, they lay the three of them, the entire dead young family, side by side. There their remains stayed as a sacred memento to survivors until Cormac rescued them, or stole them—whatever similar action it was that Lord Elgin did to the Parthenon marbles—on his last upriver expedition of goodwill, and sent them over to a museum in Edinburgh.

"When the last of Obseewit's companions, including her own mother, died of the sickness, she was left alone on the land, foraging and hunting and gradually dwindling in strength from weakening lungs. She went down to the Bay of Exploits to talk to Shanawdithit one last time before she died, and she was—I was—lucky she did so that day because Shanawdithit was moved to St. John's in a day or two, without forewarning, where she would live for another nine months before dying herself of tuberculosis.

"Obseewit's great conundrum on her way to her last visit to the Bay came from her sighting of John Peyton Sr. and Noel Boss within possible killing distance. They were talking together by Peyton's salmon operation near the mouth of a stream, leaning on their long guns. Although she was a lengthy flight of an arrow away, she felt sure of bringing down one of them. But there was insufficient cover between her and them to let her creep closer and be certain of the double kill. If she shot just one of them, she'd be forced to give up her hope of seeing Shanawdithit one last time; she'd have to flee back upriver to escape. So she left them and travelled on down.

"The two women sat on their accustomed rocks in the woods. Obseewit told her niece/sister of the chance encounter, and

Shanawdithit told her that these two men occasionally visited, separately and together, young Peyton's house where she was staying, and the presence of either of the two murderers would upset her exceedingly. They would laugh at her reaction, until Peyton Jr. shut them up with a bark of disapproval at their behaviour. Obseewit asked her if she'd thought about taking advantage of her closeness to the younger Peyton, and his trust of her, to kill him with a knife in revenge for his carrying off Demasduit and for the death of her husband and baby. She replied that he protected her and fed her, and he and his wife seemed to like her very much and treated her with dignity, and she loved, and was loved by, their children, who couldn't wait to climb up onto her lap. Shanawdithit could see that Obseewit was working to hide her anger at that response, thinking it weak and soft for a true Beothuk.

"She asked Obseewit what she'd do if she came across old Peyton and Noel Boss again on her way back. She answered that she thought she'd try to kill at least one, and with luck both of the butchers.

"Shanawdithit waited a moment and then said, 'What I see is a probable survivor shooting you dead, or, if you leave no survivor of the two, then a gang of white avengers tracking your footprints through the snow, and very likely finding you in your weakened state, and killing you. Just one more Indian gunned down by white devils.'

"'I don't mind being killed,' said Obseewit. 'I only have days of life left, anyway.' The two women stayed silent, both knowing each was musing on her own life and that of their lost people. Then Obseewit muttered, 'But why? Why would I bother killing them now? For revenge? Yes, why not just kill them for our pure and simple idea of reprisal and payback? For revenge! But that thought brings a sense of utter vainness, uselessness, pointlessness over me. What would be the point of it, after the fact? A feeling of satisfaction? Fulfillment? I cannot dredge up a feeling of that even as I vividly picture my arrows piercing their bodies. Can you, Shanawdithit?'

"'No.'

"'Then, should I kill them to stop them from murdering any more of us? Too late for that now. There are none of us left. If we were going to stop them from murdering us, we should have tried to do that before we were made extinct by their murders, and the white devils' disease, and the brittle stiffness of our own customs."

"'As your father, Gobodinwit, forever said,' murmured Shanawdithit, 'We needed to stop them, but we needed to do it the right way.'

"Obseewit stood to begin her trek upriver, and Shanawdithit to walk back to John Peyton Jr.'s house, neither knowing that, over the next nine months in the capital, St. John's, Shanawdithit would describe in words and pictures for many interested people events and characters from Beothuk history. As they said goodbye, Obseewit said, 'If the good spirits were ever to give me second chance in another life, I would do that. I would do it the right way. I would make sure that we learned and used every kind of weapon available, and I would recognize early, and use all my gifts of speech to persuade and prepare others to join me in combatting the evil of men who would conquer and enslave and murder men, women, children, and babies. I would never, never surrender in that fight. I would never give up: I would, like our unwavering and unyielding Nonobawsut, resolve to lie choking in my own blood, first."

Sir Winston Churchill looked into the fire. I rose beside him and murmured his words from his war against the conquering, enslaving, murdering Nazis: "If this long island story of ours is to end at last, let it end only when each one of us lies choking in his own blood upon the ground."

He raised his head and met my eyes with a small nod. Then he took my hand and said, "Relate my chronicle, William Cull. Tell them why."

ACKNOWLEDGEMENTS

My gratitude to Gavin Will, Amanda Will, Stephanie Porter, Geoff Frampton, and Glenn Day of Boulder Books for their help and encouragement in creating this book and presenting it to readers. My thanks to Iona Bulgin for the quality of her editing and to Tanya Montini for her superb graphic design.

Thank you again to Shirley Bussey Stead for her critique of the original manuscript and her constant support throughout the process.

I would like to acknowledge my admiration for the great Mi'kmaq people of eastern North America. I have drawn inspiration from their heroic survival and their magnificent contribution here over the millennia, concerning which they have made much progress in setting the record straight. The genetic heritage of the Beothuk that yet survives in Newfoundland may, I believe, be attributed in large measure to their cousins on this Island from time immemorial, the Mi'kmaq.

BIOGRAPHY

 Born in Newfoundland, Bill Rowe graduated in English from Memorial University and attended Oxford University as a Rhodes Scholar, obtaining an Honours M.A. in law. Elected five times to the House of Assembly, the first time at 24, Rowe served as a minister in the Government of Newfoundland and Labrador, and as leader of the Official Opposition. He practiced law in St. John's for many years, earning a Queen's Counsel designation. He has also been a long-time public affairs commentator, appearing regularly on national and local television, as well as hosting a daily radio call-in show on VOCM and writing weekly newspaper columns in *The Telegram*.

Rowe has written a dozen books of fiction and non-fiction. He is a member of the Writers' Union of Canada and has served on the executive of the Writers' Alliance of Newfoundland and Labrador. He has a son, Dorian, a daughter, Toby, and three grandchildren, Rowan, Elizabeth, and Phoebe.